# THRONE

## OF

# ICE

## AND

# BLOOD

\*\*\*

## Ruthless Enemy

*Ruthless Enemy*
*Wicked Enemy*
*Heartless Enemy*

\*\*\*

## Flame and Thorns

*Empire of Flame and Thorns*
*Throne of Ice and Blood*

# THRONE OF ICE AND BLOOD

## FLAME AND THORNS
### BOOK TWO

MARION BLACKWOOD

ISBN 978-91-989043-0-7 (ebook)
ISBN 978-91-989043-1-4 (paperback)
ISBN 978-91-989043-2-1 (hardcover)
ISBN 978-91-989043-3-8 (special edition)

This is a work of fiction. Names, characters, places, and incidents either are the product of the author's imagination or are used fictitiously. Any resemblance to actual persons, living or dead, events, or locales is entirely coincidental.

www.marionblackwood.com

# CONTENT WARNINGS

If you have specific triggers, you can find the full list of content warnings at: www.marionblackwood.com/content-warnings

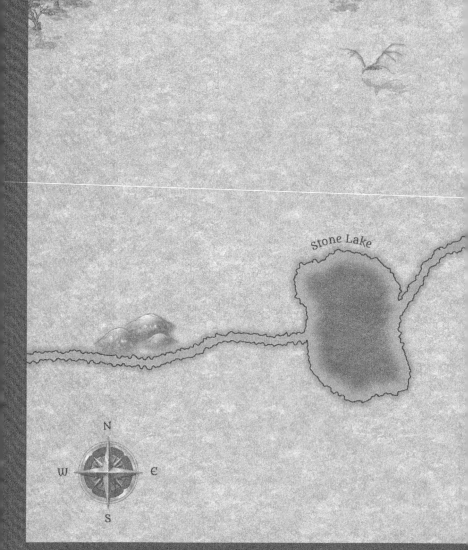

Stone Lake

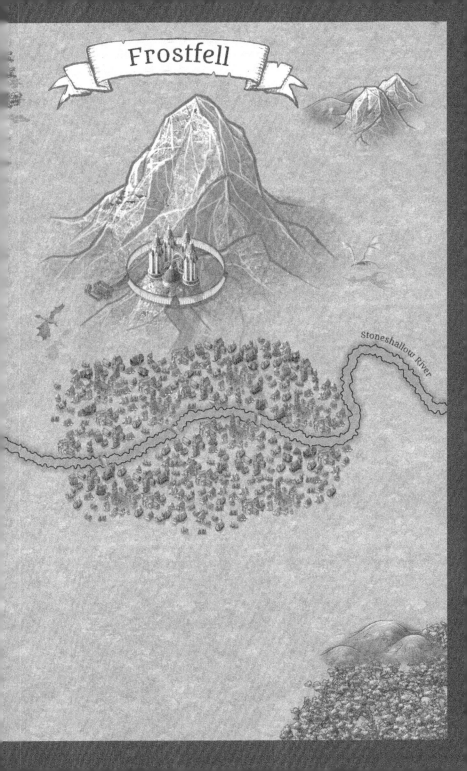

Frostfell

Stoneshallow River

*For all the people pleasers out there whose sense of self-worth is deeply connected to other people's opinions.*

*You don't have to prove anything to anyone.*

*You are enough.*

# CHAPTER ONE

I ce bites into my skin. It presses against my throat and saps my strength, making me feel like I haven't slept in weeks. For one brief moment, I consider just rolling over in bed and going back to sleep. But Goddess above, I need to get that strange ice away from my throat.

While trying to pry my eyes open, I groggily reach towards my neck. Light stabs at my eyes, and I have to squint against the brightness.

My fingers brush against something cold and hard that circles my throat.

A memory flashes through my mind.

I frown.

Then the whole storm of memories crashes down over me like a merciless cold wave.

The Atonement Trials. The Ice Palace. The winner's ceremony.

And Draven Ryat snapping an iron collar shut around my throat.

I gasp awake. All lingering grogginess evaporates like mist in the sun as I sit bolt upright in bed while my heart pounds against my ribs. Blinking furiously, I whip my head from side to side.

Pale walls made of white ice meet me. And a bed with dark gray sheets, which I'm currently occupying. As opposed to the other parts of the Ice Palace that I've seen, this bedroom has wooden floorboards that cover the ice floor. I stare at a patch of sunlight that shines in from the window somewhere to my left and paints those dark wooden boards in lighter colors. My mind churns.

I have no recollection of how I got here.

The last thing I remember is kneeling in front of Draven's feet in that throne room and silently vowing to kill him. Then a wave of exhaustion crashed over me, making me sway so much that I had to brace myself on the floor. After that, everything is black.

Panic clangs inside my skull and my heart slams against my ribs.

Yanking up my hand, I desperately run my fingers over the iron collar around my throat, trying to find the clasp. That intense panic inside me surges when I can't find one. I suck in short shallow breaths as I slide my fingers down into the small gap between the collar and my neck and try to yank it off instead.

It doesn't work.

That icy feeling of the cold iron bites into my hand as I grip the collar.

I frantically search for the clasp again.

"It won't work."

A gasp rips from my throat, and I whip my head towards the sound of the voice.

Draven Ryat is seated in an armchair in the corner of the room. The light from the window only partially hits his sharp cheekbones, leaving the rest of his face in shadow. He is only wearing a pair of black pants, and his black hair is slightly damp, making it look as if he has just stepped out of the bath. My gaze flits across his body.

He is lounging in that dark gray armchair as if it were a throne. Leaned back with his legs spread and his arms draped along the armrests, he exudes power and authority. His sharp abs and muscular chest are painted with both light and shadows from the partial sunlight that filters in through the window and hits the otherwise dark corner of the room.

A small ray hits his golden eyes, making them glint, when he nods towards the collar around my throat. "You won't be able to find a clasp. Only a dragon shifter can take off a collar like that."

I stubbornly yank against the collar again. But when it doesn't come off, I'm forced to admit that he might be telling the truth. Rage burns through my chest as I let my hand drop back down.

But then a jolt shoots through me instead when my hand meets cool silk fabric. I snap my gaze down to my body, and another wave of panic washes over me.

When I passed out in the throne room, I was wearing an elaborate silver dress. Now, I'm dressed in a simple short nightgown made of black silk. Which means that someone changed my clothes while I was unconscious.

"You changed my clothes," I blurt out.

After everything that has happened, I know that there are a million other things that I should probably have said to Draven at this particular moment. But my mind is still struggling to come to terms with the sheer magnitude of the situation that I'm in right now, so I need to focus on something smaller. Something more manageable. Something like this.

Draven cocks his head. "Yes."

There is an entirely unreadable mask on his face as he watches me. I grip the sheets harder, trying to resist the urge to pull them up to cover more of my body. Instead, I shift my position so that I'm sitting at an angle where I can face him head on without needing to twist my body to the side. Focusing on my anger, I try to push back the panic that is still clanging inside my skull.

I narrow my eyes at Draven. "You took my clothes off?"

"You've been asleep for three days." He lifts his toned shoulders in a nonchalant shrug. "I figured you would be more comfortable in that than a ballgown."

My stomach drops, and it takes everything I have not to show my shock. Three days? I've been out for *three days*?

While still trying to cover my panic and shock, I shoot Draven a hard look. "So you took it upon yourself to strip me naked while I was unconscious?"

A slow and vicious smile curls his lips. "It's nothing I haven't seen before."

My heart jerks at the reminder of that afternoon in the underground forest when he pushed me up against that rock wall and fucked me exactly the way I wanted him to. Like I was his.

"And besides," he continues. A ruthless and highly possessive glint shines in his eyes as he holds my gaze. "Would you rather it had been a random stranger who stripped you down to your underwear and changed your clothes?"

The thought of that sends a pulse of dread through me. It's followed by the infuriating realization that he's right. I couldn't very well sleep in a ballgown for three days. And I most certainly wouldn't have wanted some stranger to change my clothes.

But I will die before I ever admit that to him, so I just scoff and slide towards the edge of the bed instead.

Sheets tangle around my limbs. I shove them away impatiently before swinging my legs over the side of the bed.

"You shouldn't—" Draven begins.

I shove myself to my feet.

My legs immediately buckle.

I suck in a sharp breath between my teeth as I topple towards the floor.

But right before I can hit it, a pair of strong arms wrap around my body and hoist me back up. My heart jerks as I suddenly find myself with my cheek pressed against Draven's bare chest. His body is warm against mine. And his intoxicating scent of night mist and embers fills my lungs when I draw in a breath. It makes fire surge through my veins.

Which immediately makes me angry.

Struggling upright, I give his chest a hard shove. "Don't touch me."

"The first draining is always the hardest," he says as if I hadn't spoken.

And he doesn't let me go either. He keeps his hands on my shoulders and watches me with scrutinizing eyes until he is satisfied that I can stand on my own. Once he is, he finally releases me. But he doesn't step back.

My head spins, and my stomach aches with hunger, and exhaustion from the iron collar still clings to my bones, so I don't dare to move yet either. I need to let my body adjust after three days of lying in a bed. So instead of putting some much-needed distance between us, I settle for tilting my head back and glaring up at him.

"The first and *only* draining," I retort.

His face is an unreadable mask as he holds my gaze. "Draining you of magic is the entire purpose of a life slave."

"I am not your slave."

"That collar around your neck says otherwise."

"If you ever drain me again, I will kill you."

He slowly wraps a hand around my throat and holds me firmly in place while his eyes sear into mine. "You and I both know that if I want to take it, I can."

My heart thumps in my chest. And as much as I hate it, hate it with every fiber of my being, I know that he is right. With the iron collar both blocking my magic and sapping my strength, I would never be able to fight him off. He can do whatever he wants with me, and there is nothing I can do to stop him. He knows it. And I know it. So in the end, I just stand there with my chin raised and hold his gaze in silence.

He lets his hand drop from my throat. "But I won't."

Shock pulses through me.

"We had an audience back in the throne room," Draven continues. "Now, we don't."

I blink at him in surprise as he even takes a step back.

The shock must have been visible on my face, because Draven lets out a soft sigh and then raises his eyebrows pointedly. "I told you that I tried to save you from this, remember?"

His words from back in that throne room, his eyes so full of sorrow as he whispered soft words against my lips, drift through my mind.

*I wasn't trying to sabotage you, little rebel. I was trying to save you. From this.*

He did say that. And he *was* trying to save me by tampering with the trials so that I would lose.

Back in that throne room, I asked him a question that he never answered. So now, I ask it again.

"Why?"

His face immediately transforms into an emotionless mask again. "Does it matter?"

I'm just about to snap, *yes, it matters!* But right before the words can make it out of my mouth, I hesitate. Does his reason actually matter? He still collared me. He might have been trying to help me earlier, but when it all came down to it, he still made me his slave.

Something hard settles around my heart. Something I'm not used to. But it helps keep the panic and hopelessness away, so I lean into it.

A vicious scoff rips from my throat as I meet Draven's gaze again. "No, I guess it doesn't."

He smiles, but it's a cold smile that doesn't reach his eyes.

While drawing a hand over the collar around my throat, I fix Draven with a hard stare. "I will kill you for this."

For the briefest of moments, I swear that I can see true mirth and almost a hint of approval glitter in his eyes. But when he speaks, his tone is only filled with cruel mocking, so I immediately start to doubt that I ever saw it at all.

Raising his hand, he gives my cheek a patronizing pat. "That's the spirit."

I slap his hand away. To my surprise, it doesn't make me sway the way moving around did earlier. My legs feel steady now. The collar still saps my strength, but I no longer feel as if I'm about to collapse.

Opening my mouth, I get ready to spit a retort back in Draven's face. But right before I can say anything, my stomach growls. Loudly.

Draven flicks a glance down to it. I expect him to mock me about it, but when he speaks, his tone is suddenly serious instead.

"You haven't eaten anything in three days." He meets my gaze for a moment before he abruptly starts towards the door. "I'll get you some food."

Startled by the sudden change in his behavior, all I manage to say is, "I, uhm…"

Draven nods towards a pale wooden dresser by the white ice wall to my right. "Your clothes are in there. Stay here. I'll be back in a few minutes."

Before I can even figure out how to respond, he throws the door open and strides out. Leaning to the side, I glance out the doorway. There appears to be another larger room out there. Draven snatches up a shirt that was draped over a chair and puts it on before pulling on his boots too. Then he strides towards another door set into the wall of that room and disappears through it.

For a few seconds, all I can do is to stare after him.

Then I lurch into motion.

Sprinting across the floor, I yank out the topmost drawer of the dresser that Draven indicated. Just as promised, I find most of my clothes in there. All of them have been washed and folded into neat piles.

After throwing off the black silk nightgown, I shimmy into my tight brown pants and then pull the white shirt over my head. My knife is nowhere to be seen. No surprise there. But Draven has placed my leather boots on the floor next to the dresser, so I shove my feet into them before I hurry out of the bedroom.

Just like I assumed, the door to my bedroom leads to another room. It's bigger than the bedroom, and it looks almost like a living room or a fancy sitting room or something. There is a grand desk by one wall, and a cluster of armchairs and couches around a low table. An open door shows glimpses of a bathroom by the wall opposite me. And there is another door, this one closed, a short distance from it on the same wall. To my right is yet another door. That one is made of clear ice and leads out to a balcony. But I don't bother with any of them. Instead, I run straight towards the one that Draven used when he left.

My heart skips a beat when I shove down the handle and find it unlocked.

He left me alone and he didn't even bother to lock me in. How stupid can he be?

Flinging the door open, I dart across the threshold.

The soft white light of faelights illuminates a wide corridor made of the same white ice as the rest of this accursed castle. But as opposed to the room I just left, there are no wooden floorboards out here. Instead, only ice glitters below me and above me and around me. I quickly push the door shut behind me and then take off down the hall.

My boots pound against the pale floor and my hair flutters behind me as I sprint away. I have no idea where I am or which direction I'm supposed to be running, but there is still an overwhelming sense of hope and relief pulsing through me as I dart down the corridor and into the next hallway. I'm getting out. Right now. I can figure out how to get the iron collar off later. As long as I make it out of this castle, freedom will yet again be within my grasp.

White corridors decorated only with silver and sparkling faelights flash past around me as I weave my way through the Ice Palace. I have to duck servants and guards several times, but somehow always manage to stay just out of sight.

My muscles burn and my lungs ache as I skid around another corner.

And come face to face with a group of guards.

My heart leaps into my throat.

Throwing myself backwards, I dart back around the corner.

"What was that?" a voice comes from the corridor.

"You see someone?" another man asks.

I curse silently in my mind. With my heart thundering in my chest, I hurriedly back away. There was another corridor branching off a short distance behind me. If I can just make it there before—

The sound of boots thumping against the floor comes from around the corner.

"I'll check it out," the first voice replies.

*Shit.*

While keeping one eye on the corner, I practically run backwards until I reach the other hallway and can back into it.

My stomach lurches.

A yelp slips past my lips as my heels slam into something. Combined with my speed, the sudden obstacle makes me trip backwards. I flail my arms, desperately trying to get my balance back, but because of the long run and the lack of food and the iron around my neck, my reflexes are too slow.

I topple backwards and crash down on the ground.

Yells come from the guards, and the sound of their pounding feet gets louder as they sprint towards me.

Desperately, I shove myself into a sitting position and swing my legs over the long thing that I tripped over. I have just managed to twist around and get to my knees when I realize what it is.

A body.

My gaze snaps down to the pool of blood that has formed underneath it.

For one single second, all I can do is to stare at it. Stare at that body. That very dead body and the very incriminating pool of blood that I am currently bracing my palms in.

Then reality snaps back into me, and I yank my hands off the floor. Blood coats my palms, and small drops fly from my fingers when I move to jump to my feet.

But before I can so much as get off the ground, the group of guards skids around the corner.

They stop.

Shock pulses across their faces as they stare from me to the dead body to my blood-covered hands and then back again.

"It's not what it looks like," I blurt out.

"Get her!" the squad leader snaps.

Light glints in their silver armor as they all surge forward. I scramble back, trying to get away, but a boot takes me in the side of the ribs before I can even get halfway up from the floor. The force of it flips me over and sends me crashing back down on the bloodstained ice.

I gasp air back into my lungs and place my palms against the ground to push myself up.

Someone plants a boot between my shoulder blades and shoves me back down. I let out a huff as my chest connects with the floor again. And before the sound has even finished leaving my mouth, someone is twisting my arms up behind my back. I suck in a hiss as iron manacles are snapped shut around my wrists.

With the iron around my throat, and now the iron around both of my wrists too, my already exhausted and starving body is so weak that I can do nothing but lie there on my stomach and stare at the dead body next to me.

"Tell the captain that the Master of the Treasury is dead," one of the guards yells somewhere above me. "And that we've caught the murderer."

Blood from the now disturbed pool underneath the Master of the Treasury's corpse slowly runs towards my face where I lie with my cheek pressed against the floor, a boot on my back, handcuffs shackling my wrists, and a squad of guards from Empress Jessina and Emperor Bane's Silver Dragon Clan surrounding me with swords raised.

I heave a deep sigh.

Well… fuck.

# CHAPTER TWO

I t's quite ironic that in an entire castle made of ice, the coldest part of it is actually the only place not made of ice. Which just so happens to be the dungeon.

I stare at the iron bars that make up the entire front wall of my cell. Coldness from the stone floor seeps through the fabric of my pants and chills me to the bone. A shiver rolls through my body.

If I could just stand up, I could at least pace back and forth to try to get some warmth back. But I can't. My hands are shackled behind my back with iron manacles which, along with the collar around my throat, drain my already dwindled energy and strength. And even if they weren't, I couldn't have gotten to my feet anyway. Because the handcuffs are also locked to an iron ring set into the thick stone floor behind my back, trapping me in a kneeling position.

I blow out a long sigh.

My breath forms a small white cloud in the air before me.

The feeling of ice pressing into my throat and my wrists from the iron collar and shackles aren't exactly making it better either. While glaring at the empty stone corridor outside the bars to my cell, I once more lament the fact that this dungeon isn't made of ice as well.

Just like Isera, the Iceheart monarchs must be able to somehow control the temperature of the ice they create. Because the walls and all the floors in the palace might look like they're made of ice, but they're not cold in the way that real ice is. It's only smooth and cool. Kind of like marble.

But here, down inside the mountain, on whose slopes the Ice Palace sits, only cold stone and iron has been left to torment me.

A new sound comes from the corridor.

My gaze darts towards it.

Straining my ears, I try to hear past the voices of the guards who are talking amongst themselves in a room somewhere down the corridor. Firelight from the torches set into the walls dances across the rough stone, and there is a muted dripping of water in the corner behind me. The guards continue chatting softly.

I tilt my head slightly as I concentrate on trying to identify that new sound. But no matter how hard I try, it doesn't sound again.

Heaving a defeated sigh, I let my head drop back down. With my chin resting on my chest, I stare down into my lap while both frustration and a sudden sense of despair wash over me.

Maybe this wasn't such a good idea after all.

Mabona's tits, what was I thinking? I just ran blindly through a castle that I don't know the layout for. Until the guards hauled me down to the dungeon, I didn't even know which floor of the castle I was on. I should have made a proper plan first. I should have eaten to get some of my strength back. I should have plotted my escape route. I should have done so many things differently.

But I just… I couldn't pass up the opportunity. Who knows if Draven would ever make the same mistake of forgetting to lock the door again? I had to take the opportunity presented to me.

Annoyance ripples through me.

Why did some damn Master of the Treasury need to get murdered right in the middle of my desperate escape?

"So I hear you killed someone."

I snap my head up.

A small gasp escapes my lips when I find Draven standing right on the other side of the iron bars. He is now wearing his black dragon scale armor again, and he must have performed a half-shift too, because his wings are out. His arms are crossed over his chest, and there is a disapproving look on his face as he watches me.

"And not just someone," he continues. "The Master of the Treasury."

"It wasn't me," I protest.

He lets out a huff of laughter. "Yeah, that's what they all say."

Metal clanks as my handcuffs rattle the short chain when I try to stand up before I once again remember that I'm trapped. Frustration streaks through me, and I yank futilely against my restraints again.

"Goddess damn it, Draven," I snap. "Listen to me. I didn't do this."

He just continues watching me in silence, his face unreadable.

I try to keep my scowl firmly in place as I glare back at him, but I can't stop a hint of worry from rippling through me. What if he actually thinks that I killed that guy? I doubt murder goes unpunished in the Ice Palace. I'm already a slave. What else will they do to me if I actually go down for this?

Draven lets out a long breath and uncrosses his arms. "I know."

Metal clinks faintly as he pulls a set of keys from one of the pouches on his belt. I watch him, still a little stunned, as he unlocks the section of the iron bars that functions as a door. Giving my head a quick shake, I try to clear it while Draven strides into the cell.

"You know that I didn't kill him?" I echo.

"Yes." He moves until his boots are right in front of my knees. "His throat was slit, and you had nothing to slit it with."

Since he's now looming over me, I have to crane my neck to meet his gaze as I narrow my eyes at him. "Because that's the only reason why it couldn't have been me? Not because, oh I don't know, the fact that I would never just kill an innocent unarmed man?"

Amusement flickers in his eyes as he arches an eyebrow at me. "I distinctly remember you slashing a knife at my face back in the thorn forest."

"Yes, well..." I huff. "You weren't innocent. Or unarmed, for that matter."

A dark chuckle escapes his throat, and he tips his head to the side as if to concede that I do have a point.

I rattle my manacles again. "So, are you going to unshackle me or what?"

With a sly smile on his lips, he slowly reaches forward and draws a hand along my jaw. That devilish smile combined with the gentle touch makes lightning skitter across my skin. I draw in a sharp breath as his fingers stop underneath my chin and push upwards, tilting my head farther back.

"I haven't decided yet," Draven answers.

I grind my teeth. "But I didn't kill him."

"No. But you sprinted away like a little thief even though I told you to stay—"

"I'm not a dog."

"—in your room while I left to get you some food," he finishes as if I hadn't interrupted. And he puts extra emphasis on that last word. As if I'm supposed to be grateful that he still intends to feed me after making me his slave.

"So maybe I should leave you here for a while to teach you a lesson about disobedience." His eyes glint. "And because you look really fucking hot in handcuffs."

A jolt shoots straights through my core. It's immediately

followed by a wave of anger. I shouldn't be reacting like this to him. Not after everything that has happened. But apparently, the feelings that I had started to develop for Draven don't just magically disappear overnight. Even though everything between us is now more complicated than ever.

Clenching my jaw, I glare up at him in silence. He just stares right back at me. His hand is still underneath my chin, tilting my head back and exposing my throat to him.

"I won't beg, if that's what you're waiting for," I declare.

The silence crackles around us as he holds my gaze.

Then a soft laugh escapes his lips. "Of course you won't, little rebel."

Letting his hand drop from my chin, he instead walks around me until he can reach the manacles behind my back. Faint clinking sounds. Then two distinct clicks.

A sigh of relief comes from deep within my chest when the iron handcuffs disappear from my wrists.

Rolling my shoulders, I move my hands forward and rub at where the iron touched my skin. It helps remove the feeling of ice from before. Draven walks back around me while I brace my palms on the floor in an effort to push to my feet.

My legs don't move.

Dread sluices through my veins. I'm still too weak after the contact with so much iron, combined with several days without food, that I can't stand up yet. It's going to take another few minutes for my body to recover enough strength to stand. Let alone walk back up all those stairs that the guards hauled me down.

But I'm too frustrated and embarrassed and stubborn to tell Draven that, so I just remain there on my knees while he takes a step towards the door.

"You…" he begins, but then he trails off when he notices that I'm not following him.

His dark brows furrow as he turns and looks back at me. Then realization pulses across his face.

Averting my gaze, I clear my throat a tad awkwardly while another flicker of embarrassment sears my cheeks. Mabona's fucking tits, one day, I swear I'm going to be the strong and powerful one standing before him while he kneels on the floor.

I suck in a sharp breath in shock as a pair of muscular arms suddenly lift me up from the floor. Blinking, I snap my gaze up to Draven's face as he adjusts me in his arms until he's holding me against his chest. He doesn't look back at me. Doesn't say anything. He just strides out of the cell with me in his arms. My heart is suddenly pounding in my chest.

But the storm of strange emotions that whirl through me are quickly drowned out by confusion when Draven doesn't take a right towards the stairs. Instead, he turns left and walks down the corridor. Towards the room where the guards are still talking faintly.

I lick my lips nervously. But even if I knew what to do, I couldn't move enough to do it right now. And I refuse to show Draven that I'm worried. So I just lie there in his arms as he stalks down the hall.

A crash echoes between the rough stone walls as he kicks the door open. It slams against the wall inside the room, making the torches vibrate in their metal holders.

Three dragon shifters in silver armor jump up from the chairs they were sitting on. One of them moves so fast that he almost knocks over the table they were seated around. Paper playing cards flutter to the ground and mugs wobble on the tabletop.

"Commander," the brown-haired one blurts out as the three of them straighten to attention.

Confusion and surprise flit across their faces as they glance between him and me. Draven ignores them all. Twisting to the left, he sets me down on top of the table right next to the door. Since I'm as confused as the guards appear to be, I just stare at him as well. He keeps his hands right next to my shoulders for a few seconds, as if he's getting ready to catch me if I topple off the table. But his face is an unreadable mask, and I can't use my magic, so I have no idea what he's feeling right now.

Once Draven is satisfied that I'm not going to fall off the table, he at last turns back to the three guards from the Silver Dragon Clan.

All three of them immediately lower their chins in deference. They might be a part of Empress Jessina and Emperor Bane's clan, but Draven is the Commander of the Dread Legion, so they are his subordinates too.

"Commander," they murmur in unison.

"Who handcuffed her?" Draven demands.

They exchange a worried glance.

"I did, sir," the brown-haired one replies.

A blast of wind shoots across the room. It hits all three guards straight in the chest, making them fly backwards. The two blond ones slam into the wall behind them and collapse to the floor while the brown-haired guy hits the side of a table, flips over it, and then crashes down on the other side.

Draven stalks towards him while the two blond guards cough and struggle to their knees.

"Commander," the dark-haired one croaks as he tries to untangle himself from the chair he hit when he slid off the table. "I'm—"

His words are cut off as Draven yanks him up by the collar and slams his fist into the guy's face.

From where I'm still sitting on the table, I suck in a gasp as I stare at them with wide eyes.

The guard grunts as his head snaps back. Draven drives his fist into his face again.

"Commander," one of the blond men calls from the other side of the room. "Please—"

Lightning cracks through the room.

Shouts of alarm echo between the walls as the blond guards jump back and throw their arms up to protect themselves. Draven doesn't even look at them. His furious eyes are focused solely on the man before him as he punches him in the face again. Another lightning bolt cracks into the stone floor, and dark clouds churn inside the room.

Draven slams his fist into the guard's stomach. Then he at last releases the guy's collar. A gasp of pain rips from the man's throat as he collapses down on the floor. But it's cut off by another huff as Draven stomps his boot down on his back, forcing him flat against the stone floor.

Firelight from the torches casts dancing shadows over the man's face as he blinks and tries to suck air back into his lungs.

Relief flickers in his eyes when Draven takes his boot off his back. But it's short-lived when Draven instead places it on the back of his elbow. With his foot in place, Draven crouches down and grabs the guy's wrist.

A cry of pain shatters from the guard's throat as Draven lifts his arm upwards while still keeping his boot on the back of his elbow. If he pulls too high, he's going to snap the guy's arm in two.

"Commander, please," the guard gasps. Pain and terror shine in his eyes as he squirms on the floor underneath Draven's boot. "Please. I'm sorry. I—"

Another scream of agony rips from his lungs as Draven forces his arm higher.

And when Draven at last speaks, his voice is so cold and deadly that ice skitters down my spine.

With a firm grip on the guard's wrist, Draven stares him down with those furious golden eyes. "If you ever touch her again, I'll break your fucking hands. She's mine. Got it?"

My heart flips.

"Yes, sir," the guard gasps out. "Please. I'm sorry. Commander. Please."

Draven inches his arm upwards another breath.

A whimper spills from the guard's mouth.

Then Draven finally releases him. He curls up on the floor, cradling his arm. The other two guards just stare at their commander, their faces white with fear, from where they still cower by the back wall.

I draw in a deep breath. I'm not sure if I have breathed at all these past few minutes.

Firelight dances over Draven's black armor as he straightens again. Without a second look back at his victim, he simply strides straight towards me and slides one arm underneath my knees and the other behind my back.

Then he picks me up and stalks out the door without another word.

# CHAPTER THREE

I t isn't until we've already ascended the stairs and are halfway through the first ice corridor on the ground floor of the castle that I've recovered enough, both physically and mentally, to tell Draven that I can walk on my own. He sets me down gently but keeps sharp eyes on me, as if he's worried that I'm going to collapse.

This strange protective behavior makes my heart squeeze hard in my chest and my head feel like it's full of twisting vines. This protectiveness is so at odds with the fact that he collared me with iron and drained my magic not three days ago.

Furrowing my brows, I study him where he's still standing right in front of me. Faelight gems have been set into the ceiling, making the entire ice corridor look like it's covered by a blanket of sparkling stars. The soft white light glitters against the ice walls and casts faint reflections over Draven's impassive face. I narrow my eyes at him.

He doesn't look like he cares. But he... acts like it.

"Why?" I ask.

A ruthless glint appears in his eyes. "Because I don't like it when people touch what belongs to me."

I grind my teeth. "I don't *belong* to you."

"Yes, you do. In every way that matters."

"Enough!" I snap, suddenly feeling exhausted and fed up and vulnerable and everything all at once. Throwing my arms out, I shake my head in frustration while I hold Draven's gaze. "I know that you're baiting me. I know that you're deliberately saying that to make me angry. So just stop."

To my surprise, he doesn't try to deny it. Doesn't argue. Doesn't call me delusional or try to play it off. Instead, he just watches me in silence with those intense eyes of his.

And that is somehow worse.

I want to scream. I want to crawl into bed and pull the covers over my head. I want to murder someone. I want to bawl my eyes out.

I have never felt this off-kilter in my entire life. In the span of a few minutes, my entire life was turned upside down. Everything I thought I knew turned out to be false, and everything I had was ripped away from me. And I haven't even had time to process it. I passed out and then I woke up and was arrested for murder, and now... this. I just need the world to stop spinning out of control for one fucking second.

"Why did you do all of this?" I demand, my voice coming out more high-pitched and desperate than I would've liked.

"You're going to have to narrow that down a little."

"Why did you try to stop me from winning the Atonement Trials?"

"I've already told you. I was trying to protect you. From this."

"Then why didn't you just say that from the beginning?" All of my conflicting emotions are just bubbling over and pouring out of me like a raging flood now, so I end up practically screaming the words at him. "Everything would've been so much easier if you had just told me that the Atonement Trials were a sham!"

Frustration flits across his face. "Don't you think I know that?"

"Then why didn't you?"

Draven opens his mouth as if to reply, but apparently, he doesn't have a good answer to that question, because he just closes his mouth again and flexes his hand in frustration while annoyance blows across his features again.

However, before I can press the matter further, footsteps thud from farther down the corridor.

"Commander," a voice calls. A moment later, a messenger rounds the corner and skids to a halt a few steps away from us. He draws in a deep breath. "The Emperor and Empress have requested your presence in the throne room."

A muscle flickers in Draven's jaw, and for a second, he only continues staring me down. As if he wants to continue our argument. But then he forces out a long breath and at last turns to meet the messenger's gaze.

"I figured as much," Draven replies. He jerks his chin at the messenger in dismissal while taking a firm grip on my arm. "Tell them that I'll be right there. I just need to return my pet to where she belongs."

I whip my head around to glare at him, but before I can get a single word out, the messenger clears his throat.

"Your, uhm…" He trails off, his gaze flitting around the empty corridor for a second as he squirms uncomfortably. "Your *immediate* presence has been requested, sir."

Draven clenches his jaw. Then he grinds out, "Fine."

Relief washes over the messenger's face, and he gives Draven a nod. "Please, follow me."

I frown at the messenger's back as he turns around and starts down the hall in the direction from which he came. Draven obviously already knows how to get to the throne room, since he apparently lives in this castle. So there would be no need to have someone escort him there like this. Except as a power play to remind him that he can be summoned at will. Which strikes me as a little odd.

Draven's hand is still around my arm when he starts forward, pulling me with him. Since I was lost in thought, I stumble a little before I manage to fall into step beside him.

"Behave," he commands, his voice hard.

Snapping my gaze to him, I'm just about to growl back at him that I am not his pet. But the expression on his face stops me. His voice might be cold and ruthless, and his words might be an order, but when he meets my gaze, it looks more like a plea.

My gaze drifts to the messenger's back again where he strides along the corridor in front of us.

A sense of uneasiness slithers through my stomach. Whatever is going on right now obviously involves things that I don't understand yet. And I don't want to make the same mistake of charging blindly into something and screwing up my chances of escape.

So instead of snapping at Draven out of stubborn defiance and stupid pride, I shift my gaze back to his and give him a slow nod to signal that I understood the warning.

Relief pulses across his face for a second before that cold ruthless mask is back on his features again. But he gives my arm a small squeeze before he releases it.

We continue towards the throne room in silence after that.

I try to memorize the path we take as we weave our way through the sparkling ice castle. And I count the guards too. Most corridors we venture through are deserted, and the few times we meet someone, it's people who are dressed like servants. But to my great annoyance, most stairwells we pass are guarded by dragon shifters in silver armor. I add their positions to my mental map anyway.

Once the grand double doors to the throne room at last appear before us, I shift my gaze back to Draven again. He is walking with his back straight and his chin raised, and that usual expression of ruthless power is firmly on his features. I desperately want to reach out with my magic and push at his emotions to see what he's really feeling.

"Your Imperial Majesties," the messenger says, his voice echoing in the high-ceilinged hall, as we walk through the open doors and into the throne room. Taking a step to the side, he sweeps his arm out towards Draven. "Commander Draven Ryat."

Draven just keeps stalking right past the messenger without even glancing at him, as if he can't be bothered to give him even a second of his precious time. The messenger doesn't seem to mind. He just bows to the Icehearts and then backs out of the throne room again. Casting a glance over my shoulder, I find him closing the massive ice doors behind us while Draven and I continue towards the dais ahead.

I shift my gaze back to the two thrones ahead right before an ominous boom echoes through the room, signaling that the doors have now been shut.

Jessina and Bane Iceheart are sitting on their imposing ice thrones atop the dais. As usual, both of them are wearing impeccable clothes in shades of silver. Jessina's white hair has been pinned up with sparkling pins while Bane's black hair hangs straight down his back like a smooth black waterfall. His black eyes are fixed on me while Jessina's pale gray eyes study Draven. Their massive silver wings rustle slightly as they spread them out wider.

Draven keeps his own wings tucked in tightly. I don't know enough about dragon shifter culture to understand all of the subtleties, but this somehow feels like another power play. As if the Icehearts are spreading their wings wider to show dominance, and Draven is keeping his folded to signal that he has no intention of challenging them.

Five paces from the dais, Draven stops. It's the exact same place that Isera, Alistair, and I were standing in during the fake winner's ceremony three days ago. At just the thought of it, I get an overwhelming urge to reach up and tug at the iron collar around my throat again.

However, before I can so much as lift my hand, Draven bows to his monarchs.

There are several other gestures that I would much rather be showing the Icehearts right now, but since I have decided to refrain from being stupid for no reason, I curtsy as well. Jessina snickers faintly, which informs me that my ability to curtsy properly apparently hasn't improve while I've been unconscious.

I remain standing half a step behind Draven as we straighten again.

"Selena is awake," Emperor Bane says without preamble.

I start slightly and snap my gaze to him. This seems like an important summons, so the fact that *that* was the first thing out of his mouth takes me by surprise. His black eyes are still fixed on my face, and I have to resist the urge to fidget.

But Draven just nods and replies, "Yes."

"Alistair and Isera are not," Empress Jessina fills in. She narrows her eyes slightly as she holds Draven's gaze. "Which means that you didn't drain as much energy from her as you should have."

"I know," he replies. "Since Selena is weaker than both Isera and Alistair, I didn't want to take too much the first time and risk having her unconscious for weeks."

He turns to me and slides a hand up my throat. On instinct, I try to jerk back, but his fingers close around my throat, keeping me firmly in place. My heart lurches and then pounds hard against my ribs as a cruel smile spreads across his lips while he leans a little closer to me. There no warmth, nothing compassionate, in his eyes as he locks them on me.

"That is a mistake I'm going to have to rectify later today," Draven says, his voice as vicious as his smile.

My heart hammers in my chest as I stare up at him. Is he going back on his word? In that bedroom earlier, he said that he wasn't going to drain my magic again. But one displeased comment from the Icehearts, and he's already promising to do exactly that.

His eyes betray nothing as he holds my gaze for another second. Then he abruptly releases my throat and turns back to Jessina and Bane.

"But I assume that's not why you summoned me," he says.

Bane slides his dark eyes to Draven. "No, it's not. Three high-ranking lords from our clan, all with important positions within our court, were murdered today."

"Among them was Jonah," Empress Jessina picks up. Her pale eyes burn with fury as she clenches and unclenches her hand. "He was the most competent Master of the Treasury we have had in centuries. I cannot even articulate what a devastating loss his death is for our administration."

Bane nods in agreement while drumming his fingers on the armrest of his throne. "Three important people killed *inside* the palace... This can only mean one thing." He clenches his jaw. "The Red Hand is back."

It takes all of my willpower to keep a neutral expression on my face. But inside the safety of my own head, my mind is churning.

"Yes, it would appear so," Draven replies.

Jessina grinds her teeth. "I thought you said that the Red Hand would never dare to show his face again after you almost caught him last time. That he would spend the rest of his life in hiding and that the human rebellion had been crushed for good."

My heart skips a beat. Human rebellion? There are humans who are trying to overthrow the Iceheart Dynasty too?

"It appears as though I was wrong," Draven simply says.

Ice shoots through the air.

A gasp rips from my lungs, and I throw my arms up to protect my face while I duck and twist.

But no sharp shards of ice hit my body. Glancing up, I find

Draven standing in the exact same place as before. Seven blades of ice hover in the air a hair's breadth from his throat. He just continues watching the two monarchs with that impassive expression on his face. As if he didn't even flinch when the ice shot towards him.

Slowly lowering my arms, I straighten again and turn back so that I'm facing Bane and Jessina once more. My pulse still thrums in my ears.

"Find him," Empress Jessina grinds out between gritted teeth.

Draven inclines his head. The move almost makes him cut himself on the ice shards, so Jessina flicks her wrist, making them vanish again.

"I will deliver his corpse to you at once," Draven promises.

"No," Bane interrupts. "I want him alive. I want him shackled and kneeling at our feet. And then I want to watch the hope die in the humans' eyes when we publicly torture their greatest symbol of rebellion to death right in front of them."

Draven lowers his chin. "Consider it done."

My chest tightens. Then determination seeps into my heart as I steal a glance at Draven from the corner of my eye.

I can't let him do this. I can't let them crush the human rebellion. Alone, the Seelie Court might never stand a chance against the Iceheart Dynasty. But if I can somehow get their human rebellion in contact with our fae resistance, we might be strong enough together to make a difference.

Drawing in a long breath, I squeeze my hand into a fist.

I know what I need to do now.

I need to escape, I need to find the human rebellion, and then I need to warn the Red Hand about Draven's mission.

That cold hard wall around my heart thickens as I cast another glance at Draven. I *will* protect the Red Hand and the human rebellion. Even if it means that I have to kill Draven to do it.

# CHAPTER FOUR

Dread squeezes my lungs when we walk across the threshold and back into Draven's fancy living room. During the walk back from the throne room, I was finally able to learn how to get from Draven's rooms to the main entrance. But it is with growing hopelessness that I realize that I will never be able to get there without being caught. Almost every stairwell is guarded.

The door clicks shut behind me. I flick my gaze around the living room, trying to come up with some kind of plan for how to escape. The cluster of dark gray armchairs and couches around the low wooden table stare back at me uselessly from across the room. The desk and chair to my right don't look very promising either.

My gaze lands on the clear ice door opposite me that leads out onto a balcony. I wonder what's below that. I might be able to climb down and—

Fingers brush against the back of my neck.

I whip around while wrapping a hand around my own throat to protect it. A sharp breath of surprise escapes my lips when I find Draven standing right there, his hand still lifted from when it brushed against my neck.

Ice spreads through my veins. He is going to do what Bane and Jessina told him to do. Drain my magic more fully.

For a few seconds, we only watch each other in silence. Then he turns his hand and instead twitches two fingers at me, ordering me to come closer.

"Come here," he commands.

"Don't you fucking dare," I growl back at him.

Shaking his head in frustration, he reaches for my throat again. "I'm—"

I bolt.

Darting to the side, I aim to sprint past him and reach the door that leads out into the corridor.

His massive black wings flare out wide, blocking my way.

I suck in a gasp and skid to a halt. Throwing myself sideways, I barely manage to get out of reach before his hand can close around my wrist. My heart hammers as I whip my head from side to side in search of safety.

Draven lunges for me.

Panic blares inside my skull. Making a split-second decision, I run towards the closest door. Which leads to the bedroom that I woke up in. My feet thud against the dark wooden floorboards as I dart into the room and grab the door to throw it shut behind me.

It slams into Draven's shoulder.

He lets out a huff, and he draws his eyebrows down as he pushes the door open again.

Whirling around, I abandon my efforts to get the door shut and instead back farther into the room. Draven stalks after me. I reach out blindly and grab the closest thing I can find. Which happens to be a desk light made of glass and steel, with a faelight gem in the middle.

With a scream, I hurl it straight at Draven's face.

He simply leans a little to the right, and the desk light sails harmlessly over his shoulder instead.

The sound of shattering glass echoes through the room as the desk light hits the white ice wall behind Draven with a crash. Shards rain down and clink against the floor, along with heavier thumps from the metal base. The faelight gem flickers among the wreckage.

My chest rises and falls with short shallow breaths as I continue backing away.

Draven casts a lazy glance over his shoulder at the shattered light holder. Then he slides his gaze back to me and cocks his head. "That... was an antique."

"Don't touch me," I snarl. But the fury in my voice barely manages to mask how it trembles. "I swear to Mabona, if you touch me, I will—"

He flies across the room.

With one powerful beat of his massive wings, he has closed the distance between us. I dive sideways, trying to get out of reach. But his arms wrap around my waist, and we crash down on the floor.

I kick my heel back, aiming for his shin. But dull pain only pulses through my own foot when my heel hits his dragon scale armor. Flailing and wiggling, I try to break his grip on me before he can pin me completely.

A grunt and a low curse escape his throat as he struggles to keep hold of me. I kick and ram my elbows at him again while trying to crawl away.

Then his hands wrap tightly around my wrists at the same time as he rolls over, taking me with him. My back is pressed flat against the floor as Draven settles his weight on my hips.

Panic pulses through me, and I yank furiously against his grip on my wrists as he begins moving my hands towards his knees. A frustrated cry rips from my lungs. But it's useless. Draven simply moves my hands until he can pin them to the floor with his knees.

Once his knees are pressing down on my palms, he releases my wrists.

My heart is beating so fast that I can barely hear anything over the pounding in my ears. I think Draven is saying something, but I can't hear past the panic.

He reaches towards my throat again.

I squirm desperately underneath him while fear and anger rip at my soul. He's going to drain my magic again, and then I will be left lying helpless on the floor. I will never be able to escape. Because as long as he keeps draining my magic, I won't be able to recover enough strength to fight or run. Or to resist in any way. I won't be able to do anything to stop him. To save myself.

His hands reach my throat.

Panic blares inside my skull and my heart hammers against my ribs as I fight against his overwhelming strength.

"I will kill you for this!" I scream at him, and my voice almost cracks. "I swear I will fucking kill you for—"

The iron pressing against my throat disappears.

I gasp as my connection to my magic is restored. Strength starts trickling back into my limbs again as my energy begins building back up to normal levels as well.

Lying there on the floor, I stare up at Draven in utter shock.

He is still straddling my hips and pinning my hands under his knees. But he didn't drain my magic. Instead...

I shift my gaze to his hand, staring uncomprehendingly at the item dangling from his fingers.

An iron collar.

*The* iron collar.

*My* iron collar.

Draven's eyes are serious as he holds my gaze.

My heart thumps in my chest.

For a few seconds, it's as if time isn't moving at all.

Then reality comes crashing back down over me as Draven eases his knees off my palms and gets to his feet in one fluid motion.

With my hands now free, I move one up to my throat and draw my fingers over my neck. My eyes have already confirmed that Draven has removed the iron collar, but my mind is still trying to process it, so I need the extra touch to confirm it too.

When my fingers only meet the smooth skin of my throat, a small sob of profound relief escapes my lips.

At the sound, Draven's grip on the iron collar tightens until he is squeezing it so hard that his knuckles turn white.

Suddenly worried that he's going to put it back on me again, I scramble off the floor and get to my feet as well. But Draven only remains standing there in front of me, watching me with eyes I can't read. His muscled chest rises and falls with what looks like highly controlled breaths.

Drawing a hand over my throat again, I watch him while shock continues clanging inside my skull. "You took off my collar."

"Yes." Even his tone is unnaturally controlled.

"You trust me not to manipulate your emotions and try to escape?"

"No."

His eyes sear into mine like fire, and I can tell that he means that word with every fiber of his being. He knows that I will try to use my magic to escape now. But for some reason, he took off my collar anyway.

That unspoken question hangs in the air between us. The very silence seems to crackle with lightning.

"Why?" I manage to press out at last. It comes out like barely more than a whisper.

He draws in another highly controlled breath and tightens his grip on the collar. "Because if I have to see you in this collar one fucking second more than absolutely necessary, I'm going to start killing people."

My heart flips.

The muscles in his jaw flicker as he forces out a breath and flexes his fingers around the collar still in his hand. "Outside this room, you need to wear it. If you don't, they will torture you. But in here, when it's just us, I will take it off."

Before I can even figure out how to respond to that, he turns and walks over to the pale wooden dresser by the wall. After putting the collar into one of the lower drawers, he pulls out something made of black fabric.

"I couldn't remove it while you were unconscious because I couldn't be here every minute of every day." He shuts the drawer and turns back to me. "People sometimes come in here to clean, without my knowledge, and I couldn't risk them seeing you without it. But now that you're awake, you can hide it yourself even if I'm not here."

I stare at him, my mind still spinning with disbelief, as he walks back to me and holds out a rich black cloak.

"If you ever need to hide it, put this on," he says, offering me the garment. "The cloak clasps at the front of your throat, and it hides the part where the collar is supposed to be. No one will be able to tell if you're wearing it underneath the cloak or not."

Reaching out, I numbly take the cloak. It's soft and warm against my palm as I grip it.

"I'll let slip that I'm making you wear it to humiliate you," he continues. "It's in my clan color, so people will just think that it's my way of reminding you that I own you now."

I drag in an unsteady breath while I keep the cloak in a death grip. I feel like my head is ringing.

"Why?" I manage to press out. "Why are you doing this?"

His eyes soften for a fraction of a second. Then it's gone, and he just blows out a small sigh instead. "I've already told you. Because you don't deserve this."

A knock comes from the front door.

I whip my head towards it while panic pulses through me.

But Draven was apparently expecting it, because he just nods calmly at the cloak in my hands. "Put it on."

It takes me a second to pry it out of my own death grip. Shaking out the rich black fabric, I drape it over my shoulders and then clasp it at the front of my throat. Just like Draven said, it hides most of my throat from view.

Once it's in place, Draven nods and then walks over to the door. From where I'm standing, I can't see who is on the other side when he opens it, but it appears to be the person Draven was expecting, because he takes a step back as if to invite the person inside.

"Put it on the desk," he commands, his voice dripping with authority. Then he raises a hand and points towards the bedroom I'm standing in. "And then clean up the mess on the floor."

My gaze flits to the shattered glass and steel frame that apparently used to be an antique desk light.

A woman in a pale gray dress nods in acknowledgement as she walks past Draven. In her hands, she's holding a tray full of food. My stomach growls at the mere sight of it.

After setting down the tray on the desk, she hurries into my bedroom. She doesn't even acknowledge me. Only begins cleaning up the mess I made without a word.

Out in the living room, Draven snaps his fingers and locks eyes with me before stabbing a hand towards the tray of food. "Eat."

Since I'm too hungry to be offended by his presumptuous command, I simply walk over to the desk and sit down. Draven crosses his arms and leans one shoulder against the wall as he watches me inhale three entire plates of food and gulp down a whole pitcher of water.

The woman in the gray dress finishes cleaning up at the same time as I swallow the last bite of food. She bows to Draven before she disappears out the door again with both the now empty tray and a small bag full of clinking glass shards.

Once she has shut the door behind her, Draven turns back to me.

"Good," he says. "Your collar is off, you have eaten, and you understand the situation you're in." He nods towards the room I woke up in. "That's your bedroom." He jerks his chin towards the closed door on the other side of the living room. "That's my bedroom. The bathroom is the door next to it. Any questions?"

I almost laugh out loud. He's joking, right? I have like a million questions about a million different things.

But since I get the feeling that the answer to his question is supposed to be *no*, I decide to give him what he wants. "No."

He nods. "Good. Now stay here."

"Where are you going?"

"You heard Bane and Jessina. There is a killer on the loose."

"The Red Hand."

"Yes."

I open my mouth, but then decide that asking too many questions would be stupid since it would just make him suspicious. I already have a plan, and it's better for me if he leaves quickly so that I can get to it. So instead of asking more about the Red Hand, or telling him what I really think about his mission to kill the most important resistance fighter in this city, I blow out a sigh and give him a nod as if I have accepted my reality.

Draven watches me in silence for another few moments, as if he doesn't believe it for a second. Then he shakes his head, informing me that he is indeed not buying my act in the slightest, and straightens from the wall.

"Don't do anything stupid," he says.

Before I can retort, he stalks out the door and closes it behind him.

Two distinct clicking sounds echo between the white ice walls as he locks it too. I shoot him a glare through the door, even though he can't see it.

Then I jump up from the chair and hurry over to the balcony door instead.

I have a human resistance to find.

# CHAPTER FIVE

Winds swirl over the wide balcony, tugging at my black cloak and making my long silver hair flutter behind me. I brace my palms on the ice railing and lean forward a little so that I can look down.

The ground stares back at me from four stories up.

My stomach turns.

Shifting my gaze, I study the ice wall next to me that runs straight down to the stone ground below. Just like that ice wall that Jessina created in the hedge maze during the Atonement Trials, this one also looks to have been made by ice flames. At least in part. The wall is straight, but it's not smooth. The ice flames must have frozen the way they hit, because the entire surface of the wall is jagged and uneven. Which means that it might be possible to climb it.

My gaze slides back to the hard stone ground again.

"It's not that high," I try to persuade myself, as if that would somehow make the ground come closer. "I could totally climb that."

Another gust of wind rushes over the balcony, and I

instinctively grip the railing harder. Mabona's tits, did it really have to be windy today of all days?

I cast a glance over my shoulder. From this angle, I can only see part of the living room through the open balcony door. But the front door to Draven's quarters remains closed and locked.

Swallowing, I shift my gaze back to the world outside. I can't let this opportunity pass me by. Draven has taken off my collar, and he has left and will likely be gone for a while. If there was ever an opportunity to escape and seek out the human resistance, it's now.

My eyes sweep across the city that is visible on the other side of the defensive walls that circle the Ice Palace. Sunlight shines down from a mostly clear sky to illuminate the sprawling city that spreads out across the grasslands at the foot of the mountain. Compared to the Seelie Court, it's so big that my mind can barely comprehend its true size. Buildings made of wood and stone almost seem to gleam in the sunlight.

And somewhere in there is the human resistance and the legendary assassin known as the Red Hand.

Determination fills my heart as I gaze towards the city.

Straightening, I squeeze my hand into a fist and thump it against the ice railing while I give myself a firm nod. I have to risk it.

There looks to be a side gate set into the high defensive walls a short distance to my left, and now that I have my magic back, I should be able to get through it. All I need to do is to get down there.

My stomach turns again as I follow the uneven ice wall all the way down to the ground. I swallow once more as I try to push back the nausea. I can do this. It's just like the Atonement Trials. Just a little higher. Well, a lot higher. But hey, who's counting?

I draw in a deep breath to steady myself as I move towards the side of the balcony. After climbing up so that I'm sitting on the railing, I reach towards the closest chunk of ice that juts out a little from the wall.

Just like the rest of this castle, it's not freezing the way normal ice is. Only cool. I grip the improvised handhold tightly as I twist my body and ram my foot into a small indentation. My heart slams against my ribs.

After drawing in another bracing breath, I push off from the railing and swing myself onto the wall.

A jolt of dread shoots through my whole body, making me feel lightheaded. I squeeze my eyes shut for a second while I cling to my temporary handholds so hard that my fingers ache.

Once the sense of dread and vertigo has passed, I pry my eyes open again and focus firmly on the ice wall in front of my face. As long as I only watch that, and don't look down, I won't know just how high up I really am right now.

There is another handhold a little farther down. I shift my hand down towards it while letting one leg drop down as well in search of another foothold. Once I find it, I slowly ease my way down.

And then I climb.

My pulse thrums in my ears as I make my way down the side of the Ice Palace. I can barely force air in and out of my lungs because my mind keeps screaming at me that this is a terrible fucking idea and that I'm going to slip and plummet to my death. But it's too late to stop. I need to make it down now. One way or another. But preferably in the way that doesn't leave me broken and dying on the stones below.

A gust of wind rips through the air.

I gasp as it catches in my cloak, yanking it hard to the side. It pulls me off balance, and I miss the next foothold.

My stomach lurches as I step right into the air instead.

I cry out in panic.

Air rushes in my ears as my body drops downwards. I grip the ice hard with my hands, but the sudden yank downwards when my feet can't brace on anything rips my left hand off the chunk of ice I was holding on to.

Another wind slams into me.

Tears, from both the cold wind and the panic, sting my eyes as I scramble to get my hand back up to another handhold. My cloak whips in the wind behind me. I throw my left hand out blindly while gripping the ice hard with my right. But it's slipping.

Panic spikes through my spine.

I just need to—

My hand slips from the wall.

I don't even have time to be afraid. Instead, a strange sense of breathless disappointment washes through my entire body as I plummet downwards. I'm going to die. I'm going to hit the stones below and break my legs. Shatter my spine. Crack my skull. The fall is going to—

My feet slam into the ground after only a second.

The impact is so sudden, and so unexpected, that my knees buckle even though the force of it wasn't particularly strong. Toppling over, I crash down on the ground.

For a few seconds, all I can do is to lie there on my side and stare at the uneven gray stone that makes up the surface beneath me. My mind is convinced that I should still be falling through the air. But the rough stone underneath my cheek says otherwise.

Dragging in a shuddering breath, I slide my hand along the cold stones.

The ground.

Which was apparently a lot closer than I thought.

Pushing myself up onto my knees, I elbow a scraggly bush out of the way and then tilt my head back to look up at the ice wall before me. The handhold I slipped from stares back at me from only a short distance above me. While I was climbing, I was so focused on the wall that I never looked down to see how far up I was. I had apparently made more progress than I realized.

I suck in another ragged breath while my mind continues spinning.

My stomach turns.

I'm not dead. I'm not lying broken and paralyzed on the stones. I'm still alive. Still unharmed.

Bracing one hand on the ice wall, I lean over the bush beside me.

And then I throw up.

Repeatedly.

Every one of my limbs shakes, and my pulse is still thrumming so fast in my ears that I can barely hear anything. I wipe my mouth with the back of my hand and drag in an unsteady breath.

Once my mind has finally accepted the fact that I didn't die, I push myself up to my knees and stagger away from the wall. I don't know if guards patrol here, so I can't linger too long. The side gate that I spotted from the balcony is just a short distance away, so I flip the hood of my cloak up and sneak towards it.

As I draw closer, I realize that the gate is made of round metal bars rather than something solid. I study the color while I take up position in the shadows of the wall close to it. Based on the color, it looks to be made of iron.

Annoyance flits through me. Of course it's fucking iron.

I shift my gaze to the man standing in front of it.

He is wearing silver armor, which means that he is part of Bane and Jessina's clan rather than Draven's. Just like all adult shifters, he looks to be somewhere between twenty-five and thirty years old, so just based on his appearance, I have no idea if he is experienced or a new recruit.

Narrowing my eyes, I study his body language. He is standing too straight to be comfortable. People who are older and more experienced usually look more relaxed, because they are confident in their abilities and their orders. I drum my fingers against my thigh. If I had to guess, I would say that he is someone who is desperate to prove himself. And I sure hope that I have guessed correctly. Because my life is about to depend on it.

After making sure that the cloak covers my pointed ears, I step out of the shadows and stride straight towards the guard with confident steps.

"Why isn't this door already unlocked?" I bark with enough authority to surprise even myself.

The guard jumps in surprise and then hurries to straighten again as he turns to me and snaps to attention. "What—"

"Commander Ryat sent word half an hour ago that you were to have it open and ready for me the second I appeared," I declare, interrupting him. "Every second you waste here is another second that my mission goes unfulfilled."

Worry and panic pulse across the guard's face at the mention of Draven's name, and at the sight of my black cloak.

Turning to the right, I stab a hand towards a path that I most certainly did not come from. "You should have seen me walking towards you and already have been ready."

The moment I turn around to point, when he can no longer see my eyes, I call up my magic and shove it at the yellow spark of panic in the guard's chest. Then I blow it into a wildfire.

"I d-didn't—" he stammers.

Cutting off the flow of my magic, I turn back towards him again. "You have two seconds to open that gate before I report your insubordination to the commander."

All blood drains from the guard's face.

Metal clinks as he snatches up his ring of keys so fast that he almost drops it. Whipping around, he tries to ram the key into the lock. But his movements are so frantic that he misses it several times.

While his back is to me, I once more call up my magic. This time, I push at the bone white spark of fear in his chest. I increase it rapidly until I can see his hands shaking.

The keys rattle in his hands. But then he finally gets the door unlocked and shoves it open.

I cut off my magic right before he can turn around and see that my eyes were glowing.

"Here, I'm sorry," he blurts out. "Please, don't tell him."

Stalking forward, I growl, "Make sure that this door is always open for me before I even reach it, and I'll consider not telling him about this."

"Thank you," he gasps out as I stride right past him and out the gate.

As soon as I have passed him, I once again reach out with my magic and increase his fear. Metal clanks and rattles as he struggles to close and lock the door behind me.

A victorious grin spreads across my mouth.

It's followed by a wave of relief and pure joy.

Cool fall winds whirl across the sloping mountainside and fill my lungs as I stride away from the Ice Palace a free woman. I did it. I made it out. I will never have to go back to that suffocating castle again. Never have to wear that awful iron collar again. Never have to kneel at Draven's feet or watch the Icehearts smirk at me.

I'm free.

And now, it's time to fight back.

A path has been cut into the mountainside, and it leads down to the city below. I follow it.

Excitement pulses through me like lightning when I reach the end of the path and the first buildings appear before me. The Atonement Trials might have been a sham, but ultimately, I achieved my goal. I made it out of the Seelie Court. And now, I have a chance to start a new life.

Buildings made of wood and stone line the wide cobblestone street that I start down once I leave the small footpath behind. It's deserted. But the sound of voices comes from farther down. My heart patters against my ribs as I make my way towards it.

I have no idea how to find the Red Hand and the human resistance, so first, I just need to explore the city and get a feel for it.

Reaching up, I once again make sure that my hood is in place. As long as my pointed ears are covered, I can pass for a dragon shifter. Or a human.

Another burst of ridiculous excitement shoots through me.

Humans. I'm about to see real humans for the first time.

The soft chatter at the end of the street gets louder with every step.

My heart thumps in my chest.

This is it.

I turn the corner.

And walk right into a busy road.

People in all shapes and sizes bustle up and down the street in groups or pairs or alone. Trailing to a halt, I just stand there and stare for a while.

Two people with dark brown hair lug a large sack from an open doorway and towards a waiting cart. After swinging it back and forth, they heave it up onto the already half full cart. It lands with a thud, sending a small cloud of what looks like flour swirling into the air. They dust their hands off and then walk back into the dark wooden building to grab another one.

Across the street, a woman in a simple green dress is sweeping the porch in front of what looks like some kind of shop. She wipes her forehead with the back of her hand before leaning the broom against the stone wall of the building. Then she disappears back inside.

More people are strolling up and down the street.

"Do you need help, dear?"

I start in surprise. Realizing that my mouth was slightly open, I snap it shut and give my head a quick shake to clear it before I turn towards the source of the voice.

A short woman with a round face and a kind smile looks at

me with eyebrows raised. Her wavy blond hair ripples over her shoulders as another gust of wind swirls between the buildings.

I blink, remembering that she asked me a question.

"Uhm, no," I manage to press out at last. Then I force a smile onto my own lips and nod. "But thank you."

She nods back and pats me on the arm before she opens the door that I was standing right next to. Still trying to process everything, I once again give my head a quick shake and move away from the door that I was almost blocking.

Since just standing here is obviously drawing attention, I decide to just pick a direction and start walking. I choose the one that looks to be leading farther into the city.

Sunlight streams down from the blue sky and glints in the windows of the buildings that I pass. Small flowerpots that contain evergreens dot several of the porches, and a few of the wooden houses have even been painted in bright colors.

All around me, people are chatting and going about their day like normal. As if this isn't one of the most monumental moments in my entire life.

A woman walks out of a doorway to my right and closes it behind her. Then she staggers over to a rickety wooden chair that has been placed on the porch. It creaks as she drops into it. With a sigh, she leans back and tilts her face up towards the sun.

I stop dead in the middle of the road.

My jaw practically hits the ground when I take in her face.

It's... wrinkled.

Her cheeks are saggy and there are bags under her eyes and there are lines all over her forehead and around her eyes.

My heart is barely beating as I just stare at her in shock.

She's old.

And she's not just old. She *looks* old.

I have never seen someone look old before. It's fascinating. While the old woman sits there and soaks up the sun, I stand a short distance away and stare at her like an absolute idiot. Stare at the way her limbs look thin and frail. The way her skin seems to hang loosely around her bones. At the wrinkles and the dark spots on her skin.

Fae don't physically age like that. And neither do dragon shifters. So it's the first time that I have ever seen a physically old person. It's mind-blowing. Her entire body is a testament to the fact that she has *lived*. Proof of all the decades she has seen. All the things she has endured and experienced. It's incredible. Absolutely incredible.

It isn't until people start staring at *me* that I force myself to keep moving. But it doesn't matter. Because I meet several other old people as I continue down the next street. I stare at them too, but a little more discreetly.

Once I'm several streets deep, I have finally figured out how to tell the humans and the dragon shifters apart. Since normal dragon shifters can't perform a half-shift, no one out here has wings on display the way Draven and the Icehearts do. And there is no real difference in terms of height or physique either. Instead, the thing that sets the humans apart is something more intangible.

They all look more alive, more real, than both the dragon shifters and we fae do. Because we don't physically age, both fae and dragon shifters have an ethereal sense of timelessness to our features. The humans don't. Instead, they look like they have truly lived, even the young ones, in a way that we don't.

In all the stories about humans, no one ever mentioned this strange aura that they possess that the rest of us don't. Though I suppose the fae who were allowed to live after the dragon shifters conquered us wouldn't have had a chance to meet a human before that, so maybe that's why.

I study them intently as I walk. Apart from lack of that ethereal quality to their features, they look almost exactly like dragon shifters. They also have those strange eyes that only have one color instead of—

Panic shoots through my chest.

My eyes.

I've been covering my ears. But my turquoise and lavender eyes are just as damning. I'm the only person here who has two colors in both eyes.

*Shit*. Tugging the hood of my cloak down, I cover my eyes in enough shadow that people hopefully won't notice. The dragon shifter guard at the gate had to have noticed. But I must have manipulated his emotions enough that he truly believed that Draven had sent me even though I was fae. And I must have gotten lucky with that human woman back there on the street. Or maybe the humans don't know about fae.

I frown as I turn a corner and disappear down a far less busy street.

Is it possible that the dragon shifters have kept our entire existence a secret? Or maybe they just don't know about all of our physical characteristics since they have likely never seen any of us before. Just like I didn't know that humans didn't have the same ethereal quality to their features as we do.

Shaking my head, I continue deeper into the city. There is so much I don't know about this world that I'm now supposed to be a part of. So I study everything intently as I walk.

Now that I know which people are humans and which are shifters, I notice something else. All the fancy shops I pass are owned by dragon shifters, and all the hard manual labor is done by humans. The shifters are also dressed better. Not in terms of style, but rather quality. The clothes that the humans wear are, in general, more worn and frayed. The humans also look more tired, though I don't know if that's just because they age differently.

I frown as I note the holes in a human man's shirt as he pulls a heavy cart up the road. Maybe the shifters treat the humans like they treat us too. But why would they? Their race didn't enslave the dragon shifters the way that all of our ancestors did.

"What the fuck are you staring at?"

My heart leaps into my throat, and I whirl towards the sound of the voice.

A small breath of relief escapes me when I realize that the comment wasn't directed at me. Across the road, a little to my right, two male dragon shifters in silver armor have cornered a human man against a wall.

"Nothing," the human says. He keeps his chin lowered as he shakes his head. "I wasn't looking at you."

"Oh really?" the black-haired shifter replies. "Then why could I see your disrespectful eyes glaring at me when you thought I didn't notice?"

The human swallows. "I… uhm…"

They shove him up against the wall.

Anger flashes through me. After flicking my gaze up and down the road to make sure that no one is watching me, I summon my magic and push at the spark of anger in the shifter's chest.

To my surprise, it's not there.

I try another emotion.

The orange spark of smug superiority in his chest is so large that I actually blink in surprise. He really must think that he is better than all the humans.

Using my magic, I decrease his sense of superiority until it's barely more than a flicker.

Unfortunately, it doesn't matter.

I gasp and release my magic as he still rams his fist into the human's stomach.

Air explodes from the man's lungs, and he doubles over. But the second shifter just yanks him back up while his companion hits him again. Pain pulses across the human's face as an armored fist slams into his cheek.

And all around me, people do… nothing.

They just avert their eyes and hurry away.

Fury crashes over me like a tidal wave. I am so fucking sick of these haughty idiots and their damn entitlement. They act like bullies. And for absolutely no reason. Just because their ancestors suffered millennia ago doesn't give them the right to beat up innocent people now.

With my hood still pulled down low to hide my face, I glance around at the people hurrying away while the soldiers continue pummeling the human. Someone should do something. Someone should step in. Someone should stop this.

And then I realize that *I* am someone.

Before I even know what I'm doing, I've picked up a small pot from the windowsill next to me and thrown it at the closest dragon shifter.

The evergreen that had been planted in the pot flops back and forth in distress as the pot sails through the air.

Then it hits the dragon shifter in the back of the head.

A loud thud sounds. Followed by a crash as the pot lands on the stones behind him. His knees buckle. Then he too crashes down on the ground.

For a few seconds, the entire street is dead silent.

The human man stares at me, his blue eyes wide with disbelief. As does the remaining dragon shifter. His gaze flits down to his now unconscious partner, and then it slowly slides to me.

Logic and reason at last catch up with me.

I shouldn't have done that.

I really shouldn't have done that.

From where he's still standing pressed against the wall, the human gives me a look of gratitude.

In front of him, the dragon shifter shoots me a death stare.

He takes one slow step forward.

Then he's barreling straight towards me.

*Oh shit.*

# CHAPTER SIX

Whirling around, I sprint down the street in the other direction. Pounding feet echo behind me as the dragon shifter gives chase.

"Stop her!" he bellows at the citizens on the street.

My heart lurches.

But none of the humans step out into the road to stop me. In fact, after casting a glance towards the man I just saved and the unconscious soldier I left in my wake, they do the opposite. They leap out of my way when I hurtle down the street.

Grabbing the railing of a small porch, I swing myself around the corner of the building and sprint into a narrow alley. I need to make him lose sight of me. My heart thumps in my chest as running footstep pounds against the cobblestones far too close behind me.

I whip my head from side to side, trying to plot out an escape route. Running from pursuers? I've done that a hundred times before in the Seelie Court. The only problem is of course that, back then, I knew every street like the back of my hand. And now, I have absolutely no idea where I'm going.

The alley ends abruptly before me. I blink in shock as I skid right out into a wide square full of market stalls and people. And more soldiers in silver armor.

Panic pulses through me. I need to get out of sight before the man behind me can call out and tell them that I—

"The human in the black cloak!" the soldier behind me shouts. "Stop her!"

Three soldiers in silver armor whip their heads in our direction.

Mabona fucking damn it.

Sprinting to the left, I weave through a sea of market stalls and shocked people who gasp and stumble out of the way as I barrel past them. Colorful awnings on their wooden booths flutter in the wind, and the scent of baking bread and spiced meat drift through the air.

I dart around a wide stall selling meat pies. A sheet of fabric appears right in front of me. Shoving it up, I roll underneath it and jump to my feet at the back of the booth on the other side. A man with large round glasses scrambles out of his chair so fast that he knocks it over. It hits the ground in a clattering of wood.

"Sorry," I mumble as I duck underneath his shelves full of clocks and pocket watches.

"There!" an angry voice shouts from somewhere on my left.

A soft curse rips from my lungs as I take off down the alley of market stalls. Ducking and twisting through the crowd of people, I set course for the nearest road that leads away from this crowded square.

I let out a breath of relief when I finally detach myself from the last group of people and can run unhindered down the side street I picked.

But I only make it halfway down before dread washes through my veins like ice.

At the end of the road I'm sprinting down is a house.

Panic blares through me.

This is a dead-end street.

Screeching to a halt, I cast a panicked look over my shoulder. There is only a matter of time before the dragon shifters reach this road. And once they do, they will see me.

And I have nowhere to hide.

My heart slams against my ribs as I turn around so that I'm facing the mouth of the street while I continue backing farther towards the dead end. I'm going to have to fight them. Or manipulate their emotions. Or manipulate their emotions *and* fight them. Four of them.

If only I had my knife. Then I could… Then I could what? Take on four trained dragon shifter soldiers on my own? Goddess above, this is never going to work.

A yelp slips from my lips as a strong hand suddenly wraps around my upper arm and yanks me to the side. My stomach lurches as the ground disappears underneath my foot when I take a step to the side.

Someone curses under his breath next to me, but I don't have time to look at who it is because I'm busy falling down the short steps into some kind of cellar. The wooden steps dig into my body as I roll down them before I hit the floor with a huff.

Wood groans as the trapdoor I fell through is pulled shut. It's followed by a soft thud as the man at the top of the steps bolts it with a thick wooden bar as well.

"Ow," I groan as I roll to a stop against the side of a crate.

The man whips his head towards me and puts a finger against his lips. I snap my mouth shut right as voices echo from somewhere above.

"I swear she ran in here," someone says.

"Then where is she?" another male voice growls back. This one I recognize. It's the first shifter who was chasing me. "There's no one here."

"If you're looking for a woman in a black cloak, she pretended to run in here but then she doubled back and took the other road," a new voice says.

"Which one?"

"The one just to the left there."

Angry cursing echoes through the air but then grows fainter along with the stomping of boots.

I heave a deep sigh of relief as the soldiers who were hunting me leave to search the other street that some kind soul lied to them about. Pushing to my feet, I turn towards the other kind soul who saved me.

A human man with thin brown hair and a scraggly beard walks down the steps to the stone floor of the cellar. His blue eyes look me up and down in an assessing, but not hostile, way.

"I saw what you did for ol' Jerry back there," he says. "Was watching from the roof, ya see."

"Thank you for hiding me," I reply as I dust myself off and straighten my clothes.

"Mm-hmm." He scratches at his beard as he comes to a halt in front of me. "Got very strange eyes, you have. Don't look like no dragon shifter I've ever seen. So who are ya?"

Hesitation blows through me for a second. Revealing who I am might be risky. But at the same time, I need to find the human resistance as fast as possible. And if this guy was willing to hide me from the Silver Clan soldiers, he must at least share some of the same sentiments as the resistance. He might even be one of them. Or at least know how to contact them.

"I, uhm…" Worry flickers through me, but I ignore it and instead reach up to push my hood back. "I'm not a dragon shifter."

He sucks in a sharp breath between crooked teeth. Stumbling a step back, he stares at me with wide eyes. Or not me. Rather, he stares at my pointed ears.

"Y-you, you're one of them fae, ain't ya?" he manages to press out at last.

I nod. "Yes."

"Father Almighty."

I have no idea who Father Almighty is, but he says it the same way that I curse using our Goddess Mabona's name, so I'm assuming that it must be the human god.

"Well, ain't this something to shock my socks off," he says while shaking his head at me in disbelief. "How did you even manage to get into the city? Ain't all of yous supposed to be in some forest leagues from here?"

"Yeah, I, uhm…"

Goddess above, how am I supposed to summarize everything that has happened to me these last few weeks? How much does he even know?

"Do you know anything about the Atonement Trials?" I ask instead.

"Them competitions where they pick their life slaves?" He smacks his lips and nods. "Yep. Heard the rumors, I have."

"Okay…" I trail off, trying to figure out how to phrase this. In the end, I decide to just say it. "I'm one of them."

Blood drains from his face and he takes a step back. "You…? You're one of their life slaves?"

"I was. I escaped."

"Father Almighty." Running a hand through his beard, he tugs at the tangled hairs on his chin. "Whose?"

"Draven Ryat's."

His hand falls away from his beard as he stares at me. "The Shadow of Death? You're his?"

"I *was*," I repeat. "I escaped."

"Aw, woman. This is… You've gotta come with me. Quick."

Taking a step around me, he waves frantically with his hand while he hurries across the cellar floor and towards a door set into the wall on my right.

Hope surges inside me. He does know the resistance. He has to. Otherwise, he wouldn't be reacting like this.

With excitement coursing through my veins, I jog after him.

Metallic clicking echoes between the stone walls of the cellar as he unlocks the door and pulls it open.

"Hurry," he calls, and casts an impatient glance over his shoulder. "Ain't got much time."

I pick up the pace as he disappears across the threshold. My feet thud against the stones as I hurry into the room after him.

Blinking, I come to a halt. It looks like some kind of storage room. Wooden crates are stacked floor to ceiling, and it's dark. The only light comes from the torches that were set into the wall of the main room we just left. And the man is nowhere to be seen.

"Where…" I begin right as something creaks behind me.

I whip around.

But it's already too late.

The man, who was apparently hiding behind the wall right next to the door, has already darted back out and thrown the door shut behind him. I sprint towards it and throw my shoulder against the wood right as a metallic click sounds.

Utter darkness now fills the room.

"What are you doing?" I scream at him through the door as I bang my fist against the wood.

"The only smart thing there is," he replies from the other side. "I'm gonna give you back to the Shadow of Death and beg him for his mercy."

"No!" I slam my fist against the door again. "Don't do this! You can't—"

"Have to. If he found out that I hid you… That I helped you… He'd slaughter everyone I've ever spoken to."

Summoning my magic, I shove desperately at the spark of sympathy in his chest. But it's not there.

"Please," I beg, trying to create a spark of sympathy that I can manipulate. "He's going to kill me. He's going to torture me. You can't give me back to him. Please. I'm begging you."

I push frantically at his sympathy again. But my lies have

apparently not been enough to create any. I slam my hand against the door.

No sound comes from the other side.

Dread washes over me when I realize that he must have already left.

Wood groans in distress as I pound hard on the door and throw my shoulder against it over and over. But the door refuses to move.

"Coward!" I scream at the man who is no longer there. "You fucking coward!"

I try everything, put everything I have into it, but no matter what I do, I can't get the door open.

Something between a sob and a scream rips from my throat as I sink down to the floor and brace my back against the cold stone wall.

Goddess fucking damn him.

Goddess fucking damn it all.

Why can I never catch a fucking break?

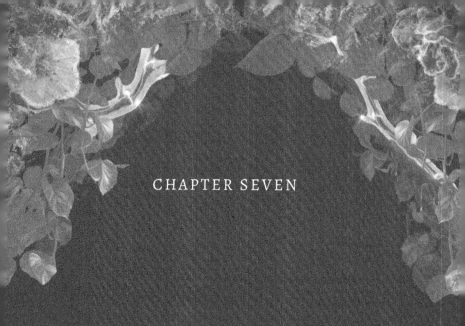

# CHAPTER SEVEN

Voices drift from the other side of the door. I leap to my feet and grab the only item that I could find in this pitch-black room that can even be remotely classified as a weapon. Which happens to be a particularly sturdy carrot.

"—can't believe you!" a woman's voice snaps. "What if I hadn't come to check up on you right this very moment? You would've handed her over to Draven fucking Ryat without even telling me about her!"

A jolt shoots through me. It's followed by a tiny sprout of hope. This woman sounds like she's very against the idea of giving me back to Draven.

"Told you already, I have," the man from before replies. "Don't want nothing to do with your little rebellion."

"It's not *little*, Dad. And if you actually have one of the fae from the palace in there, our resistance is going to make more progress in the coming weeks than we've done for the past decade."

My heart jerks in my chest. This woman is part of the rebellion. And it sounds like she wants my help.

Quickly summoning my magic, I throw it out in search of

the burgundy spark of courage. I only find one, which must belong to the woman. That grumpy man didn't seem very courageous to me. Pouring my magic into that lone spark of courage, I increase it so that the woman will feel brave and determined.

"She's fae, alright," the man replies with a huff. "Got them pointy ears and everything."

"And you just locked her in there?" his daughter replies, her voice full of exasperation. "How am I supposed to get her to trust me now?"

"Not my problem."

She heaves a frustrated sigh. "Is she armed?"

"Don't know. Didn't check."

Another deep sigh. "Father Almighty, I really hope she doesn't stab me."

Then a heavy click sounds from the lock and the door is pulled open.

I blink against the sudden torchlight that streams in through the doorway and hits me right in the face. When my eyes have adjusted, I come face to face with a woman dressed in a beige shirt, brown pants, and a nondescript brown cloak. Her red hair falls a little past her collarbones, and it brushes against the fabric of the cloak when she cocks her head.

"Is that...?" Her dark blue eyes are wide with surprise as she stares at my hand. "Were you planning to stab me with a *carrot*?"

I start slightly and glance down at the sturdy vegetable that I had forgotten that I was still holding. Looking up from my improvised weapon, I meet her eyes again and shrug. "Well, the turnips were a bit too soft, so..."

She bursts out laughing.

The sound is so full of genuine merriment that it stuns me for a second. Her father, who is still lurking in the main room, draws his eyebrows down and scowls at both me and his daughter. But he doesn't say anything.

"I like you already," the woman presses out while refilling her lungs after the burst of laughter.

Before the final word has even left her lips, I lurch into action. Cutting off the flow of magic to her courage, I instead push towards the deep blue spark of trust. It's small. But it's there. I latch on to it and pour my magic into it with a steady stream, increasing it until it's burning steadily.

Guilt twists in my stomach and nausea crawls up my throat. I have spent my life trying to prove to everyone that I am not this kind of person. That I am not someone who would manipulate people's emotions without their permission. That I would never use my magic to make people like me. And yet, here I am, doing exactly that.

Swallowing, I try to force the nausea and guilt back down. Because this is too important to leave to chance. I need to get this woman to welcome me into their resistance, and I don't have time to make her trust me the normal way. I learned my lesson during the Atonement Trials. I can't keep playing the game the way I did before. Trying not to lose is not a strategy. I need to play to win.

"I'm Kath," she continues, and gives me a little wave. Then she motions towards the man who is still scowling at us from behind her back. "Sorry about my dad. He's—"

"The only sane person in this bloody family," he interrupts with a huff.

Kath shoots him a glare over her shoulder.

Several different plans flash through my mind. Because I overheard their conversation outside the door, I already know that she is part of the resistance. So I want to tell her straight away that Draven is hunting the Red Hand, and I want to make her take me to their resistance so that I can begin helping them plot and scheme and take down the Iceheart Dynasty. But in the end, I decide to pretend as if I didn't hear anything through the door. If I know too much or push too hard this soon, it might trigger a flare of suspicion.

"So you're not planning to give me back to Draven Ryat?" I ask instead. And I make my voice tremble slightly, as if I'm as terrified of Draven as everyone here appears to be.

She snaps her head back to me, looking aghast. "God no!"

I let out a calculated breath of relief. And I keep feeding the deep blue spark of trust in her chest until it's burning so strong that I know it will remain even when I pull back my magic.

"In fact," Kath continues. "There are some people I would love for you to meet." I open my mouth to respond, but before any words can make it out, Kath hurriedly adds, "Look, I know that you have no reason to trust me." She winces apologetically. "Especially after my dad locked you in here. But I promise you, we're on the same side. We hate the Icehearts and Draven Ryat just as much as you do, and I promise, if you just hear us out, you'll see that you can trust us."

Goddess above, I have used magic to manipulate her into trusting me. And she is worried that *I* am not going to trust *them.* That cold slimy guilt twists in my gut again. I try to block it out.

While furrowing my brows a little, I pretend to think it over for a few seconds, the way a normal person would. Then I straighten, set the carrot down on the crate next to me, and give her a nod. "Alright."

Relief washes over her features. I once more have to swallow down a flash of guilt.

"Great!" A beaming smile spreads across her face as she jerks her chin. "Come with me."

Since I'm reasonably certain that I have gotten her to trust me now, I release the grip on my magic at the same time as I step out of the darkened storage room. That way, they might just think that my eyes were glowing because of the darkness and the torches reflecting against them.

"Bad decision, this is," the grumpy man mutters from where

he's now sorting through a shelf in the corner. "I'll tell ya. Very bad. Don't come crying to me when this blows up in your face."

"Yeah, yeah, I love you too, Dad," Kath replies, and she does give him a soft smile before she strides towards the steps on the other side of the room.

After flipping my hood up to hide my ears, I follow her as we walk back up them and out through the trapdoor. Kath waves me forward, and we start back out of the dead end.

Sunlight streams down from the blue sky and warms my cheeks as we make our way through the city. Murmuring voices mingle with clinking and clattering sounds coming from inside various shops, and the scent of baking bread and cooking food drifts out of several windows. My stomach rumbles in response since I threw up most of the food I ate after I fell down the castle wall. Thankfully, the grumbling of my discontented abdominal organ is drowned out by the sounds of the city.

"Your eyes are really cool," Kath says as we turn a corner and continue down another road. While still keeping one eye on the people around us, she motions at my eyes. "The two colors and the glowing... They always do that?"

"The two colors, yes. The glowing, only sometimes."

"Cool. Yeah, I suppose that's great when it's dark."

My mind churns. So, she does think that my eyes were glowing because of the darkness. They must not know as much about fae as the dragon shifters do. And I decide not to correct her about the reason for my glowing eyes. The less they know about my true powers, the better. For now, at least.

"Well, here we are," Kath announces as she stops outside a three-story building made of dark wood.

Tilting my head back, I look up at the rather impressive building. "You live here?"

"God no!" She laughs. "Wouldn't be able to afford it even if I saved up for it my whole life. This is The Black Emerald. It's a... thief bar."

Surprise pulses through me, and I turn to stare at her in surprise.

She scratches the back of her neck a little sheepishly while a mischievous smile blows across her lips. "I'll explain inside."

After jerking her chin at me, she simply walks up to the door and opens it. I cast a glance over my shoulder to check for dragon shifters before I follow her across the threshold.

The inside of the tavern is also made of dark wood. Tables and chairs occupy the front of the room while wooden booths with cushions in emerald green fabric line the walls. There is a long counter to my right, and what looks like a door to the kitchen. I sweep my gaze over the people who are eating and drinking and chatting around us while Kath and I weave our way through the spacious tavern and towards the wooden staircase at the back of the room.

People watch me with suspicious eyes at first, but as soon as they notice Kath, the suspicion evaporates and they go back to eating and drinking.

The soft murmur of voices disappears as we make our way up the stairs and then through a corridor on the second floor. My heart patters in my chest as Kath stops in front of a plain wooden door and knocks.

"Yeah?" someone calls from inside.

"It's me," Kath replies.

And before the other person can say anything else, she simply opens the door and strolls inside. I follow her.

The room we enter is a lot smaller than the tavern area downstairs. One large table takes up the floorspace in the middle of the room. There are twelve chairs around it, but only three of them are occupied. Burning candles stand in a cluster in the middle of the table, even though bright daylight falls in through the window. I quickly study the three people seated at the table.

Two men and one woman. All three of them look to be around the same age as Kath. Since humans age differently, it's hard to tell, but my best guess is that they're somewhere in their twenties.

"Where's Hector?" Kath asks as she strolls up to the table and pulls out a chair.

One of the men, a guy with red hair the same shade as Kath's and blue eyes of a very similar color too, is the one who replies.

"He's…" the guy begins, but then he trails off when his gaze slides to me. After a second's pause, he ends his sentence with a vague, "Out." Clearing his throat, he shifts his gaze back to Kath. "Who's this?"

"It's, uhm…" Surprise flits across Kath's face as she stops with her hand on the back of the empty chair and turns back to face me. "Father Almighty, I never even asked your name, did I?"

"Selena," I reply while carefully eyeing the empty chair. "My name is Selena."

"Selena," Kath echoes, and sweeps a hand towards me as if she is introducing me to the others. "This is Selena." Then she points towards the blond man seated at the table, who has been silent this whole time. "And this is Peter." She moves her hand to the woman with chin-length black hair and brown eyes seated next to him. "And Ami." Then she finally nods to the redhead. "And the suspicious one over there is my little brother Kyler."

"Hello," I say. It comes out sounding so awkward that I have to stifle a cringe.

Kyler just turns to his sister. "I'm still waiting for the part where you explain why you have brought a stranger here."

"Right." Kath shifts her gaze to me and then motions at the hood of my cloak. "Selena, would you mind…?"

I push my hood down.

Peter gasps. Ami jerks back and blinks in shock. And Kyler's mouth drops open.

"Yep," Kath says cheerfully, and then finally plops down on the empty chair she pulled out earlier. "That's why."

While I claim another empty seat at the table, Kath explains who I am.

"How do you even know that we can trust her?" Kyler says once she's finished. He cuts me an unapologetic look. "No offense."

"Dad said she saved Jerry from a shifter patrol," Kath replies.

The moment she begins that sentence, I pretend that my cloak has gotten caught under the leg of the chair and bend down while twisting to the side as if to fix it. So once the final word has left her mouth, I have already summoned my magic while they can't see my eyes. I shove it at the small sparks of trust that have appeared in their chests following Kath's declaration. With a firm push, I blow those sparks into large steady flames. Then, I release my magic and straighten again.

It did the trick. No distrust shines on their faces when they look at me now.

"Do you realize what an excellent opportunity this is?" Kath says to her friends before turning to me. "Okay, I know that I have been really cryptic and stuff. So, here's the thing…"

I pretend to be surprised while she explains what I already knew. That they are members of the human rebellion and that they are trying to take down the Iceheart Dynasty. Then the surprise becomes genuine when she explains what their current plan is.

"A heist?" I echo. "You're planning a heist?"

Wicked mischief glints in Kath's eyes. "Yes. We're going to hit their treasury and wipe out their financial leverage. It's going to cripple their entire rule."

Ami, the dark-haired woman, slides intelligent brown eyes to me. "But we haven't yet been able to figure out how we're supposed to actually get all of us into the treasury, and then out again with all the loot."

Another beaming grin spreads across Kath's face. "Which is where you come in."

Confusion ripples through me, and I frown at her. "What do you mean?"

"You can be our eyes and ears."

Silence falls over the room as the four humans turn to me with hopeful eyes. Light streams in through the window, making their eyes practically glitter. A few dust particles that drift through the air catch the light. They swirl in the draft when Peter leans forward in his chair and braces his arms on the dark wooden table. The silence is so loud that I can practically hear it ringing in my ears.

Ice seeps through my veins when I finally realize what their words mean.

"You…" I begin, but I have to swallow down the dread and panic rising like bile in my throat before I can continue. "You want me to… go back."

Sympathy floods Kath's face, but she still says, "Yes."

My hand drifts up to my throat. "Do you know what they do to me in there?"

"No." Her voice is as soft as her eyes. "But I can imagine that it's not pretty."

I draw in short shallow breaths while desperately shaking my head. "I can't go back. I have literally just escaped. I can't…" I shake my head again.

"Look," Kyler interjects. There is sympathy on his face as well, but it's almost hidden behind blazing determination as he squeezes his hand into a fist. "I know that we're asking a lot. But the truth is that we will never be able to pull off a heist without someone on the inside. We need you."

I can barely hear him over the ringing in my head.

Go back? I can't go back. If I do, there is no guarantee that I will be able to escape again after the heist. Then I will be stuck there with a collar around my neck. Forever.

"You might be free, but the rest of us aren't," Kyler continues.

"And those other fae in the palace, are you really willing to leave them there?"

Guilt explodes inside me. Isera. And Alistair. They're still trapped in there.

"Kyler," Kath admonishes.

"What?" he replies. "We *need* her."

"Yes, but…"

They continue to argue about his cutthroat persuasion tactics, but I can barely hear them, because my own mind is so loud. And the worst part is that Kyler might be right.

I thought I would just help the human resistance from the outside. Maybe even get them in contact with our own resistance back in the Seelie Court. But Kyler is right. Having a spy inside the Ice Palace is invaluable. Haven't I always said that I wanted to be more important? That I want to play a bigger part in the resistance? That I want to do something that actually makes a difference instead of just working as a lookout? This is it. This is my chance to actually do something of value. To actually prove that I am worthy. And besides, I can't leave Isera in there. Even Alistair. He might be a bully but he's still one of us. I can't just abandon them to torture and despair while I go free.

"I'll do it."

All voices cut off abruptly.

And before I can change my mind, I repeat, "I'll do it."

Relief washes over them all.

"Thank you," Kath whispers.

"But I'm going to need…"

I trail off as a jolt spikes through me. Draven. Mabona's tits, if I'm going to do this, I have to get back before Draven realizes that I'm missing.

Peter sucks in a gasp as I jump to my feet so fast that the chair topples backwards and clatters down on the floor.

"I need to hurry," I press out, flicking frantic eyes between them. "I need to make it back before they realize that I'm missing. Do you have any climbing gear?"

All four of them scramble to their feet as well.

"Climbing gear?" Kath asks, staring at me in confusion.

"I had to climb down the side of the castle to get out. I will have to climb back up it again."

"Oh." She blinks, and then whips her head to Peter. "Get a set of gloves and shoe covers for her."

He lurches into motion and sprints out of the room while Ami hurries around the table. Paper flutters as she yanks out a sheet and begins explaining how I can pass along information. Apparently, they have a drop-off location on the grounds of the castle. While Ami is still drawing a map and explaining procedures, Peter returns and shoves a pair of gloves and something else into my hands. I just grab them and the paper without looking at them before hurrying to the door.

I'm just about to throw it open when someone opens it from the outside instead. A tall and muscular man with brown hair and brown eyes steps through the door, and then stops when he almost slams right into me.

"Hector," Kath blurts out from behind me.

All four of them straighten and lower their chins slightly the way that people do when faced with authority. My gaze shifts back to the man before me. Based on the way the others are acting, this Hector guy must be the leader of this resistance.

His eyes widen when he sees my pointed ears.

But I don't have time to stop, so I just meet his eyes and deliver the warning that I set out to deliver from the beginning.

"Be careful. Draven Ryat is coming for the Red Hand."

Hector starts in surprise, but I just slip around him and dart out the door.

I need to make it back to my room before Draven gets back.

# CHAPTER EIGHT

**M**y lungs burn as I sprint the final distance along the path that leads up to the side gate. Every breath feels like I'm inhaling shards of glass, but I keep pushing myself. I have to make it. Please, Mabona, I have to make it.

Just dashing through the city like this has taken almost all of the energy I had. I have no idea how I'm supposed to make the climb up to the balcony. My gaze drifts down to the gloves and the other strange pieces of equipment that I'm still holding. Hopefully, these will be enough to get me through it.

At last, the side gate becomes visible before me. With a sob of desperation, I reach for my magic even though my energy is already draining fast. But before I can use it on the guard, he leaps into motion on his own.

While still running towards him, I blink in surprise as he unlocks the door and opens it for me.

When I get closer, I realize that it's the same guard from before. Conflicting emotions twist in my chest. Apparently, I managed to manipulate his emotions so strongly the first time that I permanently altered his perception of me. On the one hand, that makes me feel incredibly powerful. But at the same time, sharp guilt and rolling nausea hit me straight in the gut.

All my life, people have kept me at arm's length because they were afraid that I might do something like this to them. And I have been angry at them for that assumption. But now, I'm becoming the person that they always feared I was. The person I swore I wouldn't be.

Anger burns through me, and I shove the guilt aside. What's the point of having magic if I can't use it to help people? It's not like I make a habit of manipulating people's emotions. Today was just an exception. A necessity. I needed to make the guard let me out and I needed to make the humans in the resistance group trust me. It was a one-time thing. It's not like it's going to happen again. Right?

As I reach the gate, I slow to a walk so that the guard won't get too suspicious. But it appears to be an unnecessary precaution, because there is only fear in his eyes when he looks at me.

"Please, don't tell Commander Ryat about earlier," he whispers as I stalk through the open gate.

I cut him a sharp look and make my voice hard. "As long as I never have to wait for you to open the gate again, your failure stays a secret."

"You won't." He nods vigorously. "I promise."

An intoxicating burst of satisfaction pulses through me, making me feel invincible. I have to resist the urge to grin as I stride away from the gate and back to the secluded section where Draven's balcony is.

Once I reach it, I finally come to a complete stop for the first time since leaving The Black Emerald. Dragging in a deep breath to refill my lungs and slow my racing heart, I at last unfold the items in my hands.

The gloves I was given are lined with a strange material across the entire palm section as well as the fingers. I have never seen something like it before. It looks like it should be sticky, but when I poke at it with my finger, it doesn't get stuck to it.

Shaking my head, I place the gloves on the ground while I fold up the map to the drop-off location and hide it inside my shirt. Then I shake out the final two pieces of equipment. I frown. It looks like two small pouches that are shaped roughly like low shoes. Except they're stretchy, and the bottom is covered in the same odd material as the gloves.

Since I don't have time to second-guess this, I just pull them over my boots and then yank on the gloves as well. Then I reach for the closest chunk of ice that sticks out of the wall and begin climbing.

Shock pulses through me.

My hands and feet... it's like they're sticking to the ice until I pull them back off. It gives me an incredible grip. I can even just press the bottom of my shoes against the flat wall while only using my hands to grip chunks of ice, eliminating the need to find proper footholds. I doubt the material is strong enough to allow me to just walk up the side of the building, but with the help of the handholds, my shoes stick firmly. As do my hands. They only come off when I deliberately pull them away. It's almost impossible to slip.

Hope and excitement surge through me. With these, I will be able to climb in and out of the room at will. I could even use it to sneak into other windows in the castle so that I can help the resistance find a way to the treasury without Draven knowing. This is going to be perfect.

I grin as a strong gust of wind whirls around the castle, tugging at my cloak and my hair, while I remain firmly on the ice wall.

For the first time since I began my sprint back, I don't regret my decision. I will be able to leave any time I want. So I'm not really trapped here.

A massive weight lifts from my chest at just the thought of it.

This is going to work. I'm going to help the resistance find a way to the treasury, they're going to rob it, and then I'm going to leave this castle for good. The Iceheart Dynasty will be financially crippled. I will be free, and I will have gotten revenge.

My muscles tremble when I at last reach Draven's balcony again. Despite the help of the gloves and the shoe covers, scaling the side of a building still requires physical strength. Which I don't exactly have in spades right now.

With a soft groan of exertion, I drag myself over the railing and drop down on the balcony. The door is still slightly open. I stare at it, estimating how large the gap is, while I suck more air into my lungs. The gap looks to be exactly the same as the one I left. Which should hopefully mean that Draven hasn't been here and noticed it.

After taking off the gloves and the shoe covers, I send a desperate prayer to Mabona that I'm right.

And then I slink back in through the balcony door and close it behind me.

I barely dare to breathe as I straighten inside the living room.

But no angry dragon shifter storms out of the shadows.

Blowing out a long breath of relief, I hurry into my bedroom and yank open one of the drawers. I need to hide the climbing equipment. I bundle them, along with the map, into some other pieces of clothing that I doubt Draven will ever touch.

Right after I have closed the drawer and walked back into the living room, a click comes from the front door.

My heart lurches.

By Mabona, my cheeks are red after the lengthy run and my hair is windblown after the climb and I haven't even had one single second to just take a breath and compose myself. If Draven sees me like this, he's going to know that I have done something that I shouldn't.

Making a split-second decision, I sprint towards the door right across from me.

If he's going to see me looking this suspicious, I need to give him something else that he can catch me doing.

Right before the front door is pulled open, I yank open the door to Draven's bedroom and sprint inside.

My heart slams as I skid to a halt on the dark wooden floorboards inside. I draw in a deep breath. And immediately regret it. Because this entire room smells like him. And that scent reminds me of the time when he gave me his shirt. And the time when he kissed every inch of my body and wrung every drop of pleasure from my soul.

"Snooping, huh?"

I whirl around to find Draven standing in the doorway. Or *standing* isn't exactly the right word. He has his arms crossed over his muscular chest and one ankle crossed over the other while he leans one shoulder against the doorframe. His body blocks my way out of his bedroom entirely.

Draven tuts and shakes his head, but there is a mischievous glint in his eyes as he holds my gaze. "Though I suppose I shouldn't be surprised. If I remember correctly, sneaking around castles is a favorite pastime of yours."

And just like that, it feels as if we're back in the Seelie Court, throwing easy banter back and forth. It makes me want to smile. But it also confuses me. First, I hated him for trying to sabotage me during the Atonement Trials. Then, the more time we spent together, I started to have feelings for him. Then, I hated him again when he put the collar on me and made me his slave. But then he removed my collar the first chance he got and is doing what he can to protect me. And now, I don't know where we stand anymore.

I know that, logically, I should probably still hate him. But I also can't just erase all the other feelings that I have for him. Can't erase how it felt to kiss him. To fuck him solely because I wanted to. Can't erase how he makes me feel free and strong and makes me feel as if I don't have to make myself less. Can't erase how much I enjoyed our banter back in the Seelie Court. How I still feel drawn to him.

Realizing that I still haven't answered him, I give my head a quick shake and try to compose myself again.

"I wasn't snooping," I manage to press out at last.

"No?" Draven arches an eyebrow. "Then why are you blushing furiously?"

*Because I just ran through the entire city and then scaled the wall of the palace*, I reply silently, and rather smugly, in my mind. But I don't say that out loud. Instead, I let him think that I'm blushing from embarrassment by just answering with a huff.

His smirk widens. "Were you imagining me in bed?"

My heart stutters.

He chuckles. "If I remember correctly, you've done that before too."

This time, both the blush and the self-conscious huff are real as I remember my embarrassing blabbering when he surprised me back in his room in the Seelie Court. "That's not what I meant back then, and you know it."

Pushing off from the doorframe, he straightens and then saunters towards me with that devilish smile still on his lips. "Wasn't it? I distinctly remember how... *wet* you were."

My cheeks feel like they're on fire.

Draven comes to a halt in front of me and slides two fingers along my jaw. Lightning crackles over my skin at his soft touch. He places his fingers underneath my chin and then pushes upwards, tilting my head back further so that he can lock eyes with me.

"What?" He flashes me a grin. "No clever comebacks?"

"I will escape, you know."

Leaning closer, he lets out a contemplative hum. It's a low and dark sound that almost vibrates against my lips. My heart skips a beat at the feeling of it.

"Because that went so well the last time I locked you in my bedroom," Draven baits.

"I could always just handcuff you to your desk again."

His eyes glitter. "You're welcome to try, little rebel. But you and I both know that you look a lot hotter in handcuffs than I do."

My heart jerks and then beats hard to make up for it. And a jolt a fire shoots through my core.

It's immediately followed by a flash of panic. I shouldn't be doing this. I shouldn't be feeling this. And I most certainly shouldn't enjoy this bantering and the feeling of his fingers against my skin.

Draven might have shown me a scrap of mercy by taking the collar off when I'm in his quarters, but it doesn't change the fact that he is the Commander of the Dread Legion. A loyal servant to the Icehearts. He might not be draining my magic, but I am still his prisoner. I can't trust him and he can't trust me.

Blocking out all the tangled feelings I now have for Draven, I abruptly take a step back so that I can put some distance between us. It makes his hand fall away from my chin.

For one single second, he almost looks confused. As if he can't understand why I would suddenly pull back like that. Then his gaze drops down to my neck, where the collar should be, and all traces of emotion are wiped straight off his features.

With that mask of only ruthless authority on his face, he takes a step back as well and then jerks his chin towards the door. "Get some rest and then get ready. We're eating with my clan tonight."

There is nothing left of the teasing notes that laced his voice only seconds ago. Now, it's filled with unflinching command. This was not a suggestion. It was an order. From the master to his slave.

I grind my teeth and clench my fist but say nothing. After all, I'm the one who destroyed our little moment in the first place. So instead of refusing out of pointless pride, I just stalk out of his bedroom in silence.

But my treacherous heart squeezes painfully in my chest.

Everything would have been so much easier if I could just flip a switch and forget everything that has happened between me and Draven. Forget everything he made me feel during our time together in the Atonement Trials. But as I, more than anyone, already know, emotions are a lot more complicated than that. And a lot more dangerous.

# CHAPTER NINE

W hen Draven said that we would be eating dinner with his clan, I thought that meant that I would get to see the more restricted areas of the Ice Palace, which would be great for my mission to find a way to the treasury. But it was the exact opposite.

Evening winds whip through my hair and make my black cloak flutter behind me as we walk down the slope of the mountain and towards the barracks that are located outside the defensive walls. Thankfully, they're at the west side rather than the east, which means that we didn't have to use the same side gate that I snuck out of earlier. I'm pretty sure that my cover would have been blown if that guard had seen me with Draven like this.

I glance up at Draven as we walk. He has barely said a word to me since he ordered me to get some rest and get ready. And his face betrays nothing either. I watch the way the moonlight paints silver highlights in his black hair and the way it makes his eyes gleam. By Mabona, what I wouldn't give to know what goes on in that head of his sometimes.

To my surprise, he doesn't even notice that I'm studying him.

His eyes are firmly fixed on the barracks before us. And as we close the final distance, he clenches his jaw and draws in a long breath. I get the strangest feeling that he is bracing himself.

However, before I can ask him about that, he pulls the door open and just strides inside. I follow him.

The door leads to a short corridor. There are several rooms both on the left and the right of the corridor, all with doors half open, but Draven walks straight for the open doorway at the end of the hall. Cheerful voices and laughter drift out from that room, and flickering light dances over the stone walls, as if a lot of candles have been lit in there.

After pulling the front door shut behind me again, I push a few windblown strands of hair out of my face and then hurry to catch up with Draven. But apparently, I didn't need to hurry. Because Draven has stopped before the threshold.

Standing in the shadows of the open doorway, he just watches the room on the other side in silence. I quickly close the distance to him, thinking that it might be me he's waiting for. But when I come to a halt next to him, he still doesn't move. I frown up at him and then glance into the room as well.

Long tables made of dark wood run the length of the massive room. All of them are positioned in the same direction, with one short side towards this door and the smaller table that has been set perpendicular to all the others. Candles have been placed along the tabletops of each one of them, and their light casts the whole room in a warm glow.

All of the tables, except the short one at the front, are already full. I sweep my gaze over the people seated along them. All of them are dragon shifters wearing black dragon scale armor. Their armor isn't as intricate as Draven's, but the style is similar. And the fact that it's black is of course also a telltale sign that these soldiers belong to the Black Dragon Clan.

"Hold on," a female dragon shifter calls from where she is seated at the front end of a table, close to where the empty shorter table is. She leans across the table and reaches a hand towards the male shifter seated opposite her. "You've got something in your hair."

The guy blinks, his violet eyes widening in surprise, and runs a hand through his blond hair. "No, I don't."

I frown, studying him intently. I feel like I've seen him before. Then it hits me. He was one of the soldiers that I eavesdropped on back in the Golden Palace during the Atonement Trials. The guy who apparently used to be Draven's best friend before Draven sold out his entire clan to the Icehearts in exchange for power.

"Oh, wait," the woman says, and slaps her forehead as if she has just remembered something. A broad smile full of wicked mischief spreads across her face. "I thought it was a whole nest of pine needles, but it was just your hair."

Laughter erupts around the table.

The blond man huffs and pitches a piece of bread at the woman. "Very funny, Lyra."

"Oh come on, it *was* funny," the female shifter, Lyra, says with that wicked grin still on her mouth. Her orange eyes sparkle in the candlelight, and her wavy brown hair ripples over her shoulders as she flaps her hand in the air. "You flew right into that pine tree."

"I wouldn't have crashed into it if I didn't have to swerve around your crazy ass." He shakes his head at her, but amusement shines on his whole face. "Seriously, who jumps off a fucking cliff and shifts mid-air?"

Lyra grins at him. "Someone who wants to win."

"You only won because you cheated."

"Oh, come now, Galen." She winks at him. "Don't be such a sore loser."

"Sore loser? Me?" Draven's former best friend, Galen, presses a hand to his chest in a show of exaggerated shock. "You're one to talk. You're like the most competitive person I've ever met." He hikes his thumb towards a man farther down the table. "Poor Finlay over there still wishes that he had let you win in that last sparring match because of how much grief you've been giving him over it."

Another wave of laughter ripples through the room, and the woman seated next to Lyra elbows her in the ribs while Lyra rolls her eyes.

I shift my gaze back to Draven, who is still standing unmoving in the shadows. His eyes are fixed on Galen and Lyra and the others, but the expression on his face is as unreadable as ever. I desperately want to reach out with my magic and push at different emotions so that I can figure out what he's really feeling. But because we had to leave Draven's rooms, he had to put the collar back on me.

For a second, I consider just asking him outright if he's okay. But before I can make a decision, he abruptly drags in a breath and then steps out of the shadows and straight in through the doorway.

Every conversation cuts off the moment he becomes visible.

The dead silence that spreads like a plague through the room is so jarring that I almost forget to follow Draven into the room. All signs of merriment and all sounds of joy have evaporated within a matter of seconds.

Draven strides straight up to that smaller table at the front of the room and takes up position behind it. Since I'm not entirely sure what I'm supposed to be doing, I linger by the wall right inside the doorway. But none of the shifters look at me. Instead, all of them drop their gazes and bow their heads to Draven.

"First order of business, before we can start eating," Draven says without preamble. His powerful voice echoes through the massive stone room. "We have new orders."

His clan members raise their heads to look at him.

And it takes all of my willpower to stop a gasp from escaping my throat.

There is no companionship, no respect, no warmth, in any of their eyes when they look at him. Instead, their expressions are full of resentment. And not just any resentment. It's so strong that I can practically feel their acidic hatred even without using my magic. And so obvious that it's impossible to miss.

It shocks me to my core. After that conversation I eavesdropped on back in the Seelie Court, I knew that some of the people in Draven's clan resent him. But I thought they did it in secret. They don't. They resent him, and they don't even try to hide it. And I thought it was only some of his clan members. But it's not. It's all of them.

Completely stunned, all I can do is to stare at the hatred visible on everyone's features as they watch Draven.

Draven, on the other hand, either doesn't notice or doesn't care. That same blank mask of ruthless authority never leaves his face as he sweeps his gaze over all of his people.

"The Red Hand is back," he announces. "And we have been tasked with finding him."

Most people just let out an annoyed sigh, but at the front of the room, Galen clenches his jaw and squeezes his hand into a fist.

"We'll focus on the human parts of town," Draven continues. "Don't waste time on being gentle. If they don't answer, make them answer."

I snap my gaze to Draven, staring at him while anger pulses through me. And apparently, I'm not the only one. The resentment in the room is now so palpable that I can almost feel it vibrating against my skin.

"If we—" Draven begins.

Galen slams his fist down on the table, cutting him off. "Again with the Red Hand! Can't you just accept that you lost to him?"

The whole room sucks in a collective breath, and half of the soldiers turn to stare at Galen in shock. As if they can't believe that he dared to say that out loud.

Dead silence spreads across the room following his outburst.

Draven, whose expression still hasn't changed, slides his gaze to his former best friend. "What was that?"

Galen shoves to his feet. Anger pulses in his violet eyes as he glares back at Draven. "You heard me. You're fixating on the Red Hand just because he's the only one who has ever managed to outsmart you. And I'm tired of hurting people just to salvage your pride." He squeezes both hands into fists. "If anything, we should be *helping* the Red Hand."

This time, people outright gasp. Even Lyra, the spirited woman who was teasing him before, tries to reach out and grab his arm to pull him back down in his seat. But Galen doesn't back down. Fury flickers in his eyes as he holds Draven's gaze.

I stare at Galen as well. Suggesting that they should be helping the Red Hand is just one word away from outright treason.

Draven takes a slow step to the side. The entire room seems to be holding its breath as he rounds the table and starts towards his former best friend.

"Is there something you want to get off your chest, Galen?" he says, his voice cold and dripping with challenge.

Galen flicks a quick glance around the room, but he stands his ground as Draven prowls up to him.

Ruthless power pulses from Draven's entire body as he comes to a halt in front of Galen. "You know what to do. If you think Azaroth chose wrong when he made me clan leader, you need to challenge me for it. You need to kill me and release the magic so that Azaroth can choose someone else."

I don't think anyone in the entire room is breathing.

Lyra casts a worried glance between Draven and Galen, looking like she's trying to decide whether to pull Galen back into his seat or to stand up next to him and help him fight.

Draven spreads his massive black wings wide in a clear display of power as he holds Galen's gaze. "So, I'll ask again. Is there something you want to get off your chest, Galen?"

Tension crackles through the room like lightning. Galen grinds his teeth and flexes his hand. And for a moment, I think he might actually do it.

But then he drops his eyes and bows his head in submission. "No, sir."

"Good." Draven stabs a commanding hand towards Galen's empty chair. "Then sit back down."

Everyone in the room lowers their chin in submission as well while Galen sinks back down on his chair. A muscle flickers in Draven's jaw, and for a moment, he just stands there and stares out at the sea of silent soldiers.

Then he snaps, "The hunt for the Red Hand begins at sunrise."

His clan members bow their heads lower in acknowledgement of the order. Draven watches them for a second. Then he abruptly spins on his heel and stalks towards the door.

"Selena," he says, his voice still cold and clipped, as he strides past me. "Let's go. I've suddenly lost my appetite."

I'm one second away from telling him to stop treating me like a dog who is expected to follow him around, but the words die on my tongue when I see the expression on his face. It's only for a fraction of a second, and he probably thought that no one could see it from that angle. But because I was standing right by the wall, I could see his face for that one brief moment before his back is fully to me and everyone else as he stalks out the door.

And the sheer heart-wrenching pain that flickered in his eyes during that fraction of a second is so strong that it snatches the breath from my lungs.

I glance back towards the room full of silent dragon shifters as I follow Draven out.

Hatred once again pulses on their faces as they stare daggers at Draven's disappearing back.

I always thought that he didn't care that his own people hated him. But maybe this all bothers him more than he admits.

# CHAPTER TEN

T he one good thing about Draven's hunt for the Red Hand is that it gives me a lot of unsupervised time. Since Draven is gone most of the day, and sometimes at night too, I have been able to sneak out a lot. By climbing off the balcony and then in through other windows, I have searched through parts of the Ice Palace that would otherwise have been inaccessible. Like the highly guarded wing that I'm currently in.

My heart patters in my chest as I draw myself up along the white ice wall and peek around the corner. A jolt shoots through me.

Farther down the hall, two guards in silver armor are positioned on either side of a doorway. They're wearing ornate silver helmets and are holding tall spears.

I yank my head back.

Unfortunately, just because I can sneak in through a window doesn't mean that I can roam freely once inside. Especially not here. In Bane and Jessina's private wing.

While cursing silently, I hurry back down the corridor and towards the deserted and unlocked room that I climbed in through.

In the week since I was recruited by the human resistance, I have managed to provide them with precious little information of value. The Ice Palace is huge, and I don't even know which floor the treasury is supposed to be located on. That has made it difficult to concentrate my efforts. Well, that and the fact that I can't let anyone recognize me. If someone saw me and realized who I was and reported me to Draven, I would be in a world of trouble.

Stopping outside the deserted room, I reach for the handle. But then I hesitate.

The smart thing would be to climb back out the window and return to Draven's rooms before any of the no doubt numerous guards in the Icehearts' royal wing catch me. This place is most likely more well-guarded than any other part of the castle, and trying to sneak into it blind is both dangerous and stupid. But at the same time, I can't let this opportunity slip through my fingers.

I know for a fact that both Bane and Jessina are occupied elsewhere all night. Apparently, there is some kind of banquet for the court tonight. Which I know because a servant tried to get Draven to attend, but he just told the servant that he was too busy planning the hunt for the Red Hand. And with both Draven and the Icehearts busy in other parts of the palace, I can't waste this opportunity to search the royal wing.

The only problem is of course how to get in there.

I stare at the door before me for another few seconds, weighing the risks and the gains. Then I blow out a determined breath and straighten my spine. I need to at least try.

Leaving the door behind, I sneak down the corridor in the other direction. If I can't get past the guards protecting the entrance, I need to find another way in. There can't possibly be only one way into the royal wing. There has to be some kind of servants' entrance. Or an emergency exit or something.

If only Isera was here. She could probably just split one of these ice walls with her magic, and then we'd be through. Or even Alistair. He could melt a hole in one.

My heart squeezes at the thought of Isera and Alistair. I haven't seen them since I blacked out in that throne room after Draven and the Icehearts collared us all. When Draven received the orders to hunt down the Red Hand, Jessina said that Isera and Alistair hadn't woken up yet because of how much magic she and Bane drained from them. But that was a week ago. They must surely have woken up by now.

I wonder how they're doing. I can't imagine that the Icehearts are removing their collars the way that Draven does for me. I need to find a way to get to them. To talk to them. To tell them that I'm working with the human resistance. That we have a plan. And to tell them to just hold on a little longer.

But for now, I need to stay focused. So I block out my worry for Isera and Alistair and instead focus on my current problem. Getting into the royal wing without being arrested or killed.

The faelights that are set into the ceiling glimmer above me like stars as I make my way through the corridor. Outside the windows, the sky is dark. Dinner has already come and gone, and we're halfway to midnight already.

I keep my steps soft as I sneak along the ice corridor and towards the next corner. Technically, I'm heading away from the royal wing. But if I'm right, there might be another entrance somewhere on the other side. I just need to—

"Why did we have to get the boring shift?"

My heart leaps into my throat.

Just around the corner up ahead, another voice answers, "It's not the boring shift. Guarding the royal wing is a great honor."

"But guarding the banquet hall is so much more fun. This is the time of night when things always start getting really interesting."

*Oh shit.*

Those two guards are coming to relieve the ones who are

already stationed at the entrance to the royal wing. And to get there, they must pass through this corridor. The corridor that I'm currently in. The one corridor that I'm really not supposed to be in.

Alarm bells blare inside my skull as I whip my head from side to side. I'm too far away to make it back to the deserted room before the guards can spot me. And there is nothing to hide behind in this corridor. The only thing in it is the faelight gems in the ceiling. No tables. No decorations. Not even a carpet.

My gaze snags on a closed door farther down the corridor. If it's unlocked, I might be able to make it there and get inside the room right before the guards round the corner. If it's not, I'm dead.

I sprint towards it.

"I'll take an uneventful night guarding the royal wing over getting killed by the Red Hand any day," the second guard says.

Their footsteps are getting closer.

They're almost at the corner now.

My heart slams against my ribs as I hurtle down the corridor in their direction. It's all or nothing now. If I can't make it through the door, I will be too close to them to escape. The door has to be unlocked. Please, Mabona, the door has to be unlocked.

"You really think the Red Hand is gonna sneak into a crowded banquet and start killing people?" the first guard replies.

He's right around the corner.

I throw myself the final distance to the door.

"I think there have been too many throats slit inside the palace, and I don't want the next one to be mine."

My hand closes around the handle, and I shove it down in the same breath as I yank it open.

Relief crashes through me when I meet no resistance.

Leaping across the threshold, I yank the door shut as quietly as I can.

And come face to face with a pair of golden eyes.

My heart stops.

Draven Ryat jerks back in shock from where he's standing on the other side of a table covered in maps. Stunned disbelief pulses across his whole face as he stares at me.

I open my mouth.

Black wings flare out as Draven shoots across the room.

My heart jerks back into action and then pounds hard when Draven slams a hand in front of my mouth and shoves me up against the wall. His forearm is braced across my collarbones, keeping me pinned to the wall, while his other hand remains firmly over my mouth.

"Don't you think the risk is higher here, though?" the first guard says from right on the other side of the door.

"No. The Red Hand would never be stupid enough to try to assassinate the Emperor and Empress themselves. He knows he'd get slaughtered if he faced them head on."

"I sure hope so."

"No hope needed. This is the safest place in the palace."

"Still boring, though."

"Now you're just…"

Their voices grow fainter as they disappear down the hall.

Still pressed against the wall, I stare up into Draven's now furious eyes. He keeps his hand over my mouth for another few seconds before he lets it drop. But he doesn't step back. And he doesn't remove his forearm from my chest either.

"What the hell are you doing here?" he hisses at me.

I try to push myself away from the wall, but he just presses his forearm harder against my body, trapping me more firmly.

"What am *I* doing here? What are *you* doing here?" I counter.

He stabs his free hand towards the table covered in maps. "I'm working. Now answer the fucking question."

Since I can't very well tell him what I'm really doing here, I say, "I was trying to escape!" I grind my teeth and glare at him in annoyance to really help sell the lie. "But there are guards everywhere. I've been running through corridors and up and down stairs for half an hour, but I still somehow just manage to get deeper into this damn castle."

"Of course there is! What did you think was going to happen? That you would be able to just stroll out?" He shakes his head at me in disbelief. "How did you even get out of the room?"

Breaking eye contact, I turn my head to the side and clench my jaw to make him think that I'm just being stubborn.

His hand slides up my throat and then locks underneath my jaw. With a firm grip, he turns my head back so that I meet his eyes again. Unflinching command laces his voice as he demands, "Answer me, little rebel. Or this is going to be a very long night for you."

"Some woman came by to clean," I lie. "I snuck out while she was busy cleaning the bathroom."

He curses under his breath. I open my mouth to make sure that he has truly bought my lies, but before any sound can make it out, Draven abruptly releases my jaw and presses his palm over my mouth again. I struggle underneath his grip and squirm against the wall.

Draven shoots me a sharp look and shakes his head. And there is something about his expression that makes me go silent and still.

A few seconds later, faint footsteps can be heard through the door.

Realization hits me.

Of course. The two guards who were being relieved of duty. They're walking back through here to get to their next post or whatever it is that they do.

Once their footsteps are no longer audible, Draven at last takes his hand off my mouth and also lets his forearm drop from my collarbones. While he takes a half step back, I brush my hands down my rumpled clothes to make sure that the gloves and shoe covers I'm hiding in there are still in place.

Blowing out a frustrated sigh, he rakes his fingers through his hair and gives me an exasperated look. "I thought I told you to stay in your room."

"And you actually expected me to do it?" I retort. Holding his gaze, I shake my head while anger and frustration course through me as well. "You thought I was just going to obey your orders and not try to escape?"

"I'm not draining your magic. I took off your collar. I'm trying to—"

"You made me your slave, Draven! When push came to shove, you still locked that iron collar around my throat and sucked my magic out of my body."

"Look, I get that you feel betrayed."

"Do you? How could you possibly know what it feels like to be so thoroughly deceived?"

"You wanna talk about being deceived?" Pain flickers in his eyes. It's followed by something deeper. Something more like hurt. "How do you think I felt back in that underground forest? How do you think I felt when I realized that you didn't fuck me because you genuinely wanted to? That it was all an act. That you didn't really want me. That you only fucked me as a distraction to steal the ring from me."

His words hit me like a stab right through the chest.

I hadn't even realized what that must have looked like from his perspective. After what I did, of course he believes that it was all just a cunning deception.

But fucking him by that river had never been part of the plan. The plan had always just been to soak him with that slimy plant goo and get him to take his clothes off in the river so that I could steal the ring from the pouch. Nothing else.

I slept with him because I wanted to. Solely because I wanted to, even though doing so risked my plan.

My chest rises and falls as I stare up at Draven. The words are right there on my tongue, but for some reason, I can't make myself say them. Him knowing the truth won't change anything. We're still enemies. I'm still his slave. And I'm still plotting to ruin him by helping the human resistance pull off a devastating heist against the Iceheart Dynasty.

Our already far too complicated feelings for each other will only make everything worse. So in the end, I just close my mouth again.

Draven drags in a deep breath as if to compose himself. Then he takes another half step back, putting even more distance between us. And when he speaks again, there is no trace of those intense emotions in his voice or on his face.

"Listen to me. This court is brutal. In ways that you don't even know. So you need to follow my rules and stay inside our rooms. And when we're out in public, you need to behave." Reaching up, he takes my chin between his thumb and forefinger and tilts my head back so that all I can see are his serious eyes as he holds my gaze. "I don't care if you despise me behind closed doors, but out here, where people can see, you need to act as if you're my slave."

Slapping his hand away, I glare up at him so that he will understand that I truly mean every single word that I'm about to say. "I will never be your slave."

A frustrated breath rips from his lungs. For a few seconds, he looks to be debating something internally. Then he heaves another sigh, this one sounding more tired than angry. Grabbing me by the arm, he pushes the door open and then pulls me with him as he walks back out into the corridor.

"Come with me."

# CHAPTER ELEVEN

At first, I think he's going to just haul me back to his rooms and lock me in there. But instead, he escorts me down to the ground floor. I glance at him in confusion as we weave through narrow servants' corridors instead of moving through the main halls. But he says nothing, and his expression betrays nothing either.

I can't seem to figure him out. I expected him to be furious when he caught me trying to escape. And yes, to an extent, he was angry. But it seemed to be more out of concern for my safety than anything else. Which is what I don't understand. If he actually cares about me in some way, why not just *let me* escape?

It's like there are two completely separate sides of him. The ruthless Commander of the Dread Legion who obeys the Icehearts' every word. And the person who, in his very convoluted way, tried to save me from this fate. He apparently cares about me enough to do that. I just wish I knew why.

"Listen to me carefully," Draven says as he comes to a halt in front of a plain door at the end of the servants' corridor we've been traveling through. His eyes are serious as he locks them on me. "What you're about to see is going to be hard, but you can't gasp or make any sound at all that will draw their attention. If you do, they're going to make us stay. And you really don't want that. Especially since you're not wearing the collar right now."

His words, combined with the gravity of his tone, send a flare of alarm through me. Whatever is on the other side of that door must be truly awful.

"Do you understand?" Draven demands.

Dread washes through me again, but I hold his gaze as I nod. "Yes."

He keeps his eyes locked on me for another few seconds, as if to make sure that I truly understand the importance of his warning, before he gives me a nod back. Then he reaches for the handle. With careful movements, he slowly pushes it down and edges the door open a tiny crack. Then he motions for me to step forward so that I can look through the small gap.

Anxious worry snakes through my chest as I move closer. After positioning myself at an angle, I peer through the crack in the door.

At first, I don't understand what it is that I'm supposed to be looking at. Draven made it sound like there was something horrible here, but it's just a... banquet.

The room on the other side of the door is made of white ice, just like the rest of the castle, and faelight gems cover the ceiling like stars. Tables draped with white tablecloths are positioned in structured patterns across the floor, and silver candelabras line the walls. They, along with the silver candle holders on the tables, paint the room with warm light.

I sweep my gaze over the people seated at the tables. Dragon shifters dressed in beautiful garments in various colors are eating and talking with smiles on their faces.

Confusion swirls inside my skull. What is supposed to be so awful about this that Draven had to warn me not to gasp?

The tables have been placed in a pattern that points towards the high table. I shift my gaze towards it.

Jessina and Bane Iceheart are seated there at their own private table. As usual, they're dressed in silver and their massive wings are on display. Jessina laughs and then places a hand on Bane's arm while she leans in to say something. He smiles back at her.

Then my gaze drifts to the spaces on either side of their short table.

And my heart stops.

A gasp is halfway through my throat before I remember Draven's warning and snap my mouth shut, cutting off the sound before it can leave my lips.

Pain and dread and utter fucking heartache stabs at my chest like a hot knife as I stare at the two people kneeling on either side of the Icehearts' table.

Isera and Alistair.

Both of them are wearing silver garments that look more like underwear than actual clothes, leaving them practically half-naked. Their iron collars have been locked with a chain to a ring in the floor that is so tight that it forces them to kneel bowed forward slightly, and their hands have been shackled behind their backs.

I don't think I'm even breathing anymore as I shift my gaze to their faces.

They're wearing metal blindfolds which, based on the color, also look to be made of iron, as well as some kind of contraption inside their mouths. There are no straps or anything on the outside, but it looks like they have some kind of metal ring behind their teeth that forces them to keep their mouths open. No doubt so that the Icehearts can drain their magic at any time.

My heart pounds in my chest as I stare at them.

Kneeling, half-naked, handcuffed, collared, blindfolded, and unable to close their mouths. Right in the middle of a massive room full of people who can stare at them and do whatever they want to them while they can't even see what's happening around them, let alone fight back.

Next to me, Draven slowly reaches towards the handle and then closes the door softly again. I just stand there, staring at the now closed door before me. The horrors I saw on the other side forever burned into my mind.

"What are they doing?" I press out at last. It comes out like something between a whisper and a gasp.

"They're breaking them," Draven replies.

His voice is devoid of all emotion. Tearing my gaze from the door, I turn to stare at him. Once again, the expression on his face betrays nothing. He just holds my gaze, his eyes serious.

"This is what they do," he continues. "The first few weeks or months or sometimes even years when they break in their new life slaves. When the fae still try to fight back. Still try to resist. Before they eventually break and become obedient little slaves just to stop the torment and humiliation."

"They do this with all fae who win the Atonement Trials?"

"Yes."

My heart is pounding so hard that I can barely hear him anymore. Turning my head, I stare at the closed door again, as if I can see the torture that Isera and Alistair are enduring even through the pale wood that separates us from the banquet hall.

Soft fingers appear on my chin, turning my head back so that I'm facing forwards again. When I do, I find Draven standing there, closer than before. He keeps his hand on my chin, and his eyes sear into mine as he holds my gaze.

"Do you understand why I'm showing you this?" he asks.

My mind is spinning, so I can't manage to formulate a reply in time. When the seconds drag on, Draven answers the question for me.

Raising his free hand, he points towards the door. "*That* is what I'm expected to do to you as well."

My heart jerks in panic.

His grip on my chin gets firmer, as if he truly needs me to hear and understand his next words.

"So you need to act as if I have already broken you. Do you understand?" His eyes burn into my very soul. "If they think that I have failed to break you, they will eagerly try to break you themselves. And there is nothing I can do to stop them."

I draw in an unsteady breath.

"So hate me all you want, little rebel. And fight me all you want in private. But out here, in public, you need to act as if I'm your God."

# CHAPTER TWELVE

My ears are still ringing when we get back to Draven's rooms and he closes the front door behind us. I feel like I've been hit by a massive blast that knocked my head against a wall and cracked my skull open. I knew that the Icehearts were cruel, but I never expected... this.

"Where are they?"

It takes me another few seconds to realize that the words came out of my mouth. Giving my head a quick shake, I try to push out the shock and dread. After pulling myself together, I turn to face Draven, who is still standing a few steps away, watching me with unreadable eyes.

"Draven." Steel creeps into my voice as I lock eyes with him. "Where are they keeping Isera and Alistair when they're not humiliating them in public like that?"

He clenches his jaw and watches me in silence for a second.

"In the kennels," he replies at last. And before I can so much as get another word out, he adds, "But you're not going there."

"I need to see them!" I protest. "I need to talk to them."

"And say what? *Hang in there?*"

I jerk back, his mocking words hitting me like a slap. Because that was exactly what I had been planning to say.

Raking both hands through his hair, he forces out a frustrated breath while shooting me a look full of exasperation. "There is nothing you can say to them that will make this better. All it will accomplish is to put *you* in danger."

"From what?" I snap back.

"From everyone!" Taking two powerful strides forward, he closes the distance between us and grabs me by the shoulders. "You need to be careful. Everyone in this palace works for them." His eyes are burning with frustration as he locks them on me while he tightens his grip on my shoulders. "Listen to my words. *Everyone* in here works for them. So don't try to sneak out, don't get seen, and don't talk to anyone."

I have no intention of promising any of the sort, so I decide to change the subject instead. Lifting a hand, I motion in the general direction of the banquet hall. "Did you do things like that to your previous life slave?"

There is no emotion at all in his tone when he replies, "Yes. It's what's expected of me." Then pain creeps into his eyes for a fraction of a second as he adds, "But I don't want to do that to you. I can't. So please, don't do anything stupid that will draw their attention."

And there he goes again, saying things that make me think he truly cares about me. But still not giving me a reason for it. Or doing the one thing that would help me, which is to let me escape. But I decide not to venture into that dangerous subject at the moment. I'm still planning on sneaking out to find Isera and Alistair the first chance I get, so I can't risk making Draven too suspicious.

Narrowing my eyes, I study the tense expression on his face and instead ask, "Is it always like this? The humiliation and the cruelty?"

"Yes. Since they were treated like shit by the fae dragon riders, they want to balance the scales by being cruel to you now."

"But *we* didn't do anything. Isera and Alistair didn't do any of that."

"I know. But they don't care." True loathing flashes across his face for a second, and he squeezes his hand into a fist. "For them, those past crimes are enough to justify what they're doing now."

"You keep saying *they*. You don't agree?"

He gives me a pointed look. "If I did, I wouldn't have tried to save you from this, now would I?"

A sudden burst of frustration rips through my soul, and my next words come out like a shout. "So why do you serve them?" I throw my arms out in exasperation while staring up at him. "I can tell that you despise them! Despise what they do. So why do you still do their bidding?"

He opens his mouth as if to reply, but then just closes it again. Blowing out a sigh, he shakes his head and just begins turning away as if to leave.

My hand shoots out, and I grab his arm and yank him back to face me. "No! Don't do that. Don't begin answering and then change your mind halfway through. You always do that. So answer me for once! Why do you serve them?"

Anger flashes across his face. "Because I don't have any other choice."

"There is always a choice!"

"You have no idea what you're talking about." The anger on his face transforms into searing pain for a second before his expression becomes unreadable again. Clenching his jaw, he flexes his hand and draws in a controlled breath. "You don't know them like I do. You don't know what they're capable of. What they've already done. To me. And to others."

"You're just a coward!"

Hurt flits across his face for a fraction of a second.

And I immediately regret my words. Because he's right. I have no idea what he has gone through before this. I have no idea what made him betray his entire clan in exchange for power.

But before I can take it back, that flash of hurt disappears from his features and a smirk full of challenge spreads across his face instead.

"Good," he says, that smirk still on his lips as he takes a step closer. "There's that sharp tongue and that fire I've been looking for. You looked so desolate when we walked back in here that I was worried it might have gone out for good." Lifting a hand, he brushes his thumb over my bottom lip. "Glad to see it's still there."

I blink in shock, and for a few seconds, all I can do is to stare at him. Was he just baiting me? Was this whole conversation just an act to get me to snap out of the panic and dread that I felt after seeing Isera and Alistair? I hate to admit it, but if it was, it certainly worked.

A ripple of forbidden desire courses through me when he brushes his thumb over my bottom lip again.

I slap his hand away.

His eyes glint and that devilish smirk widens. "Good. Hate me. Fight me. Take it all out on me."

Grabbing the collar of his armor, I yank his face down closer to mine while a matching smirk full of challenge spreads across my own mouth. "You're going to regret that wish. Because inside these walls, I'm going to become your worst nightmare, and I won't stop until you bow down before your own personal Queen of Hell."

He slides his fingers down from my lips to instead circle my throat. A shudder ripples through my body as he slants his mouth over mine, just shy of touching. And when he speaks, his breath caresses my lips in a way that makes pleasure curl around my spine.

"As long as you act like I'm your God *outside* these walls, I welcome your hell in here, little rebel."

"Deal."

He smiles against my lips. "Deal."

But I made no promise to actually stay in here while he is out hunting the Red Hand. Because I have a resistance to help.

He wants me to fight? Fine. I'll fight. I will help the human resistance pull off this heist and cripple the Iceheart Dynasty.

And then, I am going to get Isera and Alistair and get as far away from here as possible.

## CHAPTER THIRTEEN

It took two days before I finally got a chance to sneak out while the rest of the castle is sleeping. Draven disappeared in the middle of the night, presumably something to do with the hunt for the Red Hand, and he left our rooms an hour ago. I left soon after, but through the window in my room rather than the door.

My heart patters in my chest as I close the final distance to the section known as *the kennels*. I had to use my magic to persuade one of the servants to tell me where it was, but now that I'm here, I still don't understand why it's called the kennels. It's located on the ground floor, right next to the outer wall of the palace, so I had to climb down the side of the castle and then in through a window in the corridor a short distance away.

I flick my gaze back and forth as I make my way towards the door. But to my surprise, there are no guards here. They might be on the inside though, and there is no other way for me to check than by simply opening the door.

Stopping in front of the plain door, I draw in a bracing breath. Then I push the handle down. Slowly.

My pulse thrums in my ears.

But no alarm is raised.

I carefully edge the door open wider and peer inside. No guards. After casting one last look over my shoulder, I slip in through the door and close it behind me.

A room full of cages meets me on the other side.

I stop dead in my tracks.

Cages. Not cells. *Cages.* None of them are big enough for an adult to stand upright. I stare at them while dread and rage sear through my veins.

There is only one torch in the entire room, and it's located close to the door, so the rest of the room is left in murky shadows. But if I squint, I'm fairly certain that I can make out two people sitting in the two closest cages straight ahead.

Swallowing down the storm of emotions inside me, I move towards them. As I get closer, the man in the first cage snaps his head up.

A pair of orange and green eyes and a mop of curly blond hair meet me.

Alistair.

He jerks back in shock when he sees me, and he blinks several times as if he's trying to figure out if he's hallucinating or not.

"Selena?" he presses out, his voice hoarse. His eyes are wide as he stares at me. "How are you here? Where is Draven?" Then suspicion flashes across his face, and he narrows his eyes at me. "Is this a setup?"

Coming to a halt in front of his cage, I study him while my heart squeezes painfully in my chest.

There was certainly no love lost between me and Alistair during the Atonement Trials. In my opinion, he is, and always has been, a bully. During all my time in the Seelie Court, I have only ever seen him be mean and do things to make other people feel small and weak and worthless. But regardless of his previous actions, he doesn't deserve *this*.

He is seated at the back of the cage where he has a full

view of the door. He's still only wearing those tight shorts that look like underwear. The only other thing he has with which to cover himself is a thin blanket. He has draped that over his shoulders so that it protects his naked back from the iron bars of the cage that he is leaning against. Seated with his knees drawn up to his chest, he tries to wrap as much of his body as possible with the parts of the blanket that remain.

It takes me another second to remember that he asked me a question. While trying to block out the pain that is strangling my heart, I crouch down so that I'm sitting on my knees in front of his cage instead of looming over it.

"Draven is out hunting a human rebel called the Red Hand," I reply. "I managed to sneak away after he left."

I shift my gaze to the cage right next to Alistair's.

And that pain that I was trying to block out hits me like a blow to the chest again.

Isera is seated at the back of that cage, in the exact same way that Alistair is. With a thin blanket around her shoulders, she is sitting with her knees drawn up to her chest and leaning her back against the iron bars. She is also still only dressed in those garments that look like underwear.

But as opposed to Alistair, she isn't looking at me. She is just staring blankly at the white ice wall across the room. Her long black hair hangs like dark curtains around her face, and her blue and silver eyes show no signs of life whatsoever. If it weren't for the fact that I can see her chest rising and falling, I would almost believe that she was dead.

"Isera," I say softly.

She doesn't reply. Doesn't look at me. Doesn't show any sign at all that she even heard me.

Swallowing, I shift my gaze back to Alistair. "How are you holding up?"

The moment the words are out of my mouth, I want to slap

myself. In the history of stupid questions, that one must surely rank in the top ten.

Alistair draws his eyebrows down in a scowl. "How do you think?"

I wince and then nod to tell him that I also realize that it was a dumb question. Then my gaze slides to Isera again. She still doesn't reply. Just sits there, staring at the wall.

"She's been like that ever since they put the collars on us," Alistair supplies. His eyes soften for a fraction of a second, and he heaves a sigh. "Ever since she found out what really happened to her mother after she won the last Atonement Trials."

"She hasn't said anything?"

"No. She doesn't do anything at all." The softness is replaced by an intense flash of disgust. "When the Icehearts come, she doesn't even try to fight back. She just lets them do whatever they want. Like she's a fucking doll."

"Maybe she..." Dread crashes over me when a sudden realization hits me. "Oh Goddess above. She's claustrophobic. Intensely claustrophobic."

Remembering her fear when we had to crawl through that tunnel during the Atonement Trials, I quickly snap my gaze back to her and try to get her to respond or look at me or in any way acknowledge that she has heard my offer to take away her fear. But she just continues staring at the ice wall on the other side of the room. I usually only do things like this if I have the other person's permission, but since I know what is making her disassociate like this, I decide to take matters into my own hands.

Since I'm not wearing a collar, I call up my magic and shove it towards the bone white spark of fear in her chest. I expect to find it blazing like wildfire. But to my utter shock, it's not. In fact, it's not even there at all.

Completely stunned, I release the grip on my magic and just stare at her. She's not feeling claustrophobic? But then why is she this... catatonic?

Alistair, who couldn't see that I was using my magic since my head was turned towards Isera, just answers as if I haven't already confirmed that she isn't lost in fear at all.

"It's not just when we're in these cages, though," he says. "She's like this all the time." He lets out something between a sigh and a humorless breath of amusement. "And then there is *that*."

Shifting my gaze back to him, I find him nodding towards the cage in the corner behind me. I turn around.

Shock crackles through me as I find a third person sitting there.

A gorgeous woman with flowing brown hair, pink and purple eyes, and a scar across her cheek and jaw is seated in the middle of the cage.

My jaw drops. "Lavendera?"

Lavendera Dawnwalker is sitting cross-legged there on the white ice floor with her hands resting in her lap. There is a collar around her throat as well, but as opposed to Isera and Alistair, she is wearing the same clothes that she wore when she was competing in the Atonement Trials with us. And as usual, she is staring into space as if she's not really here.

But at the sound of her name, she tilts her head back down and shifts her gaze from the part of the ceiling that she was gazing at and instead fixes it on me. For a few seconds, that vacant expression remains on her features. Then she blinks hard a couple of times, and reality seems to snap back into her.

"Selena?" she says. Her eyes widen in what looks like genuine shock. "What are you doing here?"

"What am *I* doing here?" I stare at her in disbelief. "What are *you* doing here?"

She tilts her head to the side while a considering look blows across her beautiful features, as if she is recounting everything that has happened in the two weeks since the Atonement Trials ended.

"The Icehearts flew back to get me," she says eventually. A

bitter smile tugs at her lips. "They consider tree magic too important to let it roam free."

"You mean too *dangerous*," I say.

That bitter smile on her lips widens.

"So yeah," Alistair says from behind me. His voice is laced with bitter mockery and exasperation. "You asked how I'm holding up? I've got one person who's completely catatonic and another who either just sits there staring into space or screams about how crowded it is in here."

A sharp glint flashes in Lavendera's eyes. "It *is* crowded."

"Regardless, neither of you are doing anything to fight back."

"Because it's *pointless*."

I'm stunned by the sharpness of her voice as she practically growls that final word at us. Shifting on my knees, I move so that I'm sitting at an angle where I can see both of them. Alistair is glaring at Lavendera, who looks back at him with equal steel in her eyes.

"It's pointless to fight the Icehearts," she snaps, her voice cracking through the air like a whip. "They're too powerful. Too cruel. Too vicious. They control everything. How much food we're allowed to eat. What we're allowed to drink. How many children we can have—"

A jolt shoots through me. "Wait, what?"

She continues glaring at Alistair for another second before she slides her gaze to me and shakes her head as if she doesn't understand the question. "*What*, what?"

"What do you mean they control how many children we're allowed to have?"

Still seated there cross-legged in the middle of her cage, she stares at me in silence for a few moments, as if the answer should have been obvious. Then she cocks her head while a considering look instead blows across her features. "You really don't know, do you? You've truly never suspected anything?"

"Suspected what?" Alistair snaps from my right, sounding as impatient as I feel.

"That they're sterilizing us."

My stomach drops.

For a while, only the faint hissing of the lone torch by the wall breaks the dead silence. Light from its flickering flame dances over the white ice walls, casting ominous shadows around the rest of the room.

"What?" I manage to press out at last.

Lavendera holds my gaze with serious eyes. "We didn't always only produce one child. Back before the war, we could have as many children as we wanted. But after they trapped us in the Seelie Court, they began to sterilize us after we have given birth to one child."

Ice spreads through my veins.

"Why do you think all the doctors in the Seelie Court are dragon shifters?" She shakes her head at me, as if she can't believe that I had never thought about it. "After the mother gives birth, they give her something that they say will help relieve the pain. But it actually makes us sterile."

"Why?" Alistair asks. He sounds as horrified as I feel.

"To produce strong magic users."

Nausea crawls up my throat as her words clang through my skull. "They're breeding us?"

"Yes. They think that having multiple children thins the magic in our blood, so they only let us have one to make sure that if that child is born with magic, it gets all the magic in that bloodline.

Dragging in an unsteady breath, I press a hand to my mouth. I feel like I'm going to throw up. We're not people to them. We're less than animals. A source to be controlled and bred.

And then, age-old guilt, guilt that I thought I had already buried when I left the Seelie Court, suddenly flares up inside me. They're limiting us to one child to make that child's magic stronger. Which means that I destroyed my parents completely simply by being born. More than I even knew. Not only because they sterilized my mother without her knowledge after I was born, but also because it made my magic stronger. Which ultimately ruined my parents' whole relationship.

"And besides," Lavendera continues. "How else were they supposed to keep *an entire race* contained inside just one single city? If we could have multiple children, we would outgrow the city and the resources it can provide."

I feel like the entire foundations of my world are breaking. Desperately blocking out the torrent inside me, I try to keep it from shattering completely and burying me underneath so much rubble that I will never be able to climb back out. I can't consider the full implications of this right now. I don't even know if it's actually true. If it was, we would have known. Wouldn't we?

"How do you know all this?" I ask, my voice strained from how hard I'm trying to keep it together right now.

"How do you *not*?" She shakes her head at me, almost as if she's disappointed in me. "Have you never thought about it? If we truly could only produce one child, our species would have gone extinct long ago."

"But then... won't we go extinct now?"

"Since we live for so long, it will take a while. And I assume the Icehearts are planning on lifting the restrictions once we run the risk of inbreeding." She gives me that look of absolute disbelief again. "Have you seriously never questioned any of this?"

"No," I snap as a wave of embarrassment and anger crashes over me. Because deep down, I know she's right. I should have questioned it. But instead, I reply, "I was... busy worrying about other things. Like how to survive. And eat."

A harsh laugh escapes her mouth. Then she gives me a nod, as if conceding the point. "Yeah. That's how they do it. Distract you with—"

She abruptly stops speaking in the middle of her sentence.

Her eyes go vacant for a second. Then they snap back in focus. A snarl rips from her throat, and she shoots up from the floor. But since the ceiling of the cage is so low, it only makes her bang her head against it. She crouches down and rakes her fingers through her hair, and then begins pacing bent over like that.

"Stop," she growls. "It's so crowded. It's so fucking crowded."

I stare at her, completely stunned by the abrupt change in behavior.

"Yeah, she does that," Alistair says, and heaves a deep sigh.

Lavendera continues pacing while furiously raking her fingers through her hair. My heart beats hard in my chest as I watch her. I don't know what suddenly triggered it from one second to the other, but I suppose I do understand it. If she truly has been living out in the thorn forest all her life, like people say, any kind of confinement must feel crowded. And this in particular.

My gaze shifts to Isera, who is still sitting immobile in her cage, staring at nothing. Then I flick another glance at Lavendera before I at last return my gaze to the blond fire-wielder in the cage to my right.

Alistair is right. We're in bad shape. When I snuck in here, I thought that I would be able to recruit both Isera and Alistair to the resistance. But it looks like Alistair is the only one sane enough to actually help.

So I block out all the awful things I have learned in the past few minutes and instead focus on my mission. I can't change what has happened in the past. And I don't even know for sure if Lavendera is right. It's still only her speculations. I need to focus on the things that I can change. Which is the future. I'm going to take down this whole fucking dynasty if it's the last thing I do. And for that, I'm going to need help from Alistair.

However, when I turn back to him, I only find suspicion in his green and orange eyes as he locks them on me.

"You know, you never really answered my question,

Soulstealer," he says, using the nickname he and his friends used to call me back in the Seelie Court. "How are you here? If you managed to sneak away from Draven, why did you come here instead of escaping?"

Hesitation pulses through me. If we were back in the Seelie Court, Alistair is the last person I would trust with a secret as dangerous as this.

My gaze drifts down to the collar around his neck and over the thin blanket wrapped around his half-naked body.

Determination pushes out the hesitation. Alistair and I might have had our differences in the past, but right now, we want the same thing. So I decide to be honest.

His eyes widen as I explain about my escape and my meeting with the human resistance and the planned heist to cripple the Iceheart Dynasty.

"I will get you out of here," I finish. "I promise. After the heist, I will get us all out of here. So you have to hold on. For just a little while longer."

Sitting there at the back of the cage, he watches me in silence for a few seconds. My heart pounds as I wait for him to say something. To tell me that I'm an idiot. That I should have run when I had the chance. That I should try to steal the keys to their cages from Bane and Jessina and just get us all the hell out of here. But to my surprise, he doesn't.

Drawing in a long breath, he instead says, "What do you need?"

"Maps," I reply. "There are places that I can't get into. Like the royal wing. I need to know the layout so that I can figure out where the treasury is and how to get there."

Alistair grimaces, but then nods. "They keep us blindfolded when they take us out of these cages. But I'll see if I can overhear something."

"Thank you."

He glances away and runs both hands through his curly blond

hair. "Just... promise you'll make a plan to get us out of here. Quickly."

"Of course. I'll..." I trail off as I notice something.

When he raised his arms to draw his hands through his hair, it made the blanket around him slide off his shoulders and expose his chest. My heart pounds as I stare at the vicious burn scars visible across his chest and stomach.

"Are those... burn scars?" I blurt out.

Panic flashes in Alistair's eyes as he snaps his gaze back to me while quickly pulling the blanket back around his body again. His voice is tight as he grinds out, "Yes."

"But I thought you couldn't get burned by your own fire magic."

"I can't."

"Then how—"

"Just find a way out of here." He shoots me a hard look, signaling that the discussion is over. "I'll see what I can pick up about the location of the treasury. And I'll keep an eye on Isera." Then he nods towards the cell in the corner, where Lavendera is still pacing and snarling about how crowded it is. "Her too."

"Thank you." I hold his gaze. "I'll be back as soon as I can."

He nods. Then a hint of desperation flickers in his eyes for a second, and he swallows. "Just... hurry."

And before I can reply, he braces his forearms on his knees and lowers his head to rest his forehead against them, hiding the expression on his face. My gaze shifts from him, to the catatonic Isera, to the panicking Lavendera.

I desperately want to reach out with my magic and take away all the emotions that are hurting them. But I don't even know what it is that they're feeling, let alone how it would affect them if I took that emotion away. It might just make everything worse.

So in the end, I just give them all a nod that none of them can see.

And then I slip back out the door.

# CHAPTER FOURTEEN

My heart pounds in my chest as I skid to a halt outside the front door to Draven's quarters. I had planned to climb in through the window or the balcony, but a dragon shifter flew right towards the section of the wall that I was on before I could reach it. So I panicked and jumped in through another window instead. After that, I managed to get to Draven's door without anyone seeing me, but none of that will matter if the door is locked.

With my heart still hammering against my ribs, I grab the handle and slowly push it down.

Relief washes through me like a flood. It's unlocked. One of the servants who regularly come to the room for one reason or another must have forgotten to lock it.

While sending a heartfelt prayer of thanks to Mabona, I slip in through the door and close it quietly behind me.

The living room is dark around me. Only the faint silver light of the moon that shines in through the windows and the clear balcony door illuminates the space. I cast a glance at the door to Draven's bedroom. It's closed. Just like it was when he left. And everything inside the living room looks the same as well.

I let out a long sigh of relief. He isn't back yet.

Tiptoeing across the dark wooden floorboards, I sneak back into my room and then hurry over to the dresser. Since I should already be sleeping, I throw off my normal clothes, with my climbing gear hidden inside, and then yank open the drawer to grab that short silk nightgown that is my only choice of sleepwear.

My heart jerks.

It's not there. Why isn't it there? By Mabona, please don't tell me that the servant who forgot to lock the door took it away to wash it or something. How am I supposed to explain this to Draven? That she somehow just took it off my body while I was supposed to be sleeping?

Still completely naked, I yank open another drawer to check if I just misplaced it.

"Looking for this?"

I gasp. Whipping around, I stare at the back wall of my room. Or... not at the wall. At Draven.

He is leaning casually against the pale ice wall, one ankle crossed over the other. But his eyes are intense as he watches me. He's only wearing a pair of black underwear, leaving the rest of his lethal body on full display. And he has one hand raised, his palm nonchalantly tipped forward, and from his fingers dangle a short garment. My black silk nightgown.

"Imagine my surprise when I got back from my little errand and found your room empty and your clothes missing. After I specifically told you to stay here. For your own safety." Tilting his hand, he lets the nightgown slide off his fingers and flutter to the floor in a ripple of black silk. Then he straightens, his eyes searing into me. "Where were you?"

My heart slams against my ribs. Drawing in a short breath, I start backing towards the door.

Draven narrows his eyes at me. "Don't."

I whirl around and dart back into the living room.

The booming of massive wings echoes through the room, and before I can even make it halfway to the front door, Draven flies past me. A distinct click sounds as he locks the door before turning towards where I'm now standing frozen in the middle of the living room. And when he reaches out and turns on the closest faelight, I can see the exasperation on his handsome face.

"What were you going to do? Huh?" He shakes his head before nodding towards my body. "Run out into the corridor stark naked?"

My gaze shoots down to my own body. Heat floods my cheeks when I remember that I am in fact completely naked. Meeting Draven's gaze again, I open my mouth, but I can't figure out what to say.

"Azaroth's flame," he mutters, and shakes his head again. Then his expression sharpens, and he takes a step towards me. "I'm still waiting for an answer. Where were you?"

I back away as he keeps advancing on me. But then I remember myself before I can bump into one of the dark gray couches close to the balcony door. Forcing myself to stand my ground, I raise my chin and just hold Draven's gaze as he closes the final distance between us. The soft light from the faelight gem makes his golden eyes glitter as he comes to a halt right in front of me. This close, I can count every ridge of his sharp abs and every muscle visible on his half-naked body.

"I won't ask again," he warns.

"Fine." I shoot him an annoyed look. "I was trying to get down to the kennels to see Isera and Alistair."

Frustration flashes across his face. "I told you—"

"I know what you told me. But I don't care. I wanted to see them."

He blows out a controlled breath through his nose and flexes his hand. "How did you get out?"

"When you left and then came back to get something from your room," I lie. "I snuck out then."

There is no way in hell that I would have had the time to actually sneak out during those brief moments when he was getting whatever it was that he had forgotten, but there is no way for him to know that.

"Azaroth's fucking flame," he growls. "Did anyone see you?"

"No."

He gives me a sharp look.

I throw my arms out as if in frustration. "I couldn't even make it down the stairs! There are guards in every stairwell."

I don't want him to know that I have already talked to Isera and Alistair. Or at least Alistair. And I most certainly don't want him to know that I've talked to Lavendera. Because I have a feeling that she and her tree magic is going to become our hidden weapon. The one thing that will tip the scales in our favor and get us all out of here.

Raking his fingers through his hair, he blows out a long breath of relief. "Thank God for that at least." After dropping his hands again, he locks serious eyes with me. "I've told you. *Everyone* here works for them. And if they find you sneaking around the castle, without your collar, they are going to do unspeakable things to you. Which is why I couldn't risk drawing attention to you by tearing this whole fucking castle apart with my bare hands to find you the moment I discovered that you were gone, even though every nerve inside my body was screaming at me to do exactly that."

The sheer worry and protectiveness in his voice, and the fear in his eyes, stun me so much that all I manage is to stare back at him. He truly is worried about my safety.

That realization makes my heart do strange things in my chest.

No one has ever cared about me before. And certainly not this intensely. But for some reason, and in his own twisted way, *he* does. The thought makes an unexpected burst of warmth fill my chest.

And suddenly, this all feels too intimate. Too real. And I can't handle that. Because this isn't real. Nothing between us is real. We're on opposite sides in this war, and all we have ever done is to deceive each other. So I reach for the one thing that feels safe. Feels natural without being too intimate.

Taunting challenges.

"So now what?" I bait. Raising my chin, I give him a look dripping with challenge. "You're going to punish me?" A sly smile spreads across my lips as I add in a mocking voice, "Master."

Dark desire flares up in his eyes. Closing the final distance between us, he slides his hand around my neck. With a commanding grip on my throat, he stares me down while his chest rises and falls with slow and controlled breaths.

"Do you want me to punish you, little rebel?"

A spike of forbidden pleasure shoots straight down my spine.

He slides his gaze down my utterly naked body, and when his eyes meet mine again, the fire in my veins is mirrored in his expression as well.

I once more try to remind myself that Draven and I are enemies. That I shouldn't enjoy his commanding hands on my body. That I should just block out all the confusing emotions about him that have been twisting inside me ever since the Atonement Trials. But when he's looking at me like this, like I'm the only person in this whole world who matters, it's impossible.

"How about this," he begins, his voice low and dark. "If you can manage to stay quiet, I might consider letting your insubordination slide. Just this once."

"Stay quiet for what?"

My heart skips a beat when Draven spins us around and pulls me down with him as he sits down on the dark gray sofa that was waiting behind me. He sits down farther back on the cushion and spreads his legs wide before positioning me between them. My back is pressed against his muscular chest as I try to balance my weight on the edge of the cushion right in front of him.

He lifts his legs and drapes them over mine, spreading my legs wide open and keeping them like that.

I suck in a breath as my heart jerks in my chest and heat pools at my core.

Releasing my throat, he moves his hand down to rest on the edge of the couch right between my legs. The near touch of his fingers makes every nerve inside my body go on high alert.

"For this," he whispers in my ear.

He brushes his fingers over my clit.

Lightning shoots up my spine.

"Do you accept the challenge?" he murmurs, making his breath dance over the shell of my ear, right at the same time as he brushes his middle finger over my clit again.

Pleasure pulses through me, and a moan rips from deep within my chest.

He smiles against the side of my neck. "I'll take that as a yes."

His finger circles around my clit with expert precision. A ripple rolls through my body, and I have to bite my tongue to keep another moan from spilling out. He shifts his hand so that his thumb rubs my clit instead while he slides his fingers down to my entrance.

I throw my head back against his shoulder and drag in a shuddering breath as he gently traces his fingers around my entrance while he continues his sweet torture on my clit. Desire courses through my veins like liquid fire.

He slips one finger inside me.

Throwing my hands out, I grip his knees hard.

My clit throbs with need as he shifts the position of his thumb slightly. I gasp as it rubs against it at the perfect angle.

Draven lets out a dark chuckle. His warm breath caresses the sensitive skin right below my ear, sending another shiver of pleasure down my spine.

He slides his finger out of me and then adds a second finger.

I arch my back as another bolt of pleasure crackles through my body. Tension builds inside me as Draven begins pumping his fingers while his thumb rubs my clit. Clenching my jaw, I desperately try to stop the moan building in my throat.

Another gasp rips from my lungs as Draven slides his free hand along the curve of my breast and then rolls my nipple between his fingers. Lights flicker before my eyes as the feeling of his thumb on my clit, his fingers inside me, and his other hand toying with my nipple sends me careening towards an orgasm.

Gripping his knees, I press my mouth shut as the wave of pleasure builds inside me.

Draven thrusts his fingers deep inside me and then spreads them one way before switching their positions several times.

My body jerks as a bolt of pleasure shoots through me. Squirming desperately, I try to close my legs again to relieve the intense pleasure surging through my every vein. But Draven's legs remain draped over mine, keeping my legs spread wide open before his merciless hands.

Pleasure pulses through my body as he rolls my nipple between his fingers while he tortures my pussy with his other hand. I drag in unsteady breaths through my nose as the tension inside me builds to a crackling storm. A whimper spills from my lips.

Draven angles his head so that his mouth is once more right next to my ear, and when he speaks, I can hear the wicked smile in his voice. "If you want me to gag you, just say the word."

His breath dances over my ear, making a violent shudder of pleasure course through me. The tension inside me is thrumming so furiously that my body is practically vibrating with it. He pumps his fingers inside me with commanding strokes while his thumb moves harder against my clit. I gasp air into my lungs as the edge of the orgasm draws closer.

He pinches my nipple.

Release crashes through me.

Throwing my head back, I press it against Draven's shoulder as pleasure streaks through me, setting my every nerve on fire. My legs tremble underneath his. And it's only by sheer force of will that I manage to stop myself from crying out in pleasure.

Draven keeps fucking me with his fingers through the entire orgasm, drawing it out and trying to force the moans out of my mouth. But I keep my lips pressed tightly together, even as lights flicker before my eyes and my body writhes against his.

When the final pulses of pleasure have faded and Draven removes his fingers, I gasp air into my lungs as if I haven't breathed at all in the last few minutes. My muscles feel too loose and my skin too hot. I slump back against Draven's body.

I can feel every ridge of his muscles as I lean my back against him. My chest heaves.

For a few seconds, neither of us moves or speaks. I just sit there, slumped against him while my heart hammers against my ribs and my mind tries to piece itself together. Soft white light from the faelight gem across the room makes the white ice walls glitter. I drag in another deep breath as Draven lifts his legs off mine.

Then he thrusts his hips.

Hard.

My stomach lurches as it sends me sliding right over the edge of the couch. And because my body still hasn't recovered completely from the intense orgasm, I can't make my reflexes work in time, so I just collapse to the floor.

The couch creaks behind me as Draven stands up. While I try to reorient myself and push myself up to my knees, he strides around my naked body until he's standing right in front of me.

"I have to say," he begins, his voice smug. "It was a good effort."

"Effort?" I retort as I raise my head to glare up at him. "I won."

He draws his hand along my jaw, tilting my head back further, while a devilish smirk spreads across his stupidly handsome face. "Did you forget that cute and very desperate moan that came out of your mouth the moment that my fingers brushed against your wet little cunt?" His golden eyes gleam. "I hate to break it to you, little rebel, but you lost before we even began."

Slapping his hand away, I shoot to my feet and give his chest a shove while heat sears my cheeks. "Asshole."

His hands shoot up and wrap around my wrists before I can pull them back. I yank against his grip, but he's far stronger than I am. He flashes me a self-satisfied smile as he watches me struggle against him for another few seconds before I'm forced to give up.

Once I have stopped moving, he locks eyes with me again while a serious expression descends on his features.

"Here's the deal," he begins.

"Oh I am done making deals with you for one night."

He lets out a low chuckle that vibrates in the air between us, and his eyes glint dangerously as he holds my gaze. "That's okay. It's not actually a deal. It's a command."

I narrow my eyes at him. Raising his eyebrows, he waits for me to protest. But he and I both know that he has the power to make me obey him if he really wants to, so I just click my tongue in annoyance and concede the battle. A wicked smile blows across his lips before his expression turns serious again.

"Since I clearly can't trust you to follow the simplest of rules," he gives me a pointed look, "even though they're for *your own safety*, you will now be accompanying me everywhere."

"What?"

"You heard me."

"Yes, but—"

"But what?" He arches a dark brow. "Do you have something else you need to do?"

Frustration pulses through me. How am I supposed to sneak away and search for the treasury if he takes me with him to hunt the Red Hand? Goddess damn it.

But I can't exactly tell him any of that, so I just mutter, "No."

"Good." He flashes me another satisfied smile. "Then it's settled."

I yank my hands back the moment he releases my wrists. After shooting him one more glare, I turn and begin stalking back to my bedroom. But before I can take more than two steps, Draven speaks up again.

"And where do you think you're going?"

Confusion swirls through me, and I turn back to frown at him. "Back to my bed?"

His gaze sears into me. "I said *everywhere*."

A jolt shoots through me, and fire burns through my core again. I flick a glance towards the closed door to his bedroom before I meet his intense eyes again. "I thought you didn't want me in your bed."

"I thought you climbed into it anyway."

My heart pounds against my ribs at the memory of what happened between us when he locked me in his bedroom during the Atonement Trials.

Draven nods towards the open door to my bedroom. "You have thirty seconds to go and put on your nightgown. Then I expect you in my bed."

Heat rushes through my whole body.

Licking my lips, I swallow. "Or what?"

"Or I'm going to throw you over my shoulder, carry you back there, and handcuff you to it."

Forbidden desire shoots through me.

A slow smile spreads across Draven's lips. "One."

I dart into my bedroom. Grabbing the short silk nightgown, I yank it over my head and then snatch up a pair of panties that I didn't have a chance to put on earlier. And before Draven reaches the count of thirty, I am indeed lying on the soft sheets of his luxurious bed.

The mattress shifts underneath my body as Draven lies down after shifting into his fully human form again.

"At least you're not blocking half of the bed with your wings this time," I mutter into the darkness.

Warm air hits my bare shoulder as Draven lets out a soft chuckle.

Silence falls over us. The moment I climbed onto the bed, I rolled over so that my back was to him. And for a while, I just lie there on my side and stare out at the darkened room. The mattress shifts underneath me again as Draven gets comfortable. I listen to his steady breathing while my heart does dumb things in my chest.

And before I can stop myself, I find myself saying, "Back then, you purposely shifted into your human form in the middle of the night and lifted me into your bed, didn't you?"

He doesn't reply. But his breath hitches for a second, so I know that he heard me.

"Why?" I ask, because I know that I'm right about this. There is no other explanation for it. I didn't climb into the bed back then, so the only way for me to end up there is for him to have put me there himself.

Still, he says nothing. But he doesn't deny it either.

Blowing out a sigh, I pull the covers up higher around me while indecision pulses through me. I wonder if he would help me. He obviously cares about me in some capacity, and he did try to save me from this fate. And I know that he dislikes what the Icehearts are doing to us. So if I told him about the human resistance and the heist, he might actually help me.

While Draven's breathing evens out again, I run that idea

through my head several times. But I always come back to the same conclusion.

No, he wouldn't help me.

I don't know what happened to him that made him sell out his own clan in exchange for power, but he's obviously too afraid of the Icehearts to ever dare defy them.

No. Regardless of his secret moments of kindness, I can't trust him. Not with this. Against the Iceheart Dynasty, we are on our own.

# CHAPTER FIFTEEN

When Draven said everywhere, he truly meant everywhere. It has been almost a week since he issued that command, and I honestly thought that he would be satisfied by now. That he would just do it for a day or two to prove a point. But Goddess was I wrong. Every day, he takes me with him when he goes out into the city to hunt for the Red Hand.

Torchlight dances over the dark wooden walls of the tavern we're in. The people who are renting rooms in the adjacent corridor quickly disappeared into them the moment that four dragon shifters in black armor stepped across the threshold. But the humans who were just here to eat or drink weren't as lucky. Most of them are cowering down in their seats, trying not to draw attention to themselves while Galen, Draven's former best friend who appears to still be his second-in-command, tortures a man at the bar.

I wince as another scream shatters from the human man's throat.

"Who is the Red Hand?" Galen demands, his voice hard.

The man clenches his teeth.

Two steps away, Draven is leaning nonchalantly against the bar while he watches the brutal interrogation. Galen flicks a glance at him, to which Draven responds with a nod.

Galen twists the man's arm higher up. The guy screams, bending forward where he is kneeling on the floor, and shifts his body to try to relieve the pain that the unnatural angle of his arm is causing.

Averting my eyes, I wince again as another raw cry of agony rips from his throat. The other people in the tavern cower deeper into their chairs while a few of them cast desperate glances towards the door. But the other two soldiers that Draven brought are standing on either side of the door, preventing them all from leaving.

"Who is the Red Hand?" Galen demands again.

"He's the leader of the resistance," the man gasps out at last.

Snapping my gaze back to him, I blink in surprise. That's news to me. I knew that the Red Hand was an important part of the resistance, but I didn't realize that he was the actual leader.

"We know that," Galen replies, still keeping the man's arm bent at an unnatural angle. "But who *is* he?"

"I don't know!"

"Here's the thing." He nods towards Draven. "He won't let me stop until you give us the Red Hand's name. And I do what he says." He twists the man's arm farther back. "So give me what I want."

Another cry of pain, followed by a whimper, spills from his throat as he trembles on the floor. "Please. I don't know his name. I don't know who he is. No one does."

A sudden realization hits me like a fucking lightning strike.

*I* know who the Red Hand is.

Hector.

Based on the way Kath and the other humans reacted when he walked through the door, he is their leader. And this man just confirmed that the Red Hand is the leader of the resistance. Which means that Hector is the Red Hand.

Oh by Mabona. Draven is out here torturing people in order to get them to tell him who the Red Hand really is. People who truly don't know the Red Hand's identity. If he only knew that the person who sleeps in his bed every night is the one who has the coveted answer to his question.

Determination pulses through me. No matter what happens, I have to take that secret with me to the grave. I have to keep the Red Hand safe so that we can have a shot at toppling the Iceheart Dynasty.

Another scream echoes between the dark wooden walls.

"Please," the man gasps. "Please, I'm begging you. I'm telling the truth."

Draven just watches him with merciless eyes for another few seconds. Then he flicks his wrist. Galen immediately releases the man's arm and takes a step back. Soft whimpering comes from the human as he moves his arm back into its proper place.

After studying him for another moment, Draven slides his gaze over the rest of the tavern.

Clothes rustle and gasps ripple through the room as everyone shrinks back.

But Draven just pushes off from the bar and straightens.

"Move out," he says to his soldiers, who nod and immediately start towards the door. Draven shifts his gaze to me and jerks his chin. "Selena."

I flick another glance towards the man, who remains kneeling on the floor, while Draven stalks out the door. Guilt twists my heart. If I had told Draven what I knew, I could have ended this man's suffering. In fact, I could prevent a lot of suffering for all the humans. But it would only be temporary. The work that the Red Hand and the resistance are doing is too important.

Tearing my gaze from the man on the floor, I start towards

the door as well. But I only make it one step before someone grabs my arm. My stomach lurches as the sudden pull on my arm makes me stumble into the table next to me.

"Act like you just tripped," a woman with short brown hair hisses in my ear. "This whole tavern is full of idealistic idiots, and I don't want them to know that I gave this to you." With one hand still on my arm, she uses the other to press a paper into my palm. "Give this to Commander Ryat. This is what the Red Hand looks like."

My eyes widen in shock, and I flick a glance down at the folded-up piece of paper in my hand before I meet the woman's gaze again.

Her brown eyes are serious as she holds my gaze. "Tell him that not all humans support the Red Hand. I despise him. His actions only bring trouble for the human communities."

Before I can figure out how to reply to that, she releases me and pushes me away from the table, as if she's annoyed that I tripped into her.

"Watch where you're going," she snarls, very convincingly, at me.

I quickly stuff the paper into my pocket and then hurry out the door.

Outside, I find Draven arguing with his soldiers. Or rather, with Galen. The other two dragon shifters look like they would rather be anywhere but here at this particular moment.

While Draven is otherwise occupied, I drift over to a cluster of barrels as if I just want to lean against them while I wait. But once I get there, I shift my body so that I'm standing at a better angle. And then I yank out the piece of paper that the woman gave me and flip it open.

My heart jerks when I find a hand-drawn sketch of a tall and muscular man. Just like Hector. In the sketch he is wearing nondescript gray clothes and a hood pulled up over his head. And on his face, hiding his features from view, is a red mask. It's shaped like a snarling devil. The illustration might not show any of Hector's facial features, but the height and build it shows, combined with this very distinctive mask, is incriminating enough.

Behind me, Draven continues arguing with Galen. My heart slams against my ribs as I crumple the paper in my hand again so that it won't be visible. I can't remain with my back to Draven for too long, or he will get suspicious.

So with the note hidden in my hand, I turn and lean against the barrels like I was pretending to do from the beginning.

Guilt and worry and indecision twist inside my chest again as I watch the street before me.

Humans and dragon shifters are moving up and down the cobblestones. Most of them walk with purpose, as if they have somewhere to be. But almost all humans cast looks full of wariness and poison at Draven and his soldiers.

Red light from the setting sun slants down over the buildings, painting them the color of blood. The torch that has been stuck to the barrel next to me crackles as a late afternoon wind sweeps down the street.

My mind drifts back to the man inside the tavern behind me. And then to all the humans out here who hurry past Draven and his clan members. More of them are going to get hurt. As long as Draven can't find the Red Hand, he is going to take it out on these people.

I've seen it these past few days. Seen the ruthlessness and the brutality that he and the other dragon shifters inflict on the humans in their mad search for the Red Hand.

And I could put an end to it.

If I give Draven this drawing and tell him that Hector is the Red Hand, I can prevent further suffering. But the cost of that would be devastating. It would cripple the human resistance and destroy any chance they have of overthrowing the Icehearts.

Those tangled thoughts drag up that infuriating instinct that I thought I had already buried. I want people to like me. Secretly, I want all of these humans to look at me like a hero. I want the recognition that I never received in the Seelie Court. The recognition I never received no matter how much I did for the fae rebellion there. I want the other fae resistance members to admit that they were wrong. To tell me that they should have trusted me. That they should have let me help before.

But in my heart, I know that it's a ridiculous and utterly selfish wish. It doesn't matter if people like me. It just matters that we win.

So while I keep my eyes on the humans who will now suffer because of me, I move my hand to the torch right next to me.

And then I burn the drawing of the Red Hand to ash.

"Selena, let's go."

Startled out of my thoughts, I tear my gaze away from the humans moving up and down the street and instead turn towards Draven. Galen and the other two soldiers are striding away, along the road that leads farther into the city, while Draven is facing the street that leads back to the Ice Palace.

Discreetly moving my hand behind my back, I let the remaining flakes of ash fall to the ground while I push off from the barrels and straighten. Draven, whose dark brows are drawn down in a scowl, appears to be too frustrated after his argument with his soldiers to notice what I did. After flexing his hand, he rakes it through his hair while impatiently waiting for me to reach his side.

Almost before I've closed the final distance, he starts off down the road. I jog a few steps to catch up before I can fall into step beside him. Whatever the argument was about, he's apparently not happy about it, because he just stalks forward in silence without even looking at me.

At first, I plan to just let him be. But the farther along the street we walk, the more exasperated and angry I become as well. Because at almost every public building we pass, I see dragon shifters harassing and interrogating humans in an unnecessarily harsh manner.

"You could stop this, you know," I grind out eventually, and flick a hand towards the cruel behavior around us.

Draven gives me a look from the corner of his eye. "Why would I?"

"Because it's wrong. You know it's wrong."

"No, actually, I don't. Because it serves my goal."

"These people are innocent! You know that. They don't deserve to be treated like—"

My words are cut off by a gasp as Draven suddenly grabs me and pulls me into a darkened alley. Only the deserted and very narrow pathway observes us as he pushes me up against the rough stone wall and plants his palms on the wall on either side of my head, caging me in.

"Let's get something straight." His eyes burn through my very soul as he locks them on me. "I am not a hero. I don't care about other people. I only care about getting what *I* want."

Drawing in an unsteady breath, I just stare up at him in silence while my heart beats hard against my ribs. Because I can tell that he means every word of that.

He nods towards the mouth of the alley, where on the other side, dragon shifters continue to brutally interrogate humans. "These injustices that you want me to stop? I *encourage* them. Because they serve my goal."

"To finally take down the Red Hand?" I let out a mocking scoff. "Did he really bruise your ego that much when he beat you last time?"

"It's not about my ego."

"Really? Then why are you taking it out on the civilian population like some kind of bully who got his own pants pulled down?"

"Because I don't care who gets hurt, as long as it serves my goals. This world is cruel and unfair. And if you're too kind and too trusting and too empathetic, people will only take advantage of you."

His words hit me like a knife to the gut. Because deep down, deep in the hidden corners of my soul that I try to hide from everyone, I know that he is right. All my life, I have done everything I can to please the people around me. And all anyone has ever done is to use me because of it. I have drained myself, sacrificed everything that I wanted, to make everyone else happy and to help them achieve their goals. But it didn't make the world better. It just made *me* miserable.

Draven takes one hand off the wall and brushes gentle fingers over my cheek, pushing a stray lock of hair away from it and hooking it behind my ear instead. The soft touch sends a ripple down my spine.

"So I don't wring my hands about collateral damage," he says as he holds my gaze with those intense eyes of his. "I take what I want from this world. And God help anyone who stands in my way."

My heart pounds in my chest. I know that I should be outraged. That I should berate him for his lack of morals and his complete disregard for other people. But deep inside those hidden corners of my soul, I find myself desperately craving that kind of ruthless conviction for myself. I have spent my life living for other people. What would it be like to only live for myself? To do only what I want? To take what I want from this world and to hell with everyone else?

However, I can never voice those dark and forbidden thoughts out loud. And the fact that I even have them makes me panic. Makes me feel horrified and angry with myself. So instead of admitting that I might actually understand the desperate desire that Draven has just explained, I decide to hit back.

"You don't care about anyone else, huh?" I challenge.

He flashes me a sharp smile. "No."

"Then why did you try to save *me*?"

That ruthless expression on his face falters for just one single second. But since I was watching him so closely, I saw it. And he knows that I saw it. A muscle flickers in his jaw.

Holding his gaze, I stare up at him. Waiting for him to finally explain why he cares about my safety. Daring him to tell me.

But just like before, he gives me no answer.

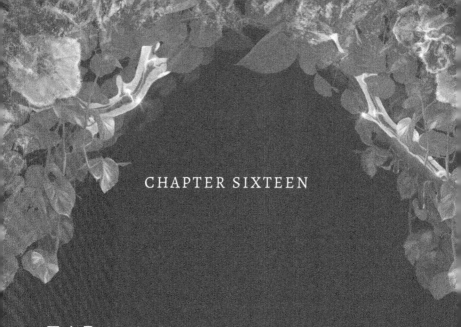

# CHAPTER SIXTEEN

W e have barely made it three steps inside the massive ice doors of the palace before a female dragon shifter with stunning green eyes hurries up to us. Or rather, to Draven. He just keeps walking, making her awkwardly run along next to him as we make our way up the stairs and towards his rooms.

"Commander," she says, looking apologetic. "Empress Jessina and Emperor Bane have noticed your absence at the last few banquets."

"Their observation has been noted," Draven simply replies.

She clears her throat self-consciously. "They are requesting your presence at the banquet tonight."

"I'm busy. Hunting down the Red Hand." He cuts her a look. "As per their own orders."

The messenger squirms underneath his hard gaze and trips on the final step, but still manages to press out, "I'm afraid they're insisting."

Draven lets out an annoyed sigh. "Fine. Consider your message delivered."

I glance at the woman, who still continues hurrying along next to Draven. Worry pulses across her whole face.

"So you will be there?" she asks.

I can practically hear the pleading in her voice. If Draven doesn't show up, the Icehearts will probably punish *her* for it.

Draven clenches his jaw and then lets out another sigh. But this one sounds more resigned than angry. "We'll be there."

My heart skips a beat. We. *We* will be there. Which means that I'm going as well.

"Thank you," the messenger whispers softly, and then bows her head to Draven before she disappears back the way we came.

Anticipation and anxiety fight like wolves inside my chest as Draven and I continue towards his rooms. This might be the perfect opportunity for me to do some sneak interrogations and find out where the treasury room is. But it will also mean that I need to put on an act in front of the Icehearts and pretend like I have accepted that Draven is my master. And I am not looking forward to that.

The moment we step inside his living room, he closes and locks the door behind us. I raise my eyebrows and shoot him an exasperated look. He just gives me a pointed look back that I can only interpret as, *you're the one who keeps sneaking out.* I let out a huff.

"I need to take a bath and wash off all this dirt and blood," he announces as he starts towards his bedroom. "That dress you wore to the collaring ceremony is still in your closet. Put it on."

I glance over my shoulder towards my room, but I find myself trailing him into his instead. Because Goddess damn it, I really can't figure him out. In private, his entire being pulses with authority and control. But the moment that Bane and Jessina call for him, he leaps to obey their orders.

"You don't want to go to this banquet," I state as I follow him across the threshold and into his bedroom.

He turns on the faelights, bathing the neat and tidy room in glowing white light. Without even looking at me, he strides over to the armor stand that holds his black dragon scale armor when

135

he's not wearing it. I lean back against the white ice wall right inside the door and cross my arms.

"No, I don't," he admits while he begins removing the pieces of armor that cover his arms and chest.

His back is still to me, so I can't see the expression on his face. But his tone is flat and emotionless. Since my collar is still on, I can't reach out and push at his emotions to see what he's really feeling.

"I don't get it," I say, frustration leaking into my voice. "Back in our city, you truly are the Shadow of Death. People tremble at the mere mention of your name." I shake my head at his muscular back. "But here, you're like a little lapdog who jumps at his masters' command."

He stops moving for a second. My heart starts pounding in my chest as he just remains standing motionless with his back still to me. Then he lifts off the final piece of the armor from his torso and drops it down on the armor stand. It lands with a heavy thud.

I can't help but feel as if I've crossed a line that perhaps shouldn't have been crossed. But I've committed now, so I find myself saying, "What happened to the guy who ordered me to bend over and put my hands on the wall?"

Draven remains standing with his back to me, now only wearing a pair of pants. The muscles in his arm shift as he flexes his hand.

My pulse thrums in my ears.

He turns around. And my breath hitches at the intensity in his eyes when he locks them on me. Fire flickers through my veins as a sly smile spreads across his lips while he prowls up to me.

I try to keep the nonchalant look on my face and to continue leaning casually against the wall with my arms crossed. But there is something about the way he moves that makes me straighten and uncross my arms so that I'm ready. But ready for what, I don't know.

Coming to a halt right in front of me, he braces one hand on the doorframe right next to me and leans closer. The light from the faelight gems glitter in his eyes as he cocks his head. That devilish smile on his lips widens.

"If that is what you want me to do, all you have to do is ask, little rebel."

My clit throbs at the dark promises dripping from his voice, and an involuntary shudder of pleasure ripples down my spine. He's not even touching me, and yet my body is suddenly pulsing with tension.

Goddess above, what am I doing? Draven is my enemy. He is actively hunting the one person who can help the human resistance take on the Iceheart Dynasty. And here I am, craving his ruthless bloodstained hands on my body. Again.

While desperately trying to block out those confusing and highly inconvenient feelings, I draw my eyebrows down in my best attempt at a scowl and let out a huff. "That's not what I meant."

His eyes gleam. "Wasn't it?"

"No. It was just an example. To demonstrate my point."

"Uh-huh." He runs his tongue along his bottom lip and then lets his hand drop from the doorframe. "Like I said. I need to take a bath."

For far too many seconds, all I can do is to stare at that hot as sin smirk on his stupid fucking mouth while ridiculous and absolutely inappropriate desire runs amok inside my very infuriating body.

He arches an eyebrow. "Are you staying for the show or...?"

It takes me another moment to process his words. And at first, I can't make sense of them. Then my gaze darts down to his hands, and I finally realize what he has been doing since he dropped his hand from the door.

Undoing the fastenings on his pants.

Heat sears my cheeks, and I snap my gaze back up to his face.

He lets out a smug chuckle.

Narrowing my eyes, I level a stare full of challenge on him. "Mark my words, oh Shadow of Death, I will put you in your place one day."

With his pants still hanging low on his hips, he lifts a hand and draws soft fingers along my jaw. And the grin on his mouth would have made the King of Hell himself proud. "Come try it, little rebel."

I slap his hand away. With a huff, I spin on my heel and stalk out of his bedroom, my cheeks still ablaze.

His satisfied laughter follows me out.

# CHAPTER SEVENTEEN

The silver dress glitters in the white faelight as I spin in a slow circle in front of the mirror to check my appearance. This is the dress that I wore to the fake winner's ceremony when Draven first snapped the collar shut around my neck and shattered everything I thought I knew about the world. And it would be so much easier to hate this particular piece of clothing if it wasn't so damn beautiful.

The dark silver bodice is covered in tiny white gems, making them look like sparkling stars. Patterns made with gleaming silver threads decorate the sheer fabric of the sleeves that end below my elbows, and the flowing pale silver skirt ripples around my legs when I move.

It's the most beautiful garment I have ever worn in my entire life. Part of me knows that I'm supposed to hate it because of what it symbolizes. But the other part of me is desperately yearning for a future where I can buy clothes like this for myself and wear them whenever I want instead of always having to wear the same shirt and pants that I have worn for the past decade.

Straightening my spine, I give myself a nod in the mirror. I'm going to make that future happen. Some day. But first, I need to get through tonight.

After brushing my hands down the smooth skirts of the dress, I leave my bedroom behind and walk out into the living room.

Draven is already there. He is once again wearing his black dragon scale armor, and as usual, his hair has been swept back from his face as if he has just carelessly run a hand through it. His massive black wings are also visible behind his broad shoulders.

Coming to a halt on the floor, I just watch him for a few seconds as he opens a small black box that he has put on the desk before him. Something made of silver glitters inside.

"No cape this time," I remark, and nod towards his armor.

He straightens and starts turning towards me. "No, no cape—"

His words are abruptly cut off mid-sentence when his breath hitches the moment his gaze lands on me.

Sparkling warmth floods my entire body at the look in his eyes. He is staring at me as if I'm the most beautiful thing he has ever seen.

Then he snaps out of his stupor and gives his head a hard shake as if to compose himself. While blinking a few times, he clears his throat.

"No," he repeats, still not sounding quite as composed as before. "No cape this time."

My gaze drifts over the armor that covers his muscular body, and that sparkling warmth suddenly drains from my soul to instead be replaced by a sobering realization.

During the commencement ball for the Atonement Trials, Draven was wearing fancy formal clothes and a cape. A cape that would get tangled up in his wings if he tried to fly. He explained that it was a statement. A way of showing others that he is so powerful that he wouldn't even need his wings to win if someone tried to attack him.

But now, he's not wearing a cape. He's not even wearing fancy formal clothes. Instead, he is wearing armor. Which means that he considers this banquet so dangerous that he can't afford to waste any of his advantages.

My heart patters in my chest as I take in his appearance again. He hasn't strapped his sword to his spine, but there is a more discreet dagger in his thigh holster.

What in Mabona's name are we about to walk into? I thought this was just supposed to be a fancy dinner.

"Come here," Draven says.

Blinking, I yank myself out of my worried musings to find Draven twitching two fingers at me. For a moment, I consider ignoring his presumptuous command. But in the end, I decide to choose my battles instead of being stubborn for no reason, so I walk over to him where he's still standing by the desk.

Silver and white gems glitter in the faelights as he lifts a breathtaking necklace from that small black box before him.

I arch an eyebrow at him. "I hate to break it to you, but that necklace doesn't match your armor at all."

A surprised laugh rips from his throat. He blinks and flicks a glance down at his own chest, looking startled by the sound that came out of it. Then he gives his head a couple of quick shakes while letting out another breath of amusement.

Locking eyes with me, he tries his best to suppress a smile and instead scowl at me. He fails miserably. "It's for you, smartass."

"Oh."

"Turn around."

My heart is suddenly pounding in my chest as I turn so that I'm standing with my back to him instead. Every nerve in my body is now on high alert.

Soft fingers brush over my shoulder. A shudder of pleasure rolls through my whole body as Draven draws his hand over the back of my neck, moving my hair to the side. I draw in an unsteady breath as he drapes my hair over my shoulder instead. Every time his fingers touch my skin, it sends lightning crackling through me.

Cool silver meets my suddenly heated skin as Draven positions the necklace around my throat. His breath caresses the back of my neck as he bends down a little to fasten the clasp. Another shiver ripples down my spine with every warm breath that dances over my skin.

"There," he says. "Done."

But his hands linger on my shoulders for another second. My heart thumps hard. Then he lets his hands slide off my shoulders. I turn to face him.

Holding his gaze, I try to read the expression on his features while I reach up and brush a hand over the beautiful necklace now resting around my throat.

"This doesn't change the fact that I'm wearing an iron collar too," I say. But my voice doesn't come out nearly as hard as I had intended it to. Instead, it comes out sounding more like a confused question.

Pain flits across Draven's face for a moment. "I know." His eyes are serious as he holds my gaze. "But it hides it a little, which will help stop me from murdering someone tonight."

My mouth drops open slightly, but before I can say anything, he breaks eye contact and instead rakes his gaze up and down my body. And the sheer possessiveness in his eyes when he does it makes heat pool at my core.

"Fuck," he growls. "That dress should be black."

My heart skips a beat. But all that makes it out of my mouth is, "So why isn't it?"

He drags his gaze up to my face again while I realize something that I hadn't noticed until now. And before he can say anything, I blurt out that realization.

"In fact, nothing in here is black." Raising a hand, I motion at the rooms around us. "All the furniture, the couches, the armchairs, even your bedsheets, are silver."

He draws his eyebrows down in a scowl. "They're not silver. They're dark gray. Which is halfway to black."

A laugh of disbelief escapes my mouth. "You can't be serious."

"We don't have time for—"

"Why is nothing in here black?"

"For the same reason they made you wear silver during the commencement ball." Before I can so much as open my mouth again, he reaches up and grips my chin while locking hard eyes on me, as if to truly make sure that I understand what he's about to say. "Now, do you remember that deal we made?"

The sudden seriousness in his tone makes a pulse of dread flutter through me. "Yes."

"Say it."

"When we're in public, I need to pretend that you have already broken me and act as if you're my master."

"Or…?"

"Or they are going to try to break me themselves."

"Exactly. This is the first real social gathering where Bane and Jessina can observe us, so they're going to scrutinize our every move. Do you understand? If they're going to believe that I've already broken you, you need to really sell it."

My pulse thrums in my ears, but I hold his gaze. "I understand."

"Good." Releasing my chin, he lets out a long breath and rakes a hand through his hair. "Then let's go."

Anxious worry sluices through my veins as I follow Draven out the door.

I have a really bad feeling about this.

# CHAPTER EIGHTEEN

E ven though I knew it was coming this time, I still have to suppress a horrified gasp when we walk into the banquet hall and see Isera and Alistair kneeling next to the Icehearts' table. Just like last time, they're half-naked, handcuffed, blindfolded with iron, and kept bowing forward by the tight chain linked from their collars to the floor.

Fury to rival the demons in hell courses through my body like liquid fire. I'm going to ram a knife through Bane and Jessina's hearts if it's the last thing I do.

"Ah, Draven," Emperor Bane says as we close the distance to the high table. "I was beginning to think that you weren't going to show."

We come to a halt below the short platform where their table is located. I remain two steps behind Draven and keep my eyes on the floor. Though to be honest, that is as much to prevent the Icehearts from seeing the rage in my eyes as it is to sell the broken slave act. I draw in a long breath and force myself to swallow down the anger.

Draven bows to his monarchs. "Apologies for my absence. Tracking down the Red Hand is requiring all of my time."

His tone is respectful and his words are polite, but I can still hear the unspoken second part of that reply. *So why are you wasting my time by forcing me to come to this banquet?*

However, the Icehearts don't appear to notice that, because all Bane says is, "Any progress?"

"No."

Bane clicks his tongue in disapproval. But before he can say anything else, Jessina switches to a topic that makes my stomach twist.

"Selena is looking very… comfortable," she says, drawing out that final word.

Since my eyes are still on the floor, I can't see the expression on her face. But she sounds extremely disappointed.

"I thought you would be in the middle of breaking her," she continues. "This is the most fun part, after all."

"Indeed," Emperor Bane picks up. "And yet, there she is. In a dress. No handcuffs. No blindfold. Nothing."

"Why would I need that?" I can practically hear the wicked smirk in Draven's voice. "When I have already broken her."

Silence falls over our section of the banquet hall. Behind us, the other dragon shifter courtiers continue eating and drinking and chatting with each other as if nothing is wrong. As if Draven and I aren't balancing on the edge of a knife right now. Light from the hundreds of candles in the room flickers in the corner of my eyes and makes the white ice floor gleam. I keep my eyes firmly on those shining reflections while resisting the urge to fidget.

"Already?" Empress Jessina says at last. She sounds more surprised than suspicious, thankfully. "How did you accomplish that?"

"I took her out to the mountainside," Draven replies. There is both cruel amusement and wicked satisfaction in his voice. "And made her strip naked. Then I shackled her to a boulder and summoned a lightning storm." He lets out a vicious laugh. "I left her naked and handcuffed in that raging storm for twelve hours. She begged for mercy at my feet after that."

A jolt shoots through me as Draven suddenly slides his hand up the back of my neck and into my hair. Taking it in a firm grip, he winds my hair around his fist and then pulls down, forcing me to raise my gaze and tilt my head back to expose my throat instead.

"Isn't that right?" he demands as he stares me down.

The ruthless expression on his face snatches the breath from my lungs. I *know* that this is an act, but I'm still having trouble convincing my mind not to panic. In this moment, Draven looks like the true Shadow of Death. The hard set to his mouth, the merciless expression on his face, the commanding hand gripping my hair, and the complete and utter authority in his tone… He looks like he's going to torture me if I don't obey his every command.

My heart slams against my ribs. Goddess above, Draven is a master at deception. To an extent that I never would have guessed.

I only need to half fake the breathless fear in my voice as I reply, "Yes, sir."

Satisfaction pulses across his face, and he releases my hair before turning back to the Icehearts.

Jessina purses her lips and drums her fingers on the armrest of the white wooden chair she is seated on. "You should have told us beforehand." Disdain and malice flood her pale gray eyes as she slides her gaze to me. "I would have liked to see that."

"Perhaps we can get a little demonstration now," Bane interjects before Draven can reply. A cruel smile spreads across his lips, and his black eyes glint in the candlelight, as he studies me for a second before locking eyes with Draven again. "Make her crawl to you and bow at your feet."

My stomach lurches, and it takes all of my willpower to stop the shock and panic from showing on my face. I just stare at

Emperor Bane while his eyes are still fixed on Draven. He can't be serious. Is he actually going to make me—

"Kneel."

The command pulses through the air and reverberates through my very soul. Tearing my gaze from the vicious emperor, I slowly turn to face the source of the voice.

Draven has taken a few steps to the side, so that there is some distance between us. Power pulses around his muscular body like black smoke as he stares me down, as if daring me to disobey his command. But for the briefest of moments, I swear I can see a flicker of pleading in his eyes.

His words from earlier echo through my head. *They're going to scrutinize our every move. You need to really sell it.*

I lower myself to my knees.

"Crawl to me," Draven commands.

The banquet hall has gone suddenly dead quiet. I can feel everyone's eyes on me. It's so intense that it feels like they're burning holes through my body. All I want to do is to scream at them. Or cut their eyes out with a knife. But I know that I have no other choice.

So I do as he says.

And crawl on my hands and knees to his feet.

Laughter erupts from somewhere halfway down the room. The moment that first burst of laughter shatters the silence, other courtiers start snickering as well.

My cheeks burn with humiliation, and rage strangles my throat. I can barely breathe through the fury as I come to a halt in front of Draven's black boots and sit back on my knees again.

"Bow," he orders, his voice dripping with command.

Sliding my hands closer to his boots, I bend forward and press my forehead against the cool ice floor.

Another wave of cruel laughter ripples through the courtiers. I squeeze my eyes shut, trying to block it out.

Emperor Bane lets out a mocking chuckle. "So pathetic. So weak. Without their dragon steel, they're nothing."

It takes everything I have to stop myself from snapping back that without their iron collars, *they* are nothing. If they weren't covered in iron, Isera and Alistair could probably take out half of the courtiers in this room with their fire and ice magic before the courtiers could even shift into their dragon forms.

"I can't wait until we've broken ours enough that they will willingly grovel in public," he says.

*Ours*. As if Isera and Alistair are nothing more than toys. Possessions to use and abuse. Suddenly, I'm glad that my forehead is pressed against the floor, because I don't think I would have been able to stop the rage from showing on my face. Even though my life depends on it.

"Your boots look a little dirty, Draven," Empress Jessina suddenly says. Her voice is full of challenge and wicked glee. "Tell her to lick them."

Ice spreads through my veins. She wants me to do *what* now?

Raising my head, I look up at Draven. But I already know what I'm going to see. A ruthless uncaring mask on his face. A mask that fools everyone. Everyone except me.

His voice is just as hard and merciless as before when he commands, "Lick my boots."

And because I know that I have no other choice than to see our little act through all the way to the end, I bow down again and lick his boots, just like he ordered me to.

Anger pulses through my whole soul. I am going to kill them for this. I am going to kill them all for this.

Jessina laughs. As do most of the other courtiers.

"Excellent work, Draven," the satisfied empress says. "Thank you for that little demonstration. It will surely be remembered as the highlight of the night. You may take your seat."

One second passes, probably while he bowed to the two of them, then he grabs me by the arm and practically yanks me up from the floor. I stumble the first few steps as he hauls me with him while he strides across the room. Once I have gotten my feet properly on the floor again, I pull discreetly against his grip to let him know that he can release me now. He doesn't.

I glance up at him.

The moment that we reach a spot where our faces are no longer visible to anyone, he clenches his jaw and flexes his hand while fury so cold that it could've frozen the sun itself crackles across his features. He looks like he's going to murder someone.

"You will need to sit on your knees next to my chair," he whispers as we make our way towards the table closest to the high table, but his words come out more like a growl. "We need to stay for at least an hour before it's acceptable for us to leave. But I need to get out of here for a few minutes first. Otherwise, I won't make it through that hour without killing everyone in this room. You need to stay, or they will get suspicious. So just sit there. I will be back soon."

Before I can even reply, we reach the table we were heading for.

Shock pulses through me when I realize that the table is full of Draven's people.

His former best friend, Galen, is sitting to the right of the only empty seat, which is at the head of the table. And Lyra, that cheerful shifter with wavy brown hair and orange eyes, is seated opposite him. Both of them are wearing black. As are eight more people sitting beside them at the long table.

All of them watch Draven with outright hostility in their eyes.

"I can't believe you made her do that," Galen hisses under his breath as Draven pulls me to a stop to the right of his empty seat at the head of the table. "In front of everyone. Have you at last lost your final shred of—"

"Shut up," Draven snarls. Lightning flashes in his eyes, and he turns to me. Finally releasing my arm, he snaps his fingers and points at the floor. "Sit."

I lower myself to the floor so that I'm sitting on my knees next to his chair, just like he said.

He locks hard eyes on Galen again. "Watch her."

"Don't you—" Galen begins retorting, but Draven grabs the collar of his shirt and yanks him halfway up from his seat.

"I'm about to murder someone," Draven growls in his face. "And unless you want that to be you, you watch her until I get back."

Galen's violet eyes are wide with what looks like genuine shock as he stares up at his commander. Then he quickly jerks his chin down in a nod.

Draven just releases his collar, shoving him back down in his seat, and stalks away without another word. His clan members watch him go with a mix of surprise and disdain on their faces.

Part of me is furious that Draven is the one who gets to storm out and be angry and then gather his composure before coming back inside. I'm the one who just crawled across the floor and licked someone's boots in front of an entire banquet hall, for Mabona's sake!

But the other part of me can barely believe my luck. Draven has left me unsupervised with his people, who hate him. Which means that I finally have a chance to get the information I need for the heist.

"Sorry you had to go through that," Lyra says from my left, her voice full of empathy. Then it disappears, and rage takes its place instead as she glances towards where Alistair and Isera are kneeling. "This whole thing is so fucked up."

"Yeah." I blow out a long sigh, trying to gather my wits and choose my words very carefully. "I almost escaped, you know. The first day when I woke up, I made it all the way to…" Scrunching up my eyebrows, I pretend to think hard. "I don't remember which floor it was, but it was close to where the treasury is."

"The third floor?" the redhead next to Lyra fills in.

Victory pulses through me. The third floor. The treasury is on the third floor. My heart pounds in my chest. Now, I just need one more thing.

"Yeah, that's the one," I reply while desperately trying to figure out how to get them to tell me *where* on the third floor it is.

Lyra furrows her brows. "How did you even get there? The northeast stairwell is like one of the most well-guarded stairwells in the entire castle."

I almost let out a whoop. For once in my life, I appear to have luck on my side. While sending a heartfelt prayer of thanks to Mabona for what must have been her divine intervention, I suppress the victorious grin that threatens to spread across my mouth.

The treasury is somewhere in the northeast corner on the third floor. Now, I can finally begin plotting out a route for the human resistance to use during their heist.

"Oh, it might not have been that then," I reply, letting some uncertainty into my voice. "I just assumed it was since that's where the Master of the Treasury was."

Lyra raises her eyebrows. "You met the Master of the Treasury?"

"Not exactly." I grimace. "I tripped over his corpse."

"Oh, right. That was the day when the Red Hand killed all three of those people."

I glance from her to Galen, who hasn't said a word since Draven left. He was tasked with watching me, but his violet eyes are still locked on the side door that Draven stalked out of. Candlelight from the silver holders on the table flickers across his features. It's difficult to read the expression on his face, but he almost looks… sad.

"What even is the deal with Draven and the Red Hand anyway?" I ask. "He seems almost obsessed with him."

At that, Galen finally tears his gaze from the door and turns his head to look at me. The sadness is gone from his features. Instead, only contempt shines in his eyes.

"It's because of his bloody ego," he huffs.

"Keep it down," a dark-haired male shifter hisses from farther down the table. He casts a worried glance towards the door that Draven left through. "He could come back any second."

"What do you mean *his ego?*" I ask before Galen can take that advice. Because I desperately want to know more about Draven's history with the Red Hand.

After casting a glance towards the door, which is still closed, Galen meets my eyes again. "Draven has always won. He has always completed every mission he has been given. Crush that rebellion. Bring that clan to heel. Burn that city. Conquer that castle. Assassinate that person. He *always* succeeds." Smug amusement flits across his face for a second. "But not with this guy. The Red Hand is the only one who has ever gotten away. The only one who has ever outsmarted him."

"And his pride won't allow that," Lyra fills in from across the table. She spins her fork in her hand before stabbing it into the piece of steak on her plate. "It's a threat to his power. Makes him look weak. That's why he's so obsessed with personally hunting down the Red Hand."

"Exactly," Galen picks up. That smug smile on his face widens a little. "But I, for one, applaud the Red Hand for the sheer size of his balls, defying the Icehearts like this."

Lyra flicks a glance towards the side door. "Something I wish our not-so-fearless leader had more of too."

Disgust flickers in Galen's eyes. "Did you know that during the first six years after he swore allegiance to the Icehearts, Draven didn't use the half-shift at all. As a gesture of respect and submission." He scoffs. "Like some kind of—"

He cuts his sentence off in a heartbeat as the side door is yanked open and Draven strides back in.

I flick my gaze towards him. His hair is slightly disheveled, as if he has been running his hands through it repeatedly. But he does look less inclined to murder someone.

Oppressive silence falls over the dining room table as Draven strides towards the head of the table. His clan members lower their chins in a show of deference as he drops down in his seat. From my place on the floor, I can see the expressions on their faces that Draven can't from his angle. Disdain and hostility once more lace their features like ice.

I let out a small sigh.

This is going to be a long hour.

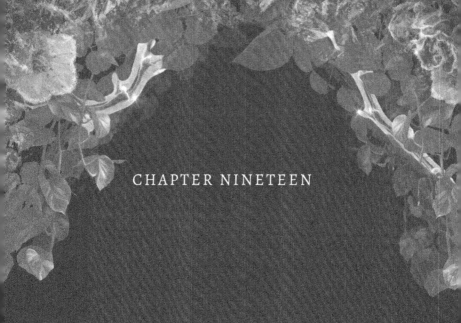

# CHAPTER NINETEEN

When we finally return to Draven's rooms, it feels as if I have a thrashing lightning storm raging inside my body. There is too much outrage. Too much anger. Too much frustration. Too fragile hope. It's just… too much.

"Are you okay?"

Whirling around, I find Draven standing only a step away. His golden eyes gleam in the faelights as he studies my face intently, as if trying to read the answer to his question there.

"What do you think?" I retort.

He doesn't get annoyed by my curt reply. Instead, he just reaches out and removes the iron collar from my throat.

A sigh of relief escapes my lips as that cold feeling disappears from my throat, and magic and strength flood back into my body. I run a hand over my throat while Draven sets the collar down on the low table by the couches next to us.

That storm of emotions tears through my soul again.

Anger crackles inside me. I just spent an hour on my knees next to Draven's chair, watching Isera and Alistair be humiliated by the Icehearts. And before that, I crawled across the floor and licked his boots in front of the entire banquet hall.

It all hits me too hard and too deep and I just… snap.

Twisting towards Draven, I give him a hard shove. "How could you let them do that to me?"

Since he was still half bent over from placing the collar on the table, the shove actually makes him stagger to the side. He blinks, looking genuinely surprised, as he straightens and turns to face me.

I shove him in the chest again. "How could *you* do this to me?"

This time, since he's standing upright, the shove does absolutely nothing to push him back. Which just infuriates me even more. I slam my palms against his armored breastplate in frustration while my voice rises to a shout.

"You made me kneel and crawl and lick your fucking boots!"

In a flash, his hands wrap around my wrists, stopping them before I can try to shove him back again. But there is no anger on his features. Only resignation.

"You know why I had to do that." His eyes are serious as he holds my gaze. "Why *we* had to do that."

"I don't care! It was the most humiliating thing I have ever had to do."

He clenches his jaw as I yank and struggle like a feral animal against his grip on my wrists. With a sigh, he suddenly takes a step forward. And since he's still keeping my wrists in a firm grip, it forces me to move back. A snarl rips from my throat, and I struggle even harder.

"Stop fighting," he presses out while still trying to keep a grip on me. "You—"

"Stop fighting?" I scream back at him. "I will not—"

He pushes me up against the wall, which surprises me enough that I cut my sentence off halfway through. I hadn't realized that we had moved so far.

Draven moves my hands away from his breastplate and instead pins them against the cool ice wall on either side of my head while he presses closer to me and braces his knee against the wall between my legs. My heart pounds in my chest as I stare up at him.

"This armor is made of dragon scales." He locks commanding eyes on me. "You're going to shatter the bones in your hands before you ever make a dent in it. So yes, stop fighting. Rin Tanaka is with her own clan, in their home, which is halfway across the continent. So if you break your hands, there is no one here who can heal you."

My chest heaves as I glare back at him. But as much as I hate to admit it, he does have a point.

Forcing out a long breath, I try to bank the burning fury inside me. It only partially works. I flex my fingers and then drag in another deep breath.

Draven still doesn't release me. He keeps pinning my hands to the wall. And his knee remains braced against the wall between my legs as well. Because of how close he's standing, the position of it makes me almost ride his thigh. The feeling of his body pressed against mine like this makes a surge of burning desire course through me. Which is incredibly frustrating when I'm trying to be angry at the infuriating bastard.

"Do you have any idea how humiliating that was for me?" I demand, trying to ignore the fire in my veins.

"I know." He clenches his jaw for a second, as if he is fighting the same fury and outrage as I am. "But it still doesn't change the fact that we had to do it. For your own safety."

"Easy for you to say. When was the last time *you* knelt in front of someone?"

"Over two hundred years ago. When I swore my allegiance to the Icehearts."

"Exactly. You don't kneel for anything or anyone, so how could you possibly know how I felt?" Yanking against his grip again, I swallow down a flash of lingering humiliation as I press out, "They *laughed* at me. The courtiers in the room, they laughed at me."

"I know," he repeats, the words coming out more like a growl. He flexes his hands around my wrists and clenches his jaw again before fixing me with a stare full of deadly promises. "I marked each and every one of their faces, and I swear to you, I will make them all crawl before the week is over."

My heart flips and my mouth drops open a little. He would actually do that? He would hunt down and humiliate members of this court just because they laughed at me?

"I know you hate me because I made you do that," he says, his intense eyes still locked on me. "So how is this for revenge?"

I frown in confusion, but before I can reply, he releases my wrists and straightens. My heart slams against my ribs as he just stands there, watching me, for a second.

Then a gasp escapes me when Draven lowers himself to his knees.

"You're right," he says, tilting his head back so that he meets my gaze. "I kneel for nothing and no one." His golden eyes burn like flames, searing right through my soul. "But for you... For you, I would kneel."

I drag in an unsteady breath. My mind is spinning and my heart is beating like a battle drum in my chest. Draven Ryat, the Shadow of Death, leader of the feared Black Dragon Clan and the Commander of the Dread Legion, is on his knees before me.

"And as for making you lick my boots," he continues, a sly smile now playing over his lips. "Allow me to settle that score as well."

My heart skips several beats, and then pounds twice as hard to make up for it, when Draven slides his hands up my legs, pushing the flowing silver skirt of my dress upwards. Lightning crackles through my veins as his hands roam across my bare legs and up towards my hips.

I gasp as he curls his fingers over the top of my panties.

With his eyes still locked firmly on mine, he begins sliding my panties down my thighs.

The feeling of that soft, thin fabric brushing against my heated skin makes a moan build inside my throat. I throw my head back and suck in a shuddering breath. Draven guides my panties down over the thickest part of my thighs. Then he releases them. They slide right down my legs and hit the floor.

Draven takes my ankles in a firm grip and lifts my legs one at a time, making me step out of the discarded garment. The feeling of his commanding hands around my ankles makes another surge of burning desire course through me. Dragging in a deep breath, I tilt my head back down to meet his gaze again.

Still on his knees, he holds my gaze with gleaming eyes for a second. Then he slides his hands back up my left leg. With a firm grip, he lifts my leg and drapes it over his shoulder. My pulse is thrumming in my ears. This close, and with my leg up like this, I can almost feel his warm breath against my now completely exposed pussy.

There is a devilish smile on his mouth when he looks at me as he adjusts his position and then leans forward.

A gasp rips from my throat as he flicks my clit with his tongue.

Throwing my head back, I brace it against the cool ice wall behind me and press my mouth shut to stop a moan from escaping my lips.

Draven draws his tongue along my pussy with a slow luxurious stroke and then swirls it around my clit.

A jolt shoots through my spine, and I squirm against the wall.

While still teasing my clit with his tongue, he slides his hands up to my hips. With a firm grip, he traps me in place as he continues his sweet torture. I suck in a shuddering breath as he rolls my clit between his lips before sliding his tongue back down my pussy.

I squirm against the wall again as he teases my entrance with his tongue. He just tightens his grip on my hips, keeping me mercilessly trapped.

Pleasure pulses inside me as he swirls his tongue around my clit again with expert precision. While dragging in desperate breaths, I blindly reach out and slide my hands through Draven's smooth black hair. Curling my fingers in his silken strands, I grip his hair hard.

A deep groan comes from his chest. It vibrates against my already throbbing clit and makes pleasure crackle through my veins. A moan spills from my lips.

Draven lets out a dark chuckle, full of wicked satisfaction, which vibrates even more against my sensitive clit.

Squirming furiously against the wall, I try to remember how to breathe as Draven takes my clit between his lips again.

I gasp as he nips at it.

His fingers dig into my hips as he holds me firmly in place while he moves down to my entrance and slides his tongue over it. A whimper escapes me.

He pushes his tongue inside me.

Lightning crackles through my veins. My entire body is thrumming with pent-up tension. I drag in unsteady breaths as Draven fucks me with his tongue. Gripping his hair hard, I moan as I tumble closer to an orgasm.

Draven angles his head and slides his tongue over my clit again.

Another whimper drips from my lips.

He lets out another smug chuckle that vibrates against my already pulsing clit.

The pent-up tension inside me is so intense that I feel like I'm going to scream if I don't get release soon.

Draven torments my clit with commanding strokes. I clench my hands harder in his hair. He slides his tongue over my clit again. And then flicks it.

Pleasure crashes through me.

Gasping up into the ceiling, I almost collapse to the floor as release pulses through my body with enough force to make my legs shake. Draven tightens his grip on my hips, holding me up and keeping me on my feet, while he continues teasing my clit with his tongue to intensify the orgasm.

Incoherent moans spill from my lips, and black spots dance before my eyes. My legs are shaking so much that I wouldn't be able to stand if it weren't for Draven's hands on my hips.

When the last of the orgasm has faded, my chest is heaving so much that all I can do is to just lean against the wall behind me and stare up into the ceiling. My heart is pounding against my ribs.

"Oh, fuck," I gasp out between heavy breaths.

Draven kisses the inside of my thigh before releasing my hips and guiding my left leg back to the floor.

It takes conscious effort to unclench my fingers and slide them back out of his hair. I throw one hand out and brace it against the wall to help me keep my balance as I tilt my head back down.

Draven is still on his knees before me. His eyes glitter in the faelight as he flashes me a devilish smile. "How was that for revenge?"

A breathless laugh bubbles from my throat, and I shake my head at him while trying to fight the smile that's spreading across my own mouth.

He raises his eyebrows, that wicked satisfaction still on his features. "What?"

I slide my free hand along his jaw. To my utter astonishment, it makes a shudder roll through his body. The sight of it makes my heart do a backflip in my chest.

A wicked grin spreads across my mouth. "I was just thinking how good you look on your knees before my feet."

Dark desire and forbidden promises glint in his eyes as he slowly stands up so that he's towering over me instead. He slides one hand around my throat, pinning me to the wall, and draws the other up my thigh. My breath hitches as his hand stops right in front of my pussy.

"Don't get cocky, little rebel." He flashes me a sly smirk. "You and I both know that I can have you begging for my cock with just a few strategic strokes of my fingers."

"A few strokes?" I taunt while raising my eyebrows. "Now who's getting cocky?"

I gasp as he flicks my still sensitive clit with his fingers.

That devilish smile on his lips grows wider. "You were saying?"

Reaching up towards the hand he keeps around my throat, I wrap my own hand around his wrist and lock eyes full of challenge on him. "I'm saying that maybe you should stop running your mouth and prove it instead."

A dark chuckle rumbles from his throat. Leaning closer, he slants his mouth over mine and whispers straight against my lips, "Gladly. When I'm done with you, your wet little cunt will—"

Loud pounding comes from the door.

It startles me so much that, for a second, I can't even figure out what is happening. Then the sound comes again, and I realize that someone is knocking frantically on the door.

"Commander," a man calls from the other side while continuing to pound on the door. "Commander."

Draven keeps his hands on my throat and my pussy, but his gaze darkens as he turns his head to glare at the door. And when he shouts back to the person on the other side of the door, his voice is dripping with threats.

"Someone had better be dead, or I'm going to rip your fucking throat out for disturbing me over nothing!"

The knocking stops immediately, and the man outside the door falls silent.

Draven tilts his head to the side in a half nod, as if satisfied that his threat worked. But right before he can turn back to me, the man outside speaks up again.

"But Commander," he calls, sounding worried and apologetic. "Someone *is* dead."

Draven continues scowling at the door for another second. Then he seems to understand what's going on, because he heaves a deep breath and turns back to me. Closing his eyes, he leans his forehead against mine for a second.

"Next time, little rebel," he whispers in promise.

Then he releases me and stalks over to the door.

After yanking my panties back on and smoothing down my dress skirt, I quickly shift my hair so that it's covering my throat and hiding the fact that I'm not wearing a collar. Draven glances back at me when he reaches the door and, apparently satisfied with my hair solution, then shoves the door open.

A male shifter in messenger clothes leaps back to avoid getting hit by the door. He wrings his hands and gives Draven another apologetic look.

"What is it?" Draven demands.

"The Red Hand has killed again."

# CHAPTER TWENTY

**B**oth anticipation and worry pulse inside me as I follow Draven and some of his soldiers towards the scene of the crime. We took the northeast stairwell. My heart patters against my ribs as we ascend the stairs.

I have to stifle a sharp breath when Draven leads us out of the stairwell as soon as we reach the third floor. This is where the treasury is. I flick my gaze around the pale ice corridor, lit by faelight gems in the ceiling. Don't tell me the humans tried to break into the treasury prematurely instead of waiting for my intel.

Boots thud against the floor around me as Draven and the other shifters hurry down the hall. We round a corner.

Blood stains the ice.

I trail to a halt while the others continue towards the man who is lying on the ground a few strides ahead. He is wearing silver armor but carries no sword. His brown hair is wet with blood from the pool of it that he's lying in, and his brown eyes are wide with shock. My gaze drifts to his neck. His throat has been slit with one precise cut.

"Seal off this entire wing," Draven snaps to his soldiers.

"Check the entire floor, and the ones above and below it too. He can't fly, which means that he's still in the building. Find him!"

"Yes, sir," his soldiers reply before darting away to follow his orders.

I scramble to the side and press myself up against the wall as two of them barrel past me.

Cold air hits the back of my neck.

Stunned, I flick a quick glance over my shoulder to find the window behind me slightly open. It's nothing more than the tiniest of cracks, and it's not visible unless you're standing right next to it the way I am. But it looks as if someone pushed it closed in a hurry without being able to properly check that it was fully closed.

Sudden realization hits me like a shovel to the face, and a gasp almost escapes my lips before I manage to suppress it. I quickly turn my head back so that I'm facing forwards again and take a discreet step to the side so that my body is blocking the window more fully.

Mabona's tits. *That's* how he does it.

I've been wondering how the Red Hand is getting in and out of the castle without anyone seeing him roaming the halls. And this is it.

It was the human resistance who gave me those special gloves and shoe covers that I use for climbing. That's what the Red Hand is using as well. That's how he can manage to get in and out undetected.

My heart beats nervously in my chest while I try my best to look neutral as I remain standing in front of the window while Draven and another one of his soldiers, a woman with white blond hair and pale blue eyes, crouch down next to the body on the floor.

Draven is certain that the Red Hand is still here since he can't fly. As long as he doesn't figure out that the Red Hand can easily scale the walls, he will keep searching for him in all the wrong places. And I have to keep it that way.

With one eye on Draven and the blond shifter, I shift my position slightly and casually stretch my arm. The moment both Draven and the woman are focused on the corpse before them, I yank the window closed. And I make sure to shuffle my feet in a way that makes my shoes squeak slightly against the smooth floor at the exact time when the window clicks shut.

My pulse thrums in my ears. But neither Draven nor the woman looks up. I breathe an inwardly sigh of relief. The window is now firmly shut. Draven will never know that that's what the Red Hand used in order to get out.

"Sir," the blond shifter says. Her gaze flits down the corridor in the other direction for a second before she meets Draven's eyes again. "We're only four corridors away from the treasury."

My heart jerks. The treasury isn't just somewhere on this floor, it's *here*. Dread washes through me. What if the humans are inside?

"This guy isn't connected to the treasury," Draven replies. A considering look blows across his features as he gazes down the corridor as well. Then he nods. "But I'll check it out anyway."

He straightens and takes a step forward. When she does the same, he gives her a look full of authority.

"Stay here and make sure that no one, and I mean *no one*, touches the body," he commands.

She immediately stops and then takes a step back towards the body while lowering her chin. "Yes, sir."

Draven slides his gaze to me and jerks his chin. "Selena."

I resist the urge to reconfirm that I have properly closed the window behind me and instead quickly follow Draven as he strides down the corridor. He slows down a little, allowing me to catch up, but says nothing as we continue down the hall and into the next one.

As soon as we have rounded the corner, he turns his head and locks eyes with me while we continue walking. "Don't touch anything."

I shoot him an exasperated and half offended look.

"I mean it," he says as he slides his gaze back to the corridor, only glancing at me occasionally as he keeps speaking. "I've already saved your troublesome ass from jail once. If you get blood on your hands now, it's going to be very hard to explain it away a second time." He nods towards my throat and lowers his voice. "Especially since you're not wearing your collar right now. So just… don't do anything to draw attention to yourself."

Since the messenger was already waiting for us outside Draven's door, we didn't get the chance to put the collar back on me. So I'm still only using my hair as cover. To be honest, it makes me feel a little nervous too. But I don't tell Draven that.

Instead, I arch an eyebrow at him. "First of all, you appeared to be liking my *ass* just fine a few minutes ago."

He chokes on his breath and snaps his gaze to me.

I flash him a smug grin before fixing him with another pointed stare. "And secondly, I'm not stupid. I'm not going to start dipping my fingers in the blood of a murder victim and paint red flowers on the wall."

He arches an eyebrow right back at me. "Need I remind you that your hands were completely *covered* in blood the last time you were near a dead body."

"That's because I tripped over him."

"My point exactly."

Drawing my eyebrows down, I let out a huff.

And before I can come up with a suitable retort, we reach the end of the corridor. A guard in silver armor meets us there. He leaps to attention the moment his gaze lands on Draven.

"Commander," he says.

Draven gives him a curt nod in reply before turning to me. "Only a select few are allowed past this point. And you are not among them. So stay here."

Frustration and disappointment rip through my chest. Goddess damn it. We're still three corridors away from the actual treasury. I was hoping that Draven would be taking me with him all the way to the treasury. But apparently, there is a limit to the amount of luck I'm allowed this particular evening.

"And behave," he adds, holding my gaze.

Since we have an audience, I decide not to argue. Letting out a soft sigh, I give him a nod.

The guard watches our exchange but doesn't appear suspicious or confused, which I suppose is a good thing.

After holding my gaze for another second, as if to once again remind me not to do anything to draw attention, Draven turns and continues down the corridor without me. I watch his broad back disappear around the corner.

The dragon shifter who is guarding the corner is still watching me.

I resist the urge to adjust my hair. I already know that my throat is completely covered. But I still take a step back and then drift down the corridor, just to put some distance between us.

Faelights gleam like stars above me as I move. This time, when I'm not so focused on Draven, I take the time to truly study the wide corridor around me.

Just like most of the hallways in this castle, it's almost entirely bare. There are no side tables, no decorations, no torches on the walls, and no soft carpets on the floor. Only the pale unforgiving ice and the glowing faelights in the ceiling.

I slide my gaze over the smooth walls.

A jolt shoots through me.

Blinking, I come to a halt halfway down the corridor and stare at a section of the wall. There are lines in it. Deep lines. Like cracks or cuts. I trace them with my eyes. They're shaped like a large rectangle. Almost like…

I suck in a sharp breath.

A door.

There's a hidden door here.

Excitement courses through my body. Goddess above, this could be it. This could be the way in and out for the human resistance. The Red Hand might be able to scale the walls undetected, but an entire host of humans will be seen. And they can't get the treasury out if they have to climb the walls. But if they can get into this corridor through a secret door, they only have to make it through three more corridors before they reach the treasury.

Now, I just need to figure out where it leads.

Still standing in front of the secret door, I flick a quick glance down the corridor. The guard in silver armor is still standing there at the end of it, watching me.

I make sure that my head is fully towards the wall, so that he won't be able to see my eyes, and then I call up my magic.

"This is such a cool door," I say.

The moment the words are out of my mouth, I shove my magic straight at the yellow-green spark of suspicion in the guard's chest. Just as I expected, my words made it flare up. I use my magic to slowly decrease it until it's almost entirely gone.

"What is it?" I ask innocently, as if it's just a question out of purely academic curiosity.

And because my magic is blocking his ability to be suspicious about my motives, he shrugs and replies, "It's an escape route in case of emergency."

"Oh, that's so clever. I'm guessing it leads out to the mountain here on this side?"

"Yeah."

Victory pulses through me, and I have to force myself to keep the innocently curious expression on my face. But all I want to do is to grin like an absolute villain. This is what I excel at. I can't believe that the fae resistance never used me for missions like this. I was born for sneaky espionage and surveillance.

For a moment, I consider asking the guard exactly where the

escape route leads out. Even though I have narrowed it down to the east side of the mountain, it's still a big mountain. The other end of this tunnel could be anywhere.

The words are right there on my tongue. But before I can get them out, footsteps sound from around the corner.

My heart leaps into my throat. Quickly cutting off the flow of my magic, I walk away from the door and instead lean casually against the wall halfway between it and the guard.

A second later, Draven comes striding back around the corner.

He studies me intently but apparently doesn't find anything to complain about, because all he says as he reaches me is, "Let's go."

"Since you're still scowling, I'm going to assume that he wasn't there," I observe, trying to bait him into telling me if he found any other humans there.

"No," Draven replies. "It was empty."

Relief washes through me. None of the humans were there.

We continue back to the other corridor. But when we get there, the dead body is not the only thing waiting for us.

Rage burns through me when I see Empress Jessina and Emperor Bane standing there with displeased expressions on their features. But that's not what triggered my anger. Both of them are holding a chain that is attached like a leash to Isera and Alistair's iron collars. They're still blindfolded but at least they're not handcuffed anymore. Though that's probably only because they wouldn't even be able to move if they were wearing iron shackles as well as the blindfold and the collar. I squeeze my hand into a fist as I watch them sway unsteadily on their feet.

"What is the meaning of this, Draven?" Empress Jessina demands.

Her massive silver wings flare in anger as she drops Alistair's leash and instead stalks up to Draven. Emperor Bane releases his grip on Isera's leash as well and follows her. Both Isera and Alistair slump back against the wall.

Draven pushes me towards it and out of the way of the two angry monarchs as he instead strides to meet them. It's only then that I remember that I'm not wearing the collar myself. If the Icehearts notice that, I'm screwed.

"The Red Hand continued his murder spree while we were all *busy at the banquet*," Draven replies.

This time, the acidity in his tone during the final part of that sentence is loud and clear for everyone to hear. Draven is not happy that they forced him to go to the banquet when he could have spent that time doing more important things.

Jessina flares her wings wider. "You do not take that tone with me. Understood?"

She and Bane come to a halt in front of Draven and draw themselves up to their full height. Both her wings and Bane's are now spread so wide that they brush the walls of the hallway.

Draven stares them down for another second before he drops his gaze and lowers his chin while he tucks his own wings in tighter in submission. "My apologies."

"I don't want your apologies," Jessina snaps. "I want results."

"This man was in charge of scheduling all the guard rotations," Bane growls while stabbing a hand towards the dead body on the floor. "Just getting someone else caught up on all of his charts and lists and schedules is going to take weeks."

"I know," Draven replies. "Again, I apologize."

"If you don't find the Red Hand soon, we will hold you personally responsible."

"And you know what that means," Jessina adds, malice dripping from her voice.

"Yes," Draven replies, his voice controlled. "And I assure you, I'm doing everything…"

While Draven and the Icehearts continue their argument, I move so that I'm standing right between Isera and Alistair. Then I brush my hands over their arms at the same time. Both of them flinch.

"It's Selena," I whisper since they're still blindfolded. Keeping my voice so low that only they will be able to hear, I continue, "The human resistance has killed again. They're picking off important people. And I have made progress on the treasury." I draw my hands down their arms again in a gesture of comfort. "You just need to hold on a little longer."

To my left, Alistair dips his chin in the briefest of nods to signal that he heard me. I glance towards Isera. She doesn't replicate the gesture. I blow out a small sigh.

Right as I'm about to move away again, a cold hand grips mine.

It takes all of my willpower not to whip my head around and stare at Isera as she gives my hand a firm squeeze.

She heard me.

My heart pounds.

She's aware of her surroundings again.

Which means that she is also aware of everything the Icehearts are doing to them.

I flick a glance over their half-naked bodies and the collars and the blindfolds and the leashes. Burning fury sears through my soul, and I squeeze Isera's hand back firmly.

And I decide, then and there, that just ruining them financially isn't enough. The humans are going to pull off this heist. But that is not enough for me. I want the Icehearts hurt. I want them to suffer. I want them to despair. I want a fucking war. I want to make them watch as this whole castle burns to the ground around their heads.

I'm going to turn this whole fucking city against them.

# CHAPTER TWENTY-ONE

The atmosphere around me is mostly cheerful. But that's about to change. The moment a group leaves one of the tables, I swipe a half full mug from it to blend in better before I continue deeper into the tavern.

Several days have passed since I made my vow to make the whole city rebel against the Icehearts, but this is the first night since then that Draven isn't sleeping right next to me. He did everything he could to sneak out silently so that I wouldn't notice that he left me unsupervised. Little does he know that I always wait for him to fall asleep first. So he disappeared to deal with whatever it is that he had to deal with, and I left soon after.

And now, I'm making my way through my fifth tavern of the night.

Both humans and dragon shifters are drinking here, though at separate tables. I eavesdrop on all of their conversations as I drift through the warm room as if in search of a table of my own.

Most of them are just talking about their day or the latest gossip in their neighborhood, but there is a group of humans in the corner that is watching the dragon shifters with wary eyes. I set course for the pale wooden table next to theirs.

While making sure to keep my eyes down and the hood of my cloak up, I slide into one of the seats at the tiny table for two next to the larger group. The rickety wooden chair creaks in alarm when I sit down. I adjust it so that I'm sitting at an angle where I can still see them while they can't see my face under the hood. Keeping my eyes on the unidentified liquid in the mug I stole earlier, I call up my magic and listen as the humans talk.

"Why do they have to drink here?" a man with a ginger beard mutters. "Can't we have one single place to ourselves?"

"This whole city is their place now," another man replies. The scar on his cheek stretches when he grimaces and then shoots another scowl at the dragon shifters three tables away. "This thing here… It's just dog pissing to mark their territory."

Reaching out with my magic, I latch on to the pale red sparks of anger in their chests and begin to steadily increase them.

"Did you know they even took our name?" a woman with curly hair says while she stares daggers at the shifters.

Ginger Beard and Scar, as well as the rest of their group, turn towards her in surprise.

"What?" Ginger Beard asks.

"Yeah," Curly Hair replies. Tearing her gaze from the dragon shifters, she looks back at her companions. "My grandma used to tell me these stories, see. Said she had once seen an old map of the world. She worked in the palace when she was a girl, she did. Cleaning down in the archives. And on that map, our city was called Stonehollow. Not Frostfell."

Their anger spikes. I feed it even more with my magic.

Scar squeezes his hand into a fist and slams it down on the table, making their mugs rattle. "The Icehearts must have changed the name after they moved their castle here."

"They didn't move it here," Ginger Beard growls. "They destroyed our ancestors' castle and then built theirs on top of its bones."

"And they will keep taking everything from us," I say softly, still keeping my head bowed and my face hidden under the hood. "Until we do something about it."

All of them snap their gazes to me. I immediately release my connection to their anger and instead shove my magic at the yellow-green sparks of suspicion. The tension bleeds out of their postures when I lower their suspicion until it almost disappears.

"I know," Curly Hair replies to my statement. Sadness blows across her features. "But we can't fight the whole Iceheart Dynasty, see. They're immortal, they can breathe fire, and they're big as buildings, they are. They might as well be gods."

Fear tries to flare up in their chests, but I quickly lower that as well.

"The Icehearts won't die of old age, no," I say. "But if someone shoves a blade through their hearts, they will die as easily as the rest of us. And besides, we have something they don't." I pause for dramatic effect. "Numbers. This is *our* city. We outnumber the shifters. If we just band together, we can overthrow them."

I push at the hope in their chests, but to my surprise, it's not there. Cutting off that flow of magic, I quickly shove it towards the burgundy sparks of courage that I hope will be there instead. Relief flickers through me when I find tiny sparks of courage burning in most of their chests. I fan them into burning wildfires.

"She's right," Ginger Beard says. He straightens his spine and raises his chin as I keep feeding his courage. "We are the silent majority. It's time we stop being silent."

The others nod vigorously as I keep increasing their courage as well. Still keeping my head low, I watch as the group of humans split up and move to other tables. I throw my magic across the whole tavern, alternating between increasing the humans' anger, lowering their fear, increasing their courage, and even increasing a few sparks of hope that pop up.

Nausea rolls through my stomach, but I do my best to swallow it down. I'm playing with these people's feelings like a musician plays a fiddle. It's not right. Manipulating people's emotions like this is not something a good person, a kind person, would do. If these people knew what I was doing to them, they would hate me. And they would be right to.

That part of me that desperately wants people to like me is fighting the small but growing part of me that just wants to be ruthless for once in my life and simply take what I want without apologizing for it.

My chest tightens with anxiety and dread. It's quickly followed by anger at my inability to just do what needs to be done without worrying about what other people might think of me.

Pushing up from the table, I decide that this is enough for tonight. I need to get back to the Ice Palace anyway. I want to check in on Isera, Alistair, and Lavendera and update them on my progress. And I can't risk waiting too long, because I don't know when Draven will return.

After cutting off the flow of my magic, I weave between the now increasingly restless humans and the confused dragon shifters who watch them with brows furrowed. I keep my head down and slip through the crowd unnoticed. Then I run back to the Ice Palace.

When I finally sneak in through the door to the kennels, I head straight for Alistair's cage. But to my surprise, he isn't there. And neither is Isera.

Drawing up short, I come to a halt on the pale ice floor and just stare at their empty cages. It's the middle of the night. What in Mabona's name could the Icehearts be subjecting them to now?

"Make it stop, make it stop, make it stop."

I snap my gaze towards the sound of the voice.

Pain pulses through my heart when I find Lavendera sitting in the middle of her cage, rocking back and forth and gripping her hair with both hands.

"Make it stop, make it stop, make it stop," she whispers over and over again.

I hurry over to her cage and drop down to my knees in front of it. "Lavendera."

She doesn't look up. I try to reach through the bars, but she's sitting too far away for me to touch her. Her fingers are squeezing the flowing brown strands of her hair so hard that her knuckles have turned white, and she keeps rocking back and forth. Pain hits me straight in the chest again.

"Lavendera, please," I whisper back. "I can help you. Just tell me what you're feeling, and I can help take that emotion away."

Her head jerks up and her gaze snaps to mine.

It's so sudden that I jerk back in shock.

"No." Her eyes are wide and panicked as she stares at me while letting her hands drop down from her hair. "Don't mess with my head. Don't you ever mess with my head. It's already too crowded. Too crowded." A sob suddenly rips from her throat, and tears line her eyes. "I'm so tired." Another sob. "Oh Goddess, you have no idea just *how* tired I am."

I just stare back at her, horrified. Do the Icehearts even understand the kind of torture they're putting her through just by locking her up like this?

"I promise," I begin. "I won't touch your emotions unless you want me to. But please…"

I trail off.

The tears are gone from Lavendera's eyes. And so is everything else.

Sitting there in the middle of the cage, she just stares at the wall behind me with vacant eyes. As if she has completely disconnected from the world around her to escape the pain.

My heart squeezes hard as I watch her.

And that ruthlessness that has been growing inside me seeps deeper into my soul, intertwining with all the rage and pain already festering in there.

I will get Lavendera out of here. I will get them all out of here. And I will burn this fucking castle to the ground.

Even if it means that I have to manipulate every single human in this city to do it.

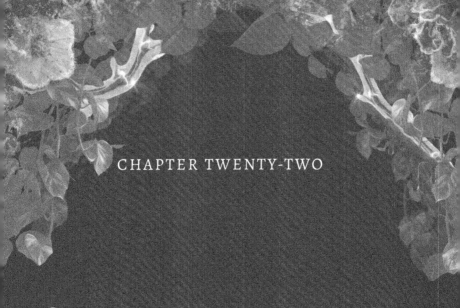

# CHAPTER TWENTY-TWO

Silently cursing the fact that I'm wearing my infuriating iron collar, I try my best to flirt the way normal people do. Which I'm quickly coming to realize is something that I might actually be quite terrible at.

The dragon shifter in front of me furrows his brows and watches me with both confusion and suspicion evident on his face. I decide to press on anyway. Draven is currently in the room that this shifter is guarding, where he is reporting his progress and plans for capturing the Red Hand, and I need to take every opportunity I can to sneakily interrogate anyone who might know where the other entrance to the emergency escape tunnel is located.

Since I can only sneak out when Draven is away, which is always at night, I haven't been able to search the mountainside for the tunnel. It's pitch black out there. I would be more likely to break my ankles trying to climb across the stones than actually finding the entrance. And since I can't go there when it's daylight, because Draven keeps me glued to his side at all other times, I need to find someone else who can give me the information that I need. Which hopefully is this guy.

"You must be incredibly skilled if you have managed to get this job," I say.

The guard before me shifts his weight, the slight move making his silver armor glint in the sunlight streaming in through the window, while he continues watching me with eyebrows knitted in confusion. "What do you mean?"

"You're guarding the Empress and Emperor's personal meeting room. They wouldn't give that position to someone who hasn't proven himself."

A hint of pride pushes out some of the confusion on his face, and he straightens his spine ever so slightly. "I suppose you're right." Then he seems to remember who he's talking to, because the satisfied smile disappears and hostility takes its place as he narrows his eyes at me. "Though what would you know about skills and work ethics, *fae*."

He spits out my race as if it tastes foul.

I suppress a snarl. This would be so much easier if I had my magic. But I keep at it anyway.

While expertly hiding my rage at his rudeness, I run my tongue along my lip for a second and then make a show of raking my gaze over his body. "Nothing. That's why I'm attracted to strong men who like to take control."

That startles him enough that he jerks back a little and blinks at me.

I don't give him even a second to recover. I need to make him feel both confused and turned on so that he won't figure out what I'm really doing when I steer the conversation back to the topic of where he was stationed before he was given this honored position. In particular, if he has ever patrolled the east side of the mountain.

So I keep a flirty expression on my face as I take a half step closer and put a hand on his arm and play on his sense of superiority and his disdain for fae. "A strong man who can put me in my place. Someone who can dominate—"

The door is yanked open.

And before I can so much as close my mouth, let alone take my hand off the guard, Draven stalks back out into the corridor.

He freezes two steps out on the floor, and his eyes lock on the hand I still have on the guard's arm. For a moment, the only sound is the faint click of the door as it swings shut behind him again. Then his expression darkens, and he drags his gaze up to the guard's face.

I yank my hand back at the same time as the guard blurts out, "Commander."

"What the hell is going on here?" Draven demands, flicking eyes that have darkened with threats between us.

"We were just having a conversation," I reply before the guard can say something stupid.

Unfortunately, he does that anyway.

"I didn't touch her," he presses out, his eyes wide with fear and pleading. "She's the one who was trying to flirt with me."

Lightning flashes in Draven's eyes, and he slowly turns to me. "Oh?" But before I can even reply, he snaps his gaze back to the guard and declares, "Jesper, you're on cleaning duty in your clan's barracks for the next five months."

Tilting my head back, I barely manage to stifle a frustrated groan. Now he's definitely never going to talk to me. And he's also going to warn all of his friends to never talk to me.

"It's not his fault," I begin, trying to mitigate the damage, as I tilt my head back down. "He didn't—"

A yelp escapes my mouth, cutting off my sentence, as I'm suddenly hoisted into the air. I suck in a sharp breath to clear my head, but the scene around me still isn't making any bloody sense.

Because Draven has just picked me up and thrown me over his shoulder.

I let out a huff as my stomach connects with his hard shoulder plate.

He just wraps an arm around the back of my thighs and starts walking.

Wiggling, I try to find purchase on the armor across his back, but my palms keep slipping. So I squeeze my hand into a fist and slam it into his back instead. It just makes pain pulse through my hand.

"What did I tell you about trying to break my armor with your hands?" Draven demands. "You'll just shatter your bones."

"Put me down," I growl back at him as he rounds the corner into an empty hallway. "What the hell do you think you're doing?"

"What does it look like?"

"Did you seriously just throw me over your shoulder and carry me away because I was *talking* to another guy?" I slam my fist against his back again and kick my legs at his stomach. "What kind of jealous territorial bullshit is this?"

"First of all, you weren't talking to him. You were *flirting* with him. And secondly, I'm not jealous."

I scoff. "Right."

My stomach lurches as he suddenly stops and lifts me off his shoulder. I blink as my feet hit the floor again. But I don't even have time to gather my wits before Draven's face is right in front of mine. Fire burns in his eyes as he stares me down.

"I'm not jealous," he repeats. And before I can retort, he presses on. "And I thought we had a deal. Act like my submissive little slave in public and fight me all you like in private."

"I am."

"Then what do you call that?" He stabs a hand towards the corridor no longer visible to our left. "Azaroth's flame, I should just put you in black armor too, because you're as bad as my own clan at just following simple orders that are for your own protection."

"Maybe you should," I bait. "That way, there would be no question who I belong to."

"There has never been a question about that."

"Really? I thought you just said that you weren't jealous and territorial when it comes to me."

He opens his mouth to retort, but then his gaze darts down the corridor. A moment later, I hear it too. Footsteps. Coming this way.

Shifting his gaze back to me, he rakes his hands through his hair and lets out a long sigh. "Let's save this argument for later. Right now, we need to get to my clan's barracks and brief them on today's plan."

"To catch the Red Hand," I fill in. It's half statement, half question, but Draven answers anyway.

"Yes, to catch the Red Hand."

And before either of us can say anything else, two courtiers round the corner. They blink at us in surprise. Draven simply starts walking while assuming that I will follow. And since he is unfortunately right that we need to keep up appearances, I do exactly that.

The walk to his clan barracks is a tense and quiet one. And all the way there, I stew in silence and curse his interruption back there.

By giving the guard cleaning duty as punishment for just speaking to me, Draven has now made sure that none of the guards from the Silver Dragon Clan are going to dare to talk to me. Which means that I can't get the information I need. And all just because of his stupid jealous bullshit.

I glance at Draven from the corner of my eye as we enter the barracks of the Black Dragon Clan.

He wants to be a territorial asshole? Fine. I'll be a fucking menace too.

"Listen up," Draven calls as he strides into the massive room where his soldiers have gathered. "We will be trying a different strategy today."

While Draven begins explaining their orders for the day, I

slink away towards one of the changing rooms that are connected to the main room. A few of the shifters cast curious glances at me when I pass them, but no one stops me. And Draven knows that there is no exit there, so he just keeps giving orders as well.

I slip into the empty changing room. People have left their normal clothes neatly folded on shelves above the empty armor stands that line the stone walls. Coming to a halt right inside the door, I quickly begin stripping off my own clothes.

If there is any place where I can do something like this as revenge, it's here. Draven's clan won't sell him out to the Icehearts, so whatever happens in this barrack will stay in this barrack.

I know that I'm being petty and stupid, but I'm frustrated that he ruined my chances to get information from the guards in the palace and I want to get back at him. Publicly. And besides, there is something that I want to hear him say out loud. Something that I want him to admit. Even though it doesn't matter. Even though I shouldn't care. Even though it won't change anything. But I still want to hear him say it.

After stripping down to my underwear, which leaves very little to the imagination, I straighten my spine and raise my chin in a confident posture even though my heart is suddenly pounding in my chest.

And then I stride straight back into the main room.

For a few seconds, Draven just keeps issuing orders, and everyone else only continues watching him.

I walk farther into the room.

Then the first few soldiers begin glancing at me. They do a double take when they realize what I'm wearing. Or rather, not wearing. Armor creaks faintly as one after the other, they all turn to stare at me.

Draven notices the commotion and finally flicks a glance in my direction.

He too does a double take.

His mouth hanging open, he stares at me with such an almost comical look of shock and disbelief on his face that I almost laugh out loud at the sight of it.

But I only get to enjoy that for a few mere seconds. Then his expression darkens like an oncoming storm.

"Eyes down!" he bellows across the room. "Anyone who raises his eyes will get them carved out."

All the men in the room quickly jerk their heads back and drop their gazes to the floor. And all the women too.

Lightning flashes in Draven's eyes, and he flexes his hand down by his side, as he advances on me. His soldiers part before him like water before an unforgiving mountain.

My heart thumps as I begin backing away. I don't want to have this conversation in front of his entire clan, so I keep moving until I have retreated through the still open door to the changing room. Draven stalks in after me and slams the door shut behind him.

"What the fuck do you think you're doing?" he demands.

"You said you wanted me to wear the black armor of your clan." I raise my eyebrows and spread my arms in challenge. "Well, here I am. I removed my other clothes, but there were no extra sets of armor here, so I went in search of one."

"You…" Cutting himself off, he draws in a long breath through his nose as if to calm himself down. Then he stabs his hand towards my clothes, which are just lying in a pile on the floor. "Put your clothes back on. Now."

"Why? I thought you weren't jealous."

"I'm not."

"Fine. Then I'll just keep flirting with everyone I come across."

"Not unless you want them to lose their eyes. And their hands."

A frustrated breath rips from my throat, and I take a step forward, closing the final distance between us, as I jab a finger against his chest while locking eyes full of challenge on him. "Just admit it."

His gaze slides down my half-naked body. A muscle flickers in his jaw, and he drags in another deep breath through his nose. But to my shock, it's not anger that flickers in his eyes. It's burning desire.

The realization sends a jolt through my body. All my life, I've avoided doing things like this. I've avoided challenging people. Avoided doing things that might make them angry. Because I didn't want them to start hating me. And deep down, that age-old fear was twisting inside me, worrying that I shouldn't be doing that to Draven either. That standing up to him would only make him dislike me.

But to my utter shock, it appears to be the exact opposite. Based on the expression on his face as he rakes his gaze over my body, this stunt I just pulled only makes him like me more. And that realization fills me with a sweeping rush of giddiness and makes me feel bold and powerful all at once.

Draven forces his gaze back up to my face. "Admit what?"

I flash him a smirk full of challenge. "Admit that you're a jealous territorial bastard who can't stand the thought of me flirting with someone else."

"You're playing with fire, little rebel."

"I thought we had already established that I'm quite adept at that."

"Put your clothes back on."

"Admit it."

He clenches his jaw and stares me down.

I stare right back at him.

Something between a frustrated sigh and a growl rips from his chest. Then he drags in a long breath.

"Fine." He works his jaw, still holding my gaze with those burning eyes of his. "I'm a jealous territorial bastard who can't stand the thought of you flirting with someone else."

My heart does a backflip in my chest, and heat floods my body.

I knew it. In the end, it won't matter, because he will always be my enemy. But I still wanted to hear him say it. *Needed* to hear him say it.

Confused and highly inconvenient feelings twist inside my chest.

Holding Draven's gaze, I draw in a short breath and press out, "Why?"

"Why what?"

"Why do you hate it when I flirt with someone else?"

"I've already told you." He slides his hand up my throat and positions it right underneath my jaw in a highly possessive move. His eyes burn through my soul as he stares me down. "Because you're mine."

I arch an eyebrow at him. "Your life slave?"

"No. *Mine*. In every sense of the word."

A shudder of pleasure and forbidden desire ripples down my spine.

The way he is looking at me right now is making me want to bare my whole soul to him. He sees me. All sides of me. He knows exactly what kind of person I am. Knows exactly what I can do. That I could try to manipulate him with my magic when he takes my collar off in his rooms. That I hate everything he stands for. That I will continue to fight him in private. And he *likes* it. In his eyes, I am enough. And not just enough. I'm somehow... more.

I suddenly can't breathe. Why did it have to be my most dangerous enemy? Why did he have to be the one to make me feel like this? Make me feel alive and seen and strong and powerful in a way that no one ever has.

With a firm grip on my throat, Draven leans down until his lips are right in front of mine. And for one single second, I don't know if he's going to kiss me or drain me of magic.

186

He does neither of those things.

"Now, put your clothes back on," he says, speaking the words directly against my mouth.

Pleasure rolls through me when his breath caresses my lips.

And before I can get my wits back, he releases me and abruptly spins on his heel. I watch as he strides back to the door. But he pauses with his hand on the handle.

Looking back over his shoulder, he meets my gaze while a smile that is pure villain spreads across his face. "Oh and, Selena?"

It takes me a second to remember how to speak, and when I do, the word comes out in an embarrassing croak. "Yes?"

His eyes glint. "You will pay for this little stunt tonight."

# CHAPTER TWENTY-THREE

**F**urniture crashes on the street. Sitting on a wooden planter a short distance away, I watch as Draven's soldiers throw chairs and side tables and books and decorations out of the windows of the houses before me. Wood cracks and ceramic shatters as the humans' treasured possessions hit the stone street below.

Apparently, the different strategy that Draven mentioned in the barracks earlier today involves destroying people's homes as much as possible while they search the buildings for the Red Hand.

Curling my fingers, I grip the edge of the wooden planter hard and grind my teeth as I watch Draven. He is standing in front of a row of silent humans. All of them have their heads bowed while he stares them down with merciless eyes.

"If you just tell me where the Red Hand is, we won't need to keep searching through your homes," Draven says.

Sounds of crashing furniture punctuate his words.

The humans standing in the row before him say nothing. But they squeeze their hands into fists and grit their teeth. Even from my position, I can practically feel the anger radiating from them.

I shake my head at Draven, even though he can't see it.

This is all so unnecessary. These people know nothing about the Red Hand. They're just ordinary people.

Forcing out a long breath, I unclench my hands from the edge of the planter and flex them to relieve the tension that had started to build up. While Draven continues threatening the humans in front of their homes, I tilt my head back and look up at the sky.

Orange and pink streaks line the heavens and paint the soft clouds in vibrant colors. It's almost sunset. Draven and his clan members have been at this all day. Barging into people's homes to check if they're hiding the Red Hand in there and destroying their possessions while Draven rounds them up outside and threatens them.

It's almost as if he is going out of his way to be as cruel and ruthless as possible. And I can't help but wonder if part of it is because of how the Icehearts are treating him. I still remember the way they berated him and threatened him in that corridor where the latest dead body was. Maybe that's why he does the same thing to the humans. As a way to take back control. To not feel so powerless.

I study the burning anger that is visible on all the humans' faces as they are forced to stand there and watch their homes be destroyed.

It's cruel. But, as much as I hate to admit it, there is one positive side effect of what Draven is doing. It's making the humans angrier. Which will make it easier for me to fan the flames of rebellion by heightening their outrage and fury even more with my magic. I need the spark of anger to already be there so that I can manipulate it. And after this, a large portion of the city will already be boiling with rage.

"Don't turn around."

I suck in a sharp breath between my teeth.

Fortunately, a bookcase hits the street right at the same time, which drowns out the sound.

It takes all of my willpower to force my features back into a normal expression and to keep my eyes on the buildings ahead as I whisper, "Kath?"

"Hello, Selena," Kath replies in an equally soft voice.

She is sitting on the other side of the planter, behind my back and a little to the left. When I pretend to sweep my gaze up and down the street, I can only just make out her red hair from the corner of my eye.

I didn't even hear her walk over and sit down. But since Kath is a member of the human resistance, and a pretty high-ranking one too, I suppose she does know how to discreetly move through a crowd.

"You're a hard woman to find," she says.

Tilting my head down, I pretend to watch the stones below so that no one will notice that my mouth is moving when I reply, "I know. I'm under almost constant surveillance. Did you get the messages I left?"

"Yes. But it has been a while since your last one now."

"I'm still trying to find the other entrance to the tunnel. But for that, I need an excuse to go out to the east side of the mountain when it's still daylight."

"I'll see what I can do."

I adjust my position a little so that it won't look suspicious that I'm sitting in the exact same way for too long. Once my mouth is once more hidden from view, I begin asking a question that I have been wondering about ever since I realized how the Red Hand is getting in and out of the Ice Palace.

"Kath?" I begin.

"Yes?"

"Why can't the Red Hand do this? If he can get inside the castle, why do you need me to find a route to the treasury?"

Her red hair swings slightly in the corner of my eye, as if she looked up and down the street to make sure that no one overheard me. Then she lets out a soft sigh. "Because the Red Hand is our secret weapon. He's not involved in the heist. The heist is *my* responsibility. He only focuses on assassinating strategic people. We could never risk him being captured just for a surveillance mission like this." A soft laugh, barely more than a whisper, escapes her lips. "And besides, he kind of just does whatever he wants."

I suppose that makes sense. The Red Hand isn't just a skilled member of the human resistance. He is their most important symbol. If he were to be captured, they wouldn't just lose a capable operative. If Draven were to arrest the Red Hand, it would gut morale and destroy the hope and revolutionary momentum that the resistance has built.

"Makes sense," I reply.

"I need to move soon, otherwise they might start to notice me," she whispers back. "Is there anything else?"

"Yes. After the heist, I need to get out of the city." I swallow down a sudden sense of dread. "Draven is going to hunt me to the ends of the world once he realizes what I've done."

"Figured as much. We'll try to set up a plan for how to get you out."

"It's not just me. There are three more fae in the palace. I'm getting them out too."

Kath falls silent. I desperately want to turn around and look at her, but I force myself to keep my eyes on the buildings ahead. The soldiers from the Black Dragon Clan are still hurling furniture and decorations out of the windows while Draven stands there in front of the humans, staring them down and daring them to protest. A loud crash echoes between the stone walls as a cabinet hits the ground. The people who were passing this part of the street hurry past while casting worried glances at the unfolding events.

"Just getting one fae out of the city will be difficult enough,"

Kath replies at last. "But four?" Her hair swings in the corner of my eye as she shakes her head.

I grip the edge of the planter hard. "I'm not leaving without them."

Once again, she falls silent. Then she lets out a soft sigh. "Then you're gonna have to convince someone I'm not even sure exists."

"Who?"

"According to my brother, who has listened to one too many bedtime stories in his life, there is supposed to be a fae woman living out here in Frostfell who helps smuggle other fae out of the city. I'm not sure if she's real or if this is just a myth, but I'll talk to my brother. If he knows where to find her, I'll leave the instructions at the drop point."

"Thank you."

"I really need to go now."

"Then you..." I trail off, because the hint of red hair has already disappeared from the corner of my eye.

A few moments later, I find Kath walking down the street in the other direction. I slide my gaze back to Draven, who is once more threatening the humans.

Drawing in a breath, I straighten my spine as resolve pulses through me.

This mysterious fae woman is real. She has to be. And I am going to find her.

I flick a glance up and down Draven's muscular body as his words from earlier echo through my skull.

*You'll pay for this little stunt tonight.*

My heart starts beating irregularly in my chest.

Yes, I will find the mystery fae. But first, I just need to survive whatever punishment Draven has in store for me tonight.

## CHAPTER TWENTY-FOUR

**W**ater drips down my body to land on the smooth ice floor. This is the only room in Draven's quarters that doesn't have wooden floorboards. Which I suppose makes sense since it is a bathroom. But still, it creates a stark contrast between the warm water in the bathtub and the cool ice floor.

Goosebumps spread across my arms, and my nipples harden, at the sudden coolness. I reach for a towel and quickly wrap it around myself.

Despite Draven's earlier threats, he didn't do anything to punish me. Once he was finished terrorizing the humans in the city, we ate a tense dinner with his clan, and then we returned to his rooms. He took a bath and then disappeared into his bedroom. So I simply took a bath too.

And as I dry myself off, I can't help but feel a little... disappointed. I know that it makes no sense, but this little war of bantering and challenges and sly threats that Draven and I have going on gives me a sense of normalcy.

My entire life right now consists of balancing on the edge of a knife. Every time I step foot outside this room, I risk death and torture for one reason or another. I'm not actually broken, but I need to pretend as if I am in front of everyone. Otherwise, the Icehearts will begin torturing me themselves. I'm helping the humans plan their heist and I'm also trying to start a full-scale rebellion on my own. If anyone finds that out, I'm dead. One mistake, in anything I do, and I'm doomed. Sometimes, the pressure of all of that is so intense that I can barely breathe.

But when I'm with Draven, that life and death threat is somehow gone. And I feel like I can breathe again. Feel like my life isn't a gigantic deathblow waiting to happen. So I was almost looking forward to seeing how he would exact his revenge after I stripped almost naked and strolled through an entire room full of his soldiers.

Letting out a long sigh, I shake my head at myself in the mirror and then wrap the towel around my body again. I left my nightgown in my room, and I don't want to put my normal clothes back on now that I have just come out of the bath.

After drawing a hand through my long silver hair, I open the bathroom door and walk back out into the living room.

My heart jerks.

I come to an abrupt halt a few strides into the living room as I find Draven waiting for me.

Only wearing a pair of black underwear, he is leaning against the desk so that he is half sitting on the edge while he has one ankle crossed over the other. The pose practically drips with casual authority, especially since his half-naked state leaves his lethally powerful body on full display. And as if that wasn't enough, he also has one hand slightly raised and is spinning a pair of handcuffs around his finger.

Heat sears through my body, and a throbbing starts between my legs.

Draven watches me with an absolutely devilish smile on his lips.

And I'm suddenly reminded that I'm just standing there, frozen on the floor. Giving my head a quick shake, I try to gather my wits. It works poorly. But I clear my throat and arch an eyebrow at him anyway.

"For someone who said he was going to punish me, you don't look very angry," I observe.

"I'm not." That burning desire from before flares up in his eyes again as he holds my gaze, and that devilish smile on his lips widens. "Do you have any idea how hot you are when you're cocky and confrontational?"

My heart skips a beat.

"Challenging me in front of my entire clan like that?" He flicks a possessive glance up and down my body. "So fucking hot. All I wanted to do was to bend you over a table and take you right then and there to show them all that you are fucking *mine*."

Heat washes through me, and my clit throbs harder. "Told you you're a territorial asshole."

"Yes, I'm a really fucking territorial asshole. Which is why I can tell you that it's the last time you ever pull a stunt like that."

"You mean this?" I unwrap my towel.

Soft gray fabric flutters through the air before the towel lands on the floor behind me, leaving me completely naked. My nipples harden again, but not from the cold this time.

Draven's eyes darken with desire.

I flash him a villainous grin.

His massive black wings explode into view as he performs a half-shift, making a small cloud of black smoke drift through the air. Before I have even finished sucking in a startled breath, Draven has flown across the room. I stumble back a step as he lands right in front of me.

Pressing the advantage, he takes a step forward, forcing me to retreat again. My heart flutters in my chest as he keeps advancing on me while I find myself backing into his bedroom.

"You troublesome little rebel," he says as he continues backing me across the room. "Do you know the torture you put me through when you walked into the room half-naked like that?"

I'm just about to open my mouth to reply, but then the back of my thighs abruptly hit the edge of Draven's bed and I lose my balance. Spinning my arms, I try to steady myself.

Draven places his palm against my chest and gives me a shove.

I topple backwards onto the bed.

Dark gray sheets crinkle underneath me as I scramble backwards while trying to sit up.

"Allow me to demonstrate," Draven continues as he climbs onto the bed as well.

My back hits the headboard with a thud.

Draven cocks his head. "Unless you don't think you can handle it, of course?"

I shoot him a grin full of challenge back. "Oh I can handle you just fine, Shadow of Death."

A dark chuckle rumbles from his chest. He jerks his chin. "Then lie down and place your hands above your head."

My pulse thrums and fire pools at my core as I obey his command and scoot down a little so that I can lie down on my back. The wooden headboard is cool against my skin as I move my hands up over my head and rest them against the headboard.

Metal glints in the lone faelight by the dresser as Draven spins the handcuffs around his finger again. Then he sits so that he is straddling my chest as he reaches up towards my wrists.

My heart jerks in anticipation when Draven locks one side of the handcuffs around my wrist. They're made of steel, not iron, so they don't block my magic or sap my strength. After threading them through the wooden bars of the headboard, he grabs my other wrist and moves it closer. Then he snaps the other manacle shut around that wrist as well. It leaves both of my hands shackled and locked to the headboard.

Draven shifts backwards until he is standing on his knees over my legs. When he meets my gaze again, there is a wicked smirk playing over his lips. "Nervous?"

I hold his gaze. "Never."

A yelp escapes my lips as Draven suddenly grabs me by the hips and yanks me downwards on the bed. Soft sheets brush against my skin as I slide down along the bed until my arms are stretched fully above my head. Because of the handcuffs trapping me to the headboard, I can't even bend my arms anymore.

I draw in a breath to steady my suddenly racing heart as Draven moves so that he is straddling my right thigh. While settling his weight on it, he uses his hand to push my other leg to the side, exposing my pussy to him.

With my heart pattering against my ribs, I glance up at the handcuffs and try pulling against them. They don't give an inch.

Sliding my gaze back to Draven, I arch a cocky eyebrow. "I knew it. I *knew* you liked handcuffs in bed."

His eyes glitter as he leans down over me, so close that I can feel his breath against my skin. A shiver of pleasure rolls down my spine as he brushes his lips along my jaw before slanting them over my mouth, just shy of touching.

"Of course I do. Anything that gives me control." He slides a hand up my throat while whispering against my lips, "And now, you are going to beg. And plead. And grovel."

"If you think it will be that easy, you—"

A gasp rips from my lungs as he draws his fingers firmly over my already throbbing clit. Moving with expert precision, he rubs his thumb over my clit again and again. I press the back of my head down on the soft mattress as pleasure begins pulsing inside me, building like a storm.

"You were saying?" Draven taunts.

And I want to answer his challenge, but unfortunately, all that makes it out of my mouth is a moan.

He lets out a smug chuckle.

While still sliding his thumb over my clit, he moves his index and middle finger down and teases my entrance. I yank against the handcuffs and curl my fingers into fists as the tension inside me builds.

A jolt shoots up my spine as Draven pushes both fingers inside me.

I gasp, staring up into his gleaming eyes. His face is still right in front of me, and he still keeps his other hand around my throat, as he studies every expression on my face.

Pleasure ripples through my veins as Draven begins thrusting his fingers in and out.

Another moan spills from my lips, along with a whimper.

The smirk on his face widens.

My heart slams against my ribs as Draven brings me closer and closer to an orgasm. I squirm against the sheets and suck in short shallow breaths as the edge draws ever closer. Draven rubs my clit with firm motions. I'm almost there. One more and then I will—

He abruptly stops moving his fingers.

I drag in a strangled breath and blink against the sudden disorientation as my orgasm starts to fade before it could even begin.

"If you think it will be that easy…" Draven taunts, echoing my own words, while wicked amusement shines on his stupidly handsome face.

My responding curse only makes it halfway out of my mouth before it's cut off by a gasp when Draven begins rubbing my clit again. Pleasure once more starts building inside me as he thrusts his fingers as well.

I drag in an unsteady breath.

I squirm underneath him and yank against the handcuffs as he brings me back towards an orgasm. Pent-up release thrums inside me as he slides his thumb over just the right spot. Pleasure builds, just waiting for release. One more second and then—

He stops moving his hands.

A snarl rips from my throat.

Draven just laughs.

And then brings me to the edge of another orgasm but stops right before release can actually crash through me.

Then he does it again.

And again.

When he does it for the seventh time in a row, I'm ready to scream my lungs out.

My whole body is practically vibrating underneath him as he stops moving his fingers right before release can find me. I gasp in ragged breaths. My chest heaves. I feel like my brain is going to melt and my body is going to explode from the pent-up tension.

"Draven," I gasp out. "Please."

He starts teasing my clit and begins slowly thrusting his fingers again.

A whimper spills from my lips.

"Oh Goddess," I plead as tension once more starts building inside me.

Draven tightens his hand around my throat and leans down to speak directly against my mouth. "Your goddess can't help you."

He curls his fingers inside me.

I gasp and yank desperately against the handcuffs.

His eyes glint as he locks them on me. "I am your God now."

Pent-up need pulses inside me like a thrashing storm. I'm going to die if I don't get release soon. I'm going to combust and my brain is going to shatter and I—

"So beg me," he commands.

"Please." The word is out of my mouth before I can stop it, but I don't even care anymore. "Draven. Please, I'm begging you."

"For what?"

"Please let me come. Oh Goddess... Oh God... Draven." Desperate moans drip from my lips as I squirm against the sheets and throw my head from side to side as the tension inside me reaches unbearable levels. "Please."

"What? No honorific?"

"Please, sir."

He curls his fingers inside me again, but he's moving them too slowly for it to make me come. Another whimper escapes me as I pull on the handcuffs and stare up into Draven's smirking face with pleading eyes.

"Beg me to fuck you," he orders.

I don't even hesitate. "Please, I'm begging you to fuck me."

A satisfied laugh rumbles from his muscular chest. It makes his warm breath caress my lips, which sends another ripple of pleasure down my spine.

He thrusts his fingers faster and rubs his thumb more firmly against my clit, sending me careening towards an orgasm. I suck in shuddering breaths as the edge draws closer. At long last, I will finally—

He stops moving again.

This time, I do scream.

A cry of pure desperation rips from my very soul as release is once again denied me. Thrashing furiously, I yank against the handcuffs while trying to get my legs into a position where I can kick the fucking bastard who dares to torment me like this.

Draven just slides his hand higher up my throat so that it's placed directly underneath my jaw. With a firm push, he closes my mouth and cuts off my frustrated scream.

There is a truly villainous expression on his face as he takes his other hand from my pussy and locks eyes with me. "And *that* is how I felt when I had to watch you saunter around half-naked and gloriously cocky in a place where I couldn't just shove you up against a wall and fuck you into the next century. So remember this feeling, because this is what I will do to you if you ever try to pull another stunt like that again."

And with that, he releases my throat and instead reaches for a key in his nightstand. My chest is still heaving and my body is vibrating with pent-up release when he at last unlocks the handcuffs and removes them before dropping them on the nightstand. They land on the dark wood with a metallic clattering sound.

For a moment, he just remains straddling me like that. The faint light from the lone faelight he had lit casts silver highlights in his messy black hair.

Then a wicked grin full of challenge slides home on his mouth, and he reaches up to give my cheek two brisk pats. "Good luck trying to sleep now, little rebel."

My mouth drops open in furious disbelief.

But Draven just climbs off me and straightens on the dark wooden floor beside the bed.

Scrambling off the bed, I growl curses at him and try to storm away. But every nerve inside my body is so tightly wound that I can barely make my limbs move in the way I want them to. I throw out a hand, bracing myself on the edge of the bed as I almost topple over.

After throwing my long hair back over my shoulder, I straighten again and start towards the door.

"And where do you think you're going?" Draven demands from a few steps away.

I cut him a glare over my shoulder. "Back to the bath. To finish what you started."

Black wings boom through the air as Draven shoots across the room and slams the door shut right before I can reach it. That villainous grin is back on his stupid mouth as he draws himself up to his full height in front of the now closed door.

"Oh I don't think so." Flicking a look up and down my tense body, he slides his tongue along his bottom lip. "I told you I would make you pay, and I keep my promises. And my threats."

Narrowing my eyes, I glare back at him where he stands, blocking the door.

His defined muscles flex and his massive wings flare out as he spreads his arms wide in a cocky gesture while he raises his eyebrows at me. "Wanna try to fight me over it?"

For one single second, I consider it. But my legs are still so unsteady and my whole fucking soul is vibrating with so much desperate tension that I don't think I would even last more than five seconds against Draven right now.

But physical strength has never been my advantage anyway. I didn't win the Atonement Trials because I was stronger than the others. I won because I was smarter. And because I know how to play dirty when I need to.

So instead of trying to leave, I do the opposite. I walk backwards until I reach Draven's bed. The mattress sways slightly underneath me as I drop down on the edge of the bed. Draven flashes me a smug smirk. Which I'm about to wipe right off his face.

"Fine," I say, challenge lacing my voice. "Then I guess you will just have to watch instead."

He blinks in shock as I spread my legs wide and start stroking my clit right there in front of him. His gaze darts down to my hand, and it takes him another few seconds to drag it back up to my face. When he does, his eyes are dark with desire and burning like smoldering flames.

"Selena." My name comes out like a growl.

I arch an eyebrow while continuing to tease my clit. "Yes?"

"You—"

I push one finger inside me.

Draven's threat, or whatever he had been about to say, is cut off as he sucks in a shuddering breath instead.

Keeping my eyebrows raised, I continue to fuck myself with my hand while I fix Draven with a stare full of challenge. "Problem?"

His cock hardens even more. With every stroke of my fingers, his cock strains harder against the dark fabric of his underwear.

I nod towards it. "That looks painful."

A muscle in his jaw flickers, and he flexes his hand. His chest heaves as he drags in another deep breath. And when his eyes once more lock on mine, there is such desperate desire in them that I forget to move my fingers for a second.

Draven uses that second well.

Shooting across the floor, he flies towards me. I throw myself to the side to evade him, but the move only makes both of us crash down on the floor. My back hits the smooth floorboards with a thud, and massive black wings flare out above us as Draven lands on his hands and knees above me.

My heart pounds hard in my chest as I stare up at him.

"You troublesome little rebel," Draven begins, as he curls his fingers against the floor. His gaze sears into me.

But before he can finish what he had been about to say, I slide my hand between our bodies and down between my legs. Letting out a calculated moan, I begin rubbing my clit again.

Just as I expected, he quickly reaches down to grab that wrist. But I'm already moving. Before his hand can wrap around my right wrist, my left hand slides across the soft membrane of his wing.

A shudder courses through his whole body, and he slams his hand back against the floor as a moan rips from deep within his chest. I show him no mercy. While brushing my fingers across his wings again, I continue pleasuring myself with my other hand.

Draven's eyes shutter, and he curls his fingers against the floor as another shudder rolls through his body. Pure pleasure pulses in his golden eyes.

The sight of it makes my heart squeeze. I still can't believe that I, of all people, am able to draw such a reaction from him.

He sucks in an unsteady breath and, with what looks like great difficulty, he reaches up and wraps a hand around my left wrist. Using his superior strength, he forces my hand away from his wing and pins it against the floor next to my head instead. I keep teasing my clit with my right hand.

"Here's the deal, Shadow of Death." My own eyes are full of

challenge as I meet his desperate gaze. "Either *you* fuck me, or you watch me fuck myself. Those are your two options."

The muscles in his toned forearm shift as he flexes his hand around my wrist. His eyes are burning with so much desire that I can almost feel the heat pulsing from his whole body.

Then he lets out a whole string of curses.

Victory pulses through me.

"Take your hand off your cunt," he orders. "Now."

Releasing me, he quickly strips out of his underwear and tosses them aside. With a firm grip on my thighs, he spreads my legs wide and positions himself between them.

Fire licks through my veins as he grabs my wrist and pins it to the floor above my head again as he leans down over me. His cock brushes against my entrance.

"You infuriating…"

He thrusts into me.

I gasp. Arching my back, I adjust my hips to create a better angle as he sheaths himself deep inside me with that single firm thrust.

"Troublesome…" he continues as he draws halfway out again. Then he thrusts hard. "Insubordinate…"

Pleasure ripples through me at the friction his cock creates when he slides out once more.

He slams into me again. "Little rebel."

A jolt shoots through my body. Lifting my free hand, I place it against his muscular chest as he pulls out and then thrusts deep again. But this time, he doesn't pull out again.

With his cock buried deep inside me, he locks intense eyes on me. "God, you're so fucking hot when you threaten me."

Warmth spreads through my whole soul, making it feel like it's bursting with sparkling fireworks. Holding his gaze, I slide my hand up to his jaw. He kisses my fingers.

"Don't ever hold back against me." His eyes burn through my very soul. "Don't ever suppress your fire."

My heart is suddenly so full that I can barely breathe.

Even though I have never been more a prisoner than I am in this castle, I feel freer than I have in my entire life right now. With him. Because for the first time ever, I don't have to make myself less. I don't have to sacrifice my own personality just to appease someone else.

With Draven, back during the Atonement Trials and here in the Ice Palace, I don't have to be afraid to take up space. I don't have to be small and unobtrusive. With him, I can be me. The *real* me. And the thought is so freeing and so dizzying at the same time that my head spins.

Pleasure pulses through my body as Draven pulls out and then thrusts back in.

My body jerks slightly with every commanding thrust as he starts up a firm pace. But his hand trapping my wrist against the ground helps keep me in place. I slide my other hand up the back of his neck and into his soft hair. His wings flare wider as I rake my fingers down his back instead.

Tension once more builds inside me as Draven fucks me hard.

And this time, he doesn't stop.

I slide my fingers over his wing, making him moan and shudder and break his pace for a few moments.

Wicked approval and a sly promise of revenge flicker in his eyes as he picks up the pace, pounding into me with even more commanding thrusts.

Pleasure streaks up my spine like lightning with every thrust of his thick cock.

He shifts his angle slightly.

A gasp rips from my throat at the insane friction it creates.

Draven leans down and steals the gasp from my lips with a savage kiss. I bite his bottom lip and draw my fingers down his wing in retaliation. He moans into my mouth.

The tension inside me turns into a thrumming storm as he

fucks me just the way I want him to. As if I'm his. As if every inch of my body belongs to him and him alone.

I squirm on the floor as I soar towards an orgasm.

Draven slams into me, hitting a spot deep inside.

Pleasure crackles through me like a lightning storm as release finally finds me.

After all the edging and denied orgasms, the long-awaited release hits me so hard that my vision goes black for a second. My clit throbs and my inner walls flutter around Draven's thick cock as he continues fucking me through the waves of pleasure.

Gasps and incoherent moan drip from my lips.

They're drowned out as a deep groan rips from Draven's chest.

His cock pulses inside me as release crashes into him as well.

And when pleasure floods his handsome face, everything feels so right, so perfect, that the rest of the world just drops away. For those precious moments, it's just me and him. Our bodies and souls joined as one.

Leaning down, he kisses me with such aching softness that my heart almost bursts.

"So fucking perfect," he whispers against my lips. "You're so fucking perfect."

A small noise comes from the back of my throat.

And as I kiss him back, I can't for the life of me understand how I'm supposed to make myself remember that one crucial fact that I must never allow myself to forget.

That Draven and I are supposed to be enemies.

# CHAPTER TWENTY-FIVE

T he back of my neck prickles. Again. It takes all of my willpower to just keep walking casually down the street. I have already checked that I'm not being followed, but I still can't help but feel as if I'm being watched.

Part of me wonders if it's my subconscious trying to tell me that this is a stupid risk. That Kath was right and that Kyler has just listened to one too many bedtime stories in his life. Could there actually be another fae from the Seelie Court living in this city? If there is, then where did she come from? How did she get out of the Seelie Court? Is she a previous winner of the Atonement Trials who somehow managed to escape? But then why would she stay in the city?

That paranoia pulses through me again.

While continuing down the street, I cast a discreet glance over my shoulder.

But just as I already confirmed the last time I did that, Draven is in fact not lurking there behind me, waiting to catch me and drag me back to the castle.

After I pulled that stunt in his barracks a few days ago, and the incredible but very treasonous sex that followed it, Draven has kept a close eye on me. It wasn't until today that he finally snuck away during the night when he thought I was sleeping. Luckily for me, Kath had managed to drop off instructions for me during those days when Draven was glued to my side. So now, I know where to find this mysterious fae woman. If she exists, that is.

I sweep my gaze over the street behind me again, but no Shadow of Death materializes from the darkness. And no other dragon shifters or humans either, for that matter. Only the trees that line the wide street stare back at me like silent sentries. Their barren branches rustle as a strong fall wind whirls between the houses.

Drawing my hood up further, I turn my gaze back to the road ahead.

The map that Kyler drew has led me to a part of Frostfell called Ember Hill, which, from the looks of it, appears to be one of the richer parts of the city. Grand houses, with actual lawns and fences around the property, tower over me on both sides of the street. During the summer, when all the trees that line this street are covered in vibrant leaves, this area is probably really beautiful. Now, with the barren trees and bushes on both the street and in the yards, it has an almost haunted atmosphere.

Glancing down, I check the hand-drawn map I'm carrying once more. According to Kyler, the mysterious fae woman is supposed to live in the white marble house with the blue door up ahead. I suppress the urge to yet again check the street behind me and instead continue walking until I reach the indicated house.

Just like the other houses on this street, there is a short stone wall around the property. Though it looks to be more for aesthetic purposes than to keep invaders out, because it's low enough for me to jump over, if I want to. But seeing as that would be rather rude, I decide to use the small gate instead.

It swings open on silent hinges. I cast one last look over my shoulder to check that the street is still empty. It is. After drawing in a bracing breath, I turn back to the house and stride in through the gate.

The grass surrounding the mansion-like house is well-kept, and bushes and trees and flowerbeds have been placed in an artful pattern throughout the entire yard. Since it's fall, none of them are in bloom. But it still makes me think that the person who lives here values nature. Could it actually be a fae?

Nervous apprehension sweeps over me as I close the final distance to the dark blue door. No light comes from the windows. Mabona's tits, what am I even supposed to say? It's the bloody middle of the night and I'm just showing up at her house unannounced. What if it's a dragon shifter who lives here? What if she thinks I'm a burglar and has me arrested instead?

Coming to a halt right in front of the door, I lick my lips and draw in another long breath to steady my nerves.

This is a stupid risk. Coming here is an incredibly stupid risk.

But that still doesn't change the fact that I need to do this.

If I'm going to get Isera, Lavendera, and Alistair out of this city, I need this mysterious fae woman.

Straightening my spine, I raise a determined hand and knock on the door.

Nothing happens.

I knock again.

For another few seconds, only a dark and silent house watches me.

Then flickering candlelight appears in one of the upstairs windows.

My heart lurches.

Standing there on the porch, I watch that flickering candlelight move to another room. Then it disappears for a little while before it appears again on the ground floor as the person who is carrying it walks towards the door.

*Please be real, please be real, please be real*, I beg silently in my mind.

The lock clicks.

I hold my breath.

Warm candlelight spills out into the darkness as the door opens. I blink against it while quickly trying to assess the person now standing before me in the hallway inside.

A blond woman frowns at me from the other side of the threshold. She looks to be somewhere between twenty-five and thirty, and she has that ethereal essence that both we and the dragon shifters have. Which means that she's not human, at least. Though I could probably have guessed that from the size of this house. No humans live in places like this in Frostfell.

"Yes?" the woman asks, sounding confused.

Her flowing hair covers her ears, so the moment that my vision has adjusted somewhat to the light from the small candelabra that she is holding, I quickly study her eyes.

They look… dark blue. But they could also be a mix of dark blue and another similar color, like violet or black. It's impossible to tell because of the murky darkness around us and the flickering light from the candles.

Worry pulses through me. I can't tell if she's fae or a dragon shifter.

The second stretches on.

Goddess damn it, I need to make a decision. Should I risk it?

The woman opens her mouth again to say something else, since I still haven't replied.

"I'm looking for a fae woman who is supposed to live here," I blurt out before she can get another word out.

She furrows her brows in even deeper confusion, and then lets out a small laugh while shaking her head. "A fae woman? The only fae I know are the ones who live in the Ice Palace."

Defeat and disappointment sink into my stomach like a block of ice. Of course it was too good to be true.

"Oh," I say, and begin turning away before she can realize that I am one of those fae she just mentioned. "Sorry, I must have—"

Her hand shoots out and grabs my arm in a shockingly strong grip. I whip my head back to stare at her. She has moved the candelabra up higher, and now that the light is more directly in her face, I can tell that her eyes are indeed only one color. Dark blue.

"Your eyes," she says, her voice suddenly sharp, as she moves the candelabra closer to my face.

For one brief second, I consider using my magic to lower the suspicion that must surely be burning inside her now. But I quickly discard that idea since it would only make my eyes glow, which would be clear proof that I am indeed fae.

"Yeah, sorry, I have pretty terrible eyesight," I say instead while I try to discreetly pull my arm out of her grip. "I must have read the address wrong when—"

"Lower your hood," the woman demands.

Alarm spikes through me. "I really—"

"You have five seconds to lower your hood before I scream like a banshee that you're trying to rob me. And how do you think that will end for you?"

My heart pounds in my chest as I stare into her blue eyes, which are now filled with such merciless steel that I almost forget to breathe. She's right. If she screams, it will wake the whole neighborhood. And I can't fight my way out of here against this whole street of dragon shifters. But as long as it's only this one woman, I still have a chance. So I decide to do as she says.

Slowly raising my hands, I lower my hood enough to show her my pointed ears.

She cocks her head, a sharp glint now present in her eyes. "Interesting. Very interesting."

My stomach lurches as she suddenly yanks me towards her. I stumble across the threshold and into the hallway, almost toppling over when she releases her grip on my arm. While I quickly straighten again, she slams the front door shut behind us and locks it.

Dread pulses through my body. This cannot be good.

Reaching for my magic, I spin around to face the blond woman again.

But then I jerk back, shock crackling through my veins.

Because the blond woman is gone.

My mind spins and my mouth drops open as I stare at the person now standing before me instead.

It's still a woman who looks to be between twenty-five and thirty with that timeless look that marks her as not human.

But her long blond hair is now black, and her eyes…

Her eyes are yellow and violet. Both colors mixed in both eyes like swirls of paint. Which means…

"You're fae," I blurt out.

She smiles a slow feline smile, which makes her look more like a smirking cat than a person, as she watches me. "And so are you."

"B-but how…" I glance from side to side, but the elegant hallway is empty apart from us. I meet her eyes again while shaking my head. "The blond woman?"

"A glamour." She lets out a smug chuckle and arches a dark eyebrow. "Very useful magical ability for someone such as me."

"But I don't understand. Who are you?"

"My name is Nysara."

"No, I mean, *who* are you? How did you get here? Why do you live here? How did you even get out of the Seelie Court?"

Nysara gives me another one of those slow smiles. "Oh child, I am not from the Seelie Court."

For a few seconds, all I can do is to just stand there on the pale wooden floorboards and stare at her. My pulse is thrumming so hard that I can hear it pounding in my ears. Then at last, my spinning mind catches up and I realize what she's actually telling me.

"You're from the Unseelie Court." The words come out as little more than a whisper.

"Yes," Nysara replies. She flicks her gaze up and down my body. "You look like you're about to faint. Perhaps we should sit down."

Before I can even open my mouth to respond, she is already walking towards the doorway to my left. Candlelight dances over the pale walls as she brings the candelabra with her. Giving my head a quick shake, I try to snap out of my stupor and scramble after her.

She leads me into an elegant dining room. A grand table with eight chairs around it takes up most of the floor space in the middle of the room. Nysara glides towards it and sets the candelabra down on the smooth tabletop. Then she claims a seat. I sit down opposite her while she reaches for a crystal decanter that is waiting on a silver tray beside where she set the candelabra.

"Wine?" she asks without even looking at me.

My first instinct is to politely decline since I don't want to be troublesome. But I get the feeling that I'm going to need a glass of wine to help me through this conversation.

"Yes, please," I reply.

A soft laugh ripples from her throat. "So polite."

I would have assumed that that's a good thing, but the way she says it makes it sound like an insult. However, I don't have the brain capacity left to think about that, because there are a million other questions ringing inside my skull right now. Drawing in a long breath, I try to gather my wits enough to figure out which question to ask first. In the end, Nysara decides for me.

"So," she begins while she pours dark red wine into two gleaming glasses. "You are one of the life slaves from the palace, and you have come here without a collar, which means that you are here to beg for my help to get out of the city. Am I right?"

"Yes. And no."

She raises her eyebrows in surprise. After she has finished pouring the wine, she sets the crystal decanter down on the silver tray again. Then she slides one of the glasses towards me before picking up the other and taking a sip.

"Oh?" she asks.

"I'm here because I need you to get *all* of us out of the city," I say, and then add, "Please."

"All of you, huh? Then where are the others?"

"Still trapped in the castle. But I'm working on a way to get them out. I just need to know that we can get out of the city once we're out of the palace."

"I see."

"So can you help? Please. I don't really have any money or anything to give you in return, but…" Desperation leaks into my voice as I hold her gaze and pathetically repeat, "Please."

Silence falls over the dining room. Nysara watches me with eyes I can't read. Then she takes another sip of wine. Candlelight glitters in her yellow and violet eyes as she sets her glass down and cocks her head.

"Well, normally, I require something in return for my services." She lifts her slender shoulders in a nonchalant shrug. "Or at least a little groveling." Clicking her tongue, she brushes her long black hair back behind her shoulder. "But fortunately for you, my job is both to spy on the dragon shifters and to do everything I can to sabotage the Icehearts. And taking away all of their life slaves would certainly fall into that second category."

Relief washes through me. Followed by confusion. "Wait, your *job*?"

"Yes." She raises her chin, pride lacing her tone as she looks down at me. "I am here on a mission from the Unseelie King himself."

I blink at her, my mouth dropping open a little.

That seems to have been the reaction she was hoping for,

because one of those smug feline smiles spreads across her lips as she leans back in her chair.

"The Unseelie King is alive?" I breathe.

"Yes."

"What happened? To your court? After they conquered us, what happened to you?"

"Nothing. The Unseelie Court is still the majestic independent fae realm that it always has and always will be."

My heart is slamming so hard against my ribs that Nysara must surely hear it. The Unseelie Court is free. The dragon shifters never conquered it. During all these millennia, while we have been trapped in the forest of thorns, the Unseelie Court has been out there.

And done... nothing.

"Why?" It comes out as little more than a whisper.

"Because our court is both stronger and smarter than yours."

I drag my gaze back up to her face. "No, I mean, why didn't you help us? If you have been free all this time, why did you never try to help us?"

She frowns, as if she's genuinely confused why I would even ask that. Narrowing her eyes, she studies my face intently. "You must not know a lot about our history."

"I know nothing of our history. The dragon shifters burned everything and killed everyone but the children when they conquered us."

Clicking her tongue, she traces her finger along the rim of her glass. "Yes, well, that is unfortunate."

"Unfortunate?" I snap, anger crackling through me, as I sit forward in my chair. "We have—"

"Let's get something straight." That merciless steel creeps back into her eyes as she locks them on me. "You are in *my* home, begging for *my* help, so you do not raise your voice at me. Is that clear?"

With great effort, I swallow down my anger and sit back in my seat again. Lowering my chin slightly, I force out, "I'm sorry."

"That's better."

Under the table, I squeeze my hand into a fist. But I keep my mouth shut. Because by Mabona, I really do need Nysara's help.

"So, to answer your question," she begins. "There are two reasons for why we have never tried to help you. The first one is because relations between our two courts have always been strained, to say the least. And the second, and most important, reason is because we do not get involved in other people's problems. We protect our own realm. What everyone else does outside of it is not our concern."

The most infuriating part of it all is that I actually understand her reasoning. Staying out of other people's problems is most likely the reason why their court was never conquered in the first place. It still pisses me off, though.

But I can't tell her that, so I force that rage down and instead decide to ask another question. A question that will be crucial for my plan to launch a successful rebellion and finally free our court too.

"I understand," I reply in response to her explanation. Then I raise my gaze and meet her eyes again. "But since you know what actually happened back then, can you at least tell me how the dragon shifters managed to conquer us? If all of our ancestors were dragon riders who controlled them with dragon steel, then how did they manage to overthrow us? How did they manage to get the dragon steel off and kill us all?"

Once again, she frowns deeply in what looks like genuine confusion. "What do you mean all of you?"

I just stare back at her, equally bewildered. "How did they manage to conquer us when our ancestors controlled them all with dragon steel?"

For another few seconds, we only stare at each other. A strong fall wind sweeps past on the lawn outside, making the tree branches rattle and scrape against the window.

"Malachi's balls," she says at last, a curse using the name of our Goddess Mabona's dark counterpart, Malachi, the King of Hell and Mabona's former lover. "You really don't know anything, do you?"

"What?" I demand, my heart now beating even harder.

She leans back in her seat again and watches me, as if she's seeing me with new eyes. "Yes, most of the Seelie fae were dragon riders. But only a small portion of them used dragon steel to bend the shifters to their will. The rest were voluntary and mutually beneficial partnerships between fae and dragon shifters."

I think my ears are ringing. "What... what are you saying?"

"Only a small minority used dragon steel. Mostly the disgruntled and entitled ones who had been deemed unworthy by the dragon shifters and been rejected when they asked them about a partnership the traditional way."

"A small minority..." It feels as if someone set off an explosion right next to me, and I was just hit with the massive shock wave.

"Yes."

"A small minority," I repeat. My heart is pounding. It feels like my whole world is tilting on its axis, turning everything upside down, and I have to grip the edge of the table so that I don't fall off the chair. "They have spent millennia punishing *everyone* in the Seelie Court because of something that a few entitled assholes did?"

"Well, to be fair, dragon shifters are among the most fierce and proud races, and they did not take kindly to being mind-controlled. And they have very long memories. If anyone can hold a grudge longer than an Unseelie fae, it's a dragon shifter."

But I can barely hear her over the sound of my own pounding heart and the shattering of my whole world view.

A sob rips from my chest. "I have suffered my entire life because of something that my ancestors might not even have done?"

All my life, people have been telling me things about myself. Telling me that I will only ever be able to have one child. That I am a descendant of wicked people. That all fae are inherently evil. That *I* am evil.

And I just… believed them.

I believed them when they told me all of that. I believed them when they told me that we broke a treaty and betrayed all the dragon shifters when we found the dragon steel. That the dragon shifters did the right thing when they punished all of our wicked ancestors.

Gripping the edge of the table harder, I suck in desperate breaths. But it barely feels as if any oxygen is making it into my lungs.

Every day, I find out something else that turns my world upside down. Every day, I learn that everything I thought I knew is false. That the world is different from what I have been taught.

Goddess above, I can't breathe. I can't—

Loud pounding comes from the front door.

My heart leaps into my throat, and I jump up from the chair.

With great effort, I shove all of my panic and confusion and heartbreak over what Nysara has told me to the back of my mind. I can't afford to think about that right now. I need to focus on what I came here to do. Isera, Lavendera, Alistair, and I need a way out of the city. That is what is most important right now. Not all the lies that I have been told about myself.

"Nysara," a male voice calls from the other side of the door. He sounds worried rather than angry. "Are you there?"

"Malachi's balls," Nysara curses, annoyance flitting across her beautiful features as she gets to her feet. "It's my neighbor. My overly worried and very much in love with me neighbor." Raising a slender arm, she points towards the other side of the house while she strides back into the hallway. "Go out the back door."

I scramble after her into the hallway. "But my request. Will you help us—"

"Yes. If you can get here after you escape the castle, I can cast a temporary glamour to make you all look like dragon shifters so that you can get out of the city."

Skidding to a halt on the floor of the hallway, I jerk back in shock as I find the blond dragon shifter woman from before standing there in front of me instead of Nysara.

However, her voice is still the same when she demands, "When are you escaping?"

"Nysara," the man outside calls again. He sounds on the verge of hysteria. "Please say something. Are you injured? Do I need to break the door down?"

"I don't know yet," I reply to Nysara's question.

"Then come back and tell me when you do." She stabs a hand towards a door at the other end of the hall. "Now, get out."

Loud pounding comes from the front door again.

I give Nysara a nod and then dart towards the back door. Pulling my hood up, I unlock the door and slip out.

"Karleus," Nysara says from inside the house. Her voice is now husky and seductive. "What in Azaroth's name are you doing here at this time of night?"

"I saw the light burning in your window," the man, Karleus, replies. "And I thought you might have fallen ill or injured yourself or that you had forgotten to blow out the candles and I was worried that—"

I quietly close the back door behind me and sprint across the lawn.

Cold night winds tug at my cloak as I jump over the small stone fence at the back of Nysara's property and then disappear down the street in the other direction.

One mission done.

Once we get out of the castle, we now have a way out of the city.

But my work tonight is not finished. I'm going to turn this whole damn city into a boiling pot of anger and resentment, so that when the humans pull off their heist, it will be the spark that sets an entire rebellion ablaze.

# CHAPTER TWENTY-SIX

Warmth from the roaring hearth flows across the already packed tavern, making me sweat underneath my thick black cloak. I push the fabric away from my legs and arms as much as I can where I'm seated in one of the booths at the back of the room. But unfortunately, I can't lower the hood since it's the only thing keeping my pointed ears and my glowing two-colored eyes hidden from the rest of the patrons here.

While cupping my hands around a mug of ale that I swiped from a deserted table when I arrived, I keep my head slightly bowed to further shield my eyes from view as I continue to pour my magic into the pale red flames of anger that now burn intently in everyone's chests.

When I got here, most humans in this tavern were just tired from a long day at work. Some were even in a fairly good mood. But after a few strategic whispers to a few strategic tables in the middle, and a steady stream of my magic, this entire tavern is now pulsing with pent-up rage. I keep feeding it.

"We need to do something," a human man whispers to his companion at the table next to mine. "This is our city. It was our city long before the Icehearts came with their Silver Clan and took everything. Our ancestors built it with their sweat and blood and tears. And now, we are second-class citizens in our own home. We need to take it back."

His companion nods, but there is worry in his voice when he replies, "I agree. But would we even stand a chance? They're fucking dragons, mate."

"I know. But we are the majority."

I let the connection to everyone's anger fade and instead push at the tiny sparks of courage in these two men's chests. Pouring my magic into them, I let those courageous sparks flare into wildfires.

The first man thumps his fist against the table while determination pulses across his face. "Come on, let's start tonight. I have an idea."

Chairs scrape against the wooden floorboards as the two of them shoot to their feet and stride towards the door with determined steps.

Bowing my head even more, I hide the villainous smile that spreads across my lips.

All around me, people are discussing and arguing and complaining with angry voices. Even though I have already cut off my steady flow of magic, the effect of it still remains. Because once I blow that spark of rage into a massive fire, it takes time for it to die down on its own.

Firelight from the hearth flickers across the pale wooden furniture and the angry faces all around me. I can't hear what all groups are saying, but because I set the stage with my strategic whispers earlier, I'm assuming that most of them are angry at the Iceheart Dynasty.

"Azaroth's flame, I hate them so fucking much," a male voice snaps to my left.

My heart leaps into my throat. Only dragon shifters curse by Azaroth. While still keeping my head down and my hood up, I discreetly glance towards the left.

The empty table where the two human men used to sit is still unoccupied, which now allows me to see the table behind it. Four male dragon shifters are seated there. Two with brown hair, one with blond hair, and one with silver hair. All of them look incredibly angry.

I curse silently in my mind. I didn't know that there were dragon shifters in this tavern too. When I manipulated people's anger, I did it to everyone in here since that was the most efficient option. But that means that I have been increasing these dragon shifters' anger as well.

"If they hadn't used dragon steel on us, we wouldn't have to live in this fucking city full of dirty, wrinkly, and uncivilized humans," the brown-haired one with orange eyes continues.

"That's right," the blond one growls while clenching his fist. "If we didn't have to fight that fucking war to free ourselves, we wouldn't have had to burn our ancestral lands to the ground."

My heart skips a beat. They burned their homeland in the war?

A sudden thought crackles through me.

Is that why they went back and took Lavendera too? Because they found out that she has tree magic and they're planning to use her to restore their homeland?

"Fuck, did you see that silver-haired bitch at the banquet?" Orange Eyes says. "All dressed up in a pretty ballgown, as if she isn't a savage like the rest of her people. Fuck, I hate her so much."

"At least Commander Ryat put her in her place," Blondie says.

Orange Eyes snickers. "Watching her crawl and lick his boots was the most satisfying thing I've seen all year."

The other three laugh. It's a mocking and vicious sound.

My head goes unnaturally silent. Because I suddenly realize who they're talking about.

Me.

They are talking about *me*.

The shifter with silver hair leans back in his seat and stretches his arms above his head. "Agreed."

"If she was my slave, I would fucking humiliate her," Orange Eyes continues, his voice laced with malice. "I would rip that fucking dress off her and make her walk naked everywhere. Nah, actually, I wouldn't even let her walk. I'd make her crawl on all fours everywhere. That'd teach her. That'd show her that she's nothing more than a filthy savage animal."

The others laugh again.

Pain pulses through my entire chest, and treacherous tears press against my eyes.

These people hate me. They don't even know me. But they *hate* me.

Iron bands squeeze around my heart until I can barely breathe through a sudden sense of searing hurt.

Deep down, I know that it's ridiculous and pathetic and that I shouldn't feel like this. But hearing how much these people hate me, people who have never even spoken to me and who know absolutely nothing about me, hurts. Deeply.

That desperate little girl inside me still wants people to like me. It's stupid, I know that. I shouldn't care about other people's opinions of me. But I do.

I guess that's what happens when you grow up being taught that everything is your fault and that you need to atone.

Bitterness floods my veins, and I desperately lean into that hardness that I started to build around my heart at the end of the Atonement Trials.

Why should I care what these people think?

Why is their opinion of me worth more than my own, when I know myself better than they do?

"That's it!" a man suddenly screams somewhere to my right. "I've fucking had it!"

I whip my head towards him. As does the rest of the tavern.

A muscular human man in stained worker's clothes is stalking towards the four dragon shifters on my left.

"This is our pub," he declares, and stabs a hand at the shifters. "Go drink somewhere else."

Wood grinds against wood as the four dragon shifters push back their chairs and shoot to their feet, rage pulsing across their faces as well.

"Your pub?" Orange Eyes echoes.

"Yeah," the human replies, he swings his arm to the side and points to the door instead. "So go find your own."

My heart patters against my ribs. Mabona's tits. They're going to start a fight right here. I can't get caught in the middle of this.

Sliding out of my chair, I discreetly try to slink away. But I'm trapped between them and the wall. I flick my gaze from side to side as two more humans close in on the shifters.

"You heard him," one of them says.

Keeping my head down, I hurry past behind him while the shifters are focused on the humans.

"Back off!" the silver-haired shifter bellows right as I dart past.

Something heavy hits me in the side.

I gasp and stumble sideways as one of the humans suddenly slams into me from the side after he was shoved back by the dragon shifter. The shove catches him so off guard that he doesn't even try to stay on his feet. He topples backwards, crashing into me and making us both hit the floor.

Steel rings as the four shifters grab the swords that they had kept leaning against their table.

Panic pulses through me. Pushing against the human's weight, I try to free myself from his body. He finally rolls off me and jumps to his feet. I suck in a deep breath to refill my lungs and sit up as well.

A collective gasp echoes across the tavern.

I whip my head up, expecting to find that the shifters have

started killing the human men who confronted them. But instead, I find something worse.

They're all staring at me.

Yanking a hand up, I reach for the hood of my cloak. Terror washes through me like ice when I don't find it. It was knocked down when I hit the ground, and now, my head is fully visible.

And so are my ears.

"You," the brown-haired shifter with orange eyes says, sounding both shocked and furious at the same time. His gaze is locked on me.

I swallow.

"Everybody out!" Blondie bellows, and swings his sword through the air until it's pointed towards the door. "Now!"

For a moment, everything is dead silent and still.

My heart pounds in my chest where I still remain on the floor. And for one single second, I'm convinced that the humans in this tavern will come to my aid.

But they don't.

Even with the rage I have built up inside them with my magic, they still decide that trying to fight four dragon shifters with swords while they themselves are unarmed, just to help a fae woman who they don't even know, would be stupid.

Boots thud against the pale wooden floorboards as they all run out the door instead, leaving me alone with four dragon shifters. Firelight from the burning hearth glints against the swords they're pointing at me.

I scramble to my feet.

"Don't even think about it," Silver Hair says when I flick a glance towards the still open door to the tavern.

And with one step to the side, he has put himself firmly between me and the only exit.

Fear spreads through my body like poison as I back across the room instead.

These people have spent a good portion of their night talking about how much they hate me and what they would do to me if I was their slave, and now they have me cornered and alone.

Whipping my head from side to side, I try to find a stray knife on one of the tables around me. But only mugs and spoons and bowls stare back at me uselessly.

The rage that I unwittingly increased in their chests earlier burns in their eyes as they advance on me.

Calling up my magic, I push at those pale red flames of anger in their chests and decrease them until they're only tiny sparks.

But to my horror, all that does is to sharpen their expressions into something cold and ruthless instead. Without the burning anger making them uncoordinated and lost in blind rage, they instead start thinking tactically and spread out so that they are coming at me from all sides.

I drag in panicked breaths as I have to stop backing away when Silver Hair sprints across the room so that he is behind me instead. Blondie now blocks the route to the door while the two brown-haired ones advance from the other side. Cold calculation shines in their eyes now that I have removed their blinding rage.

Oh Goddess, I shouldn't have decreased their anger. I shouldn't have increased it in the first place. I should have seen that there were dragon shifters in here earlier. I should have left sooner. I should have done a million things differently. And now, I'm going to die.

Fear and terror crackles through my body like lightning. I need to use my magic or find a weapon or an escape. Or something. Anything. But I can't think properly. I need to—

The two brown-haired men lunge at me.

I leap back. My body hits the table behind me hard enough to make the chairs topple. Wooden clattering echoes between the pale walls as the chairs hit the ground while I throw myself to the side. A sword cuts through the air in the space where my chest used to be mere seconds ago.

Orange Eyes snarls as he yanks his sword back and spins towards me.

"My ancestors lived like animals because of you," he growls as he advances on me. "They were forced to humiliate themselves and our entire family line because of your mind-control and your fucking dragon steel. And half of them died in the Liberation War." His eyes gleam with malice as he stares me down while stalking towards me. "I should do the same to you."

The back of my neck prickles.

On instinct, I duck and dive to the side right before Blondie can grab me from behind. His arms whoosh through the air where I used to stand while I roll to my feet two steps away. But Silver Hair was already moving.

The moment I leap to my feet again, he is already behind me. Panic pulses through my body when he grabs my arms from behind. Kicking blindly, I try to hit his shin or his crotch or anything I can reach. A hiss rips from his throat as my heel slams into something. But his grip on my arms only gets harder.

Reaching for my magic, I try to think of something that will help me. Some kind of emotion that will make them release me. But before I can even come up with something, pain spikes through my cheek and my head snaps to the side as Orange Eyes backhands me across the mouth.

The sudden hit makes my ears ring, and I lose the grip on my magic. Blinking furiously, I yank against the hands keeping my arms trapped while I kick blindly at anything within reach.

But then I stop suddenly when cold steel presses against the base of my throat.

When my vision clears, I find Orange Eyes standing in front of me with his sword at my throat. The other brown-haired man and the blond one have taken up position next to Silver Hair. Cold malice pulses from their entire souls as they stare me down.

Orange Eyes presses the tip of his sword harder against my skin. "This is going to hurt."

Terror freezes my whole body. I can't think. I can't fight. I can't flee. I can't do anything other than stare at the sword before me while my heart is threatening to crack my ribs. He's going to kill me.

A scream of agony splits the air. In the dead silence, it's so shockingly loud that it makes my ears ring. For one second, I fear that the scream might have been mine.

But then the sword that Orange Eyes is holding starts moving.

It falls straight down to the floor.

And so does his hand.

## CHAPTER TWENTY-SEVEN

Utter shock clangs inside my skull as I watch his severed hand fall to the floor. It lands with a thud, which is drowned out by the metallic clattering as the sword hits the pale wooden floorboards. And by the scream that comes out of his throat too, of course.

A grunt sounds from right next to me.

I flinch as blood splatters my left cheek.

The hands gripping my arms disappear as Silver Hair yells something while whirling around towards the other brown-haired shifter who was standing on my left. His quick movements as he releases my arms while turning makes me spin in that direction as well.

My eyes widen as I come face to face with the brown-haired shifter. His mouth is open in shock. And a sword sticks out of his throat.

A wet sliding sound fills the single second of dead silence as it's yanked back out. The shifter collapses to the ground right before my feet. I stare down at him while Orange Eyes continues screaming his lungs out and clutching his severed wrist.

In the brief pauses between his screaming, I hear a whooshing sound. While I'm still staring dumbfounded down at the dead man before me, a head thuds down on the floor beside him. Not a body. Just a head. The head of a male shifter with silver hair.

Then the body hits.

And more screaming starts.

I drag my gaze back up to the source of all this carnage.

The Shadow of Death stands there before me, his massive black wings spread wide and his sword stained with blood. His golden eyes burn with such fury and vengeance that it stops my heart for a second. But he's not looking at me.

Dark clouds gather around him and white lightning crackles down his arms as he shifts his gaze between my two remaining assailants.

Blondie cuts and runs towards the door.

Orange Eyes drops to his knees.

With barely more than a glance, Draven yanks out a knife from his thigh holster and throws it at Blondie. It hits him straight through the back of his neck. A gurgle sounds. Then he crashes to the ground, his body spasming.

Draven slides his gaze to my face.

I suck in a sharp breath at the furious intensity of his stare.

Then he sees the blood splattered across my cheek, and his expression darkens into death itself. The storm clouds whip around him like thrashing snakes, and lightning cracks into the floor.

"Please," Orange Eyes begs on the ground, still desperately clutching his bleeding stump. "Please, don't—"

Draven cuts his head off.

It hits the floor with a wet thud and rolls halfway before it comes to a halt next to Silver Hair's severed head. His body tips forward and crashes down as well. The dark clouds disappear and the lightning stops.

Then everything is dead silent.

My heart pounds as I just stand there on the blood-soaked

floor and stare at Draven. Across the room, the fire in the hearth still burns brightly, casting dancing light across the pale wooden walls.

In one fluid motion, Draven wipes the blood off his sword and slams it back into its sheath while he closes the distance between us.

I tense up, bracing myself for… For what? For him to grab me and handcuff me? For him to yell at me? For him to threaten me and demand to know what the hell I'm doing here?

He does none of those things.

Instead, he cups my cheeks with such heartbreaking gentleness that I almost sob.

Turning my head from side to side, he studies my face with those intense eyes of his. "Are you hurt?"

Out of all the things I had expected him to say, that hadn't even been on the list. I thought he would be furious. Instead, he's asking if I'm hurt.

"Selena, look at me." Worry pulses in his eyes as he wipes something off my cheek. "Are you hurt?"

I blink again, still trying to wrap my head around this whole situation. And then I finally remember that there was blood splattered across my face. Draven is still cupping my cheeks, but I shake my head as best as I can.

"No," I finally reply. "The blood wasn't mine."

Relief washes over his features. For another few seconds, he just holds me like that. Then he drags in a breath and lets his hands drop from my cheeks. Taking a step back, he gives his head a quick shake as if to clear it.

"We need to go," he says as he strides over to Blondie's corpse and yanks his knife out of the guy's neck. After wiping off the blade and sticking it back in his thigh holster, he turns back to me. "Now."

Pulling myself out of my stunned stupor, I give my own head a few quick shakes to clear it as well and then hurry across the floor towards where Draven is. He sweeps his gaze around the room one more time, presumably to check that no one witnessed what he did, and then he stalks out onto the street. I follow him.

But instead of continuing away from the tavern, he comes to a halt right outside on the street. It's so sudden that I slam right into him after exiting the tavern.

His hands shoot out and grab my arms to steady me. I quickly pull my arms out of his grip and take a step back. But I'm only met by an unreadable expression when I tilt my head back and look up at him again.

"Do you trust me?" he asks.

The question catches me completely off guard, and I shock myself by replying, "Yes."

That blank mask on his face cracks for the briefest of moments as shock pulses across his features as well. Then he wipes the expression off his face and instead crouches down.

My heart flips as he slides one arm behind my knees and the other behind my back. Heat creeps into my cheeks as he lifts me into his arms as if it's the most natural thing in the world.

I open my mouth to ask what in Mabona's name he's doing.

But only a gasp makes it out as he flaps his wings and launches into the air.

My stomach lurches as we shoot up from the ground. Throwing my arms around his neck, I grip him tightly and squeeze my eyes shut as the city grows smaller beneath us.

A soft laugh rolls from his chest. "Afraid of heights?"

With great effort, I pry my eyes open again. Winds rush around us, tugging at my cloak and my hair as Draven flies us even higher. Light from the bright moon casts silver highlights in his black hair.

I shoot him a glare and try to sound convincing as I reply, "No. I got over all of that when I spent hours being flown here from the Seelie Court by dragons who gripped me with their talons."

A smirk plays over Draven's lips. "Is that right?"

"Yes, and you—"

My retort is cut off when I suck in a sharp breath between my teeth as Draven abruptly flaps his wings hard, bringing us even higher. I tighten my arms around his neck and press my cheek against his shoulder while squeezing my eyes shut again.

Draven chuckles. "You were saying?"

"Bastard," I mutter against his neck before forcing myself to raise my head and open my eyes again. When I do, I find him smirking at me.

His eyes glitter in the moonlight as he arches a dark brow at me. "Do you really think that insulting me is your best move here, little rebel?"

I give him a pointed look back. "I thought we had already established that being snarky and disrespectful is my natural state."

A short laugh escapes his lips, and he shakes his head at me.

Winds wash over us as he flies us towards the gleaming ice castle on the mountain slope. I keep my arms around his neck, but his own arms are so steady underneath me that I finally dare to look at the landscape around us.

A strange sense of freedom and peace flows through my veins as I gaze out at the moonlit plains that stretch out around the city. Up here, it feels as if I have the entire world at my feet. As if anything is possible. Lakes shine like pools of silver in the moonlight, and distant forests look like dark pillows in the grassland. Countless stars sparkle above us like silver dust.

The horizon feels endless. As if I could just fly straight for it and disappear from all of the pain and struggle and danger that has surrounded me every day of my life.

Tearing my gaze from the horizon, I shift it back to Draven.

My heart almost leaps out of my chest when I find him studying me.

Then it starts thumping hard when I see the look in his eyes.

He is watching me as if I am the only thing in this world. As if the stunning landscape around us pales in comparison to my face. As if he could spend his entire life watching the expression on my face when I marvel at the world around us.

And the sight of it makes my heart tighten and my lungs stop.

The way he is looking at me is implying too many things. Things I can't dare to let myself consider.

So I drag in a strangled breath and blurt out something that I know will ruin the moment. "Why aren't you angry with me? I tried to escape from you and almost got myself killed in the process. Why aren't you angry?"

Just as I thought, that incredible look on his face disappears in a heartbeat. And instead, some of that fire from before returns to his eyes as he locks them on mine.

"Oh I am angry," he replies, his voice now filled with steel. "I'm just saving it for when we're behind closed doors."

My answer is cut off by a gasp as Draven suddenly dives downwards. My stomach lurches as we speed down through the air. I squeeze my eyes shut again and my arms tighten around him.

But just as abruptly as it began, the downward plummet stops. And so does the beating of his wings.

Prying my eyes open, I find us standing on the balcony to Draven's rooms. Or rather, Draven standing on it while he still holds me in his arms. I swallow as he stalks in through the door and then sets me down on the living room floor.

I'm still breathless from the sudden dive, so I take a few seconds to drag air into my lungs while Draven shuts the balcony door behind us. While he locks it as well, I turn on the faelights so that we can see better and then take off my cloak and toss it across the back of the sofa. Then I run my fingers through my windblown hair a couple of times.

Draven straightens by the door.

"Now…" he begins.

And his whole demeanor changes in the span of a second. Gone is that wonderful look from when he watched me gaze at the landscape. The man who turns to face me now is not an ordinary dragon shifter. It's the Shadow of Death. The Commander of the Dread Legion. A man who gives orders and expects them to be obeyed.

Drawing himself up to his full height, he crosses his muscular arms over his broad chest and levels a commanding stare on me.

"What the hell were you thinking?" he demands.

His presumptuous tone, as if he's speaking to some fresh recruit that he commands, immediately sets my teeth on edge.

"We had a deal," he continues, his voice hard. Uncrossing his arms, he motions at the living room around us. "In here, you can do whatever the hell you want." He shifts his hand and stabs it towards the door. "But out in public, you need to—"

"Act as if I'm your slave," I snap, interrupting him. "I know."

"Clearly you don't."

Since I can't tell him what I was really doing out there, I need to make him think that I was only trying to escape. So I throw my arms out in frustration and raise my voice. "What did you expect? Huh? That I would just stay here like your slave forever? That I would never try to escape?"

"I expected you to use your head!"

That stuns me enough that I just draw back and blink at him. He forces out a frustrated breath and stalks forward, closing the distance between us. The soft faelights gleam against the white ice walls, creating a surreal calm around us while everything inside me feels like it's a thrashing stormy sea. My heart pounds so hard that I can hear it in my ears.

Draven comes to a halt in front of me, barely a step away. Taking my chin in a firm grip, he tilts my head back so that I meet his gaze. His eyes are hard as steel as he locks them on me.

"I expected you to use your head," he repeats. "You're smart. Way smarter than most people give you credit for."

"How would you know?" I slap his hand away from my chin. "You don't even know me."

For a moment, I swear I see a flicker of hurt in his eyes. But then he just arches an eyebrow at me. "I watched you win the Atonement Trials. Remember?" Holding my gaze, he shakes his head as if in disbelief. "A tournament that, in terms of just pure magic type, you shouldn't even have made it past the first power demonstration. But because you're so damn smart and sneaky and cunning, you managed to win the whole bloody thing. Even despite all of my interference."

I know that we're fighting, and I know that he's angry, but his unexpected praise hits something deep inside my chest. Something that makes it hard to breathe. Because everyone else only sees the pathetic girl with weak and untrustworthy emotion magic who is desperate to be liked. But Draven... he sees *that* instead.

He reaches for my chin again, but then changes his mind halfway up and just lets his arm drop again. Flexing his hand, he drags in a long breath through his nose.

"So I expected you to use that brilliant mind of yours," he continues, pushing our argument back on track again. "What were you planning to do? Huh? Walk back to the Seelie Court? Do you even know where it is? Or how to get there? And how were you even going to get out of the city? The Silver Clan guards every road out of here. And they patrol the skies around the city too. You wouldn't even have made it a hundred yards out onto the plains before they spotted you."

Since I can't tell him that I wasn't really trying to escape, I just cross my arms and glare up at him in angry silence.

He forces out a breath and rakes his hands through his hair before once again shaking his head at me. "Azaroth's flame, you could have been killed."

"I know."

"Do you? What would you have done if I hadn't shown up right at that moment?"

"I…" I begin but then trail off as a sudden thought blows through my mind. Narrowing my eyes, I study Draven with a suspicious gaze. "Speaking of… How did you find me?"

He opens his mouth but then just frowns instead. Drawing his eyebrows down, he levels a scowl at me. But he looks distinctly uncomfortable.

"I just happened to be passing by and heard the ruckus," he tries to say convincingly before quickly adding, "But that's not the point. The point is—"

"No," I interrupt. Uncrossing my arms, I stab two fingers against his chest while annoyance and dread and anticipation all twist inside my chest like snakes. My heart is suddenly pounding again. "Don't try to change the subject. How did you find me?"

"I've already told you. I heard the fight."

"Don't give me that fucking excuse again!" I stab my fingers against his muscular chest once more while I level a searing gaze on him. "How did you know that I was in danger and where to find me?"

Reaching up, he wraps a strong hand around my wrist and yanks my hand down from his chest. "This conversation is over."

"No, it's not. This is the third time now. First, you saved me when Jeb and Tommen attacked me in my room during the Atonement Trials. Then, you saved me again when I was about to be killed by a wolfbear out in the thorn forest. And now, right when I was about to get killed by a group of dragon shifters, you magically show up again." I hold his gaze with dead serious eyes. "How did you know that I was in danger and where to find me?"

He releases my wrist and starts stalking away towards his bedroom.

"Don't you dare walk away from me!" I scream at his back.

He just keeps walking.

"How did you find me?" I yell again.

He flexes his hand as he stalks away.

A snarl rips from my throat. Lurching forward, I close the short distance between us again and grab his arm. With all my strength, I yank on it, spinning him back around to face me.

"How did you know that I was in danger?" I shout at him again. "How did you know where I was?"

"Because you're my mate!"

I jerk back as if his words had been a physical hit. Releasing his arm, I stagger a step back while the air seems to freeze in my lungs. My head is ringing. And everything else is unnaturally silent.

Draven stands there just one step in front of me. His chest heaves as if he has sprinted across half the continent. And the utter desperation on his face as he looks at me strangles what little air I had left in my lungs.

"What?" is all that makes it out of my mouth. It's barely more than a broken whisper.

"You're my mate." Draven drags in an unsteady breath and then slowly shakes his head. "When Jeb and Tommen attacked you, when the wolfbear attacked you, when those four assholes attacked you tonight... I could feel your fear."

"You can feel my emotions?"

"No, I can't feel all your emotions. I can't even feel all your fear. Right now, I can only feel the strongest of your emotions. Which is the sheer undiluted terror that comes when you're about to die."

My heart is beating so hard that I can barely even hear Draven over the loud pounding in my ears.

"That's how I knew you were in danger," he continues. "And where to find you."

I stare back at him. I can't remember if I have been breathing, so I drag in a deep breath. Apparently, I hadn't breathed in a while because my lungs expand in relief. I force in another breath while the massive bells inside my skull continue clanging.

"Because I'm your mate," I finish for him, the words coming out in a strangled whisper.

That pain and desperation flicker across Draven's face for a moment. Then he repeats, so softly that my heart aches, "Because you're my mate."

Staggering another step back, I grip the dark grey armchair next to me for support. My fingers dig into the soft cushion as I force air into my lungs while my mind keeps spinning.

I know about the concept of fated mates. Two people who are destined to be with each other and who share a deeper connection than just normal love. Two souls drawn to each other in some epic bond. While I have never actually talked to a fae who has found their fated mate, both our race and dragon shifters have them. Though they're much more common among the dragon shifters. And I had no idea that a cross-species connection was even possible.

And most importantly, I *hate* the concept of fated mates. Free will is too important to me. I hate the thought of someone else, some other power out in the universe, deciding who I can and can't love.

"No," I blurt out. It comes out as a desperate sob. "I'm not your mate! I don't want to be your mate!"

Pure hurt pulses across Draven's face. He swallows but says nothing.

And part of me knows that I should feel bad about that. Part of me knows that what I just said was cruel. But that part of me is currently suffocating underneath a tidal wave of utter panic and devastation.

All my life, I have lived by someone else's rules. I have never had any freedom. For anything. I haven't been allowed to choose my job or my clothes or where to live or even when to eat. Everything has been controlled by someone else. So the thought that someone else, some mystical power, has chosen who I'm supposed to love threatens to destroy me.

I can't breathe. I want to rip my heart out of my chest. I want to bawl my eyes out.

After an entire lifetime of having no choices, no say in my own life, the knowledge that even my ability to choose who to love has been taken from me is going to break me.

"How did…" I begin.

But then I trail off as a realization, a horrifying realization, crackles through my whole body like a vicious lightning bolt. It's so intense that I think I gasp. Gripping the back of the armchair harder, I try to steady myself as I force in a deep breath and then drag my gaze back to Draven.

"Is that why you tried to stop me from winning the Atonement Trials?" I breathe, my eyes wide as I stare at him. "Is that why you tried to save me from this fate? Because I'm your mate?"

Draven opens his mouth to reply, but then he appears to change his mind and instead just shifts his weight awkwardly and glances away. Which I suppose is answer enough.

Something between a sob and a broken laugh rips from my throat.

All this time, I actually thought that he had tried to save me from this fate because he genuinely cared about me. Because he saw something in me. Because he got to know me during the Atonement Trials and began to like me for who I was. Began to like me because he saw who I really am. Saw the parts of me that no one else ever does. And liked it.

But instead… Instead, he only tried to save me because this damn mate bond between us was forcing his instincts to protect me.

Something small and very fragile inside my chest just… cracks.

And the pain of it is so intense that I have to bend over and brace one hand on my thigh as I drag in a shuddering breath. Prying my other hand off the armchair, I press it over my heart and grip my shirt hard. But it does nothing to stem the pain that bleeds from that fragile shattered piece inside me.

I thought that I had finally met someone who genuinely saw me and understood me and wanted to be close to me instead of keeping me at arm's length because of my magic type. But now I will never know what Draven and I might have been to each other. What we might have felt about each other on our own. Because the fucking universe has already decided for us what we should feel.

"Selena," Draven whispers, and his hand brushes against my arm so gently that I almost start crying.

Instead, I pull anger around me like a shield as I straighten and slap his hand away. "Don't touch me."

Hurt pulses in his eyes again, but he lets his hand drop. And he says nothing.

Shaking my head, I start backing towards my bedroom. "I will sleep in this room tonight."

"Don't," he begins, desperation lacing his voice.

That utter desperation shocks me enough that I hesitate. Which only makes me even more angry, so I end up snapping, "You're going to force me to sleep in your bed? Because I'm your mate and that means I belong to you?"

He rocks back slightly as if I had slapped him.

Regret and guilt worm their way through my chest. I stamp them out.

Draven swallows and then draws in a breath as if bracing himself. "No, I'm not. I'm *asking you* to sleep in my bed."

"Why?"

"Because I felt your fear. I felt every second of your heart-wrenching terror when you thought you were going to die, and I just... I just need to know that you're safe." Desperation shines in his eyes as he holds my gaze. "Please."

My heart squeezes hard.

And deep down, I know that I'm being cruel and utterly

unfair. I know that I'm taking my pain and anger out on the wrong person. After all, it's not Draven's fault that I'm his mate. He had as little choice in this as I did.

So in the end, I find myself whispering, "Okay."

Relief washes over his features, and he gives me a small nod. Then he disappears into his bedroom without another word.

After I have gotten ready for the night and put on that short black nightgown, I slip into Draven's room.

Part of me is hoping that he has already fallen asleep. But the moment I step across the threshold, his intense eyes immediately lock on me. As if he was worried that I was going to go back on my word and sleep in the other room anyway.

Pushing the dark gray cover aside, I climb into bed and roll over on my side so that my back is to Draven. He says nothing. Neither do I.

Oppressive silence hangs over the entire room.

Just like every night, Draven has shifted into his fully human form and sleeps only on his side of the bed while I remain firmly on mine. But tonight, I can feel his eyes burning holes through my body as I lie there with my back to him. I half expect him to wrap his arms around me and pull me close. Part of me wants him to. The other part wants to scream into the abyss until I taste blood.

Because I don't know what's real anymore.

I've felt drawn to Draven for weeks now, and I thought that it was because part of me liked him. Liked who he is. Even the ruthless and domineering sides of him. Especially the ruthless and domineering sides of him.

But now I don't know anymore. Did I only feel drawn to him because of this accursed mate bond?

A sudden and bitterly ironic realization crawls up my throat like bile.

This, what I'm feeling right now, must be what my parents felt all the time while I was growing up. This maddening sensation of never knowing if their feelings were real or if they were just the result of me unwittingly manipulating them with my magic.

In fact, this must be how *everyone* feels when they're around me.

Harsh laughter, tasting of blood and acid, escapes my throat. Tears sting my eyes as I bury my cheek deeper in the pillow.

After what I did to my parents, I suppose I deserve this.

At least the universe has a fucking sense of humor.

# CHAPTER TWENTY-EIGHT

**S**trong arms are wrapped around me. I blink, trying to remember where I am. A pale ice wall on the other side of a room with dark wooden floorboards. A soft bed with dark gray sheets. And a warm muscular body pressed tightly against my back.

That confused sleepiness is swept away like mist by a strong morning wind, and I'm suddenly wide awake.

Draven.

At some point during the night, he did what I suspected he wanted to do last night. He wrapped his arms around me and pulled me close.

Since I'm only wearing that short silk nightgown, and he is only wearing a pair of underwear, I can feel every ridge and every curve of his body as he holds me tightly. His forearm is positioned along my chest, between my breasts, and his hand is resting straight over my heart. As if he needs to feel it beating in there to reassure himself that I'm still alive.

And it all feels so… natural.

Part of me wants to be shocked and outraged that he wrapped his arms around me. That I can feel his muscular chest rise and fall against my back. That I can feel his cock pressing against my ass. That he touches me this intimately. But the other part of me never wants to leave this bed. Wants him to hold me like this every night. Because it feels *right*.

My chest tightens as an entire wave of conflicting feelings crash over me.

Dragging in a strangled breath, I try to keep from drowning underneath the weight of it all.

My feelings for Draven were already complicated before he revealed the truth about this stupid mate bond. I feel free and strong and powerful when I'm with him. Which is an incredibly impressive feat considering that I am literally his prisoner right now. But there is something about him, something about how he sees me and how he treats me, that makes me feel, for the first time in my life, that I don't have to hold myself back. I don't have to make myself smaller for him to accept me. On the contrary, he challenges me to take up even more space. To say what I really think. Do what I really want. Be who I really am.

But at the same time, he ranks in the top three of my biggest enemies. He and Bane and Jessina are the biggest threats to our resistance movement and the biggest obstacles to freeing the Seelie Court. In order to overthrow the Iceheart Dynasty, we would need to neutralize Draven. Which means either capture him or kill him. Or turn him. But from what I've seen, he has no intention of ever leaving the Icehearts. He is actively, and with almost single-minded determination, hunting the most important human resistance fighter. He is standing in the way of everything I want to achieve.

And as if that wasn't enough, now I find out that I'm his fated mate. Which means that those feelings I had started to develop might not even be real. They might just be a side effect of the mate bond. Just like his feelings for me.

I heave a frustrated sigh. Goddess damn it. Why does everything have to be so fucking complicated?

Draven stirs behind me. I wait for him to yank his arms back and scramble out of bed when he realizes what he's doing. But he doesn't.

A low contented groan comes from deep within his chest, and he pulls me even closer and buries his face in my neck.

My heart does a backflip in my chest.

Draven draws in a deep breath through his nose, as if he is breathing me in, and when he lets it out, his warm breath caresses the sensitive skin on my neck. A pleasant shudder rolls down my spine.

He stiffens behind me.

For a few heart-pounding seconds, he remains still as a statue. Then he does what I assumed he would. He yanks his arms back and quickly rolls back to his side of the bed.

The sudden loss of his warm body against mine is like having a bucket of ice water dumped over me. I quickly scramble out of bed as well.

My heart patters against my ribs as I straighten on the floor. Draven is standing on the other side of the bed, watching me with such a raw expression on his handsome face that I feel like someone is strangling my heart again.

How much of those emotions in his eyes are his actual feelings and how much is just an involuntary instinct caused by the mate bond?

Every day, I find out something that shatters my worldview over and over again. Is anything even real?

Draven opens his mouth to say something, but I can't bear to hear what it is. So before he can get a single word out, I blurt out a question that I know will just make everything worse. But I ask it anyway.

"Are you sterilizing us?"

Draven flinches as if I had slapped him. Pain flickers in his eyes for a second, but when he replies, there is steel in his voice. "*I* am not sterilizing anyone." His tone softens. "But yes, they have created a selective breeding system to produce stronger magical bloodlines."

After what Lavendera told me down in the kennels, I already knew that it was true. That the shifters are sterilizing us after we have given birth to one child both to keep our population from outgrowing the city and also to create stronger magic users for them to drain. But hearing Draven confirm it like that is like a blow to the chest.

Staggering back a step, I have to brace myself on the nightstand as I draw in an unsteady breath and echo, "*A selective breeding system.*"

Draven winces. "That's not what I meant."

"That's exactly what you meant," I accuse, anger rising inside me to cover the pain. I pull it eagerly around me like a shield to stop my heart from breaking completely. "You're breeding us. Like cattle!"

"*I* am not doing any of that," Draven replies, the steel returning to his voice as he holds my gaze with serious eyes. "And I don't approve of it either."

"But you're helping them! You're keeping them in power. You're serving them, for Mabona's sake. Like an eager little lapdog."

Draven forces out a frustrated breath and stalks around the bed, closing the distance between us. "I have already told you. I don't have a choice."

"Everyone has a choice!" I snap as he comes to a halt in front of me. Raising a hand, I stab an accusatory finger against his firm chest. "And whether you want to admit it or not, you are *choosing* to serve them. The consequences if you don't do as they say might be awful, which is why you feel like you don't have a choice, but you do have a choice."

Anger flashes in his eyes like lightning. Opening his mouth, he gets ready to retort. But he must see the truth in my words, because in the end, he just closes his mouth again and flexes his hand in annoyance while forcing out another frustrated breath.

Raking his fingers through his hair, he shakes his head and instead changes the subject. "What about your own blind trust?"

I stare back at him. "*My* blind trust?"

"Yes! I know that you're smart, which is why I can't for the life of me figure out why you didn't use that brilliant mind of yours *before* you entered the Atonement Trials."

"We were *all* fooled by the Atonement Trials," I snap back.

"That's because you never question anything!" Desperation now drowns out the anger as he shakes his head in disbelief. "Like why did no one ever come back to visit after they won the tournament? Or send a letter or something? If people have been winning the Atonement Trials for centuries, how come not one single person ever contacted the loved ones they left behind?"

His words are a knife straight to the gut. Because he's right. I had never even thought about that. Let alone questioned it.

That desperation pulses in his eyes as he holds my gaze. "If you had just questioned things before it was too late, none of this would have happened. So I need you to start using that head of yours. I need you to start questioning things that don't make sense. Please."

My head is pounding. It feels as if giant metal bells are clanging somewhere in there inside my skull. It's so loud that I can barely hear anything.

Because Draven is right. Goddess damn it, as much as I hate to admit it, Draven is right.

There are so many things that I never questioned. So many things that I just accepted as fact. Simply because someone told me that it was true.

But now that I look back on it from the outside, I realize that everything I know, everything that all fae know in the Seelie Court, has been taught to us by dragon shifters. There were no fae teachers at school. Only dragon shifters. They taught us everything we know. Everything we know about our own history, our culture, and our biology. Everything.

Panic crawls up my throat.

I suck in a breath. But no air makes it into my lungs. I drag in another panicked breath, but just like the last one, it never makes it past my throat. Another wave of panic slams into me, and I desperately try to force air into my lungs. But it feels as if an iron fist is gripping my windpipe, strangling me.

Stumbling backwards, I crash back first into the pale ice wall behind me. No matter how fast I breathe, nothing makes it down into my lungs. I throw my hands out and brace myself against the cool wall behind me while I desperately try to breathe through the panic.

Draven's hand appears underneath my chin, raising my head. Worry swirls in his eyes when I meet his gaze.

"Selena," he begins.

"Nothing is real," I gasp out.

My chest heaves as I suck in rapid breaths that never make it past my throat. I curl my fingers into fists against the wall as my legs wobble.

"Selena," Draven says, more forcefully this time. "You need to slow your breathing."

But I can barely even process his words because I still can't get any air through my throat and down into my lungs. My hands begin to tingle. Panic crackles through me. I suck in even faster breaths.

"Nothing is real," I gasp out again. A choked sob rips from my constricted throat. "Goddess above, nothing is real."

It all just crashes down on top of me at the same time. The truth about the Atonement Trials. What really happened to Isera's mother and all the other fae who won. That we are biologically able to have more than one child but that the Icehearts are sterilizing us after we have given birth to one child in order to create stronger magic users. That only a small minority of our ancestors committed the crime of using dragon steel and that the rest of them were innocent. That I have been taught that I am inherently evil and that I need to atone for that when the truth is that I am being punished for a crime that has nothing to do with me. That the Unseelie King is still alive. That the Unseelie Court has been free all this time. That Draven and I are only drawn to each other because we are fated mates.

One lie after another. One shocking truth after the other. One blow after another that shatters everything I thought I knew about the world. About us. About me.

My knees buckle.

Draven's hands immediately appear on my hip and my arm, keeping me upright.

"I can't breathe," I gasp out between rapid breaths that keep stopping in my throat.

"Selena." Draven's voice cuts through the air like the crack of a whip. Utter command pulses in his eyes as he locks them on me. "I need you to take a breath and hold it."

"Hold it?" I press out, still sucking in rapid breaths while the panic inside me keeps mounting. My entire arms are tingling now. My hands shake and my head is spinning. "No. I need air."

"I've helped soldiers through panic attacks all my life. I need you to trust me." He braces his knee on the wall between my legs to help keep me upright while he cups my cheeks with both hands. "So take a breath and hold it."

And his eyes are so steady, so calm and confident, that I suck in as much air as I can and then hold it. My heart pounds like a battle drum in my chest, and blood rushes in my ears. Draven keeps his eyes firmly locked on me.

"Good," he says. "Now, let it out."

I gasp out the air in my throat.

"Take another breath and hold it," Draven commands.

So I do.

After a few seconds, he tells me to let it out. I obey.

"Good." Draven takes his hands from my cheeks and instead reaches down and grips my wrists. "You need to stop your mind from spinning out of control and instead ground yourself in the present." With steady moves, he raises my hands and places them against his bare chest. "So close your eyes, and take a deep breath, hold it for a few seconds, then let it out and tell me what you feel."

My chest is still heaving as my instincts are telling me to breathe rapidly, but I force myself to suck in another breath and hold it. Then I close my eyes. My arms are still tingling, and it reaches all the way up to my collarbones. Draven places his hands on my hips, holding me steady. I let the breath out.

"Tell me what you feel," Draven says.

"Your hands on my hips."

"Good. And?"

I curl my fingers against his chest before relaxing them again and pressing my palms against his firm muscles. "Your chest."

"Good. Take another breath."

I draw in a breath. To my relief, this one makes it almost all the way down to my lungs. But I make myself hold it for a few seconds before letting it out again.

"Describe how it feels," Draven says.

My mind is still spinning and trying to drag me back into that terrible panicked state, but I force myself to concentrate on only this specific moment in time. What does it feel like?

"Your chest is warm," I whisper.

It's as if sensation is returning to my hands for the first time in minutes. Goddess above, I can't believe that I didn't notice how warm his body is before. Still keeping my eyes closed, I press my palms harder against his muscular chest.

"And firm," I continue.

"Take another breath."

This one actually makes it all the way down into my lungs. I almost gasp at the feeling but manage to hold the breath for another few seconds before letting it out. That tingling sensation in my arms starts to fade.

"Your hands are steady," I continue, suddenly able to feel the comforting weight of his hands on my hips. Then I realize that I can feel the wall behind my back. "The wall is cool against my skin." I can feel the wooden floorboards underneath my bare feet too. "And the floor is hard."

Without being told to, I take a deep breath that makes my lungs expand fully. Then I slowly let it out and do it again. My hands and arms are no longer tingling.

A breath of profound relief comes from Draven's chest.

My heart flips as I suddenly feel his forehead against mine. But I don't open my eyes.

"Good," he whispers against my lips as he flexes his fingers on my hips.

For quite a while we just stand like that. His hands on my hips and my hands on his chest. His forehead against mine while we breathe slowly and deeply.

The overwhelming panic from before drains away with every second until it eventually fades completely. I drag in a long steadying breath.

"Are you okay?" Draven asks against my mouth.

"Yes." The word comes out as a whisper.

But Draven nods anyway. Then he straightens, taking his forehead off mine. I open my eyes at last. And to my embarrassment, tears begin streaming down my cheeks.

"I'm sorry," I stammer while desperately trying to wipe them off.

Seriousness descends on his features as he cups my cheeks again and uses his thumbs to wipe away the tears while he levels a commanding stare on me. "Don't ever apologize for crying. It's not a weakness. It's a sign that you've had to be strong for too long."

A sob rips from my throat, and a steady warmth fills my whole chest.

"I don't know what's real anymore," I whisper. But the tears have stopped. And the panic is gone.

A soft smile blows across Draven's lips. "Then focus on how much you hate me. Because you know that *that* is real at least."

Something between a sob and a broken laugh escapes my mouth, and I manage a small smile.

The smile stays on Draven's lips too as he bends down and kisses my forehead. Then he lets his hands drop from my cheeks and steps back.

He opens his mouth to say something else, but right before he can, loud knocking comes from the door.

"Commander!" a voice calls. "We just got word that the Red Hand has been spotted outside the palace. On the east side of the mountain."

My heart leaps into my throat.

But then my mind catches up. The east side. That's the side where the emergency tunnel leads out. The side that I told Kath I needed an excuse to search. She must have spread a rumor that the Red Hand was there, knowing that Draven would take me with him when he went to investigate it. Mabona's tits, she's brilliant.

Draven frowns at the door, and the messenger outside it, in confusion. But I'm already wiping the final tears from my cheeks. I need to pull myself together. I can break down and cry once I have successfully launched a rebellion against the Iceheart Dynasty and left Frostfell behind.

But for now, I need to keep all of those lies and world-shattering truths buried deep inside me. I need to keep it together for a little while longer. Because I have a secret entrance to find.

# CHAPTER TWENTY-NINE

Wind rushes in my ears as Draven flies us across the unforgiving mountainside on the east side of the Ice Palace. Just like last night, he carries me in his arms while his massive wings boom around us. My arms around his neck are less tight than last night, but my stomach still lurches when he banks sharply and then sweeps down towards the ground.

"You're doing that on purpose, aren't you?" I mutter.

He casts a sideways glance at me, and the smirk on his mouth is answer enough.

"Bastard," I huff.

A thud sounds as Draven's boots connect with the rocky ground. He flares his wings and rustles them once before tucking them in tighter by his back. Then he carefully sets me down on the ground as well.

My heart still patters against my ribs after the sharp dive through the air, so I draw in a deep breath to remind my body that I'm on solid ground again while I rake my fingers through my windblown hair to smooth it down.

But right before I can take a step back, Draven's hand shoots out and wraps around my throat. I start, blinking at him in

255

surprise. And for one insane second, I think he's going to pull me close and kiss me. But he does something even more surprising.

The feeling of cold ice around my throat disappears, and magic and strength floods back into my body, as Draven removes the iron collar from around my throat. A sigh of relief escapes my mouth.

Lost for words, I just raise my eyebrows at him in silent question while running a hand over my throat to rub off the last of the coldness.

Draven just slips the collar into one of his belt pouches while giving me a look that I can't read. "Wearing an iron collar that drains your energy right after you've had a panic attack is... not ideal." He casts a glance over his shoulder towards the Ice Palace in the distance before returning his gaze to me. "You had to wear it when we left. But out here, no one can see it." He nods towards my throat. "Especially not underneath the cloak."

I pull the black cloak tighter around me and adjust the clasp at the front so that it truly covers the parts of my throat where the collar is supposed to be.

"Just don't... wander off," Draven finishes, and gives me a pointed look.

"Wander off?" Spreading my arms, I shoot him an exasperated look back. "How am I supposed to manage that? The only ones who can wander anywhere out here are mountain goats."

As if they actually heard me talking about them, two mountain goats let out a smug bleat and then practically skip away across the uneven mountain slope. Gray clouds cover the heavens, painting the sharp rocks and steep inclines in bleak hues, and strong winds rush over the almost barren landscape. How the goats can be so happy in this kind of environment is beyond me.

I'm exaggerating about the inability to wander, but not by much. As I sweep a glance over the mountain side around us, I realize that the only way to get here without flying requires quite a bit of climbing. The human rebels have climbing gear, but it's still going to be dangerous and time consuming for them to get to the entrance out here. If I can find it, that is.

"You're the one who tried to escape literally *last night*," Draven replies while arching an eyebrow at me.

I return my gaze to him and tilt my head to the side before nodding, conceding the point.

"Well, would you look at that?" A smirk full of mischief and challenge blows across Draven's lips as he reaches out and draws two fingers along my jaw before giving my chin a little push upwards. "You really are learning to obey my commands without question."

With a huff, I shove his hand away and mutter, "Arrogant asshole."

His smirk only widens.

Then he takes a step back and motions at the mountainside around us while a serious expression descends on his features. "There are a few parts I need to check out. Stay here."

His wings rustle as he spreads them wide again, as if preparing to take off.

"Do you really think he's here?" I blurt out before he can fly off. "The Red Hand, I mean."

"No." Draven lets out something between an annoyed huff and a chuckle. "But I need to check it anyway."

Before I can ask why, he launches into the air. Tilting my head back, I watch him as he flies towards a spot a little higher up on the slope. In his black armor and with his massive black wings, he truly looks like the Shadow of Death as he flies over the gray landscape.

Narrowing my eyes, I study him as he examines something up there.

Part of me had hoped that he would fly so far that I would be out of sight, because then I could begin searching for the entrance to the emergency tunnel without him seeing it. But the other part of me has already come to the conclusion that it wouldn't have mattered. There is no way that I would have been able to find a hidden door out here before he came back anyway. I can barely move over this terrain, and I have no idea where to even start searching.

My mind churns as I sweep my gaze over the unforgiving landscape. How in Mabona's name am I supposed to find the door?

Another cold wind whirls around the mountain, making the branches on the few brittle and barren bushes rattle over the rocks. A short distance below, a group of mountain goats skip past while bleating happily. I shake my head at them before sliding my gaze back to Draven.

A sudden idea hits me.

*There are a few parts I need to check out.* That's what he said. A few parts.

My heart starts beating excitedly. What are the chances that one of those locations, that he no doubt needs to check to make sure that they haven't been compromised, is actually the hidden door?

Draven straightens and spreads his wings.

A sense of panicked urgency pulses through me as I quickly try to memorize his exact location. Mabona's tits, I wish I could have brought some paper so that I could draw the map out here. But there was no way for me to do that without tipping Draven off.

While he flies to another spot a short distance away from the first one, I whip my head from side to side, desperately trying to mark any specific rock formations or patterns of bushes that will help guide the humans to the right spot.

Relief flickers through me when I notice a cluster of strangely shaped boulders a short distance to my left. Using that as the deciding landmark, I try to estimate the distance between this location and both the city and the castle. Once I'm confident that

I will be able to draw a fairly accurate map for the human resistance later, I shift my gaze back to Draven.

While I watch him check out another location a short distance from the first, my mind starts processing all the revelations that I have been hit with lately.

Now that I've had some time to adjust and I'm no longer drowning in the sea of lies that used to be my worldview, I can see it more clearly. Almost from a distance. And as much as I hate Bane and Jessina with all my heart and soul, I do understand how they have managed to keep this system running for so long.

They set it up perfectly.

They isolated us completely. Not only did they physically trap us in a city that we can't leave, they also controlled the entire flow of information. They killed all the adults and burned all the history books. And then they taught us what *they* wanted us to know.

They controlled our birthrates so that our population wouldn't outgrow the city, and so that our magical bloodlines would be stronger and provide more magic for them to drain. And they taught us that only having one child was how our biology worked so that we wouldn't riot. All the doctors are dragon shifters, so there was no way for us to know.

And all the teachers were shifters too. Those teachers taught us about our history and our culture and race in the way that they wanted us to learn it. Taught us that we are inherently evil. That we are backstabbing deceivers who broke a peace treaty and enslaved all the dragon shifters. That we need to spend the rest of our life atoning for that. And because we had no one else to ask about our history, what they told us became the truth.

They kept us weak and distracted by not allowing us enough food. And drunk and distracted by allowing us as much alcohol as we wanted. Who is going to worry about whether our schoolteachers are lying to us when our stomachs are constantly aching with hunger and our minds are fuzzy with alcohol?

Shaking my head, I let out something between a huff and a sigh. Goddess damn it, if I hadn't suffered all of my life because of it, I would almost be a little impressed.

If you want to control people, isolating them is really the smartest move you can make. As long as you control their food supply, their healthcare, their education, and, most of all, their access to information and the outside world, it will be almost impossible for them to fight back.

And Jessina and Bane figured all of that out, which means one thing that I must never forget. They are incredibly intelligent. I need to be very careful not to underestimate them.

"Why have you never used your magic against me?"

I nearly leap out of my skin.

While I was busy contemplating Jessina and Bane's strategic genius, Draven must have walked back from the final location he checked. When he flies, I can hear his wings booming through the air. But apparently, the infuriating dragon shifter can walk much more quietly than a man his size should be able to.

Turning to face him, I draw in a breath and try to get my heart rate to slow again.

"What?" I ask, my mind still trying to catch up.

Draven is standing only a step away, and there is a considering look on his handsome face as he watches me.

"It's been weeks," he begins, his voice as serious as his eyes as he holds my gaze. "And I've been taking off your collar every evening when we get back to our rooms. But you have never, not even once, used your magic to try to manipulate my emotions so that you can escape."

My heart suddenly starts pounding in my chest.

"Why?" Draven presses.

The answer to his question is twofold. The first reason is of course that I am not actually trying to escape. But I can't tell him that. Obviously.

But the problem is that the second, much bigger, reason is

also something that I would prefer not to tell him. Especially now. However, between the two, it's the least incriminating one, so I have no other choice than to share that one.

My pulse thrums as I hold his gaze and lick my lips nervously. "Because…" I drag in a deep breath and then force out the sentence all at once. "Because you're the only thing that's real."

He blinks, genuine shock pulsing across his face. Then his brows furrow in confusion. "What do you mean?"

After everything that has happened between us, I don't know why admitting this is making me feel so nervous and vulnerable. I say it anyway. "All my life, I've been desperately trying to get people to accept me and trust me and like me. I have only ever spoken and behaved in a way that they would approve of. But not with you. With you, I have only ever been me. But if I start manipulating your emotions, our interactions won't be real." A small and bitter sigh escapes my lips as I shrug. "But I suppose that's ruined now anyway."

For a few seconds, he only watches me with confusion swirling in his eyes. Then realization dawns, and he actually flinches when he understands what I meant. The mate bond. The mate bond has already ruined everything.

I lift my shoulders in another shrug. "So that's why I never—"

A yelp rips from my lips and cuts off my sentence as Draven grabs my arm and yanks me to the side.

A fraction of a second later, an arrow shoots past in the space where my head used to be. It grazes the outside of Draven's arm since he also leaned to the side when he pulled me out of the way, and it produces a faint scraping sound as it skids off his dragon scale armor. Wooden cracking follows it as the arrow smacks into the boulder a short distance behind us.

I whirl around to face our attackers while dread pulses through me. By Mabona, don't tell me that Kath and the others spread that rumor in order to lure Draven here so that they could try to kill him.

But to my shock, it's not humans I'm faced with when I spin around.

It's six dragon shifters in purple armor.

Panic clangs inside my skull as I stare at them. And more importantly, at the six drawn bows that are pointed straight at us.

I gasp as six arrows shoot through the air.

# CHAPTER THIRTY

Storm winds barrel across the mountainside as Draven summons his magic and blasts the arrows out of the air. But before they have even finished clattering against the rocks, the six men from the Purple Dragon Clan loose another volley of arrows.

"Fucking hell," Draven growls.

Dark clouds billow around him as he sends another blast of wind straight at the attackers. They duck down behind jutting rocks but shoot more arrows before Draven has even managed to knock the previous ones aside. I leap to the side as one almost gets all the way to us before another storm wind manages to blow it aside.

"Just shift into a dragon and fry them!" I snap as I scramble upright again.

"I can't," Draven forces out between clenched teeth while he sends winds barreling across the mountainside. "If I shift, they will shift." He jerks his chin in the direction of the palace. "And then *they* will see it."

"What—"

"Just trust me!"

There it is again. *Trust me.* And for some strange reason, I do.

So instead of arguing, I jerk my chin down in a nod of acknowledgment.

Lightning cracks into stone as Draven shoots consecutive bolts at the men hiding behind the rocks. Their yelps are drowned out by the rushing winds as they throw themselves to the side. Five of them make it. One doesn't. His body collapses to the ground, his limbs twitching uncontrollably after being hit by a lightning strike.

The other five scream something that sounds like a furious battle cry.

Wood clatters against stone as they toss their bows to the side and sprint towards us while drawing their swords.

Draven lets out another curse and pulls his own sword from the scabbard strapped to his spine. He flicks a glance at me.

I brace myself for the moment I know is coming. The moment when he orders me to run and hide.

"You owe me nothing." He slides his gaze back to our attackers and drops into a battle stance. "But any help you can provide will be invaluable."

It takes me a second to process his words. Help. He's asking me to help.

I broke down and cried and had a panic attack not an hour ago, and yet he still doesn't see me as weak. He knows how dangerous and powerful I can be and he's asking me to help him fight.

That thought sends a pulse of steady warmth through my soul, and I feel like my whole chest is expanding.

Dark clouds thrash in the rushing winds and lightning cracks through the air around us while I call up my own magic. Draven launches himself at the first attacker. And I go with him.

Even though I don't have a weapon, I dart to the side and swing as if I'm attacking the guy with a massive sword. He whips his gaze between me and Draven, who is swinging an actual sword at him, and confusion pulses across his whole face.

I shove my magic at it, turning it into a wildfire.

With his confusion now blown out of proportion, his movements are slow and uncoordinated as he tries to evade Draven's very real weapon while I stop my attack with my fake one.

Spinning around, I shove at the worry in the other four people's chests while the tip of Draven's sword makes contact with the first guy's throat. Blood streams down his skin and stains his purple armor as the guy drops his own blade and reaches towards his throat. But Draven's cut was too deep, so his knees buckle while wet gurgles spill from his mouth.

Then the stunned moment breaks, and the other four attack all at once. Three of them go for Draven. The last one lunges at me.

I dive to the side as he swipes his sword at me. Steel whooshes through the air over my head as I roll into a crouch. Twisting around, I find Draven trying to fight three people at once while the fourth whips back towards me.

The one behind Draven rams a knife towards his spine.

Panic blares inside me.

While leaping to my feet, I blast the worry that the guy is feeling into a huge wildfire. It makes him hesitate instead right before his knife can strike, giving Draven the second he needed to whip around. Draven cuts the guy's head off with one powerful strike. Relief washes through me. But it's short-lived as my own attacker swings at me again.

I suck in a sharp breath through my teeth as I find him much closer than I expected. His sword glints in the gray light as it barrels straight for my neck.

A blast of wind slams into his side.

The sword is knocked off course right before it can hit me as the guy stumbles to the side from the force of Draven's wind. I scramble out of reach while Draven sends lightning strikes at his own two attackers. They leap back to avoid it.

But right as it strikes, I shove my magic at the bone white sparks of fear in their chests. Pouring a furious torrent, I blow it into sheer blind terror.

They scream, stumbling over themselves to get away. Draven knocks one of them down with a blast of wind while he rams his sword through the other's chest. Then he whirls towards the one he knocked down, but I don't have time to see what he does, because my own attacker has recovered. And he is furious.

Rage burns in his green eyes as he swings at me hard and fast.

Switching tactics, I latch on to that already raging flame of anger and make it even bigger, which makes him put even more force into his swing. I duck, and because he put too much blind anger behind his swing, the missed strike forces his entire body off balance. I dart to the side, aiming to get out from between him and the boulder. But he recovers quicker than I expected.

Alarm blares inside my skull as he thrusts his sword towards my side. Diving forward, I barely manage to escape the sharp edge. Air explodes from my lungs as I hit the ground hard. I try to roll over on my back so that I can see where he is, but a boot slams down on my cloak.

A choked huff makes it out of my mouth as the clasp digs into my throat when the cloak stops while I continue moving. I gasp in a breath and try to yank the cloak out from underneath his boot.

Steel glints above me.

Panic pulses through my veins as a sword speeds towards my chest.

Metal clangs against stone as the sword flies from the man's grip and slams into the boulder next to me at the same time as he staggers to the side. The blast of wind forced him off my cloak, and I suck in a deep breath as I yank the fabric back and roll out of reach.

Black clouds twist around Draven like thrashing demons and lightning crackles through the air as he advances on the remaining soldier from the Purple Dragon Clan. The soldier staggers a step back, his gaze flitting to his dead comrades around him.

I pour a massive torrent of magic into his fear.

A bloodcurdling scream rips from his throat, and he drops his blade.

Draven just rams his sword through the man's heart.

The scream is cut off by wet gurgling. Then a sliding sound as Draven yanks his sword back out. Pieces of purple armor that cracked from the insane strength in Draven's thrust fall to the ground and hit the stones with faint clinking sounds. They're drowned out by a loud thud as the man collapses to the ground as well.

Then everything is silent.

Draven turns to me and holds out his free hand. I take it and let him help me to my feet. He keeps hold of it for another few seconds while he flicks an appraising look up and down my body.

"Azaroth's flame," he says, sounding both surprised and impressed. "For someone who has spent her life avoiding conflicts, you sure know how to read a battle."

A surprised laugh erupts from my chest. "I have—"

Black smoke explodes across the mountainside. It's blown away as another strong fall wind sweeps over the landscape.

Dread seeps through my veins like ice as the smoke clears to reveal six more members of the Purple Dragon Clan standing on the mountainside a short distance away. Except these are no longer in their human form. They have shifted into dragons.

My heart slams against my ribs as I stare at the six purple dragons before us.

Draven heaves an endless sigh. "Fuck." Then he gives me a

quick look before he starts striding towards them. "Watch out for the flames."

Before I can so much as open my mouth to reply, black smoke once again explodes into the air. I scramble back as it washes over me.

A second later, Draven in his massive black dragon form shoots out of the smoke and up into the air.

The six purple dragons roar as they take flight as well. The combined booming of all their wings sends blasts of wind slamming down towards the ground and throws me off balance. I stumble towards the closest boulder as seven dragons hover in the air above.

Draven is massive, and dark clouds that crackle with lightning surround him. But there is still only one of him and six of them. I have never seen Draven fight other dragons, so I have no idea what kind of odds these are for him.

My heart pounds in my chest as I stare up at the seven dragons above. The moment seems suspended in time as they all just hover there, watching each other.

Then a massive torrent of fire shoots through the air.

Instinctively, I duck down behind the boulder as the sky above me turns red and orange. Even from this distance, the heat of it washes down over me. Everything inside of me is screaming at me to run and hide, but I force myself to straighten again as I gape up at the scene above.

Draven's massive jaws are open, and he is breathing that endless storm of fire that shoots straight at the six purple dragons. They immediately try to scatter, but one of them gets hit by the flames.

Otherworldly cries cut through the air as the purple dragon is engulfed by Draven's flames. It thrashes desperately while trying to escape into the clear air. The dark storm clouds spread wider over the mountainside as the other five arrange themselves into some kind of formation. Draven snaps his jaws shut, cutting off the torrent of fire and swings his head towards them right as they all speed forward.

With two booming flaps of his wings, he shoots upwards right before they reach him.

More animalistic screams echo through the air as Draven sinks his claws into the backs of two of the purple dragons who were flying past below him. They cry out and whip their heads back and forth, frantically trying to bite Draven's legs as he shakes them hard. The claws buried in their backs make their flesh rip open with each vicious shake.

Blood falls from the sky, splattering on the ground before me.

I scramble back as a chunk of flesh hits the stones only a stride in front of my boots.

Draven at last releases the two purple dragons, who fall towards the ground before they manage to spread their wings again, while the other four dragons make a coordinated attack. They speed through the air, coming from all sides.

I gasp as fear streaks through me.

Purely on instinct, I reach for my magic. I have no idea if I can even manipulate their emotions when they're in full dragon form, but I have to do something. I can't let them hurt him.

Throwing my magic out, I reach for the sparks of worry that I hope I will find in the purple dragons' chests after what Draven did to their other friends. To my shock, it connects. It feels slightly different than it does with a person. Wilder, in a sense. But it's still there. I shove my magic at them.

But apparently, I didn't need to.

Before the four purple dragons can get within striking distance of Draven, the black storm clouds explode around him, blanketing the whole area. White bolts of lightning flash relentlessly. In the otherwise almost pitch-black darkness of the clouds, it's so blinding that I have to squeeze my eyes shut.

Releasing the sparks of worry in the dragons' chests, I instead reach for their fear. Just as I suspected, it's already burning high. I pour even more magic at it.

Once the lightning has stopped flashing behind my closed lids, I release the grip on my magic and pry my eyes open again.

A scream rips from my lungs.

One of the purple dragons is speeding right towards me, jaws open and fire building at the back of its throat.

For one single second, it's as if time itself stops moving. All I can do is to stare at those open jaws full of gleaming teeth and the vibrating orange light that builds at the back of the dragon's throat. Because I know that there is no way in hell that I will be able to evade that torrent of fire.

Then something black and massive slams into it from the side.

I gasp and stagger back as Draven snaps his jaws shut around the purple dragon's neck.

And rips its head off.

Blood rains to the ground from the severed neck as Draven unclenches his jaws. I stare dumbfounded as the now headless body crashes to the ground with a boom that makes the stones underneath my feet shake. The head falls from Draven's jaws and lands next to it a second later.

With massive wings booming through the air, and his huge body like a shield between me and our attackers, Draven swings his head back towards the other five and lets out a bellow so furious that it makes the very mountain tremble.

My heart slams against my ribs.

And suddenly, I understand exactly why even his own people call him the Shadow of Death.

The surviving five dragons, two of whom are bleeding heavily from Draven's earlier attack, hesitate where they hover a short distance away.

But they never get the chance to decide if they're going to

attack or flee, because two massive silver dragons suddenly shoot out of the black storm clouds around them.

I stumble back as Empress Jessina and Emperor Bane in their dragon forms crash into the purple dragons, ripping the throats out of the two who were already bleeding and who were too slow to dodge. The other three immediately swerve and try to escape across the mountain.

Bane and Jessina swing their heads towards them and, in a terrifyingly synchronized move, open their jaws and breathe ice flames at them.

A rushing, crackling sound fills the air as the two massive torrents of ice fire hit the fleeing dragons.

My jaw drops as the ice wraps around their bodies, freezing their wings and trapping them inside of it. They plummet to the ground.

And *shatter*.

Shock clangs inside my skull as I watch the bodies of the three ice-encased dragons break into pieces on the sharp rocks below. My heart is pounding so hard in my chest that I can barely hear anything else.

This is why the Silver Dragon Clan has managed to bring all the other dragon clans to heel. This is why they rule. I always knew that their rare ice flames were dangerous, but I didn't realize just how devastating they could be to other dragons.

Completely stunned, all I can do is to stare at Draven and the Icehearts while a wave of hopelessness crashes over me. The humans back in that tavern were right. The dragon shifters might as well be gods. How the hell are we, a bunch of fae who can't even leave our court and humans with no magical abilities, supposed to win a war against an army of dragons who can do *that*?

The storm clouds disappear from the sky as Draven instead shoots straight towards the ground. I jump back in shock as he slams down right in front of me, creating a huge black cloud as he shifts out of his dragon form.

A second later, he stalks out of the dark mist in his half-shift form.

"What the hell was that?" he bellows at me, his voice filled with rage.

It shocks me so much that I actually flinch. But when I snap my gaze to his face, there is no anger there. Quite the opposite. His eyes are pulsing with panic, desperation, and pleading as he comes to a halt in front of me and grabs me by the collar as if he is furious with me.

I flick a glance towards Jessina and Bane, who are now landing on the ground behind Draven's back. Smoke explodes across the mountainside as they shift as well.

The moment that the smoke obscures their view, Draven yanks out my iron collar from his belt pouch and snaps it closed around my neck before they can see that I wasn't wearing one.

"No matter what happens, don't interfere," he whispers, his voice laced with the same panic and desperation that I can see in his eyes.

I open my mouth to reply, but before I can get even one syllable out, Draven presses on.

"If you care about me in any way, don't do anything. Don't say anything." He tightens his grip on my cloak while his pleading eyes sear into mine. "Please. I'm begging you."

His words hit me like a blow to the chest.

*Please. I'm begging you.*

Draven doesn't beg. Ever. What the hell is going on here?

Footsteps thud against stone as Jessina and Bane stride out of the disappearing smoke. Their silver garments and their huge silver wings gleam in the gray light of the overcast sky.

"Now, fall as if I threw you down," Draven orders in a hurried whisper. "And stay on your knees."

My stomach lurches as he uses his grip on my cloak to shove

me back. I do as he says and let myself tumble to the ground. Pebbles dig into my shins as I scramble up to my knees while Draven wipes the desperation off his features and instead lets a mask of fury descend on his face.

"If you ever get in my way like that again, I will fucking kill you," he snaps at me, his voice now once again only filled with merciless rage.

"I'm sorry," I reply, playing along and making sure to sound scared.

"Draven," Empress Jessina says from where she and Bane are still standing behind his back. Her tone is sharp.

But Draven shows no fear or dread as he turns around to face them. From where I sit on my knees, I can see them fully now that Draven's body isn't blocking the view. Worry washes through me when I notice their expressions.

Displeasure pulses in their eyes as they fix them on Draven. He only walks up to them and bows his head in acknowledgement and greeting.

"Yes, Empress?" he replies as he raises his chin again.

"Drop the arrogance," she snaps back, her pale gray eyes flashing with cold fury. "You know exactly why we are here."

Draven closes his mouth and just looks back at them in silence.

"It has been weeks, and you still haven't been able to capture the Red Hand," Jessina says, her tone laced with that freezing rage. "Half of the humans in the city have now suddenly started refusing to work. And now *this*…" She stabs a hand towards the corpse of the purple dragon shifter that Draven bit the head off. "The Purple Clan is rebelling! You're supposed to keep them all underneath our heel, and yet you let them attack you like this."

Still, Draven says nothing.

"You know the cost of failure," Emperor Bane says. His black eyes glint, and a slow and bone-chillingly cruel smile spreads across his mouth. "Don't you, Draven?"

My heart pounds as I watch them. For a few moments, Draven only stands there. Then he dips his chin in the shallowest of nods and walks a short distance to the side. Turning his back to the Icehearts, and to me, he spreads his wings wide.

I stare in confusion at the strange gesture. Emperor Bane removes something from his belt and then moves so that he is standing directly behind Draven, but still a short distance away. Then he pulls his arm back and snaps his wrist.

A gasp rips from my lungs as a thin metal whip cracks against Draven's right wing.

He flinches and squeezes his hand into a fist but says nothing.

Clenching my jaw, I press my mouth shut to stop the threat that I was about to scream at Bane when he snaps the whip across Draven's other wing as well. Draven asked me, *begged* me, not to interfere. If I do, it will probably only make things worse for him. So I force myself to do exactly what he told me to. Nothing.

Still on my knees, I sit there and watch uselessly as Bane whips Draven's wings over and over again. That thin metal whip cracks against the thin membrane of his wings until it tears through it. Blood slides down the few untouched parts of Draven's wings as the metal whip rips them open, leaving jagged holes and torn shreds.

I squeeze my hands into fists, digging my nails into my palms to keep myself from launching across the stones and ripping Bane's throat out with my bare hands. Fury, the likes of which could burn down hell itself, roars inside me like a thunderstorm.

Next to Bane, Empress Jessina is simply standing and watching her mate whip Draven's wings into bloody shreds. There is a mildly entertained look on her face. As if this is a common pastime for her.

Draven's muscular body jerks with each strike of the whip, and he is clenching his fists hard, but no sound escapes his lips. No screams. No cries. No groans of pain. No whimpers. Nothing.

Cold hands wrap around my heart, strangling it so hard that my chest aches, as I watch him flinch with each strike. It's followed by intense guilt that twists between my ribs like cold snakes. Because this is my fault. I'm the one who has been destroying clues that would lead to the Red Hand and I'm the one who has been manipulating the humans' emotions every time I sneak down to the city, causing them to protest and refuse to work. And now, Draven is paying for that.

My heart cracks a little more every time the whip strikes.

Only when Draven's wings have been rendered completely useless does Emperor Bane finally stop. Torn strips of membrane hang down in shreds, and blood coats everything that remains. It slides down the tips of his wings and drips down on the ground below, painting the gray stones red.

Draven remains standing completely still while Bane rolls up the thin metal whip and hooks it to his belt.

"Don't fail us again," Emperor Bane declares.

"Or do," Jessina adds. A slow and vicious smile curls her lips. "Because next time, it's my turn with the whip."

Bane chuckles. Then the two of them spread their gleaming silver wings and launch into the air.

My head is pounding with so much rage that I can hear the blood rushing in my ears as I watch the two Icehearts fly back to their palace. Then I drag my gaze back to Draven, who still remains standing in the exact same spot. I want to rush over to him, but I don't dare. If he's not moving, there is a reason for that.

In the sky, Bane and Jessina grow smaller as they close the distance to the castle. Then they at last disappear from view.

The moment they're gone, Draven sucks in a shuddering breath.

Then his knees buckle.

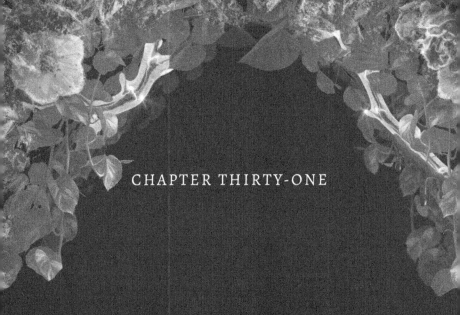

# CHAPTER THIRTY-ONE

A gony rips through my heart as I sprint across the stones and drop down in front of Draven. He's on his knees, his palms pressed against the ground before him and his head bowed. His shredded wings sag on either side of him, the tips brushing against the bloodstained ground.

"Draven." I reach towards him but then stop. I don't dare to touch him in case it will just make it worse, so I let my hand drop back down into my lap as I plead, "Please, take off my collar. I can take away your pain."

He drags in another shuddering breath. And now that I'm this close to him, I can see that his entire body is trembling with pain. His wings twitch.

"Draven, please," I beg.

When he still doesn't respond, I gently cup his cheeks and tilt his head up, forcing him to look at me.

A pang hits me straight in the heart, like a violent stab with a blade, as my gaze finds his. His beautiful golden eyes are glassy with pain.

"Please," I whisper, my voice breaking.

"No," he gasps out. Drawing in another unsteady breath, he

slowly sits up straighter while holding my gaze with those agony-filled eyes. "Not out here. Taking it off earlier was a stupid risk. They almost saw..." He drags in another breath. "They almost saw it."

Desperation crashes over me, and I hold his face more firmly as I lock dead serious eyes on him. "Then drain my magic. It heals you, right? Our magic lets you live longer because it constantly heals your body, right? So take it!"

His eyes widen, as if he can't believe that I'm offering it. Then a soft smile blows across his mouth. "I thought you said that you were going to kill me if I ever did that again."

"And now I will kill you if you *don't* do it."

A soft breath of amusement escapes his chest, but all he says is, "I can't."

Frustration rips through me, and I drop my hands from his cheeks and slap my own thighs instead. "Goddess damn it, stop being such a fucking idiot! I am *offering*, you thickheaded overgrown bat, so just take it!"

A broken laugh rips from his chest, and he raises one hand and draws his fingers along my jaw while that flicker of mirth pushes out the pain in his eyes for a second. "So stubborn, little rebel." Then his expression turns somber again, and he lets his hand drop. "But I can't. And I can't make Rin heal them either. If my wings heal too quickly, Bane and Jessina will just whip them again. I need to let them heal on their own."

"Which takes how long?" I demand.

"About a week. But I only need about two hours before my wings have stopped bleeding enough for me to be able to shift into my fully human form."

"Does that remove the pain?"

"Yes."

I study his face. If he wasn't in so much pain right now, he would probably have been able to deliver that lie without giving himself away. "Liar."

He grimaces, confirming that it was indeed a lie. "It stops people from seeing that my wings are shredded, and that's what's most important."

I shake my head at him but don't argue. Instead, I ask, "What do you need me to do?"

"We need to get back to the castle, but every nerve inside my body is on fire right now, so walking... requires effort. So just..." He works his jaw, as if he hates asking for help. "Just make sure I don't crack my head open if I fall."

I stare at him in disbelief. "Walk? You're planning to *walk* back to the castle?"

"Not that way." He jerks his chin at the long stretch of sharp rocks and steep slopes that make up the mountainside between us and the Ice Palace before flicking a glance towards one of the locations he checked out earlier. "There's a tunnel."

My heart jerks. The tunnel. It *is* here.

While I follow his gaze towards it, he braces himself on the ground and then pushes to his feet. A groan of pain rips from his throat as he tries to raise his shredded wings. But it only makes him sway on his feet.

I jump up from the ground and slide my arm around his waist while pressing my body against the side of his to brace him. He blinks and looks down at me. There is an expression I really can't read on his handsome face. And for a moment, I get the feeling that he is about to say something. But in the end, he just closes his mouth. I drape his arm over my shoulders. He lets me. Then we start towards the tunnel.

The entrance to the emergency escape tunnel is hidden behind a cluster of rocks. I mark it on my mental map as I help Draven through it. His steps are slow and his body is still shaking from the agony that must be burning through him.

As we leave the gray sky behind and move deeper into the torchlit tunnel, I flick a glance at Draven's wings. They're still drooping by his sides, as if he can't hold them up properly. They

278

produce rustling and scraping sounds as they drag across the floor when we walk. Blood still slides down from the shredded membrane, leaving a red trail on the stone floor behind us.

My heart aches.

I completed my mission and found the entrance to the tunnel.

But at what cost?

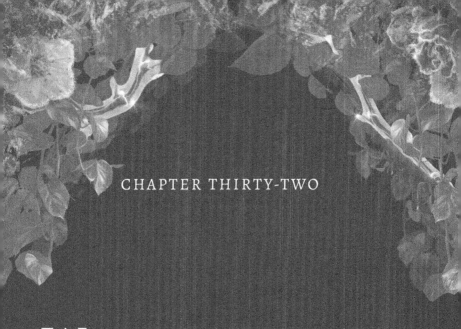

# CHAPTER THIRTY-TWO

When we at last close the door to his rooms behind us, Draven looks like he's about to pass out. The guard in the corridor at the other end of the emergency escape tunnel tried to lecture us that we weren't authorized to use that tunnel. But then he took one look at Draven's ruined wings and promptly snapped his mouth shut. He didn't even ask what happened. Just let us walk out of there. Which makes me think that it's not the first time the shifters from the Silver Dragon Clan have seen Draven like this. And that makes me want to set something on fire.

Draven sways on his feet as I guide him towards the closest couch. With every step through the tunnel and then the castle, he has been transferring more and more of his weight to me. I don't think he's even aware of it. But moving must have been causing him enormous amounts of pain, especially since he has been forced to drag his already shredded wings along the rough floor the entire time, so I just grit my teeth against the strain that the weight of his massive body is causing on mine and support him as much as I can as I haul him the final distance to the couch.

When I finally set him down so that he is seated on it, his eyes are sliding in and out of focus.

After gently easing his arm off my shoulders, I move so that I'm standing right in front of him where he sits on the couch. Then I drop down to my knees between his spread legs.

"Remove my collar," I say. It's not a request. It's an order.

Draven blinks hard, trying to focus on my face. Dragging in an unsteady breath, he grits his teeth and lifts his hands towards my throat. He fumbles several times before he finally manages to take the iron collar off. It slips from his fingers and hits the dark wooden floorboards with a thud.

The moment that it's off, I summon my magic and latch on to the violet flame of pain in his chest.

A gasp rips from my throat.

His pain is so strong that my vision blacks out and my lungs cease working. Scrambling to remember my training, I desperately try to slam up that mental wall that I use to separate my own emotions from what other people are feeling.

Draven's hand shoots up and grips my jaw, and his voice is panicked when he demands, "Does this hurt you?"

I finally slam the mental wall in place, cutting his searing pain off from my own senses. My heart still pounds from the memory of that intense mind-shattering agony, and I have to drag in a deep breath to center myself. Then I shove everything I have into decreasing the roaring flame of pain in Draven's chest.

Normally, I decrease emotions slower and at a steadier pace. But I can't function knowing that Draven is enduring this kind of world-ending pain, so I just snuff it out in one giant push. Like slamming the lid onto a burning pot. It requires an enormous amount of magical energy, but I don't even care anymore.

Especially not when a gasp of pure relief rips from Draven's chest.

I keep pouring my magic into him, forcing the pain to stay

like that. Like the tiniest of sparks that he will barely be able to feel.

Then his eyes snap back to mine, and he tightens his grip on my jaw while urgency bleeds into his tone. "Answer me. Does taking away my pain hurt you?"

"No," I reply, holding his gaze steadily.

It's almost the truth, anyway. While decreasing his pain, I can still feel it. But because I've spent over a century and a half developing my powers, I can also keep it there behind my mental wall. I know it's there, but I also recognize that the feeling doesn't belong to me, so it doesn't affect me in the way that it would him.

Draven keeps staring down at me, as if trying to read any lies in my eyes. But since it is more or less the truth, he finally drags in another deep breath and nods. Releasing my chin, he looks from side to side at the torn and bloody wings that droop down over the edges of the couch to brush against the floor. He clenches his jaw, as if bracing himself, and then tentatively raises his wings.

Shock pulses across his face when he manages to lift them up so that they are resting against the soft cushions of the couch instead.

He turns his stunned gaze to me. "I don't feel any pain. At all."

"I know," I reply.

In the dim light of the room, my glowing eyes light up his face and reflect in his own eyes. I keep pouring my magic into him. He stares at me as if I'm the Goddess Mabona herself. As if I'm the most extraordinary thing he has ever seen in his entire life.

"Thank you," he breathes, his voice choked and full of deep gratitude.

A small smile blows across my lips. "You're welcome, Shadow of Death."

He cups my cheek with one hand while an answering smile tugs at his own lips. My spine tingles as he brushes his thumb over my cheekbone. The way he is looking at me is making my heart beat erratically.

Bracing my palms on his thighs, I push myself up from the floor between his knees and move to one side. He blinks in surprise as I throw one leg over his thighs and then sit down so that I'm straddling his lap instead.

"What are you doing?" he asks, his voice still barely more than a whisper.

I slide my hands along his sharp cheekbones and into his soft black hair. "I won't be able to keep blocking out your pain the entire day. I will eventually run out of energy." Leaning forward, I kiss that sensitive spot beneath his ear. "So I'm giving you another memory to hold on to until my energy has recharged."

A shudder rolls down his spine as I kiss my way along his jaw. His strong hands appear on my hips and then slide up my sides, holding me firmly on his lap. I rake my fingers through his hair and then down the back of his neck as I brush my lips over the column of his throat.

He lets out a moan from deep within his chest.

While still pouring my magic into him, I push his armor down a little and kiss his collarbones. Another shiver courses through him. I kiss my way back up his throat while I trace teasing circles on the back of his neck.

Then I slide my hands up into his hair again and press my lips against his. While kissing him deeply, I roll my hips against him.

He moans into my mouth, and his fingers grip my sides tighter.

I tease the tip of my tongue along his bottom lip and roll my hips again. He drags in a shuddering breath and presses my body more firmly down on his lap. His mouth is greedy as he kisses me back with desperate need. I thread my fingers through his hair and meet that burning need as our tongues tangle.

While still blocking out all of his pain, I use my lips, my tongue, my fingers, and every part of my body to distract him from the memories of the bloody violence that the Icehearts inflicted on him. I kiss him and stroke his cheeks and play with his hair until all he can feel is pleasure thrumming through his whole soul.

Because the thought of him in pain makes my heart crack like brittle glass.

I don't know if it's because of the mate bond or because I do genuinely care about him, but I simply can't bear the thought of him enduring that kind of blinding agony.

My heart aches and my entire chest feels like it's filled with a tangled nest of emotions that don't fit together. I care about Draven, but I don't know if those feelings are real or if it's just a side effect of the mate bond. And regardless of which it is, I'm not supposed to care about him at all. Because he's the enemy.

The humans need to pull off their heist and I need to make the entire human population in Frostfell rise up and rebel against the Icehearts. It's the only way to kickstart a revolution that will hopefully let me free the Seelie Court.

But now the thought of that also makes my heart clench in fear and panic.

Because if I help them successfully pull off the heist, make the entire city rebel, and then escape with Isera, Alistair, and Lavendera, then that will mean that Draven has failed. Epically.

And if this is how the Icehearts punish him just for the lack of quick results, what will they do to him if I actually complete my mission?

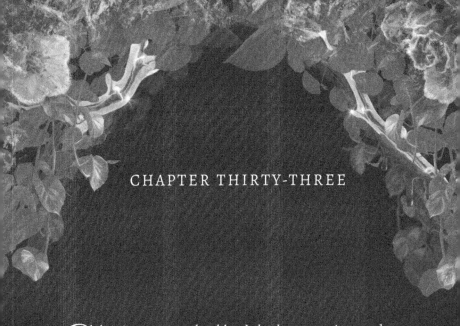

# CHAPTER THIRTY-THREE

G lancing over my shoulder, I check once again to make sure that the pale ice corridor behind me is clear. But just as the other times I've snuck down here, the hallway outside the kennels is unguarded. I quickly close the final distance to the door.

In the week that it took for Draven's wings to heal completely, he never left in the middle of the night to hunt the Red Hand. For obvious reasons. So I didn't have any opportunities to sneak out and leave the information about the tunnel at the drop-off point. But even if he had given me an opportunity, I wouldn't have left. Because... I don't know. Maybe because I don't like the thought of leaving him vulnerable.

Once his wings had stopped bleeding, he shifted into his fully human form and then just went about his duties as if nothing was wrong. He commanded his clan, conducted searches for the Red Hand down in the city, updated the Icehearts on his progress. And all the while, he showed no signs of weakness. Even I, who knew that he was in pain, could read none of that on his face.

But every day when we returned to his rooms, he let that blank mask slip. My heart still aches at the memory of how exhausted he looked then. So the moment we were hidden behind closed doors and he finally took off my collar, I spent the entire evening, and as far into the night as I could manage before passing out, using my magic to block out his pain.

Today was the first time he used the half-shift since the whipping. His wings had healed completely, and when he spread them wide, they once again looked as powerful and imposing as before. As if nothing had happened. But *I* know what happened. And I do not forget.

Stopping outside the door to the kennels, I slowly push the handle down and edge the door open the tiniest of cracks. There have never been any guards inside the kennels before, but I still need to make sure. I sweep my gaze over the large room inside. But no guards leap out of the shadows. Only an empty floor and the cages cast in murky darkness by the walls await me in there.

I slip inside.

It took me this entire week to decide if I was even going to do this. An overwhelming sense of guilt would crash over me every time I thought about sneaking down to the drop-off point and sharing my information about the tunnel with the human resistance. Because when they pull off the heist, Draven will no doubt be punished for it. And I don't want them to hurt him. But at the same time, can I really stop our entire rebellion?

In the end, I built as many stone walls around my heart as possible and decided that I couldn't justify abandoning my mission to free my entire court, even if it means that Draven will be punished. We have suffered for too long in the Seelie Court. It needs to stop.

So after dropping off the information about the tunnel entrance, I decided to head over to the kennels to update Isera, Lavendera, and Alistair on what's going on. And because I need their help with something.

A soft click comes from the door as I close it gently behind me. While sneaking deeper into the room, I glance towards Lavendera.

Except she's not there.

Trailing to a halt, I blink at her empty cage in stunned surprise.

Then I remember what I overheard down in the city. That the Icehearts burned their own homeland. That must be why they took Lavendera. Goddess above, I wonder what they're doing to her.

Dread washes through me as horrifying images flash through my mind about the torture they are likely subjecting her to in order to break her and force her to use her tree magic for their benefit.

Squeezing my hand into a fist, I straighten my spine as steely determination pulses through me. Giving the humans the information about the tunnel was the right move. We need to pull off this heist and then get out of here. No more delaying and handwringing. I need to get Lavendera, Isera, and Alistair out of here as soon as possible.

A faint sound drifts through the room. Now that I'm standing completely still, I can hear it clearly. Tearing my gaze from Lavendera's empty cage, I hurry the final distance across the floor to where Isera and Alistair are imprisoned.

Two figures are visible there in the murky darkness of their cages.

But the moment I can see them clearly, I stop dead in my tracks.

My mouth drops open as I realize what that sound is.

Alistair is crying.

He is on his hands and knees in the middle of the cage, with his head bowed forward and his fingers clenched into fists against the pale ice floor. His lean muscular body trembles and convulses as desperate sobs rip from his throat.

For a few seconds, all I can do is to stand there, frozen on the floor, and stare at him in utter shock.

Alistair Geller, the biggest bully in the entire Seelie Court and the man who threatened to kill us all in the Atonement Trials if we got in his way, is bawling his eyes out.

I can't process the concept. I thought I was the only one who broke down and cried like this.

"Do you have a plan?"

A jolt shoots through me, snapping me out of my stunned stupor, and I flick my gaze towards the sound of the commanding voice.

Isera is seated at the back of her cage. Just like last time, she has a blanket draped over her shoulders and back so that it protects her half-naked body from the iron bars that she is leaning back against. But other than that, nothing else about her is the same.

That blank and vacant expression is gone from her face. In its place is something that sends a chill down my spine.

During the Atonement Trials, Isera was always a no-nonsense kind of person. She never let people walk all over her and she didn't care about anyone's opinion. People called her *ice lady* for a reason. But there was still a sense of warmth beneath that cool exterior. A sense that she wasn't actually as cold-hearted as she pretended to be.

But now…

My breath catches as I stare at Isera.

There is nothing, no warmth, no compassion, no sense of a caring soul, on her face. Her silver and blue eyes are as cold as the space between the stars, and her expression is one of merciless vengeance and ruthless fury. She doesn't even look fae anymore. She looks like a bloodthirsty goddess who has risen from the freezing pits of another world, come to claim her revenge on this land.

And it fucking terrifies me.

"Well?" she demands, her cold eyes locked on me. "Do you have a plan or not?"

"I... Yes." I stare at her, still trying to process this change in her. Then I tentatively ask, "Your claustrophobia? How—"

"As long as the walls aren't solid and I can see out, I'm fine." She gives me a pointed look and once again demands, "The plan?"

"It's... uhm..." I cast an uncertain glance at Alistair, who is still bawling his eyes out. "Shouldn't we...?"

Making a decision, I turn away from Isera and instead drop to my knees in front of Alistair's cage. We might not be friends, but I hate seeing him like this.

"Alistair," I begin, my voice gentle.

Isera clicks her tongue in annoyance. I ignore her.

Alistair sucks in a ragged breath and gasps out, "I don't know how much more of this I can take."

"There is nothing you can do," Isera interjects before I can reply. "I did try to help him through it earlier." That cool expression remains on her face as she slides her gaze to me. "In case you were wondering." She shrugs. "But his emotions are fried after weeks of their psychological torture. It's all bubbling over. And there is nothing you can do to help him."

I cut her a hard stare and yank the top of my cloak away from my throat, showing her that I'm not wearing a collar. Her eyes widen in shock. It's the first emotion I've seen that cracks through that icy fury on her face. Even if it's just for a moment.

"I told you I have a plan," I say before shifting my gaze back to Alistair. "Tell me what you're feeling. Is it pain? Fear?"

Alistair gasps in something like a sob, his body still shaking uncontrollably. "Hopelessness."

Calling up my magic, I immediately shove it straight at the black flame of despair in his chest.

It's so massive that I actually gasp. While yanking up my

mental wall to separate his feelings from mine, I begin steadily decreasing that black flame.

A sense of stunned realization pulses through me while I work.

Back in the Seelie Court, I always assumed that Alistair didn't really have a lot of emotions. But when I latched on to the rage in his chest during the Atonement Trials, I found it so strong that it shocked me to my core. And now, his despair is a raging inferno.

As I study Alistair's shaking body, I realize that my first impression of him was completely wrong. Alistair isn't the emotionless person I assumed he was. It's the exact opposite. I'm starting to think that maybe Alistair feels too much. That he actually feels emotions deeper than everyone else.

Alistair at last drags in a deep breath as I force his despair down into the tiniest of sparks. But he remains on his hands and knees like that for a little while longer, drawing air back into his lungs. His body finally stops trembling.

I sweep my gaze over him.

Just like Isera, he is also still half-naked.

My gaze widens as I stare at his bare back. When I was here last time, I noticed that he had burn scars all over his chest and stomach. And now that I can clearly see his back for the first time, I realize that there are burn scars all over his back too.

A cold hand wraps around my heart. Where did all these scars come from?

At long last, he raises his head and takes his hands off the floor so that he is sitting upright on his knees instead. Surprise pulses in his orange and green eyes when he sees my glowing eyes, and he flicks a quick look down at my throat before meeting my gaze again. He draws in an unsteady breath.

"Thank you," he says, his voice brimming with sincerity.

I give him a slow nod in acknowledgement and then carefully begin releasing my magic. I'm worried that the hopelessness will flare up again as soon as I stop manipulating it. But to my relief, it doesn't. Apparently, just breaking the spiral of despair like that allowed Alistair to get his emotions back under control.

My eyes stop glowing as I release my magic completely.

For a few seconds, only the faint hissing of the torch by the wall behind me breaks the silence. Then Isera lets out something that almost sounds like an amused breath.

"Well, aren't you full of surprises," she says.

I shift my gaze to her. "I told you that I would get you out of here. And I meant it."

Both of them listen intently while I fill them in on my discoveries and plans for the heist and our escape. A tiny glimmer of hope returns to Alistair's eyes with every word I speak while a cold smile full of ruthless anticipation spreads across Isera's mouth.

"The only thing we still need is information about the layout and guards inside the treasury," I finish. "I can't get there. But you can."

"Are you forgetting that we're still blindfolded every time we leave these cages?" Alistair points out.

"Not unless we pretend as if they have broken us," Isera says, a scheming look on her face. Her eyes are sharp as she locks them on Alistair. "Can you handle that?"

"Can *you*?" he shoots back.

"I would slaughter every single person in this castle, innocent or not, if it meant getting my revenge. I can handle it."

Another chill runs down my spine, because I can tell that she means every word of that.

She shifts her cold determined gaze to me. "So yes, we'll get the information for you."

I give her a nod in acknowledgement. Then I turn back to Alistair. "Will you be okay?"

He clears his throat a bit self-consciously but nods. "Yeah, I'll be fine."

Picking up the thin blanket from the floor, he scoots

backwards and drapes it over his shoulders before leaning back against the iron bars. A huff of bitter laughter escapes his chest, and he shakes his head.

"It's just so fucking ironic," he says. "I won the Atonement Trials to escape this exact sort of thing."

I frown at him. "What do you mean?"

Resentment washes over his features for a second. Then he scoffs again before glancing between me and Isera. "Do you have any idea what it was like to grow up in our city with fire magic?"

I blink at him in surprise. I had always assumed that it was a great advantage. It's a strong and dangerous physical element. Especially compared to my emotion magic.

Alistair lets out a harsh laugh, as if he could read all of that on my face. "Yeah, that's what I thought."

"Just cut to the fucking chase," Isera snaps. "What are you trying to say?"

"Don't you get it?" He cuts a hard look at both of us. "Fire is *their* element. As soon as my friends, my family, my neighbors, every fucking fae in our court, found out that I had fire magic, they shunned me. After all, if I was born with the incredibly rare fire magic, it must mean that I secretly agree with the dragon shifters. Right?" He scoffs and shakes his head. "Or that I'm one of them."

My heart patters in my chest as I stare at him.

"And how do you think the shifters from the Red Dragon Clan reacted when they found out that I could wield their element?" Alistair continues. "And for them, it's not just their normal dragon fire. Their clan magic is lava magic, for fuck's sake. It's like having fire magic twice." That searing rage bleeds into both his voice and his eyes. "So how do you think they reacted when they realized that a filthy fae could wield their sacred fire?" A cold humorless laugh rips from his chest. "They've been beating me up all my life. Always cornering me when there is an entire squad of them so that I won't have any chance of winning. Beating me, humiliating me, trying to make me apologize for polluting their sacred element."

Isera, who has just listened with that impassive mask on her face up until now, draws back a little while something almost like recognition or understanding flashes across her face. But she buries it quickly underneath that cold expression again.

My gaze flits down to the burn scars across Alistair's chest and stomach, and pain spears through my heart. I meet his rage-filled eyes again. "Are they the ones who burned you?"

"This?" He motions down at the vicious burn scars across his skin, and a harsh laugh once again rips from his lungs. "No." That fury in his eyes burns hotter as he leans forward a little. "This is the work of our own people."

Horror washes through my veins. "What?"

"They were so desperate to prove to the dragon shifters that they were good people. That they were nothing like their wicked ancestors. That they were good little fae. That they were virtuous and self-sacrificing and that they prioritized the dragon shifters above themselves, above all fae, now."

My heart pounds against my ribs.

"And they did it by sacrificing their own people in the name of goodness." Disgust laces Alistair's tone as he practically spits out that final word. "So they would hold me down and burn me with torches in front of the dragon shifters to show them what good people they were. To show them that they were on the dragon shifters' side. That they would happily punish me to satisfy the dragon shifters." He scoffs. "Punish me for simply the crime of being born with fire magic."

Bile crawls up my throat. I feel like I'm going to throw up.

I have always seen our people as just... good. Even though they treated me like the plague for something that I had no control over, I have never thought of them as evil. The dragon shifters were the evil ones. They were the ones who were being cruel. And we, our entire court, were the good ones.

But apparently, the world is a lot more complicated than that. *People* are a lot more complicated than that.

Even when we are all facing the same outside cruelty, there are some who are willing to sell out their friends and neighbors just so that the people who hate us all will approve of them. Something between bitterness and amusement pulses through me. Maybe I'm not the only person in our court who has grown up with a desperate need to be liked.

"If you point them out, I could always just shove an ice shard through their throats," Isera says.

The casual offer yanks me out of my bleak thoughts and pulls me back to the present.

Alistair lets out a surprised laugh as the two of us turn towards Isera. And based on the expression on her face, she was actually serious about that offer.

Some of the anger and tension bleeds out of Alistair's body, and he lets out another small chuckle while giving Isera a nod. "I might actually take you up on that someday, ice lady."

She just tips her head to the side in a half nod, acknowledging it.

An exhausted burst of laughter escapes my own throat. Adjusting my position, I scoot back so that I'm leaning my back against the cage opposite Alistair's and then draw my knees up. While resting my elbows on my knees, I rake my fingers through my hair.

Everything inside me is just full of conflicting emotions.

After the visit to the mountainside, and the dragon battle I witnessed there, I'm no longer confident that we will actually be able to win a war against the dragon shifters on our own. And I feel guilty for helping the humans plot their heist and for bringing Frostfell to the brink of open rebellion, because now I know what the Icehearts will do to Draven if he fails. I'm still in shock over all the lies that I have been taught my whole life. I'm desperate to get Isera, Alistair, and Lavendera out of here. I feel guilty for using my magic to manipulate Kath and the other humans to trust me. And it breaks my heart that every shifter in this city hates me even though they don't know me.

"How do you deal with it?"

It takes me a second to realize that the words came out of my own mouth.

Clearing my throat, I raise my head and let my hands drop from my hair as I meet Isera and Alistair's eyes again. "How do you handle the fact that everyone hates us?"

"Not very gracefully, obviously," Alistair replies with a shrug. But there is light in his eyes again now. "Since I've spent my entire life bullying people and making them feel small in retaliation for how they've been treating me."

A surprised laugh erupts from my chest. There is a small smile on Alistair's lips as he just lifts his toned shoulders in another unapologetic shrug.

But Isera's voice is serious when she replies, "I have already told you this. Back inside that maze during the Atonement Trials. Remember?"

I shift my gaze to her and raise my eyebrows in silent question.

She sighs. "It doesn't matter what you do, some people will always hate you. You could do everything they ask, give them everything you have, and it would still never be enough. They will still hate you. Either because of their own insecurities. Or because they have been taught to hate you." Bitterness laces her tone as she adds, "Just like we have been taught to hate ourselves."

Her words hit a spot deep inside. Like a dagger straight to the chest. Uncomfortable emotions twist inside me like snakes. Because deep down, I know that she's right.

It's impossible to be liked by everyone. There are always people who will hate you for one reason or another. Be it what your magic type is or what you look like or who your family is or what your job is or even something as ridiculous as what kind of food you prefer. Regardless of the reason, there will always be people out there who want to make others feel like shit just so that they can feel better about themselves.

Unfortunately, just shrugging off their hatred is easier said than done. At least for me.

"So how do you deal with it?" I ask, meeting Isera's eyes.

Determination and an unshakable belief in herself seem to pulse from her entire being as she holds my gaze. "By reminding myself that I have nothing to prove."

And because she says it with such confidence, as if it's the most natural thing in the world, I suddenly find myself smiling.

Yeah. Maybe she's right. Maybe I need to stop apologizing for who I am and for what I do. Maybe it's time to stop second-guessing myself. To stop trying to make everyone like me.

Back during the Atonement Trials, I self-righteously thought to myself that I was nothing like Alistair. That I didn't have to do what he did in order to win. Now, I'm first of all beginning to realize that I didn't even know Alistair at all. And secondly, I'm starting to think that being more like him isn't necessarily a bad thing. Maybe I need to be more like them all.

More like Alistair.

More like Isera.

More like Draven.

Maybe it's time that I start doing what they do. What everyone else in this messed up world of ours seems to be doing.

Take what I want and to hell with everyone else.

# CHAPTER THIRTY-FOUR

"Our presence has been requested at the event tonight." Sitting upright on the bed, I meet Draven's gaze and arch an eyebrow. "*Our* presence?"

He rolls his eyes. "Fine. *My* presence has been requested. Which means that you're coming too."

I flash him a sly smile and lie back down on the bed. "Yes, sir."

He misses a step and almost stumbles. Straightening again, he adjusts the towel that is slung low around his hips and then rakes a hand through his messy black hair. Since he has just come out of the bath, his hair is still wet, and a few drops of water slide down his chiseled abs. His eyes darken with lust as he runs his gaze over my body where I'm lying on my side on his dark gray sheets.

"You really need to be careful," he warns, his eyes glinting and his voice full of wicked promises. "Saying things like that while you're lying on my bed, wearing only a tiny black nightgown."

"What, this?" I draw my hand up my bare thigh, pushing the silken fabric up towards my hip. That sly smile is still on my lips as I raise my eyebrows in teasing challenge. "I thought you said back when you were holding me captive in your room during the

Atonement Trials that the sight of my body in a tiny little nightgown does absolutely nothing to you."

He flexes his hand and clenches his jaw as his gaze follows my fingers up towards my hip. Then he drags his gaze back to my face and draws in a deep breath before shaking his head at me. "Oh you really are a menace."

I let out a smug chuckle and then roll off the bed. While striding towards the door, I wink at him. "I really thought you had learned that by now."

"I see that sharp tongue of yours is back."

"Did you miss it?"

"Yes." He studies me intently as I close the distance between us. "You're... different. These past few days, it feels as if you've gotten your spark back."

That's because I have. After my conversation with Isera and Alistair, I feel as if a great weight has been lifted off my shoulders. It didn't solve the problem that my connection with Draven is probably only a result of the mate bond, but it at least made me decide that it's time to stop feeling so guilty about what I have to do. I have to help the humans pull off this heist and I have to make Frostfell rebel so that I can launch a revolution that will finally free the Seelie Court. No matter the consequences.

And just deciding that has given me back the power that I have been handing over to other people all my life just because I have let their opinions of me determine how I feel about myself. But now that I have decided to just take what I want for once, and to hell with everyone else, I feel better. Stronger. More in control.

But I can't tell Draven that, of course, so I just flash him a teasing smile. "Just wait until I use that spark to burn down this room around your head."

A dark chuckle rumbles from his chest. "Come try it, little rebel."

I shoot him a grin full of challenge as I saunter past him towards the door.

But before I can take so much as a step past him, his hand shoots out and he grabs my arm. Keeping my upper arm in a firm grip, he arches an eyebrow at me. "And where do you think you're going?"

"To change into that damn silver ballgown I always have to wear."

"No. Not tonight." Releasing my arm, he strides over to his closet and yanks open the door. "Tonight, you're wearing this."

My heart skips a beat as he pulls out a stunning black dress with golden details. Drawing in an unsteady breath, I flick my gaze between the breathtaking dress and the satisfied smile on Draven's face.

"It's black," I state, remembering what he told me about why the Icehearts always insist that we fae wear silver.

Still only wearing that low slung towel, he walks back across the floor and holds out the dress to me. "Yes, it is."

My heart pounds as I take it. "Won't they get angry?"

"Let them." He slides his hand up my throat. With a possessive grip, he tilts my head back and then leans down so that his lips almost brush mine. "You are mine. It's time the world knows that."

Anxious anticipation ripples through me as Draven and I at last walk into one of the smaller ballrooms on the ground floor. Faelights glitter in the ceiling, making the carved ice pillars around the room shimmer. Food and drinks are waiting on silver trays that have been placed on the tables along the walls, but very few people are eating and drinking. Instead, everyone is watching each other with suspicious eyes. As if this kind of event isn't normal.

It took a lot longer than it should have to put on that black dress and get ready. But that was mostly because Draven simply tossed his towel on the bed, leaving him naked right in front of me, as he started putting on his clothes and armor. I could barely concentrate on my own clothes when his muscles flexed every time he lifted a piece of armor and secured it to his toned body. And the smug glances he cast in my direction informed me that he knew exactly what he was doing. Revenge for the 'yes, sir' comment, most likely.

But I still can't help but worry about Bane and Jessina's reaction to my dress as I follow Draven deeper into the room.

My heart leaps when I spot the Icehearts. And more importantly, the two people next to them.

Isera and Alistair are standing two steps behind them. Their heads are bowed and their shoulders are slumped submissively, but they are wearing actual clothes. No handcuffs. No blindfolds. No strange contraptions in their mouths. Only the iron collars around their throats.

A wave of anticipation washes over me.

This means that they have managed to fool Jessina and Bane into thinking that they have broken them. Which means that they might have information about the treasury.

My heart patters against my ribs as Draven and I close the final distance to them.

Jessina's sharp gray eyes immediately dart to my dress.

"She's wearing black," she states when we come to a halt in front of her and Bane.

"Yes," Draven simply replies.

Tense silence falls over our small group. I can almost hear it crackling in the air between us.

Then Jessina clicks her tongue. "It makes her look even more pale and sickly." She flicks her wrist in a dismissive gesture. "I approve."

I have to suppress both a sigh of relief and an annoyed scowl.

Standing a step behind Draven, I keep my chin lowered and my eyes on the floor.

"Everyone else is having fun, I see," Draven says, obvious sarcasm in his voice.

All around us, dragon shifters in beautiful clothes of all colors are standing tense by the thick ice walls. The dance floor in the middle of the small ballroom is completely deserted. Everyone is just watching each other, and us, warily.

Bane lets out a low and vicious chuckle. "Yes, look at them squirm. Wondering why they're here."

"Why *are* they here?" Draven asks in a casual voice.

Jessina lets out a smug huff of amusement. "So that we can make them nervous, of course."

"The attack on you by the Purple Clan last week was unacceptable," Emperor Bane picks up. I can't see his face since I'm still looking at the floor, but he sounds furious. "It's time to remind the other clans of their subservience to us."

"Next week, we will host a grand ball, which all the clan leaders will be required to attend," Empress Jessina continues. "And during it, they will all kneel and re-swear their oaths to us."

"And we will deliver those summons directly to their people tonight," Bane finishes. "Let's go."

Without another word, Jessina and Bane start striding towards the closest courtier. Isera and Alistair don't follow. They remain standing in the exact same position that they have been in this whole time.

Draven turns to me. "Behave."

I suppress the urge to roll my eyes, even though he wouldn't be able to see it.

While the three of them stalk away to intimidate people, I discreetly move so that I'm standing next to Isera and Alistair instead.

"We have the information," Isera whispers without preamble.

"Yeah, and I should win a fucking award for the stellar acting I've pulled off these past few days," Alistair adds.

"Shut it," Isera snaps. "And stay on topic."

I memorize all the details as Isera explains what the layout and guard situation look like around the treasury. It's not... encouraging. There are eight guards in the three corridors between the hidden door and the treasury. And there are no windows and no hiding spaces at all in the final two hallways. Just long corridors filled with guards.

"All in all, way too many guards," Alistair summarizes rather superfluously at the end.

"Unless someone kills them all," Isera adds, her voice now once more laced with that cold ruthless edge.

"And who would that be?" Alistair huffs under his breath. "You're still collared, ice lady. And we're talking eight dragon shifters. With swords. And probably elite training. Who would be dumb enough to try to assassinate them?"

A wicked smirk spreads across my mouth. "Actually, I think I know exactly who."

# CHAPTER THIRTY-FIVE

While Draven and the Icehearts continue moving through the room, delivering orders and intimidating people, I drift away from Isera and Alistair. I need to figure out how to get word to the Red Hand, and I don't know when I will be left unsupervised like this again. My gaze darts between the main door and the one that leads out to some kind of patio. Can I make it to the drop point and back before Draven notices that I'm missing?

"Look at him follow them like a fucking dog on a leash," a man growls quietly from somewhere behind me. "It makes me sick."

"Well, to be fair, this is literally his job," a woman replies.

"No, it's not. His job is to lead our clan."

Glancing over my shoulder, I find two dragon shifters in black armor standing side by side. A man and a woman. I immediately recognize them as Galen, Draven's former best friend, and that usually so cheerful soldier Lyra. However, Lyra doesn't look particularly happy right now. Though it's nothing compared to the scorching glare that Galen is shooting in Draven's direction.

Both of them start slightly when they realize that I'm looking at them, but then they relax again when they see that it's just me.

"Wanna join?" Galen offers, a humorless smile blowing across his lips. "I'm sure you hate him too."

I move so that I'm standing close to them, but not right next to them, just in case that would look suspicious. Then I follow their gazes towards where Draven is now standing on the other side of the room. Since the dance floor in the middle of the silver-sparkling room is still empty, I can see the other side clearly.

Empress Jessina and Emperor Bane are speaking to a man in a dark blue suit. Worry shines on his whole face as he looks at them while nodding fervently. Draven is standing on the man's other side, which means that he can't see what Draven is doing unless he takes his eyes off the Icehearts. Which I'm sure is a very deliberate power play. Draven's massive black wings are spread wide as he looms there like the Shadow of Death that he is.

"Pathetic," Galen scoffs next to me.

Memories of Emperor Bane whipping Draven's wings into bloody shreds, and Jessina casually mentioning that it's her turn next time, flashes before my eyes. I keep my gaze on Draven as I reply, "I'm sure he's just doing what he thinks is best."

From the corner of my eye, I can see both Galen and Lyra turn to stare at me in surprise.

"Great," Galen huffs, his voice dripping with sarcasm. "And now you're defending him. Looks like he really has broken you."

Oh if he only knew that it's the exact opposite. That Draven is the only person that I have never made myself small for. The first person that I have never had to hold back against or watch my mouth around.

But I can't exactly tell them that, so I say nothing. Galen doesn't seem to mind, or even notice, because he just keeps speaking.

"*Doing what he thinks is best,*" he echoes mockingly, bitterness lacing his tone. "Do you know what that is, according to Draven?"

I flick a glance at him, but his furious violet eyes are still locked on Draven across the room. When I don't immediately reply, he answers for me.

"Nothing," he spits out.

"What do you mean?" I ask.

Two courtiers in glittering dresses walk past in front of us, heading for the table of food by the wall to our right. I drop my gaze, and Galen and Lyra keep their mouths shut until they have passed out of earshot.

Then Galen heaves a frustrated sigh. "Do you know what he did the day that the Silver Clan came to our islands?"

It doesn't sound like he is waiting for an actual answer, so I don't say anything.

Just as I expected, Galen keeps talking anyway. And when he does, disgust drips from every word. "Nothing. He did nothing. The Icehearts landed in the middle of town, demanding to speak to our leader. Draven went there. They told him to swear allegiance to them. And he did." A scoff, full of disbelief and contempt, rips from his throat, and he shakes his head while still staring at Draven across the room. "He just got down on his knees and swore allegiance. He didn't even try to fight." He spits out a low and vicious curse. "Fucking coward."

My mind immediately goes back to that battle I witnessed out on the mountainside, and how Bane and Jessina decimated the dragons from the Purple Clan with their ice flames. How their ice froze their wings and encased their bodies. How they just fell from the sky and shattered on the rocks below.

He was probably trying to save his clan from that same fate.

"I'm sure there was a reason," I say softly.

Galen scoffs again. But before he can say anything else, my gaze snags on someone by the table to my right, and a small gasp rips from my lungs. Thankfully, it was partially drowned out by Galen's scoff, so he and Lyra don't appear to have heard it.

Stunned shock pulses through me as I stare at the blond human man who is clearing dirty plates off the table while keeping his head and eyes down. My heart pounds in my chest.

It's Peter. One of the members of the human resistance that I met that first day when Kath brought me to their tavern. He's the one who gave me the climbing gear.

Confusion whirls inside my skull as I stare at him. What in Mabona's name is he doing here?

Then understanding slams into me.

Oh Mabona's fucking tits. *This* is how they get to the drop point.

I've always been wondering how the humans have been able to drop off instructions and pick up information at a location inside the palace's defensive walls. And this must be it. Peter most likely works a low-level job in the kitchens here, which lets him access the palace grounds but not anything important inside the castle.

"Sorry, I need to get something to eat," I tell Galen and Lyra.

Without waiting for them to respond, I walk over to the table that Peter is clearing and casually start inspecting the food.

"Peter," I whisper.

To his credit, he doesn't so much as flinch in surprise. He just keeps gathering up the empty plates with his head down.

"You shouldn't be talking to me," he breathes back, barely moving his lips.

"I know. But I have important information that needs to be delivered as soon as possible." I turn one of the silver trays, pretending to look at the small pastries at the back of it. "There are eight guards between the hidden door and the treasury. All armed and well-trained. Fighting in a group will be suicide. Tell the Red Hand that he needs to assassinate them before the rest of you get there."

Peter dips his chin in a barely perceptible nod.

"And there is to be a ball next week," I continue whispering.

"I know."

"All the clan leaders will be there. Including Draven and the Icehearts."

He flicks a quick glance at me. Apparently, that was news to him. Then he quickly finishes gathering up the plates.

"I'll let the rest know." Straightening, he grabs all the plates and starts hurrying away. "Incoming."

I frown, trying to figure out what he meant by that last word.

Then I can feel it.

A powerful presence looming behind me. It sends a ripple down my spine.

"What did I tell you about flirting with other people?" Draven says from behind my back.

His dark voice, laced with both threats and wicked promises, makes heat wash through me.

While turning around to face him, I run through several options in my head for how to make sure that Draven doesn't become suspicious of Peter.

"I wasn't flirting with him," I say. Then I flash him a sly smile. "I was asking if he could help me kill some guards so that I can escape."

A surprised huff of amusement rips from Draven's chest. Then he tilts his head to the side, as if conceding the point. "Well, that's better than flirting at least, so I'll take it."

Sometimes, the truth really is the best lie.

Taking a step closer, he places two fingers underneath my chin and pushes upwards, making me crane my neck and meet his intense gaze. "Because if you were flirting with him, he would wake up without his hands tomorrow."

"Ah, threats of torture." I give him a knowing smile. "So romantic."

His eyes glitter in the shimmering faelights and the burning candles around the room. Then a mischievous glint flashes in those beautiful eyes of his, and he lets his hand drop from my chin and instead grabs my wrist.

I stumble a step in surprise as he suddenly begins leading me out onto the empty dance floor.

"What are you doing?" I protest, trying to pull my wrist out of his grip.

He gives me a devilish smile as he pulls us to a halt in the middle of the dance floor and then spins me towards him. "You wanted romance."

My heart skips a beat as he slides his right hand along the side of my ribs and then places it possessively on my lower back while he grips my hand with his other. Drawing in an unsteady breath, I look up into his eyes.

"I still don't know how to dance," I whisper, feeling everyone's stunned gaze on us.

That devilish smile on his lips widens. "Good thing you've become quite adept at obeying my orders without question then."

Before I can so much as open my mouth to retort, he moves us into a dance that no one else is performing. In fact, I can barely hear the soft string music from the two musicians in the corner. Though to be fair, that might be because my heart is pounding in my chest.

All around us, people are staring. Courtiers and servants and Draven's own people. I don't even dare to glance in Jessina and Bane's direction to see how they are reacting. Worry flits through my chest, and I swallow.

"Are you supposed to dance with your slave?" I ask, meeting his gaze again.

And the utter confidence and complete certainty on his face blows away that worry inside me like a strong wind. Draven pulls me closer, pressing his palm more tightly against my lower back.

"You're mine," he says, mischief sparkling in his eyes. "I can do whatever I want with you."

A huff of amusement escapes me, and I roll my eyes. "Right."

He spins us around so abruptly that my breath catches. I draw in an unsteady breath to refill my lungs as Draven pulls me closer again.

"Careful with those eye rolls, little rebel," he warns. "Wouldn't want anyone to realize that you're not actually my submissive little plaything."

I let the hint of a smirk blow across my lips and make my voice deliberately seductive as I reply, "Yes, sir."

His fingers grip the smooth black fabric of my dress harder, and he works his jaw. Letting out a controlled breath, he shakes his head at me while his gaze, burning with lust, sears through my very soul. "Such a little menace."

Lightning crackles through my veins as he slides his hand up the side of my ribs and brushes his thumb right underneath the curve of my breast. A shudder of pleasure rolls down my spine. A satisfied smirk spreads across Draven's mouth. I attempt to glare at him, but it's undone when he makes my heart skip a beat by caressing the side of my ribs again.

I hold his gaze, watching the way the light gleams in his eyes. The rest of the room disappears around us. It's just me and him. His hands on my body. His eyes, burning with desire, on mine. I can feel his very soul calling to mine, and all I want to do is to grab the front of his armor and yank his stupid troublesome mouth down to mine and kiss him until he can't breathe.

Because I can't fucking breathe either.

Indecision rips at my chest.

Should I tell him? After the torture and humiliation I have seen the Icehearts subject Draven to, he must surely hate them as much as I do. If I told him about the heist and the rebellion, he would want to help me. Wouldn't he? He must want out of here as much as I do.

And he has been standing up to them more and more. First

this black dress and now dancing with me in front of everyone. Maybe he is finally ready to fight back.

My mind drifts back to what Galen said earlier. That Draven didn't even try to fight when the Icehearts came to their home and demanded his allegiance. That he just got down on his knees and surrendered. It doesn't sound anything like Draven. But then again, I didn't know him two hundred years ago. He was only eighty-six back then. Maybe this confidence and power that he now exudes came later.

So if I ask him now to join me and help me crush the Iceheart Dynasty, he might say yes.

Fear draws its icy fingers down my spine.

Can I really take that risk? If I'm wrong, and Draven still doesn't dare to go against the Icehearts, I will be dooming not only the Red Hand, but the entire resistance. The human one and our fae one.

Swallowing, I gaze up into Draven's eyes, trying to read his mind.

But they betray nothing.

And I can't stop thinking about that blinding, world-ending, completely mind-shattering pain that I felt when I connected to Draven's emotions after Bane had whipped his wings to shreds. *That* is what Draven is risking if he simply fails them. So what would they do to him if they caught him actively trying to bring them down? A shiver of fear rolls down my spine at just the thought of it.

I stare up at him while indecision fights desperately inside me.

"Have you…" I begin before I even know what I'm doing. But I decide that I need to know. I need to ask this much, at least. So I clear my throat and try again. But I keep my voice soft, so that only he can hear. "Have you ever considered leaving?"

His dark brows furrow slightly. "Leaving what?"

"This." I flick a glance around the room, and to my surprise, realize that other people have started dancing as well. Tearing my gaze from the courtiers now filling the dance floor, I meet Draven's eyes again. "Leaving the Icehearts' service."

He clenches his jaw, as if in frustration, and glances away for a second before returning his gaze to me. "I can't leave."

"You've never even considered it?" I ask, trying to read the tense emotions on his face.

"Of course I have." He forces out another tight breath. "But I can't."

"Why not?"

He opens his mouth as if to reply, but then just closes it again and heaves a long, frustrated breath. "I tried once. It didn't... They..." He expels another forceful sigh and then meets my gaze head on. And when he speaks again, there is no doubt that he means every single word. "I can't leave."

Disappointment sinks into my stomach like a block of ice.

Because that answers my question.

Should I tell him about the heist and the rebellion?

The answer is no. No, I can't tell him. Ever.

It might be because he doesn't want them to whip his wings again, or he might be trying to keep the Icehearts from torturing his clan the way they are torturing him, or some other kind of logical but very inconvenient reason, but the fact of the matter remains that Draven will not go against the Icehearts.

Which means that I will need to help the humans pull off this heist, start a rebellion among the entire population of Frostfell, and then escape with Isera, Alistair, and Lavendera. And leave Draven to his fate. Because no matter how much I have tried to convince myself otherwise lately, Draven and I are on opposite sides in this war.

We are, and always will be, enemies.

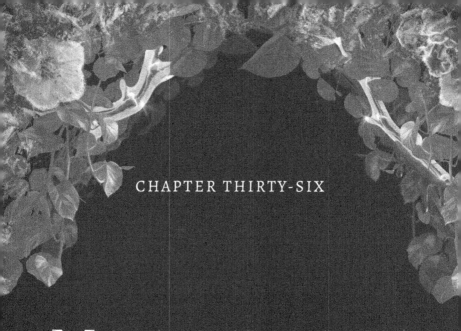

# CHAPTER THIRTY-SIX

**M**y heart aches as I stand there awkwardly on Draven's bedroom floor, watching him strip out of his armor. The beautiful black and gold dress that I wore tonight is already back in his closet. I brush my hand down the short silk nightgown I'm now wearing again.

This somehow feels like the beginning of the end. We have all the information we need for the heist and our escape. Now, all that is left is carrying it out.

Back in that ballroom, I made the decision to cut ties with Draven. To leave him to his fate and return to my own people. To my own side in this war. But making the decision still doesn't make the actual act any easier. Especially when my feelings for Draven are already tangled and complicated as it is due to this Goddess damned mate bond.

"Is none of it real?" I find myself asking, my voice coming out much more confused and desperate than I had intended.

Draven drops the final piece of his armor onto the stand with a thud and then turns to face me, now only wearing a pair of black underwear. His brows are furrowed in genuine confusion as he meets my gaze.

"What do you mean?" he asks.

"The... emotions," I begin uncertainly. "That you have for me. Are they real or just the product of the mate bond? And how do you know the difference? How do you know which ones are real and which ones are forced? Fake? Or is all of it fake?"

The words just tumble out of my mouth one after the other. But once I started, I couldn't stop. My heart aches, for multiple different reasons, and I just want someone to hold me and tell me that everything will be okay. But not even my own mother has done that for me, not once, since the day she found out about my magic. The only one who has ever come to save me is Draven. He has saved my life three times already. And the thought that he only did it because of this mate bond, and not because he truly cared about me, threatens to crack something fragile inside my chest.

Because if all of his feelings are artificial, something forced upon him by the universe, then that will mean that I have been right all along. That I am on my own. And I always have been.

Draven's expression softens, and he closes the distance between us.

Tilting my head back, I draw in an unsteady breath and meet his gaze. "Is it all fake?"

Pain flickers in his eyes. Then he slides his hands over my cheeks and into my hair as he holds me steady while his eyes sear into mine. I barely dare to breathe.

His serious eyes burn through my soul. "Does this feel fake to you?"

And then he kisses me.

Slowly and deeply and achingly passionately.

A broken noise comes from the back of my throat. Sliding my hands up his bare chest, I lock them behind his neck and yank him closer. A moan rips from his chest as I kiss him back furiously.

He drops his hands from my hair and instead grabs the hem

of my nightgown. With a firm pull, he yanks it upwards. I gasp in a breath as he breaks the kiss while pulling the fabric over my head. His eyes are wild with lust as he tosses the black silken garment to the floor and then closes the distance between us again.

Fire licks through my veins as he slips one hand around the back of my neck and the other around my waist and then yanks me back to him. My tits press against his bare chest as he holds me tight while his lips ravage mine. I moan into his mouth and rake my fingers down his muscular back.

His wings flare wider. I smile against his lips and move my hands up to his wings, gently tracing my fingers over the soft membrane.

A shudder rolls through his entire body, and he slides his hand up from the back of my neck and into my hair, taking it in a commanding grip and tilting my head back further. My heart flutters as he tangles his tongue with mine, completely dominating my mouth, while I trace my fingers across his wings. The most delicious moans rip from his lungs when my fingers brush the soft surface.

He releases my hair and waist and pulls back from the furious kiss. The sudden loss of his mouth against mine leaves me disoriented for a second. Then a jolt shoots through my body as his fingers curl over the top of my panties.

A devilish glint appears in his eyes as he takes the thin fabric of my panties in a firm grip.

Then he rips them open.

My heart flips and heat shoots straight through my core as my torn panties fall to the floor around my ankles.

Locking eyes with Draven, I grab the top of his underwear and try to do the same to him. But apparently, it's not as easy as he made it look.

A dark laugh rumbles from his chest, and he grips the back of my neck and yanks me into a possessive kiss. Still laughing against my mouth, he slides his other hand underneath his underwear and then just pushes them down his legs instead. Once he has stepped out of them and kicked them aside, I immediately wrap my hand around his thick cock and slide it up and down before teasing his tip with my thumb in retaliation.

To my satisfaction, it draws another one of those delicious moans from his throat.

He bites my bottom lip in revenge while growling, "Such a fucking troublesome little menace, aren't you?"

I laugh against his lips and slide my hand up and down his cock again at the same time as I use my other hand to caress his wing. His knees buckle for a moment. He forces out a long, steadying breath through his nose as he straightens.

"Now you've done it," he threatens against my mouth.

Grabbing the back of my thighs, he lifts me up from the floor and guides my legs around his hips. I'm forced to release his cock and instead lock my fingers behind the back of his neck. His mouth dominates mine with savage kisses as he carries me towards his bed.

He tries to throw me down on it, but I keep my legs wrapped firmly around his waist. A curse that is half exasperation, half approval rumbles from his chest. After slipping one arm around my back, he climbs onto the bed and then leans forward to lay me down on it instead.

Once my back is resting against the soft mattress, he slides his arm out from underneath me and straightens so that he is sitting on his knees. Then he grabs my ankles, which I still kept locked behind his back, and forces my legs away from his waist.

With a firm grip on my ankles, he spreads my legs wide before pressing them down against the bed. Then he slides his confident hands up my calves and towards my thighs instead. Lightning skitters across my skin at his possessive touch, and my clit aches with need.

I try to close my legs so that I can press my thighs together to help ease the throbbing in my clit, but Draven places his hands on the inside of my thighs and forces my legs to remain spread wide.

Then he leans down and drags his tongue along my pussy.

A jolt shoots up my spine, and I gasp as I arch up from the bed.

Draven's fingers dig into my thighs as he holds me trapped while he swirls his tongue around my aching clit. Pleasure spears through me, and a moan rips from my lips. I slide my hands through his hair, gripping it hard.

He tortures my clit with slow and luxurious strokes of his tongue until I'm squirming and panting on his sheets.

"Draven," I gasp.

His teeth scrape against my throbbing clit. Lightning shoots up my spine. Gripping his hair harder, I squirm and wiggle my hips.

"Draven." His name drips from my mouth like a moan. "Draven, please."

He lets out a dark chuckle that vibrates against my sensitive clit. "Oh I do so love hearing you beg."

Straightening, he releases my thighs and instead grips my wrists. After forcing my hands away from his hair, he pins them to the mattress above my head as he leans down over me.

The tip of his cock brushes against my entrance.

Another moan escapes me. My body is so tightly wound that it feels like my very soul is vibrating. Draven claims my lips with a possessive kiss, stealing that moan and the very air from my lungs.

Then he thrusts into me.

I gasp into his mouth as he sheaths himself inside me fully with that one powerful thrust. Pleasure pulses through me at the feeling of him filling me completely.

While still stealing my breath with demanding kisses, he draws his cock out and then slams back in again. My body jolts on the soft sheets. I groan in pleasure and curl my fingers. Draven tightens his grip on my wrists and then thrusts into me again.

I drag in a shuddering breath at the incredible friction it creates. Tension builds inside me as Draven starts up a commanding pace. I adjust my hips, creating an even better angle.

Pleasure crackles through me, making lights flicker in my brain.

I yank against Draven's grip on my wrists.

"Please," I moan. "Please let me touch you."

He keeps pounding into me for another few seconds, denying my request. Then he whispers against my mouth, "Fuck, you're so pretty when you beg."

His strong hands disappear from my wrists as he releases me and instead braces himself on the mattress. I slide one hand up his throat and take a firm grip right underneath his jaw.

Lust flares up in his eyes like fire.

"I will make you regret that," I promise, a wicked smile on my lips.

He lets out a dark chuckle.

"Don't think for one second, oh Shadow of Death, that I won't —" My words are cut off by a gasp as Draven's cock hits a spot deep inside me.

Pleasure shoots up my spine, and I have to move my hand from his throat to his shoulder so that I can dig my fingers into it hard in an effort to hold myself together as Draven thrusts into me, hitting that spot over and over again. A smirk shines on his lips. But I can't even spare the effort to glare at the smug bastard, because pleasure thrums inside my whole body, making my brain feel like it's melting.

My body jerks back and forth on the smooth sheets, and I career towards an orgasm as the pent-up tension inside me soars.

Draven takes one hand from the mattress and slides it along the curve of my breast. Then he rolls my nipple between his fingers. A desperate moan spills from my lips. I gasp air into my lungs and squirm furiously underneath him as the mounting pleasure becomes almost unbearable.

He keeps fucking me hard and dominantly and completely without mercy. Exactly the way I want him to. As if I am, and always has been, his.

His cock hits that perfect spot inside me again at the same time as he pinches my hard and aching nipple.

Release explodes through me.

I gasp as pleasure sweeps through my veins, intense enough to make my legs shake. I dig my fingers into Draven's muscular shoulder as he continues fucking me through the orgasm. Black spots dance before my eyes. I feel like my heart is going to give out.

Draven watches it all. Drinking it in. His eyes sear through me as he studies every emotion on my face, as if he is burning it into his mind forever.

With great effort, I manage to raise my free hand while my brain continues flickering with pleasure. I drag in a ragged breath and then slide my hand over Draven's wing.

Pleasure pulses across his face, and a groan rips from deep within his chest, as he comes.

I continue caressing his wing while release crashes through his body as well. Desperate groans spill from his mouth. I stare at his face, completely transfixed.

I still can't truly believe that I can manage to draw these moans and shudders and these raw emotions from him. It's intoxicating. It makes me feel drunk with power.

When the final waves of pleasure have at last faded from our bodies, we just remain like that for another few seconds. My hand unmoving against his wing. His cock still buried deep inside me. His eyes on mine and mine on his. Our chests heave.

Then he leans down and kisses me so gently that my heart almost breaks all over again.

Pulling out, he twists sideways and then lies down on the bed next to me. But he doesn't move to his side of the bed. And neither do I. Lying there beside him in the middle of the bed, I drag in deep breaths and try to convince myself that this didn't mean anything. That I shouldn't have done this. That we shouldn't have done this.

Draven drapes his arm over my body and pulls me closer, holding me tightly against his warm body.

A small and broken whimper escapes my lips.

He rests his chin on the top of my head while he holds me close, as if he fears that I will disappear if he lets me go. Oh if he only knew how right he is. It's only a matter of days now. Then I will be gone.

"I am a selfish person, Selena." He lets out a long breath that ruffles my hair. "And as much as I wanted to make sure that you never won the Atonement Trials, I'm secretly glad that you were stubborn and brilliant enough to win it despite all my sabotaging."

My heart slams against my ribs.

He draws in a deep breath, breathing me in, and tightens his arms around me. "Because it allowed me to have this time with you."

Something very fragile inside my chest just cracks wide open, and I have to bite my bottom lip hard to stop the sound that almost makes it out of my mouth.

And all the while, I force my mind to keep repeating one sentence over and over again.

We are enemies.

We are enemies.

We are enemies.

## CHAPTER THIRTY-SEVEN

We have a date. At last, after all my spying and sneaking around and all their plotting and scheming, we have finally decided when the heist is happening. During the grand ball that the Icehearts are hosting. Which is now only four days away.

Both anticipation and dread pulse through my veins as I sneak down the deserted street.

For weeks, I have felt as if I have all the time in the world to do this. To get it right. To think things through before I make any big decisions. And now, I'm suddenly out of time. In four days, the heist is happening. In four days, I'm escaping with Isera, Alistair, and Lavendera. In four days, I will destroy everything that Draven is working for and then leave him to be tortured by the Icehearts.

A cold hand grips my heart, squeezing hard.

But there is no other way. We need to do this during the ball, because it's the only time when all the clan leaders, as well as Draven and the Icehearts, will all be occupied elsewhere. No one will be thinking about what the humans in the city are doing. All of their attention will be on each other. It's the perfect opportunity.

It's also so dreadfully soon.

Shaking my head, I try to push those uncomfortable feelings aside. I have already decided that I need to stop feeling guilty. That I need to start being a little ruthless. So I force out a determined breath and block out the doubt in my heart as I continue towards Nysara's house.

Just like last time, the wide street is dark and deserted since it's the middle of the night. Only the barren trees watch me as I sneak towards the grand house with the dark blue door. When I pass her neighbor's house, I stop for a second and scan the windows. The last thing I need is him showing up again. Especially tonight.

But no candles are burning in the windows, so I hurry past his house and towards the gate in the low stone wall around Nysara's property. It swings open on silent hinges as I sneak through.

The back of my neck prickles. My heart leaps, and I quickly cast a glance over my shoulder. But Draven isn't there. He left our bedroom an hour ago, sneaking out to no doubt hunt the Red Hand while he thought I was sleeping. Which, admittedly, means that he is most likely somewhere here in the city. But I seriously doubt that he would be searching for the Red Hand in a fancy neighborhood like Ember Hill.

Still, I scan the empty street behind me twice more before I return my gaze to the house ahead.

Shaking my head, I skulk along the path and towards Nysara's front door. I don't know what it is about this street, this whole place, but I somehow always feel as if I'm being watched.

While I knock on Nysara's carved wooden door, I can't help but wonder if that is because of Nysara herself. She said that her mission here is to spy on the dragon shifters, so it wouldn't surprise me if she has some kind of secret Unseelie power set up over this street.

Candlelight flickers to life in the same upstairs window as last time. I watch as it moves from room to room before it reaches the hallway. Then the door is opened and a blond dragon shifter looks out at me in confusion.

The moment her blue eyes lock on my face, that fake confusion disappears and a sly feline smile spreads across her lips instead. However, she doesn't drop her glamour.

"Well, do you have a date?" she asks, getting straight to the point.

"Yes," I reply. "During the ball in four days."

She raises her eyebrows at me. "Which just so happens to be the exact same day and time that the human resistance will pull off their heist." She gives me a knowing smile. "I'm sure that's no coincidence."

My heart jerks, and I blink at her in shock. "How did you know that?"

"I've already told you. It's my job to know what is happening in this city."

"Fair enough. We will be using a secret tunnel to get in and out. It leads to the east side of the mountain. Is there any chance that you could meet us there?"

"No." She raises her chin and looks down at me. "If you want my help, you have to come to me."

Disappointment washes over me. Though I can't say that I'm surprised. During our brief interactions, I've gotten the sense that Nysara is an incredibly proud woman. Still, it was worth a shot. Getting four fae across the city unseen after the heist won't be easy. But we apparently don't have much of a choice.

"Fine," I reply. "We'll come to you."

She gives me another one of those cat-like smiles. "Good luck."

Then she shuts the door in my face.

I shake my head at the dark blue door and the Unseelie fae in disguise who is now heading back to her bedroom. She might be strange, and a little rude, but we will never make it out of Frostfell without her help.

After giving her a nod that she can't see, I turn back towards the street.

And nearly leap out of my skin.

For one single second, I swear that I see a person standing behind me. But once the sudden panic has stopped screaming in my mind, I realize that it's only a cluster of branches from the thick tree by the window.

Tilting my head up, I shoot a glare up towards Nysara's bedroom. I swear I can almost hear her laughing at me. With a huff, I shake my head again. I really wonder what other abilities this odd Unseelie woman has.

As I hurry back to the street, I amend that statement.

I really wonder what other abilities *all* Unseelie fae have. Since we have been cut off from the rest of the world for so long, I have no idea what the Unseelie Court is like. They might wield some kind of powers or possess abilities that we used to have too before the dragon shifters took over and erased our history. Abilities that they could teach us again. They might be able to help us recover some of the power that we have lost, which will be crucial if we're going to free our court.

A cold fall wind whirls down the street. I pull the hood of my cloak more firmly around my face as I start weaving my way through the city. And every time I pass any humans, I manipulate their emotions. I increase their anger and frustration and determination, making them furious and bold. Fanning the flames of rebellion.

And while I work, I let my mind churn, because this visit to Nysara and her little trick with the tree have given me an idea.

I didn't really have much of a plan after the escape, apart from somehow getting word to the Seelie Court about what is happening out here. But now I'm starting to think that the best course of action would be to make my way to the Unseelie Court.

Nysara said that the Unseelie Court doesn't get involved in other people's problems, so I doubt I will be able to convince them to help us fight the dragon shifters. If they had been inclined to do so, they would've done it millennia ago. But they might still be able to teach us things so that we can fight the dragon shifters on our own. Not only teach us about magic or whatever other powers we fae might have, but also about our history and what the political situation is like across the rest of the continent. There might even be others who—

I stop dead in the middle of the street as a memory hits me like a lightning bolt.

A memory of a creature shaped like a woman but made of the woods, and her sharp voice as she hissed two sentences at me.

*You hate the dragon shifters. We hate them more.*

The dryads.

Mabona's tits, we might be able to get the dryads to help us!

A sudden burst of excitement explodes through my chest. And for the first time in a long time, I feel hope. Hope that we might actually win. If I can get the Unseelie Court to teach me and the dryads to help me fight, we might actually stand a chance against the Iceheart Dynasty.

As I start walking again, I let a wicked grin spread across my mouth.

In the taverns I pass, humans, who are still refusing to work for the dragon shifters, are drowning their rage and resentment in alcohol. I increase those emotions, turning them into wildfires. Angry voices spill out from the windows. Human voices demanding an end to oppression. Declaring that this is their city. That they are the silent majority. That they need to stop being silent. That they need to resist. To fight back. I keep pouring my magic into them all as I pass, until the emotions are so strong that I can almost see them burning in the darkness.

That smile on my mouth turns vicious.

I can feel it with every step. This entire city is on the brink of war. A furious uprising bubbles like acid among the whole human population. All it needs is one spark. One person to light a match, and then this entire city will go up in flames.

This heist in four days will be the event that pushes them all across the final line.

And then I will be that spark.

# CHAPTER THIRTY-EIGHT

My heart pounds in my chest as I put on that breathtaking black and gold dress that Draven gave me a week ago. I try to swallow down a wave of dread, but it works poorly. My fingers are trembling slightly as I twist the hair closest to my face into the two coils that I always fasten behind my head to keep any hair from getting in my face and blocking my vision. Thankfully, Draven is too busy putting on his armor to notice.

"I'm going to have to leave you on your own for periods of time tonight," Draven says over his shoulder.

My heart jerks. *Tonight.* Yes, the grand ball and the humans' sneaky heist and our daring escape all goes down tonight. Or rather, right now. Because the moment that Draven and I have finished getting dressed, we're leaving for the ball.

It feels as if I have a cluster of thorny vines twisting between my ribs and strangling my heart, so it takes enormous effort to keep my voice light and teasing as I say, "Oh? And here I was, thinking that I commanded all of your attention."

"You do."

His reply is so immediate, and so genuine, that I have to stifle a sharp breath between my teeth. Fucking hell, it feels as if he just punched me in the heart. Letting my hands drop from my now finished hair, I turn around to face him.

He is still standing with his back to me, putting on his armor, but his hands are frozen halfway to a clasp at the side of his chest. As if he too has just realized what he said.

The silence in the room is so palpable that I swear I can hear it crackling in the air.

Then Draven clears his throat and finishes with, "But Bane and Jessina have tasked me with privately threatening some of the more difficult clan leaders into submission, so I need to go and do that too."

Which is actually great for me since it will give me a chance to slip away and escape once the heist is done. But I can't tell him that, of course, so I let a deliberately sly smile spread across my lips and keep the teasing note in my voice as I say, "Oh, don't worry. I will just find someone else to flirt with in the meantime."

At that, he at last turns around. His mouth is already open, ready to retort, but then his gaze lands on me. And his breath hitches.

My heart twists painfully.

Draven flicks his gaze up and down my body in this stunning black dress. Then he seems to remember that his mouth is still open. Snapping his mouth shut, he returns his gaze to my face and starts towards me. But that fire in his eyes remains.

"You do that," Draven at last replies as he comes to a halt in front of me.

A shudder of pleasure rolls down my spine as he slides his hand along my jaw, cupping my cheek, and then draws his thumb over my bottom lip. His eyes glint in the faelights as a wicked smile full of forbidden promises curls his lips.

"But anyone who flirts back will lose his hands. Or his tongue." His villainous smirk widens. "Or both."

A soft laugh escapes my lips.

It's followed by a wave of sorrow that threatens to crush me.

Because this is it.

This is our last goodbye.

After we leave this room, we will be out in public. Which means that I have a role to play and Draven has duties to attend. And then I will escape. Disappear like a thief in the night without so much as a word.

My heart aches.

Despite Draven's adamant refusal to leave or do anything to fight the Icehearts, he has still helped me in every way he could. He has saved my life more than once. He has protected me from torture and humiliation. He has made my life here in the Ice Palace bearable.

And deep inside that broken heart of mine, I know that he doesn't deserve this. He doesn't deserve to be left behind to take the blame for our crimes. He doesn't deserve to be betrayed like this. Especially not by me.

But I don't know what else to do. I can't stay here as a slave all my life just so that the Icehearts won't punish Draven. I need to do this. Not just for me, but for Isera and Lavendera and Alistair too. And for everyone in the Seelie Court.

So no matter how much I hate the reality we live in, I can't change the fact that it *is* our reality.

I need to do this.

Draven, oblivious to the internal battle I just fought, gives me a satisfied smile and then lets his hand drop from my cheek. He takes a step back, not knowing that this is the last time we will ever be this close. The last time we will ever speak this casually to each other. The last chance we have to say goodbye.

A bolt of panic spears through my chest, and my hand shoots out to grab his wrist before he can leave.

He turns back to me and raises his eyebrows in surprise.

"It wasn't an act," I say. My heart is pounding so loudly that I can barely hear my own voice. But I need to say this. I need him to know this. "Back in that underground forest. I didn't have sex with you as a distraction to steal the ring. It was the exact opposite."

Shock and confusion and a heartbreaking flicker of hope pulse in his eyes.

"I had stolen the ring before you had even gotten into the water," I continue, the words tumbling out of my mouth. "And I was supposed to slip away and escape while you were busy washing off in the river. Fucking you was never part of the plan. It was the opposite. It was an incredibly dangerous and reckless choice that only increased the risk of you realizing that I had stolen the ring. But I did it anyway. Because I wanted to." I hold his gaze with serious eyes, to make sure that he understands that I truly mean every word. "I did it solely because I wanted to. Because I wanted *you*."

He draws in a short unsteady breath.

I release his wrist and quickly take a step back, putting a little distance between our bodies. Because if I stand too close to him right now, I will never be able to leave.

Clearing my throat, I glance away as I finish with, "I just wanted you to know that."

I still don't know how much of what I feel for Draven is real and how much is just forced on me by the mate bond. But Goddess above, I know one thing.

Betraying him tonight is going to shatter what's left of my heart.

# CHAPTER THIRTY-NINE

The clash between the beautiful ballroom and the actual atmosphere inside it is so jarring that I still haven't fully adjusted to it, despite having spent two hours in here. It's one of the grandest rooms I have ever seen. Imposing columns of ice stretch up towards the impossibly high vaulted ceiling, which is covered entirely in faelight gems. If I tilt my head back, it's like gazing up into a pool of liquid starlight. Decorations in silver and ice are on display, and there is an entire band of musicians waiting at the edge of the massive dance floor.

At a grand ball like this, I would expect to see people dancing and laughing and enjoying themselves. But instead, everyone is standing silent and tense on the shining ice floor. Anger and resignation and dread and resentment and a whole storm of emotions hang over the room like a death shroud while everyone drinks nervously from crystal goblets in order to pass the time.

I shift my gaze to the front of the room, where a raised dais is located. Atop it are two thrones made of carved ice. Emperor Bane and Empress Jessina are seated on top of them, their massive silver wings spread wide and their fancy silver garments glittering in the faelights.

Then a clock chimes, marking that another full hour has passed.

A ripple goes through the gathered crowd.

I draw in a sharp breath as I watch a female dragon shifter in purple armor detach herself from a group farther down and start towards the raised dais. It's the leader of the Purple Dragon Clan. The clan who ambushed and tried to kill Draven out on the mountainside.

Everyone seems to be holding their breath as she comes to a halt on the floor in front of the two ice thrones. Jessina and Bane look down at her with haughty expressions. She lowers herself to one knee and bows her head.

"I, Diana Artemisia, do hereby renew my oaths of loyalty and swear allegiance to the Iceheart Dynasty on behalf of the Purple Dragon Clan," she says, her voice carrying across the sea of silent spectators.

I shift my gaze to Jessina and Bane, who say nothing. A ripple of worry goes through the crowd. When Gremar Fireclaw, the leader of the Red Dragon Clan, swore his allegiance an hour ago, they accepted it straight away. But not this time.

"Diana," Empress Jessina says, drawing out the syllables as if she is talking to a small and stupid child. "Did you really think that would be enough? After the... *disrespect* your clan showed us last week."

Most people don't know about the Purple Clan's attack on Draven, but Diana most certainly does. However, she says nothing. Only remains on one knee with her head bowed.

"If you want to earn our forgiveness," Emperor Bane picks up, a vicious smile spreading across his lips, "you need to grovel for it."

Diana drops down on both knees and presses her forehead to the floor. I swallow down the bile rising in my throat as I watch her grovel for forgiveness at their feet. Once the Icehearts are finally satisfied, they let her return to her people.

But no other clan leader steps forward. Everyone just continues standing there on the polished ice floor, nervously drinking sparkling wine and watching each other and their monarchs. The tension in the room is so thick that I could have cut it with a knife.

"Why are they drawing it out like this?" I whisper to Draven.

Draven has been standing right next to me like this for the past two hours. After what he said back in his bedroom, I had expected him to move around the crowd more. But he hasn't left my side for one single second. And that is now starting to worry me.

The heist began the moment that the ball did. That was two hours ago, which means that the humans must have at least reached the entrance to the tunnel out there on the mountainside. If they moved fast, they might already be inside the palace. Once they're done emptying the treasury, they're going to create a distraction so that the rest of us will have a chance to slip away in the chaos. But I won't be able to do that if Draven remains glued to my side all evening.

"It's a power play," Draven replies. "They only let one clan swear allegiance every hour so that it will take eight hours to get through us all. And we can't enjoy ourselves at the ball in the meantime, because no one is in a festive mood. All we can do is to just stand here in tense silence for eight hours. It's a psychological trick to wear us down and demonstrate the kind of power they have over us."

I turn to glance at him in surprise. "That's… terrifyingly clever."

He lets out a humorless breath. "I know. I'm the one who suggested it."

The doors to the patio are shoved open, shattering the crackling silence. A broad-shouldered man in brown dragon scale armor stalks outside in what looks like frustration.

That finally breaks the spell. A murmur spreads through the

room as everyone starts talking softly. No one is dancing or having fun, but they're at least speaking and moving around now. I draw in a deep breath as the tension in the room eases a little.

A few moments later, Galen comes striding towards us from the direction that the leader of the Brown Dragon Clan came from before he stalked out onto the patio. I move a little to the side to give them space while Galen comes to a halt in front of Draven.

Galen flicks a discreet but pointed glance towards the still open doors to the patio, and when he speaks, he keeps his voice low enough that only we can hear. "He says that he won't do it. Says that the stones will bend before he does."

"The Brown Clan is being stubborn?" Draven lets out a huff of amusement and rolls his eyes. "What a shocker."

A smile begins forming on Galen's mouth. "I know, right?"

Then, as if he suddenly remembers that he's not supposed to be friends with Draven anymore, he snaps his mouth shut and wipes any trace of amusement off his features. His brows pull down into a scowl instead.

Draven's behavior immediately changes as well. He straightens his spine, and that blank mask descends over his face as he looks back at Galen with commanding eyes.

"I'll handle it," Draven declares. Then he jerks his chin towards the main door instead. "Take all of our people and go back to the barracks."

The scowl on Galen's face deepens. "Why?"

"Since when do you question orders?"

"Since you became a spineless coward."

Draven clenches his jaw. "Just do as I say."

Galen bows his head in a way that is just the tiniest bit mocking. "Yes, sir."

While Galen strides away to obey, Draven forces out a long and highly controlled breath.

I glance up at him. "Why are you sending them away?"

Draven draws in another breath and turns to me. To my surprise, there is no frustration left on his face. Not one trace. By Mabona, he really is an excellent actor.

"I might be the Commander of the Dread Legion," he begins. "But I'm also the leader of the Black Dragon Clan." He flicks a glance towards the two ice thrones and the smug monarchs seated on them. "Which means that at the end of the night, I need to get down on my knees and swear allegiance too."

Understanding washes through me.

"And you would rather your people didn't see that," I finish for him.

He just slides his gaze back to me, but the look in his eyes is confirmation enough. My heart suddenly aches again. Draven clears his throat.

"I need to go and deal with this," he says, and nods towards the open doors to the patio. "I have a feeling that it's going to take almost the entire hour. The stubbornness of the Brown Clan is legendary." Then a hint of light returns to his eyes as he adds, "If you flirt with anyone while I'm gone..."

Despite it all, a small chuckle escapes my lips. "You'll cut out their tongue. Or their hands. Or both. Yes, yes, I know."

"See? You really are learning."

I have to suppress another smile and an eye roll. Draven just flashes me a knowing smirk and strides away.

So as to not draw attention, I remain standing there with my head slightly bowed like a good little life slave for at least ten minutes. It works like a charm as people continue talking quietly amongst themselves while forgetting that I'm even there.

Once I'm sure that I have become more or less invisible, I quickly sweep my gaze over the room. People are still talking in hushed voices where they're standing throughout the large room. A messenger hurries across the floor and whispers something to Bane and Jessina, who smile like satisfied cats. While they're distracted, I begin slowly moving around the room and towards where Isera and Alistair are standing close to the dais.

While getting dressed, I managed to hide my climbing gear underneath my dress. So once the humans start the distraction, we should all be able to use it to get out of here. The only problem is that we need to take turns climbing and then drop the climbing gear back down for the next person. And we also need to somehow get Lavendera out of the kennels.

Anxious worry pulses through me. There are so many things that can go wrong. What if the distraction isn't enough to draw the Icehearts away from the ballroom? What if we're spotted while climbing up the wall? Indecision slices through my chest. Maybe we should just try to make a run for it through the side gate instead of using the secret tunnel? That way, we'll be closer to where Nysara is waiting with her glamour.

But can we really make it out that way without the guard raising the alarm? I might have manipulated his emotions so that he's terrified of me, but will that be enough when I have three other fae with me? And I won't even be able to use my magic this time. And neither will Isera, Alistair, or Lavendera, since we're all wearing iron collars. Goddess above, I wish there had been a way for us to get the collars off before we escape. But this is it. This is our one chance. And we have to take it.

Tension crackles through my every nerve like lightning as I try to move as casually as possible on my way through the ballroom. I flick another glance at Isera and Alistair.

The air is yanked straight out of my lungs as I find both Isera and Alistair staring at me with full-blown panic in their eyes. My heart rate picks up until I can practically feel it thrumming in my chest. Moving as quickly as I can without drawing attention, I adjust my course and instead make my way straight towards my two partners in crime. The crowd around me continues talking softly, as if my mind isn't suddenly screaming in alarm.

Why are they looking so panicked? Don't tell me that

Lavendera was taken somewhere else before the others left the kennels. Or that Draven has somehow figured out what I'm doing.

While Jessina and Bane are preoccupied with grinning and congratulating each other about something, I come to a halt as close to Isera as I can without drawing the Icehearts' attention.

"What is it?" I whisper, hoping that she can hear me.

She keeps her gaze focused on the wall across the room, and her mouth is barely moving when she replies, "Bane just said that the trap worked."

My heart stops beating. There is a sudden rushing sound in my ears, and I feel as if the whole room is tilting to the side.

"What trap?" I breathe, my mouth suddenly dry as sand.

"They have caught the human resistance."

# CHAPTER FORTY

Wind rips at my dress as I scale the wall of the castle at breakneck speed. Panic and dread clang inside my skull like giant bells. This cannot be happening. This cannot be happening. My hair flutters behind me as I climb desperately to reach the windows of the corridor that is between the door to the secret tunnel and the one that continues towards the treasury.

Isera said that she overheard the messenger tell the Icehearts that their soldiers successfully cornered the humans from both sides the moment they stepped out of the door, and that they are now trapped there in the corridor. It can't be true. It can't possibly be true. How would they have found out? We were so careful. We have been planning for so long. It simply cannot be true.

But if it is, I need to try to do something to help them escape. Especially the Red Hand. If the human resistance loses the Red Hand, there is no telling what will happen.

My stomach lurches, and a gasp rips from my lungs as the smooth fabric of my dress skirt ends up between my shoe and the wall, causing me to slip.

I grip the jagged ice hard with my hands as I drop downwards.

A huff tears from my throat as my arms take the brunt of the weight. The long dress skirt tangles around my legs. Panic pulses through my veins. Gritting my teeth, I try to pull myself back up while trying to kick the flowing fabric out of the way.

Another wind whirls around the castle.

My hair and dress are swept to the side. I shake my head to get the strands of hair out of my face, but the wind at least managed to finally move the dress skirt aside.

Relief flows through my shoulders and arms as I finally regain purchase with my feet.

My heart pounds against my ribs.

For a second, I just cling to the wall like that and close my eyes while drawing in a deep steadying breath. Then I start upwards again. I don't have any more seconds to waste. If the guards really have cornered the humans, I need to help them before it's too late.

When I finally reach the window, I realize that it's already open.

My heart leaps.

The Red Hand. He's already here.

Fuck. I need to hurry.

Yanking the window fully open, I heave myself up and practically roll in through the window. My dress rustles around me, snagging on the latch. I yank the fabric free and then leap to my feet while pulling off my climbing gear and hiding it underneath my dress again.

From around the corner, the muffled sounds of a struggle can be heard. Last time I was here, there was a guard standing by this corner. He's not there now. Which, while ultimately good for me, is a bad sign since it means that he has gotten involved in the ambush against the humans.

I dart towards the corner. My heart pounds in my chest.

Drawing myself up by the wall, I edge forward and glance around the corner.

My heart drops.

The pale ice corridor around the corner is packed with dragon shifters in silver armor. And humans. Panic clangs inside my skull as I stare at the furious battle taking place there.

Kath and Kyler are fighting back to back, both of them carrying a pair of knives. Ami and Peter are desperately trying to push back the wall of dragon shifters who are blocking the door to the emergency escape tunnel, preventing them all from just running back out. Ami's black hair whips around her chin as she darts from side to side, trying futilely to stab at the guards with a small knife.

The rest of the humans who were there to help carry everything in the treasury are fighting with equal fury around them. But it's a losing battle. The dragon shifters are all wearing their silver dragon scale armor while the humans are only wearing clothes made of thin fabric. And all the shifters have swords, which gives them better reach against the humans' smaller daggers.

I whip my gaze from side to side, trying to come up with something that can help them. Some way of distracting the guards so that the humans can get the door open and get at least a small chance to escape back out through the tunnel.

But there is nothing.

I don't have any weapons, I can't access my magic, and there is nothing in the corridor that I can use. No side tables, no decorations, not even a wall sconce that I can rip off and chuck at the window as a distraction.

An idea flashes through my mind. It's an absolutely stupid idea. But it's all I've got.

I can use myself as a distraction. If I can get them to chase me, it might create an opening for the humans. And the guards can't use the half-shift, so if I climb back out the window before they can get to me, I might be able to make it back down to the ground.

It's dumb and insane and a ridiculous risk. But I have to do something.

Straightening my spine, I take a determined step around the corner.

But I only make it that one step before I freeze in place on the floor when I hear a sharp voice cut through the noise of the fight.

"Enough! I served them up to you on a silver platter, and you can't even complete the simple task of arresting them. I refuse to be punished for your incompetence."

Twisting tree branches explode into view across the entire corridor, snaking around the humans and trapping them in place.

My heart stops and ice washes through my veins as I stare at the woman who strides out of the fray.

Her long brown hair ripples down her back as she stalks across the ice floor. The faelights in the ceiling illuminate her gorgeous features as well as the vicious scar across her cheek and jaw.

My mind cannot process what I'm seeing.

Then those stunning pink and purple eyes snap towards me and lock straight on my face, and reality slams into me like a blow to the chest.

Lavendera.

Before her name has even finished reverberating through my skull, a branch shoots out and wraps around my waist.

I gasp in shock, snapping out of my stupor and slam my hands down on the branch now encircling my waist.

"Round them up," Lavendera snaps to the guards as she strides down the corridor towards me.

She pushes her palms upwards in the air, and a thick nest of tree branches rises behind her, cutting both of us off from the rest of the corridor.

Alarm screams inside my head as I desperately pound against

the wood and kick and wiggle. The branch tightens around my waist.

"You shouldn't have come here," Lavendera says as she closes the final distance between us. Her voice is hard, but her eyes are filled with sorrow.

"You sold us out!" I scream back in her face, fury and desperation lacing every word.

A wave of sadness washes over her beautiful face, and when she speaks, her voice is softer. Almost gentle. "No, I didn't sell you out. I was never on your side to begin with."

Her words clang inside my skull for several seconds, like the echo of a giant bell, before I finally process what she is actually telling me. I suck in an unsteady breath, my whole worldview tilting sideways again.

"You work for them." It's not really a question, but Lavendera answers anyway.

"Yes."

Blood pounds in my ears as I stare at her. "For how long? Did you work for them during the Atonement Trials too?"

"Yes. My job is to make sure that the strongest magic users move on to the next trial." A sad smile blows across her lips, and she cocks her head as she holds my gaze. As if she can't believe that I haven't realized this earlier. "Why do you think I killed Maximus? He cheated. We all knew it, but no one could prove it. So I had to enforce the rules on their behalf."

And suddenly, a whole flood of things that never really made sense become crystal clear.

"You led Alistair, Isera, and Trevor to the rings," I blurt out. "You *led* them there. Because they were the strongest magic users."

"Yes. But then Trevor dropped out on his own because of his head injury. So then someone else had to win." Another small smile tugs at her lips. "That's why I didn't take the ring from you when I found you at the edge of the forest."

I feel like my soul is crumbling in on itself. Swallowing down the dread crawling up my throat, I press out, "That's why you knew so much. About the sterilization and the magical bloodline breeding."

"Yes."

"No!" I scream as fury spears through me. Fighting desperately, I slam my fists down on the thick branch trapping me, trying to shatter it. "How can you even use magic? You're wearing an iron collar too, for Mabona's sake!"

Lavendera draws her fingers over the metal collar around her throat. "It's not real iron. It was just a way to make sure that you wouldn't become suspicious of me."

"Why?" The word rips out of my throat, raw and dripping with anger and despair. "Why did you do this to us? Why are you doing this to us?"

Deep sorrow swirls in her pink and purple eyes, but she says nothing.

"How did you even know what we were planning?" I snap while still banging my fists on the wood and wiggling furiously. "You weren't even there when I told Isera and Alistair about the plan!"

"I followed you to that blond dragon shifter on Ember Hill. Both times. The first, I could only watch from the trees in the street. But the second time, I heard your entire conversation. That cluster of branches that made you jump and that you glared at before leaving… that was me."

"No!" I scream again as hopelessness and desperation threaten to drag me under and drown me in their cold dark depths. I pound against the branch keeping me trapped while locking eyes full of pain and disbelief on Lavendera. "You can't do this! You can't be one of them! You can't—"

My voice breaks, and a sob rips from my throat.

"After everything I have done to get to this point," I press out, my voice desperate and broken. "After all the risks I have taken and all the miracles I have already pulled off, after all the promises that I have made to Isera and Alistair, this can't be how it ends. Betrayed by my own people!" I stare at Lavendera as pain cuts through my chest. "By someone I thought was my friend."

Hurt, and a sense of deep recognition, flashes across her face for a second.

Then the branch abruptly disappears from my waist.

"Go," she says.

I stagger upright after the sudden drop, and stare at her in shock.

"I will give you a head start, because…" That profound sorrow and deep pain swirls in her eyes for a second. Then she jerks her chin towards the corridor I came from. "Just go."

Before I can so much as open my mouth to answer, she spins on her heel and stalks back towards the fight.

The wall of branches that she raised between them and us drops down into the floor again, revealing that all the humans are now shackled and on their knees. Peter has blood trickling down the side of his face while Ami keeps her head bowed. Kath stares daggers at the guards around them, but next to her, Kyler is white with fear and looks like he's going to throw up.

I quickly scan all their faces while I back towards the corner.

There is no sign of that telltale red demon mask that the Red Hand always wears, and I can't see Hector's face among the captured group either.

Which means that he is still somewhere between here and the treasury.

Indecision cleaves my chest as I race back down the other corridor. The open window that both he and I climbed in through appears on my right, and for a second, I have almost managed to convince myself to use this head start that Lavendera has given me to escape on my own. But I can't.

If I leave, Isera and Alistair will still be trapped here. And if I don't warn the Red Hand, he will be captured and then killed. It will gut the resistance.

I know that Draven won't let them kill me, so even if I'm captured, I will still survive. But the Red Hand certainly won't.

My heart hammers in my chest as I sprint down the corridor and towards the treasury.

I have to warn him.

# CHAPTER FORTY-ONE

**M**y feet thud against the floor as I sprint down the corridor. With every step, the sounds of dragon shifters barking orders to the captured humans grow fainter. The dress whips around my legs as I skid around the next corner.

I jump, throwing an arm out to catch myself on the wall as I nearly trip over the body lying slumped against the wall. Scrambling upright again, I stare at the male dragon shifter in silver armor. His gray eyes are still wide with shock, but they're staring unseeing at the wall opposite him. There is a red smear down the wall that ends behind him where he sits, leaning against the wall. As if someone shoved a sword through his chest and he just slid down the wall when his knees buckled.

Skirting around his outstretched legs, I take off down the corridor again.

Faelight gems shine in the ceiling, providing the only light since there are no windows in here. But they are bright enough that I can see the next two guards long before I reach them. They are lying on their stomachs, straight across the floor of the corridor. Pools of blood spread out around their heads. But since

I can't see the front of their bodies, I don't know what wounds they died from.

My pulse thrums in my ears as I leap over the two corpses and sprint towards the next corner. Panic streaks through my body like lightning. I need to make it to the Red Hand, and then both of us need to make it back out into that corridor with windows again so that we can climb out, before Lavendera and the others realize that I went this way. This is the only path out from the treasury. If they come hunting us here, we will be trapped with no way out.

Grabbing the edge of the wall, I swing myself around the next corner. My heart leaps.

Two more bodies lie slumped in the corridor before me. Blood stains the ice floor and their silver armor red. One of them has had his throat slit in the Red Hand's signature move. But the other looks to have put up more of a fight, because his entire chest has been cut open in one long slash.

I swallow down a flash of bile at the sight of the intestines that spill out of his stomach.

Pushing myself hard, I race towards the next corner.

There are supposed to be three corridors and eight guards between the secret door and the treasury. Those two guards make five dead in total. And this is the third corridor. Which means that when I round the corner up ahead, I will reach the treasury. And the remaining three guards.

With every step, the noise of a struggle becomes louder.

My heart jerks.

Please let there still be time. Goddess above, please let there still be enough time to get back out again.

We got lucky that Draven was forced to deal with the stubborn leader of the Brown Dragon Clan. But the moment he comes back and finds out what has happened, he's going to fly straight here. And the Red Hand might be skilled, but he has nothing on Draven.

At the end of the day, Hector is still just a human, even behind his larger-than-life persona of the Red Hand. And Draven is... Draven. Powerful, skilled, ruthless Draven with his massive wings and his storm magic and his skills with a sword. If he were to catch us, I don't think even I would be able to convince him to let Hector go. Not after all of the pain and humiliation he has suffered because of his failure to capture him.

Cold hands wrap around my heart, squeezing hard, as I imagine the look of utter betrayal on Draven's face when he finds out what I have done. What I tried to do. And what I was willing to leave him to be punished for.

Using every smidgen of willpower I have, I shove those thoughts to the back of my mind. I can't think about that right now. I have to get us out of here. Right now. Before it's too late.

I skid around the final corner, practically crashing into the ice wall on the opposite side.

And screech to a halt in the middle of a battle.

One dragon shifter in silver armor is already lying dead on the floor. The other two are fighting furiously against a tall and muscular man in a dark gray cloak and clothes. And on his face is that signature red devil's mask that I saw in the drawing.

Relief crashes over me.

The Red Hand.

Hector.

He's still alive.

Steel clangs as one of the guards slams his sword towards Hector's neck while the other swings at him from the other side. Hector yanks up a pair of long daggers, blocking both strikes simultaneously. With a flick of his left wrist, he slides the sword off his blade and rams his dagger into the side of the guard's neck.

A gasp rips from his throat, but it comes out like more of a wet gurgle, as he drops his sword and reaches for his throat. But Hector must have punctured his carotid artery, because blood gushes out of the wound and spills between his fingers in a torrent of red.

The other guard tries to leap back, but Hector was already moving.

Not even looking at the dying guard, he whips around and rams his other dagger straight into the remaining dragon shifter's heart. I stare in shock. The amount of force it must have taken to pierce dragon scale armor like that is insane.

It has been less than five seconds since I skidded around the corner, but the insane level of fighting skills that the Red Hand has just displayed is incredible. No wonder Draven has been so obsessed with capturing him. He is going to be a real asset to the resistance I'm planning to rebuild. *If* I can get him out before Draven gets here, that is.

"Hector!" I call as I shove myself away from the wall that I crashed into when I flew around the corner.

Hector whips towards me, and then jerks back in shock.

I wince, realizing that I probably shouldn't have yelled his real name like that. But everyone in here is already dead, so there is no one left to hear it.

As if on cue, the two guards he just killed hit the floor with a thud. Blood quickly spreads across the pale floor around them.

"It's a trap," I continue as I hurry towards him, speaking so fast that I'm almost tripping over the words. "The Icehearts knew we were coming. Everyone else has already been captured. We need to get out. Now."

I can't see his face because of the mask, but a jolt of shock goes through his entire body, and he whips his head in the direction of the secret door three corridors away.

"We need to—" I begin.

"MAN DOWN!" a male voice bellows so loudly that it echoes down the halls all the way to us. "They're heading for the treasury!"

348

Panic crackles up my spine with the force of a lightning bolt, and for a moment, I can't make my brain work.

They have seen the dead bodies.

They know we're here.

They are coming.

"We're trapped," I blurt out.

Goddess above, there is no other way out of here. We are trapped in here. And they are coming.

My mind spins out of control as those thoughts clang through me like death knells.

Then one single breath of clarity pushes through the screaming panic.

Whirling back towards Hector, I stab a hand towards the open door to the treasury. Glowing golden reflections, as if light is shining down on mountains of gold, spill out of the gap in the door.

"Hide!" I snap at the Red Hand while bending down to snatch up a sword from one of the dead guards. "I'll pretend that it was me who did it. Once they take me away, run back to the window and get the hell out of here."

Spinning around, I face the corridor again and adjust the sword in my hand.

The sound of pounding boots echoes from around the corner, beating in tune with my hammering pulse.

A gloved hand grabs my shoulder and yanks me back around. I blink, coming face to face with the Red Hand, who is shaking his head furiously.

"Stop trying to be a hero!" I snarl at him, panic and frustration thrashing inside me like a storm. "This is the only way! Draven won't let them kill me. But he will kill *you*. He has been hunting you day and night for months! You are the face of the rebellion. I'm not. They need you. We all need you." Raising the sword, I stab it in the direction of the treasury again. "So hide in there and let me take the damn fall for this!"

"The midway guards are down as well!" someone yells from the corridor right before this one. "They have reached the treasury."

Boots pound against the floor as they race towards us.

I try to spin towards them, but Hector grabs my arm and yanks me back to face him again.

"Stop being so fucking stubborn!" he snaps as he reaches up and yanks his mask off.

I jerk back in shock.

And then the world just... stops.

Because it's not Hector who stares back at me from underneath the mask.

It's Draven Ryat.

# CHAPTER FORTY-TWO

"You…" I stammer.

It feels as if my head is an empty shell, echoing after a violent explosion. I stare up into Draven's golden eyes, but my mind refuses to process what I'm seeing.

This has to be some kind of trick. A ruse. Draven has dressed up as the Red Hand in an effort to catch him.

But blood-filled images quickly flash through my mind, disproving that theory. I literally watched Draven slaughter these guards. He wouldn't have done that if he was only pretending. Which can only mean…

"*You* are the Red Hand," I gasp out.

I feel like someone just smashed the floor beneath my feet and sent me plummeting down into the unknown abyss below.

"Yes," Draven replies, shoving his daggers back in their sheaths.

"What—"

"Not the time for this conversation, little rebel."

Shouts and pounding footsteps echo from right around the corner.

Draven grabs me by the throat and yanks me closer. I suck in another gasp as he quickly removes the iron collar from my throat and throws it down on the floor. It hits the ice with a clanking sound while Draven rips off his dark gray cloak and snatches up the remaining sword from the ground.

"We're going to have to fight our way out of here," he says. Smoke explodes through the air as he shifts into a half-shift and spreads his massive wings. "Get ready."

Before the final word has even left his mouth, a horde of dragon shifters in silver armor surges around the corner.

Tossing the sword to the ground, I yank the two daggers from Draven's belt instead. I don't know how to fight with a sword. If we're going to have any chance of surviving this, I need weapons that I can actually wield.

Draven doesn't even flinch or worry for one second about what I was doing when I dropped the sword and stole his knives.

He just gives me a quick nod of approval. "Don't hold back."

Before I can reply, the first wave of guards reaches us.

But then they hesitate for a moment when they notice that it's Draven. Summoning my magic, I shove it at those sparks of confusion in their chests until it makes them even more hesitant and disoriented. Draven swings his sword and cuts the head off the first man.

That snaps the others out of their stupor, and they lurch forward. I keep my magic pouring into them anyway since it makes them clumsy and uncertain. Draven rams his sword towards one man's chest, but the other six all swarm towards him at the same time, so he's forced to abandon the strike.

Storm winds crash through the room.

Six of the attackers are flung backwards by Draven's magic, but the final one, who was standing closest to me, dives forward right before the storm wind can hit him.

Air explodes from my lungs as he slams right into me, knocking both of us back and sending us crashing in through the doorway to the treasury. The pain that shoots through my shoulder blades when I hit the ice floor hard makes me lose my grip on my magic.

Draven whips his head towards us, but I can barely see it over the body of the dragon shifter who lands on me a second later. Rolling sideways, I shove him off me and gasp in a breath.

"I'm fine!" I call to Draven.

But he doesn't have time to reply, because the other six guards have recovered and launched themselves at him again.

I scramble up from the floor right at the same time as my attacker. His brown hair is disheveled, and surprise and confusion swirl in his eyes as he stares at me. For a moment, we just stand there facing each other.

Golden light fills the large room around us. Rows upon rows of shelves line the walls, and all of them are practically bursting with treasure. Gold and silver and gems and all manners of precious objects fill the shelves, and piles of coins occupy parts of the floor. In the middle of the room are pedestals that display gleaming artifacts. And all of it is lit by the sparkling faelight gems in the ceiling, which reflect against the precious metal and makes it seem like the whole room is glowing.

I'm surrounded by the entirety of the Iceheart Dynasty's accumulated wealth. The treasure that the human resistance tried so hard to steal. And I can do nothing to complete their doomed mission. Because it's all too late.

Alarm spikes through my spine as the guard lunges at me.

Leaping back, I yank up my daggers to block his strike. His sword slams into my intersecting blades so hard that I stagger backwards. Twisting sideways, he slides his sword free and feints to the right before striking to the left. I barely manage to see it coming in time to dodge.

Pain spears through me as his sword slices along the side of my ribs. A gash appears in the smooth black fabric of my dress, and blood spills out from the cut in my side. I gasp in pain. Resisting the urge to drop one of the knives and press a hand to the wound, I instead use the precious moment when his sword is still out of position from the strike to ram my own dagger towards his throat.

His eyes widen in surprise, but he jerks back in time, and my blade whooshes through the empty air instead. Warm blood slides down the side of my ribs as I twist with the missed strike and duck underneath his retaliating sword. It passes only a breath over my head.

Panic crackles through my every nerve as I jerk upright and jump back to evade another strike.

My heart pounds and my mind is screaming at me. Because I know, without a doubt, that I am outclassed against this man. He's an elite guard in the Silver Dragon Clan, and he has probably been training with that sword since childhood. And I'm a fish cutter with emotion magic. I will never win this duel.

Outside in the corridor, black storm clouds and winds whirl between the ice walls. Lightning bolts flash and steel clashes as Draven fights the other six guards on his own.

I throw myself sideways as my attacker rams his sword straight towards my chest. Pain pulses through my wounded side as I hit the row of shelves along the wall. Golden cups topple over and plummet to the floor in a clatter of metal. I shove myself away from the shelf, making a bowl of gems wobble right on the edge. It crashes down as the guard's sword hits it a moment later, missing me by a hair's breadth.

My mind screams in panic as I try to scramble out of reach. I need to—

He launches himself at me.

For the second time tonight, air explodes from my lungs as this damn guard slams right into my chest. But this time, he is ready for it. I'm not.

His arms wrap around my body, pinning my own arms to my sides, as I topple backwards. The impact as I hit the floor knocks one of the daggers from my hands. I gasp as the guard lands on top of me, his arms still locked around me. But that fortunately also traps them underneath my body and immobilizes the sword in his hand so that it's pressed against my side instead.

He seems to realize that too because he shifts his legs so that he is straddling me instead and then jerks upright while pulling his arms out from underneath me. In order to do that, he has to release his sword. And I use that second when he draws back to my full advantage.

Yanking up my right hand, I slam my remaining knife towards his throat.

Shock flashes across his features, and he jerks backwards.

A snarl rips from my throat when my blade yet again only cuts through empty air. This guy is too well-trained. His reflexes are too damn quick.

Still straddling me, his hand shoots towards his sword. But my hand is closer. Slamming my free hand outwards, I manage to shove the sword away right before his fingers can brush the hilt. It scrapes against the ice floor as it slides across the room before hitting a pile of coins.

Anger crackles in the guard's eyes as he snaps his gaze back to me. But he doesn't have time to do anything other than dodge again when I ram my remaining blade towards the side of his neck.

Throwing himself sideways, he evades the dagger. But by doing so, he also lifts his weight from my hips as he leans to the side. Twisting in the same direction, I shove my hips upwards at the same time as I slam my free hand into his shoulder. And because he was already leaning sideways, the move makes him tilt even more to the side.

My heart leaps in my chest, and I scramble backwards to get out from underneath him.

A snarl rips from his lungs as he lurches back towards me.

His hand closes around my ankle right before I can pull it out of reach. I gasp as he yanks hard. The skirt of my dress bunches around my thighs as I slide back along the floor. I kick my other foot, desperately trying to break his grip. He pulls again and drags me fully back to him with one hard yank.

I swing my dagger blindly above me as he once again tries to straddle me. But he expertly shoves my wrist aside before it can hit. Then his weight lands on my hips and his hands close around my throat.

Terror rips through my chest as he squeezes hard, cutting off my air.

My mind screams in panic, and I struggle furiously. But the blind panic is making me stupid, and all I manage to do is to slam my flailing arms and legs into the shelves beside me. A sack topples over, landing on its side on the shelf. Tiny pearls trickle out from the opening as the string comes partly undone. They clatter to the floor and roll across the smooth ice.

The guard isn't wasting a single second. He knows exactly how to strangle someone to death and keeps applying pressure in all the critical spots.

Black stars dance before my eyes and panic screams inside me.

*Think!* Goddess damn it, I need to think.

Clarity cuts through the blinding panic for a second.

Yanking up my dagger, I ram it right through the guard's wrist.

And the moment it hits, I summon my magic and throw everything I have into the pale red spark of pain that flares up in his chest.

He gasps and jerks back as I turn that small spark of pain into agony so deep that it will make him wish for death. A bloodcurdling scream rips from his lungs as I yank the blade back out. His hands disappear from my throat as he instead grips his bleeding wrist.

I suck air back into my lungs. Coughing desperately, I blink against the black spots that float before my eyes and draw in ragged breaths. But I can't waste this moment. Lurching upwards, I slam my entire body into his while I stab the blade towards his throat.

But even with the world-ending pain I'm pouring inside him, his instincts take over and he manages to slam his hand against my wrist and redirect the blow before it can strike. However, the move made him crash down on his side on the floor.

Scrambling to my knees, I shove him over on his back and ram the blade at his throat again. His hands fly up, gripping my wrist and stopping the blade.

I snarl in frustration as I try to force the blade down into his neck. But he's too strong.

The crackling of lightning and clashing of swords echo from outside the door, drowning out the faint clattering of pearls that keep trickling out of the bag right above me. Putting all of my strength into it, I bend forward as I try to drive the point of the blade home. But the guard keeps his hands around my wrist, holding it immobile, even though his eyes are glassy with pain from my magic.

With a cry of frustration, I yank my other hand up and slam my fist right into his injured wrist. Then I shove with my magic again.

An earsplitting scream shatters from his lungs as I magnify the pain.

And the moment he opens his mouth, I yank my hand up and rip the string off the bag above us.

A torrent of tiny pearls pours out of the bag and streams down right into the guard's open mouth.

Releasing my grip on his pain, I instead force my magic straight into the spark of bone white fear that flickers to life in his chest. His eyes almost bulge out of his head as he tries to scream in sheer panic and fear. But that only makes him swallow even more pearls. I increase his terror to the point that it must feel like he is drowning in a sea of beads, gasping in tiny round pearls instead of air.

And while he is thrashing in panic underneath me, I finally yank my wrist out of his grip and then slam the dagger down right through his throat. He gasps and jerks. The flood of pearls is still pouring down over his mouth. I yank my blade back out.

My stomach turns as tiny pearls roll out of the wound in his throat.

Only when his eyes have glassed over completely and I feel my magic disconnect from the now nonexistent emotions in his chest do I dare to move from my position. The final dregs of pearls trickle out, hitting his already full mouth and roll down his cheeks before clattering across the ice floor. I scramble away from him, suddenly feeling sick.

By Mabona, that must have been a truly horrible way to die.

Drawing in a strained breath through my aching throat, I try to reorient myself. Flashing lightning and clashing steel still come from the corridor outside. Reality trickles back into me. Draven. I need to help him.

The wound in my side has mostly stopped bleeding, but blood still covers the bare skin around it. I try my best not to disturb the wound as I stagger to my feet and then hurry back towards the open door.

Four dead guards in silver armor lie scattered across the floor while Draven is fighting the remaining two close to the door. They're coming at him from both sides, trying to force him into splitting his focus. He moves like a shadow, whipping back and forth to meet each of their strikes right before they can hit.

I flick my gaze between the three of them. One of the guards has his back to me.

Shifting the dagger to my left hand, I sneak up behind him.

"Behind!" his companion yells as he notices me.

But it's already too late.

I ram my dagger through the side of his neck.

The shouted warning also caused the second guard to lose sight of Draven for a moment. He gasps in a wet gurgling breath as Draven slits his throat.

Both guards collapse to the ground, their bodies twitching slightly before growing still.

Then everything is suddenly dead silent.

My chest heaves. So does Draven's. Blood is splattered across his face and hands, and the dark gray clothes he is no doubt wearing to hide his armor underneath are stained with blood too. I have no idea if it's his or someone else's.

Then Draven's gaze snaps down to the slice in my dress and the blood across my skin. He opens his mouth. But right before any words can make it out, another voice cuts through the silence.

"It's Commander Ryat!" a voice bellows from the corner leading out into the next corridor.

Whipping my head towards it, I find a messenger standing there with wide eyes.

He stares at Draven and the slaughter around us in shock, even as he continues yelling, "He's helping the rebels and—"

A lightning bolt cracks through the air.

The messenger stiffens as it hits him straight in the chest. Then he topples backwards, his limbs twitching even in death.

"Fuck," Draven growls. Dragging a blood-soaked hand through his hair, he pushes a few strands out of his face. "Hopefully no one heard that."

Snapping out of my stupor, I lurch into motion. "We need to get to a window. Before reinforcements get here."

"I know." He flicks a glance towards the treasury before meeting my gaze again. "He's dead?"

"Very."

"Good." After sweeping his gaze over everyone else to make sure that they're dead too, he jerks his chin. "Then let's go."

Exhaustion washes over me as we sprint back through the

corridor. My body is using up a lot of energy to heal that wound in my side. I need to eat something. I need to eat *a lot*. And soon.

By some miracle, the rest of the corridors are empty.

Lavendera and the other guards must have left with the human prisoners before their companions realized that we were in the treasury.

Cold evening winds wash in through the window as Draven shoves it open fully and then turns back to me.

A muted sense of understanding washes through me. This is how the Red Hand was getting in and out of restricted parts of the Ice Palace. He wasn't climbing in. He was flying.

"Come here," Draven says.

That mind-shattering sense of shock that I have been suppressing during the fight starts to press back into me, so I just numbly walk over to Draven.

With heartbreakingly gentle movements, he lifts me into his arms and holds me to his chest. Then he tucks his wings in tight and leaps right out through the window.

My stomach lurches as we free fall for a moment.

Then his massive wings spread out wide, and he flies us away. After everything that has happened tonight, I have no idea where he is taking me. But I'm too exhausted and too shocked to ask. So I just lie there in his arms and try to wrap my mind around that single world-altering revelation.

Draven Ryat is the Red Hand.

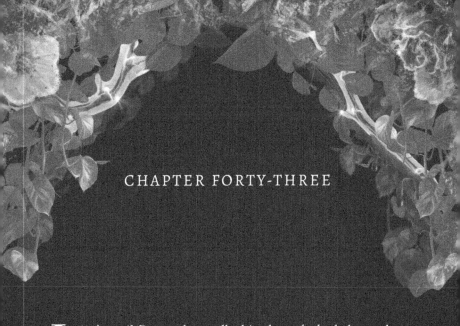

# CHAPTER FORTY-THREE

I t isn't until Draven has walked in through the balcony door and set me down in the middle of the living room that I finally realize where we are. Frowning, I glance at the wooden floorboards and the dark gray fabric of the furniture. He brought me back to his rooms?

"You need to change into better clothes," Draven declares as he disappears into the bathroom. Water splashes as he washes the blood off his hands and face. Then he strides towards one of the drawers by the wall. "And I need to clean that wound so that it can heal faster. Take off your dress."

But my mind still cannot accept what I have just learned, so all that makes it out of my mouth is, "You're the Red Hand."

Draven yanks open a drawer and begins pulling out what looks like some sort of medical kit. But he glances over his shoulder at my words, and disbelief flits across his face. "Are we really going to have this conversation right now?"

I stare back at him with equal disbelief. "Yes!"

"They might be coming for us."

"Then let's go."

"I need to treat your wound first."

"Exactly. Then you can do that and talk at the same time." Holding his gaze, I shake my head and just repeat, "You are the Red Hand."

He shoves the drawer shut again and strides back to me with a bunch of supplies in his arms. "Yes." Objects clatter as he drops the items on his desk and then jerks his chin towards the chair next to it. "Sit."

While staggering over to the chair, I blurt out, "Why didn't you tell me that you were working for the human resistance?"

"I'm not working for the human resistance. I didn't even know that they were planning a damn heist tonight until they circulated word through their network earlier this week, asking me to help them by killing the guards outside the treasury." He locks piercing eyes on me as he then retorts with, "Why didn't you tell me that *you* were working for the rebellion?"

I open my mouth to snap back at him, but then I realize that he has a point. Why am I expecting him to trust me with these kinds of dangerous secrets when I don't trust him with mine? If I had actually told him about all of this, like I have been considering doing for weeks now, he would probably have told me about his own secret missions as well. I let out a humorless huff of laughter. I guess we both have some trust issues to work on.

"When did you even have the opportunity to sneak around and do this kind of work for them?" he asks.

"When you snuck out during the night to hunt the Red Hand. Or rather, to *be* the Red Hand, I suppose." I shake my head at him. "I can't believe you've actually been helping them all this time."

Then a small yelp slips from my lips as Draven grabs me by the hips and pushes me down in the chair that I had already forgotten that I was supposed to sit down on. After I'm seated, he drags over another chair and sits down next to me. His fingers are gentle as he pushes the torn fabric aside and inspects the wound.

"My goals have occasionally aligned with the humans' missions," Draven continues while he reaches for a bottle on the desk. "So yes, I've helped them as the Red Hand on occasion. But my own mission has always been to destabilize Frostfell as much as possible. And it's so much easier to get things done when I work alone, so in this city, I never actually joined the resistance." He lets out something between an annoyed sigh and a huff of laughter while he pulls the stopper out of the bottle and pours some of it on a clean piece of cloth. "I learned that from my first attempt, which isn't going nearly as well."

For a few seconds, I just stare at him. He leans forward and runs the piece of cloth over my wound. A hiss escapes my lips as the liquid he poured on it stings when it comes into contact with my open wound. Then a sudden realization hits me.

"Mabona's tits." I gape at Draven while he quickly cleans the dried blood from my wound. "*That's* why you were so unnecessarily cruel to the humans in your supposed search for the Red Hand. You were trying to make them angry. You were purposely trying to turn the whole city against the Icehearts."

"Yes." He tosses the now red piece of cloth on the table and meets my gaze. "This needs stitching."

"Then stitch it."

"I have nothing that will dull the pain."

"I can handle it."

He holds my gaze for a few seconds before giving me a slow nod. Then he turns back towards the supplies. Faint metallic rattling sounds as he picks up a small box and fishes out a needle. While he reaches for the spool of thread, something else he said finally makes it through my mind.

"Wait," I begin, staring at him in confusion. "What do you mean, in *this* city, you never joined the rebellion?"

He threads the needle, avoiding my gaze. "Exactly what I said."

It suddenly feels as if time itself stops. I can hear every beat of my heart. It pounds in my ears like giant bells. Sitting there on the chair, I stare at Draven while understanding washes through me like cold water.

"No," I breathe.

Draven says nothing, only draws the thread through the eye of the needle and then leans forward.

"The mask is white," I say, speaking the first half of the code phrase that we use back in the Seelie Court to secretly communicate that we are members of the fae resistance.

Draven looks up and meets my gaze.

My heart thumps in my chest.

"And very hard to take off," he replies, speaking the second half of the code phrase that signals that he is also a member of the resistance and that it's safe to talk.

Something between a gasp and an unsteady breath rips from my lungs. My head is pounding.

"This is going to sting," Draven says, and then without waiting for me to reply, pushes the needle through my skin.

The pulse of pain jolts me out of my shock and snaps me back to the present.

Gripping the edge of the desk hard, I try to keep my wits about me as I stare at Draven in open-mouthed shock. "You're a member of our resistance."

"Yes," he confirms. Then his gaze flicks up to me for a second before he continues stitching my wound. "Why do you think I was there that day?"

My mind spins as I stare at him. "What day?"

"That day when you threw your drink in my face." His gaze remains focused on the needle, but I can hear the truth clang in every word as he says, "I was one of the people in masks running down the stairs. After ditching the mask and cloak, I came back in through the side door to stall the patrol. And then I found you there."

"No," I breathe again, even though I know that he is telling the truth.

A small smile tugs at his lips as he meets my gaze again and shakes his head at me as if in disbelief. "Why else would I have been there? I'm the fucking Commander of the Dread Legion. What would I be doing in a random tavern in the Seelie Court on a random afternoon?"

Pain pulses through my side as Draven continues stitching, but I can barely feel it. I can barely feel anything other than shock. And fury at my own stupidity. How could I not have seen it earlier? How could I not have figured it out sooner?

"And then there you were, already trying to distract the patrol," Draven picks up. "But I couldn't let the squad leader punish you for that, so I had to intervene." A short laugh escapes his lips. "And then you threw your drink in my face." He shakes his head. "Azaroth's flame, little rebel, it has been decades since someone managed to surprise me like that."

Little rebel. He has been calling me *little rebel* all this time, for Mabona's sake. How could I not have figured it out?

Then his expression turns serious as he meets my gaze again. "I have watched you for years. Seen the way you always try to help and always put everyone else first. And seen how people distrust you and hate you for something that isn't your fault. And I felt a connection. I knew that I had found someone who understood what it's like to be hated for something that you haven't chosen."

My heart squeezes tight.

Draven holds my gaze with those intense eyes of his. I feel like he is waiting for me to say something, but I can't make my lips move. He lets out a small sigh and continues stitching. But he keeps speaking.

"I tried to get you promoted," he says. "To move you up the chain and into more important positions in the resistance. But the other leaders didn't trust you. They refused. And because I can't be there all the time, I needed them to work efficiently without me so that I could get you all to finally launch your rebellion to bring down the Icehearts. So I had to let you remain a lookout." He ties off the thread and then puts the needle back on the table. "But I watched you."

Emotions twist inside my chest like strangling vines.

Draven stands up from the chair. I scramble to my feet as well.

"And then I found you kneeling on that field and realized that you had signed up for this farce of a trial," he continues. "I did everything I could to make you drop out without blowing my cover."

I drag in an unsteady breath, my chest feeling far too crowded.

Something almost like pain flickers in Draven's eyes for a moment. Reaching up, he slides his fingers gently over my jaw and then cups my cheek. "I've been falling for you for years, from afar, but then I truly got to know you during the Atonement Trials." A wistful smile blows across his handsome face. "And then that day when you patted my cheek and said *good talk*, I fell in love with you utterly and completely."

My heart jerks in my chest, and a broken noise comes from the back of my throat. Love. He *loves* me? I feel as if there is not enough air left in the room. My heart feels like it is both swelling with light and cracking like fragile glass at the same time.

Draven holds my gaze. "I didn't even know that we were mates until that day when the mate bond snapped into place. And after that, it was almost impossible to keep my hands off you. To stay away from you." Pain flickers in his eyes again, and he drops his hand from my cheek and takes a step back. "And now, you need to leave."

The sudden loss of his warm hand against my cheek leaves me breathless, as if I have been plunged into an icy lake. But Draven is already moving.

"Go and change into your normal clothes," he orders while he strides towards a cabinet by the bookshelf. "I'll get you some food. You'll need it so that your wound can heal."

I stagger towards my room, feeling shellshocked. As I quickly strip out of the dress and change into my pants and shirt and boots, I try desperately to reshape my world so that everything makes sense again.

But no matter how hard I try, nothing makes sense.

Draven is secretly working with both the human rebellion and the fae resistance. And has been for years. Decades. All this time, I have considered him my worst enemy, when in reality, he has done more for my cause than anyone else. And far more than me. He has been risking his life for years while secretly trying to kickstart rebellions from all sides. But at the same time, he has been obeying the Icehearts' every word. It doesn't make sense.

My heart aches as I walk back into the living room, now dressed in more practical clothes. Draven has thrown off those dark gray clothes that he was using as a disguise, revealing his black dragon scale armor underneath, and has strapped his massive sword down his spine as well. He has also managed to grab some dried meat and cheese from his cabinet. It waits on the desk in a small pile.

"Eat," he commands, and points towards it.

I numbly drop down in the chair and begin inhaling the food. My mind still spins. I shake my head while still trying to gather my wits.

"Goddess above," I breathe between bites. "I wish you would've told me."

Regret pulses across his face as he stands there next to me, watching me gulp down the food. He swallows and glances away for a second. "I was trying to protect you." Then he draws in a deep breath and meets my gaze head on. "But I was wrong. You don't need protecting." A wicked smile, full of approval, spreads across his face. "It's the world that needs protection from you."

I swallow down the final bite of cheese and then grab the last strip of dried meat. Energy is already flowing back into my body.

Draven heaves a sigh and rakes his hand through his hair. "I'm sorry for not trusting you. In hindsight, I know I should have. But I was terrified that it would only put you in even more danger. You've seen what they've done to Isera and Alistair. I've been keeping my own people in the dark for the same reason. The Icehearts are more vicious than you can imagine."

After swallowing the final bite of food, I give Draven a small smile. "Well, to be fair, I could have chosen to trust you too. But I didn't. So you're not the only one to blame." I give him a pointed look. "I wish you would have warned me about Lavendera, though."

A jolt shoots through his body, and he stands up straight while panic pulses across his face. "Lavendera?"

"Yeah." I scowl in annoyance at the memory. "She's the one who sold us out. Why didn't you tell me that she worked for the Icehearts?"

He opens his mouth to reply, but then just closes it again. Frustration and alarm swirl in his eyes as he casts a hurried look towards the door. "You've talked to Lavendera about this?"

"Well, yes and—"

Panic shines on his whole face as he snaps his gaze back to me. "I need to get you out. Now."

A massive force crashes into the front door.

# CHAPTER FORTY-FOUR

The whole door vibrates as someone throws his entire body weight against it once more while he bellows, "Commander Ryat! You have been accused of helping the human rebels. Their Imperial Majesties are demanding an explanation."

I jump up from the chair as another thud comes from the door.

"Fuck," Draven growls as he shoves a knife into my hand. "Someone heard the messenger's warning and ran to tell Bane and Jessina."

My gaze snaps down to the knife. It's not just any knife. It's my knife. The one I brought here from the Seelie Court.

A yelp escapes me as Draven scoops me up into his arms while I was busy looking at the knife. I whip my gaze up to his face as he runs back out onto the balcony and leaps off it.

My stomach lurches.

But his wings flare out, and then we're flying.

"I need to get you and my clan out," he says as he banks hard and sets course for the barracks outside the defensive walls on the west side.

"No!" I protest. "Not without Isera and Alistair."

His gaze burns through my soul as he locks hard eyes on me. "It's either leave without them or not leave at all."

"I'm not leaving them!" I growl back at him.

I made them a promise, Goddess damn it. And I intend to keep it. I swore that I would get them out. Alistair is already on the verge of breaking, and Isera is falling deeper into that terrifying coldness with every passing day here. I can't leave them to this fate. I refuse to.

Draven glares down at me. I glare right back.

"Azaroth's fucking flame," he curses. Then he swerves hard, heading towards the doors to the patio outside the ballroom instead.

A jolt shoots through me as Draven lands hard on the ground outside the doors. Through the slight gap in them, the sounds of chatting voices drift out into the night. The people in there have no idea what is happening. No idea that their commander has just betrayed them.

Setting me down on the ground, he leans forward slightly and glances in through the closest window. After a few seconds, he pulls back.

"Bane and Jessina aren't here," he says as he turns back to me. "Which means that they are out searching for me. I might be able to buy us some time."

I nod. "Alright. I'll get Isera and Alistair out."

Steel laces his voice as he levels a commanding stare on me and declares, "You have two minutes. Then I will come in there and drag you out myself. Even if I have to kill everyone in the entire ballroom to do it. Isera and Alistair included."

"Fine," I snap back.

"Don't make me regret this."

Before I can retort, he launches into the air.

Not wasting a second, I run over to the door and slip inside.

The courtiers and the leaders of the other dragon clans are still standing in clusters around the room. But now that the

Icehearts are no longer here, the atmosphere is much less tense. Just like before, most people are sipping from glasses filled with alcohol to pass the time.

My heart patters against my ribs as I sweep my gaze over the crowd. Isera and Alistair are still standing in the same spot as before. Close to the raised dais with the two ice thrones. Their heads are bowed and their eyes are on the floor in that submissive way that the Icehearts prefer, which means that they won't be able to see me.

Worry flits around inside my ribcage like erratic birds.

How the hell am I supposed to sneak the only two fae in here out of an entire ballroom filled with dragon shifters without anyone noticing?

My gaze darts between all the glasses in everyone's hands.

An idea begins to form.

*That* might work.

Keeping my head down, so that no one can see my glowing eyes, I summon my magic. I used up a lot of energy during the fight up at the treasury, and my body is also using it to heal the wound in my side. But because Draven cleaned it and stitched it up, it needs less effort to heal properly. And because he gave me food and allowed me to sit and rest while he treated the wound, I have managed to recover most of the energy I lost. It has to be enough.

Sending a desperate prayer to Mabona, I plead silently in my mind. *Please let it be enough. Please let this work.*

Then I throw my magic across the entire room.

Sparks of intoxication meet me from every chest. Some are tiny. Others are bigger. But everyone in here has at least sipped a little alcohol.

Drawing in a deep breath, I close my eyes briefly to compose myself. Then I shove my magic at everyone in the room.

I have never tried to manipulate this many people at the same time. It has to work. Please, Mabona, it has to work.

Magic flows through the connections that I've made to their feelings of drunkenness and makes them flare up. Not into the massive wildfires I can normally create. But enough that people start laughing too loudly and swaying a little on their feet. As if they are much more intoxicated than they really are.

A sort of merry chaos quickly spreads through the room.

With my heart fluttering nervously in my chest, and my energy draining at a steady pace, I hurry through the throng. When I'm almost at the dais, Isera finally glances up. She blinks in surprise at the seemingly very drunk dragon shifters around her.

"We're getting out," I hiss at the two of them. "Right now."

Alistair snaps his head up as well.

And neither of them hesitates. Lurching into motion, they hurry after me as I start back towards the door. My pulse thrums in my ears. All around us, people are talking too loudly and stumbling and slapping each other on the arm and giggling. I fervently pray that none of them will notice us. Magic flows out of me. I need to release it soon, or it will take too long for my energy to build back up.

We pass the table by the outer wall where drinks and bites of food have been placed on gleaming silver trays. Two dragon shifters in elegant suits are leaning against the table. Their eyes slide in an out of focus, as if they can't keep their vision straight because of how drunk I'm making them feel. I keep my head bowed, trying to stay as invisible as possible while I pass them.

"Hey," the black-haired one suddenly says. His hand shoots out and reaches for Isera's arm, but he's too clumsy to actually grab her. While straightening after the failed grab, he rakes his gaze up and down her body. "Why did they give you clothes again? I prefer you half-naked."

Isera picks up a knife from the cutlery that has been laid out on the table.

And rams it into his throat.

I gasp.

Blood spurts from his carotid artery when she yanks the knife back out. It splatters across Isera's face, but she doesn't so much as flinch. She just whirls towards the guy's companion and rams the knife into his throat as well.

In the span of a few seconds, two dragon shifters collapse to the floor, their life bleeding out of them.

Isera's blue and silver eyes are so cold and devoid of all sense of remorse that a chill races down my spine. She just spins towards the next group of dragon shifters, who haven't even noticed the slaughter yet, while flexing her hand on the handle of the knife.

But before she can take so much as a step towards them, Alistair rushes forward and wraps his arms around her waist from behind. Lifting her off the floor, he spins back towards me while carrying Isera.

She struggles hard against his grip, and her voice is vicious as she snarls, "I want them dead. I want them *all* dead."

"We will kill them," he snaps at her while hauling her towards the open doors to the patio. "I swear we will fucking kill them all for what they did to us. But first, we need to get the hell out of here."

Isera growls curses but stops fighting so hard. With a grunt, Alistair half shoves, half throws Isera out the door. While he hurries out onto the patio as well, I flick my gaze across the ballroom again.

Glittering faelights shimmer against the decorations and glitter in the jewelry that the female courtiers are wearing. Everyone is still laughing and stumbling as if they're severely drunk. No one has noticed a thing.

An unexpected pulse of pride ripples through me. I might be way stronger with my magic than even I knew.

Darting out onto the patio, I cut off the flow to my magic and then close the doors behind me again.

A pair of commanding golden eyes stare down at me from only a step away.

Draven.

His face is splattered with a few drops of blood, but he looks otherwise unharmed.

"With ten seconds to spare," he announces. Then he jerks his chin while starting towards the side gate on the west side. "Any problems?"

I open my mouth to reply.

A shriek cuts through the night as someone inside the ballroom screams in shock. Now that my magic is no longer clouding their senses, someone must have noticed the two dead bodies that Isera left behind.

"Uhm…" is all I manage to reply while giving Draven an apologetic grimace.

"Azaroth's fucking flame," he growls.

We sprint towards the barracks.

# CHAPTER FORTY-FIVE

The door bangs against the wall as Draven throws it open and runs inside. Isera, Alistair, and I hurry after him into the Black Dragon Clan's barracks. Torches are burning along the wall, their flickering light dancing across the stone walls, and the soft murmur of voices comes from several rooms along the corridor.

"Everyone into the gathering hall!" Draven bellows, his voice cutting through the calm atmosphere like an explosion. "Now!"

Clattering and rustling and creaking sound from the rooms as everyone leaps to their feet and scrambles out the doors. They cast surprised glances at us when they make it into the corridor, but they don't stop. Instead, they just hurry into the massive gathering hall like Draven ordered.

Draven turns to Alistair. "You, watch the skies." His gaze shifts to Isera. "And you, watch the road. If there's even a hint of anyone coming this way, you run back in here and tell me."

To my surprise, they don't argue. Or even look offended that Draven is giving them orders. They just jerk their chins down in a nod and dart back out the door. They have probably realized that Draven is their only ticket out of here.

The final few soldiers scramble out of their rooms, putting on their armor while they run. Draven stalks after them towards the gathering hall. I follow him.

"We don't have much time, so I'm only going to say this once," Draven declares as he strides inside and positions himself at the front of the room.

I take up position by a medical cabinet on the wall next to the door. Everyone else, all the soldiers in Draven's clan, have already formed orderly ranks throughout the entire room. They watch him with a mix of confusion and suspicion on their faces.

"You're all leaving," Draven says, his voice echoing between the stone walls. "Right now. You have two minutes to grab what you can't bear to leave behind. Then all of you are flying back to our islands."

Shock crackles like lightning through the room of dragon shifters.

Galen draws back in confusion and blinks at his commander. "What?"

"Don't stop for anything or anyone," Draven continues as if he hadn't spoken. "Don't obey any orders from outsiders. And if anyone, and I mean *anyone*, comes and tries to get you to return here or to force you back into the Icehearts' service, you fight like hell. Understood?"

"What?" Galen replies, that shock and utter confusion still pulsing across his face. "No. What the hell are you talking about?"

"You no longer serve the Iceheart Dynasty. Go home."

"What does—"

"Draven is the Red Hand," I cut in, my voice slicing through the confusion in the room like a blade.

Everyone stops talking. Galen and Lyra and all the others turn to stare at me. Draven shoots me an exasperated look. I just shoot one right back at him. His people deserve to know that. *He* deserves to not be hated by his people for something that he hasn't even done.

I shift my gaze back to the stunned soldiers. "And the Icehearts have just figured that out. Which is why we all need to leave. Right now."

"You heard her," Draven says, also turning his attention back to his clan. "So grab your shit and get ready to leave. You fly out in force."

No one moves.

"That's an order," Draven growls in frustration.

But they all just keep staring at him in shock.

"*You* are the Red Hand?" Galen says. It's something between a question and a stunned statement. "You've been secretly working against the Icehearts?" A flash of anger pulses across his face and bleeds into his tone as he demands, "Why the hell haven't you said anything?"

"Because I couldn't endanger you like that," Draven snaps back. "Now get a move on!"

"Endanger us? If we had known that you—"

"Do you know why I never used the half-shift during those first six years?" Draven cuts him off, frustration lacing his every word.

Galen frowns and shakes his head in confusion. "Because you were being submissive and letting them show dominance?"

"Because they whipped my wings. Every day. For six fucking years."

The entire room sucks in a sharp breath. Lyra's orange eyes are wide with horror. Next to her, Galen staggers a step back as if Draven had physically hit him.

"That's what they did to *me*, and I'm someone they need," Draven continues. "To them, you are all expendable. So what do you think they would have done to you if you had gotten caught helping the human rebels?"

Everyone just stares at him, their eyes wide.

"But now it doesn't matter anyway," Draven continues. "Because they have figured out that I'm the Red Hand. And they will punish you in order to teach me a lesson." A hint of panic bleeds into his voice as he shoots a glance at the clock on the wall. "So you need to go. Now!"

Clothes rustle as everyone begins to move. But then they all stop again when Lyra speaks up.

Her eyes are intense as she holds Draven's gaze. "You keep saying *you*."

Dread crackles through my veins like ice, and I snap my gaze to Draven. Because Lyra is right. I hadn't even noticed it until now. Draven isn't saying '*we* need to leave'. He always says '*you* need to leave'.

"Why aren't you saying '*we* need to leave'?" Lyra demands.

The other soldiers, now frozen mid-step, also turn to Draven.

He forces out a frustrated breath and flexes his hand as he growls, "Because I can't leave."

"What?" I snap. Pushing off from the wall, I stalk towards him while panic rips at my chest. "What the hell does that mean?"

"I've already told you," he replies, his voice tight, as he turns to meet my gaze. "I can't leave."

"Why the hell not?"

He opens his mouth to reply but then just closes it again and forces out yet another frustrated breath. "I can't say."

"That's not good enough!"

"I literally cannot say!" Desperation flashes in his eyes as he stares down at me. "So you either have to figure it out in the next thirty seconds, or you leave without me."

I jerk back, stunned by the pure desperation on his face.

Panic and dread rip at my chest at every second that ticks by, bringing the Icehearts closer to finding us. But I'm not leaving without Draven.

My mind churns.

He can't leave, but he can't say why. What the hell does that even mean?

Something he said weeks ago, the day that I had a panic

attack, resurfaces in my mind. Something that I thought was about something else.

*I need you to start questioning things that don't make sense. Please.*

That's what he said to me.

So what is it that doesn't make sense?

Everything. Nothing makes sense.

Draven is one of the most powerful dragon shifters in the world. The leader of the Black Dragon Clan. Storm powers. Capable of a half-shift. Why would he be unable to leave?

In fact, why would he even serve the Icehearts in the first place? And why would he just bow to them without a fight when they came to his islands? Everything I know about Draven tells me that he would never do that. He's proud and arrogant and domineering. He would never willingly bow down without even putting up a fight. So why did he?

His words clang through my skull again.

*I can't say. I literally cannot say.*

Memories flood my brain. Memories of all those times when I asked him a question and he opened his mouth as if to reply, but then only closed it again. He has been doing that a lot. As if he wanted to reply but... physically can't.

And then the biggest question of all.

Why would someone like Draven Ryat be obeying the Icehearts like a loyal little dog?

I gasp, and my mouth drops open as I stagger a step back when a sudden realization hits me like a blow to the chest. My heart pounds as I stare back at Draven.

"Fucking hell," I blurt out, my pulse pounding in my ears. "They're using dragon steel, aren't they?"

Draven opens his mouth but then closes it again. But relief washes over his features.

I drag in an unsteady breath. "Oh by all the gods, I'm right, aren't I?"

"What?" Galen presses out, sounding both confused and

suddenly terrified. Staring at Draven, he shakes his head as if in disbelief. "No. That can't… They… It's not possible. They destroyed all the dragon steel after the Liberation War. And even if they had any, they wouldn't be able to use it." His eyes are desperate. Panicked. "They can't even touch it. *We* can't even touch it. No dragon shifter can."

And then the final piece clicks into place.

I gasp as all those loose ends and strange behaviors and shocking secrets finally stop spinning in my mind, and a clear image emerges. Understanding floods my veins.

"Lavendera," I breathe. "Oh Mabona's tits. They're using Lavendera, aren't they?"

A shockwave pulses through the whole Black Dragon Clan.

But I pay them no mind. My eyes are solely focused on Draven. He doesn't reply, but I know that I'm right.

Goddess above, the Icehearts have somehow convinced Lavendera to put the dragon steel on Draven. And as fae, she can channel her magic through the metal to control Draven. She can force him to do whatever she says.

"Where?" I demand, panic rising inside me again, as I stare back at Draven. "Where is it? I've seen you naked multiple times, and you're not wearing a necklace or a collar or a bracelet or anything at all. So where is it?"

Once again, he opens his mouth but then just closes it again. Forcing out a frustrated sigh, he fixes me with a pointed look and then flexes his hand. I snap my gaze down to it.

"Your right hand?" I ask.

He just stares back at me.

"Your forearm?" I press.

He lets out a soft breath.

"It's *in* your right forearm?"

Relief washes over his features.

"Oh fucking hell." Panic now pulses inside me like a thrashing storm. We're losing time. Fast. "How are we supposed to get it out?"

"You have to cut it out," Galen declares as he suddenly runs up to us with Lyra on his heels.

The other dragon shifters are still staring at Draven with a mix of horror, guilt, and panic in their eyes. Steel sings as Galen yanks out a knife from his belt and shoves it into my hand.

I gape at him. "Me?"

"You're fae. You're the only one of us who can touch it." He casts a panicked glance at the clock. "Do it. Now!"

"And the rest of you, what are you still doing here?" Draven bellows, speaking for the first time since this shocking revelation. "Grab your shit and get ready to leave!"

They lurch into motion. Boots pound against the floor as they run to finally obey his commands.

Gripping the hilt of the knife hard, I grab Draven's wrist and pull his forearm towards me. Galen deftly removes the armor so that I can reach Draven's skin. My heart beats so loudly that I can barely hear myself think as I stare down at his forearm. The dragon steel can't be on the inside of his arm. There are too many large veins there. And the skin is too thin. It has to be on the outside. But where?

"Just do it," Draven says.

"Fuck," I snap.

Placing the tip of the knife at the top of his forearm, right below the elbow, I press down and cut a deep gash.

Draven sucks in a sharp breath between his teeth.

I immediately summon my magic and slam it at the violet flame of pain in his chest. While decreasing it, I draw the blade down his forearm.

Nausea crawls up my throat as the skin splits open.

But then I see it.

Something hard, the color of steel, becomes visible right

above the bone. It shimmers faintly, as if it's glowing from within.

Next to me, Lyra gasps.

"How long?" Galen stammers. "How long have you had this inside you?"

But Draven still can't answer. I flick my gaze up to his face. He just looks back at me, his gaze steady.

Handing the blade to the stunned Galen, I reach towards that shimmering metal at the bottom of the cut. Pain flares up inside Draven as my fingers dig into the wound, but I pour more magic down the connection to drown it out. Blood coats my fingers. I feel like I'm going to be sick.

Then I finally get my fingers around the long piece of shimmering metal. It's strangely warm to the touch. I look up at Draven. He gives me a nod.

Gripping it tightly, I yank upwards.

It comes free with a sickening *snap*, as if it was stuck to the bone.

The pain in Draven's chest spikes again, but I immediately lower it with my magic once more.

And in my hand, I hold a long piece of shimmering dragon steel. The moment it loses contact with Draven's body, that glowing shimmer disappears. And so does that strange warmth that was in the metal before.

Draven heaves a sigh of relief from the very depths of his soul.

Raw emotions swirl in his beautiful golden eyes as he meets my gaze again.

"Thank you," he whispers.

My heart almost shatters, and all I manage is a nod.

He turns to Galen and Lyra, who stand there next to me, still staring at Draven in shock and desperation.

"Since before they even landed on our island," Draven replies, finally answering Galen's question. "An entire horde of them ambushed me when I was out training. They tied me up and used Lavendera to put the dragon steel in. Then they made her order me in advance to publicly surrender when they came back days later."

Galen draws in an unsteady breath.

"They also made sure that I couldn't tell anyone about the dragon steel. Or Lavendera." His gaze flits to me. "That's why I couldn't warn you that she worked for them. In fact, that's why I couldn't do a lot of things. I tried to escape once, so they made Lavendera order me that if I leave, even if it's on a sanctioned mission, I always have to return to the Icehearts within three days. And I tried to tell some of the fae during the last Atonement Trials that it was a sham. So they made Lavendera kill the fae I had told and then order me to never reveal the truth to another fae." Pain flashes across his face. "And once a fae has channeled magic through the dragon steel and given an order, it remains active until the fae cancels it."

My heart aches, and pain twists inside my chest. For him. For what he has had to endure. For all the anger I have directed against him. Anger over things that he had no control over.

That terrible hurt in his eyes deepens as he turns to Galen. "I thought you, of all people, would figure it out. Two fucking centuries ago. You were my best friend. You knew me better than anyone. How could you ever believe that I would just sell out our clan like that?"

Galen flinches. Pain and guilt pulse across his whole face as he stares helplessly at Draven. "I just… I don't…"

Draven lets out a humorless huff of laughter. "Once I realized that all of you thought that I had simply become a… What was it you called me? A spineless coward? A worthless traitor? Well, regardless, after that, it was easier to just let you all hate me."

Galen looks as if Draven has just ripped his heart out.

Next to him, Lyra opens her mouth. "Draven, I—"

The door bangs open.

My heart jerks as Alistair sprints down the corridor with Isera on his heels. Panic is written all over his face.

"They're coming!"

# CHAPTER FORTY-SIX

B lood runs down Draven's arm from the wound, but he just snatches out a bandage from the medical cabinet and wraps it around his forearm before slamming the pieces of armor back in place.

"Outside!" Draven yells across the barracks. "Now!"

Alistair and Isera skid to a halt in front of us, glancing in confusion at the blood on the floor but asking no questions. I grab another couple of bandages and wrap them around the piece of dragon steel. Then I tie it to my belt. There is no way in hell that I'm leaving it here for the Icehearts to use against someone else.

"Get ready," Draven says to Galen and Lyra. "We're going to have to fight our way out." His gaze shifts to Alistair and Isera. "And you're going to help us."

Alistair jerks back in alarm as Draven grabs him by the throat. But before Alistair can so much as try to fight him off, Draven yanks him closer. And then removes his collar.

A gasp of relief rips from Alistair's lungs.

Isera, who probably thought that he was going to drain Alistair's magic, blinks in shock.

The iron collar clangs against the stone floor as Draven tosses it aside and whirls towards Isera. With a few quick moves, he removes her collar as well and throws it down on the ground.

For a second, and for the first time since she snapped out of her stupor, there is a hint of something other than ruthless ice in Isera's eyes. Something almost like gratitude. Or hope.

Draven gives the two of them a commanding stare. "You're the two strongest magic users in the entire Seelie Court. Prove it."

Then he's striding towards the door.

The rest of us lurch into motion as well. My pulse thrums in my ears as the six of us hurry down the corridor and back into the night outside. All the soldiers from the Black Dragon Clan are already waiting out there on the stones. I whip my head towards the castle as I jog out the door.

My heart leaps into my throat as I spot two people in silver clothes striding towards us. Their massive silver wings are spread wide, but they're walking. As if they want to make Draven tremble in fear at seeing their approach. They're not in any hurry since they think that he is still wearing the dragon steel and therefore can't leave. I watch them for another second. This is going to get violent. Fast.

"Fly straight for the Western Isles," Draven calls to his people. "Don't stop. Don't slow down. Don't look back. Now, shift!"

The ranks of soldiers sprint across the mountainside, putting distance between each other. Then the first people start shifting. Smoke billows across the stones as the soldiers shift into their dragon forms. Black dragons shoot up from the smoke and soar up towards the sky.

Alarm bells blare from the ice walls.

"Lyra, take Alistair," Draven orders. "Galen, you take Isera. We need to buy the others time."

"Take?" Alistair blurts out. "What the hell do you mean *take*?"

"It means climb on, hold on tight, and use your fucking magic to help us fight," Draven snaps. Then his gaze shifts to me. "You're with me. Get on."

Before I can even open my mouth to reply, let alone actually process what he's saying, he shifts into a dragon.

Smoke explodes around us as Lyra and Galen do the same. Massive wings flap, blowing the smoke away. I gape at Draven, who lowers himself to the ground next to me. Isera and Alistair remain equally frozen. Draven roars at us.

Snapping out of my stupor, I flick a quick glance at my fellow fae. They meet my gaze for one single second. Then the three of us are climbing up on the dragons before us.

Disbelief clangs inside my whole skull as I settle myself in the space where Draven's neck meets the rest of his body. It's shaped almost as if it's made for someone to sit there. With my heart pounding in my chest, I grip the spikes on his neck and clench my thighs tightly to stay in place.

Draven swings his head towards the Icehearts, roars a challenge, and then shoots into the sky.

My stomach drops and a surge goes through my body as we shoot upwards. Winds rip at my clothes and hair. On either side of us, Galen and Lyra, with Isera and Alistair seated on their backs, fly up from the ground as well.

Silver dragons surge over the castle's defensive walls. Then smoke explodes across the mountainside again as Empress Jessina and Emperor Bane shift into dragons as well. Their massive silver bodies gleam in the moonlight as they roar in fury. Then they shoot straight towards us.

I gasp as Draven veers sharply to the left. Galen and Lyra bank hard in the other direction.

A second later, ice flames streak past in the space we used to occupy. Bane roars in anger again and opens his jaws. Ice flames shoot towards us.

And slam right into a thick wall made of ice.

Atop Galen's back, Isera stares at Bane as if she is going to rip the dragon emperor's heart out with her bare hands. The freezing and utterly otherworldly fury on her face snatches the breath from my lungs and makes fear ripple down my spine. Whatever held Isera together back in the Seelie Court has snapped now. And I have no idea what she is planning to do anymore.

Fire crackles through the air as Draven breathes flames back at the Icehearts at the same time as Galen and Lyra do the same. The fire shoots towards them from three directions, joined a second later by a massive torrent of flames from Alistair.

It forces the Icehearts to dodge, breaking their headlong flight towards us.

But dragons from the Silver Clan are soaring over the ice walls and heading straight for us. In a matter of moments, we'll be outnumbered. I whip my head from side to side. The other dragons from the Black Dragon Clan are speeding towards the horizon, just like Draven ordered. We only need to buy them a few more minutes.

But then *we* also need to get out. And how we're supposed to do that, I have no idea.

My stomach lurches, and I press my legs harder against Draven's scales, as he turns sharply and flies around the Icehearts, coming up at them from behind. As if they have done this move several times before, Lyra and Galen do the same from the other directions.

Black clouds gather around us as Draven summons his magic. I grip his spikes tighter as lightning cracks through the air, missing Jessina's wings by a hair's breadth. She roars in outrage and shoots ice flames in our direction. Draven dives right on time.

But then the other silver dragons reach us.

My body jerks back and forth as Draven veers and dives and twists to evade the mass of dragons now attacking us. Black clouds and storm winds and lightning flash around us, forcing parts of the attackers back.

Fire and ice clash in the air, lighting up the night sky and making explosions echo across the landscape.

Lyra breathes fire at her attackers while Alistair works in perfect tandem with her and uses his fire magic to protect her from the dragons that try to swarm her from behind.

Isera, on the other hand, isn't protecting anyone. She is attacking Bane with such fury that the mountain itself trembles. Ice shoots through the air like massive spears, aiming for Bane's wings in a relentless hail of attacks. And it's all he can do to block them all with his own ice flames.

Draven swerves around a cluster of attackers, slashing them with his claws. One of them screams. Draven clamps his jaws around the silver dragon's neck and rips his throat out. Blood rains down over the mountainside, followed by the body of the silver dragon that slams into the stones with a thud that echoes against the ice walls.

And all I can do is to just sit there uselessly on his back. I don't have any magic that can help them fight the way Isera and Alistair can. But Goddess damn it, I need to do something.

Silver flashes all around me as the horde of dragon shifters try to overwhelm us with sheer numbers. Just Bane and Jessina alone are dangerous enough. We need to get the rest of these shifters away from us. Especially before they can get any more dragons out here.

An idea flashes through my mind.

"Draven!" I scream over the rushing winds. "Take us out over the city."

He rips his claws into another dragon while sending bolts of lightning straight at Jessina and dodging another attack from the side.

"Trust me!" I yell.

He lets out a roar and then breathes a torrent of fire in a long wall before us. As if they could understand him, Lyra and Galen immediately disengage and follow him as we race towards the city.

"Take us down lower," I call at him.

Rooftops flash past right below us as Draven dives so that he is flying right above the buildings. The crowds of humans, who had come out onto the streets to see what was happening up by the castle, scream in fear and duck down.

"The Red Hand has been captured!" I bellow over and over again at the top of my lungs as we soar past street after street. "The human resistance has been captured! They're about to be executed!"

And then I summon my magic.

I don't even know if this will work. It's going to require an enormous amount of energy. And even if I am somehow strong enough to do it, it's only going to work for a few seconds. So I need to make this count.

Gritting my teeth, I reach deep into my energy reserves.

And then I shove my magic across the entire city of Frostfell.

It latches on to the pale red flames of anger that I have been building in the humans' chests for weeks now. Those flames have flared up even brighter at the news that the Icehearts are about to execute the Red Hand and the rest of the resistance.

I push with everything I have.

And for ten glorious seconds, anger soars into blazing rage in every chest.

Then my energy runs out, and I gasp as I slump forward over Draven's neck, barely able to keep my grip on his spikes. I stare down desperately at the streets we fly over while the silver dragons chase us from behind.

For a few moments, nothing happens.

Then the city… snaps.

Screams of fury, screams of decades, of centuries, worth of suppressed anger and outrage, tear through the silent streets. Humans pour out onto the stones like a massive flood. Sprinting through the city, they carry everything that can be used as a weapon while they scream battle cries that echo of blood and reckoning.

Rage burns through the whole city as the entire human population storms the Ice Palace.

Tilting my head back, I scream up into the sky. Scream out of exhaustion. Out of relief. And out of sheer fucking revenge.

The spark is lit.

The rebellion has ignited.

Half of the silver dragons that were chasing us are forced to break off and fly back towards the castle.

Draven lets out a roar that sounds like approval, and banks hard, turning so that we're once again facing our enemies. Galen and Lyra do the same and then fly up so that they're flanking us.

Across the rooftops, speeding towards us, are Bane and Jessina. Even in their dragon forms, I can read the rage in their eyes as they fly towards us with the other half of their soldiers.

This took half of their current numbers out of play, but more dragons are already taking flight from the Ice Palace. We need to get out of the city. And we need to do it now.

Draven, Lyra, and Galen all open their jaws while Isera and Alistair get ready with their magic as well.

But then Bane and Jessina screech to a halt mid-air. All the other dragons have to swerve around them to keep from crashing into them. I stare at the scene before me in shock. Both Jessina and Bane are whipping their heads from side to side, as if they're searching for us.

But we're right in front of them. They should be able to see us.

Then I notice that Draven's black scales are shimmering slightly. I snap my gaze to Lyra and Alistair. The two of them are shimmering as well. And so are Galen and Isera. Glancing down, I stare at my own hands that are still gripping Draven's spikes. I am shimmering too.

What the hell is going on?

Jessina lets out a roar of frustration and starts flying back and forth with jerky movements while swinging her head from side to side. Around her, Bane and the other dragons are doing the same.

They're searching for us. Why can't they see where…

Realization hits.

Jerking my head down, I stare down at the part of the city that we are currently hovering over.

Ember Hill.

And there, on a well-kept lawn in front of a house with a dark blue door, stands an Unseelie fae with long black hair. Her yellow and violet eyes are glowing as she looks up at us.

A giddy laugh escapes my lungs.

She's glamouring us. She's making us look like part of the night sky or the buildings or something that makes us appear invisible.

"This is our chance!" I call to my allies. "We're being glamoured."

Draven doesn't hesitate for a second. Flapping his wings hard, he starts towards the western horizon.

Raising one hand to my brow, I give Nysara a salute in thanks. I swear that I can almost see the feline smirk on her lips.

Galen and Lyra fly up beside us as we speed across the city.

Bane has flown too far away, but Jessina snaps her head towards us. We might be invisible, and any sound might be drowned out by everyone's booming wings, but they can still *feel* the rushing air that Draven, Lyra, and Galen create when they streak past.

Dread crackles through me as Jessina swings her head in our direction and opens her jaws wide.

"Watch out!" I scream.

A massive torrent of ice flames shoots from her mouth as she turns her head from one side to the other, breathing the ice fire like a wide wall. It speeds towards us through the sky.

Alistair and Isera whip around and shove their magic at it.

Searing flames burn through the ice on Alistair's side, making it melt and stopping its momentum so that the rest crashes down like blocks of ice over the buildings below, while Isera throws a barrier of ice towards the ones on our side.

It hits Jessina's ice flames with a *crack* that echoes across the whole countryside.

Both attacks hit with furious force, and ice explodes as the two walls collide. Shards and chunks of it are blown outwards in both directions with enough force to smash through windows in the city below.

I gasp as one of them hits me in the back, but because of my tight grip on Draven's spikes, I manage to keep it from knocking me off his back.

Jessina roars in frustration and swivels her head as we speed away.

Relief washes over me when the city disappears from below us and we're instead flying across the fields and farmlands that surround Frostfell. And with every beat of their wings, they take us closer and closer to that open horizon.

Exhaustion laces my body, but I manage a smile at that glittering night sky ahead.

We did it. We got out. Isera and Alistair are free. Draven is free. The entire Black Dragon Clan is free. *I* am free.

The heist might have failed, but I still managed to make the entire human population inside Frostfell rise up and rebel against the Iceheart Dynasty. Their city is in chaos. They have lost the Commander of the Dread Legion. And Draven is on my side.

I lit the match that sparked the rebellion in Frostfell, and with Draven's help, this might just be the start. We might be able to free the Seelie Court and find a way to topple the entire Iceheart Dynasty and kill Bane and Jessina for good.

And now that we are no longer enemies, I might finally be able to allow myself to consider what he told me back there in his bedroom. That he has fallen in love with me. That he is in love with me.

Just the thought of that makes my heart squeeze tight.

I still hate that we're fated mates. I hate that I didn't get a choice. That I wasn't allowed to choose him on my own. But now that we have time, now that I know the truth, I might be able to at least start figuring out how much of our emotions are real and how much of them were forced upon us by the mate bond.

A smile, full of fragile hope, spreads across my lips.

This might—

Draven banks, and I feel myself sliding to the side. Gripping the spike harder, I try to force myself to stay on as I press my thighs harder against his scales. Goddess above, I'm tired. I'm so tired that I can barely move my legs.

Thankfully, Draven straightens again, which stops me from sliding.

I stare down at my legs. Then I cough. It's wet, forcing me to wipe it off with the back of my hand.

Confusion swirls inside me when the back of my hand is red when I return it to the spike before me. I try to adjust my position again, but my legs refuse to move.

Why is…?

Reaching behind me, I pat my back where the chunk of ice hit me earlier.

My heart stops as my hand meets something hard and sharp that sticks out of my back. Everything inside me suddenly goes unnaturally silent.

Glancing over my shoulder, I see a huge shard of ice sticking out of my spine. But I can't feel it.

I cough again and then look back down at my legs.

In fact, I can't feel anything below the waist.

I gasp out a breath, and blood sprays down over my shirt.

"Draven," I try to call, but my voice comes out as a hoarse whisper that is drowned out by the rushing winds.

I cough more blood onto my chest.

There is a strange silence inside my head as I reach back and touch the shard of ice that appears to have severed my spine. As if this isn't happening to me. As if I'm watching it from outside my body.

Draven banks again as he sets course for the Western Sea.

My legs are just draped uselessly over his neck, and since I can't grip with my thighs, I simply start sliding to the side when he turns.

"Draven," I croak, and cough up more blood. "I can't feel my legs."

He's still banking. I slide farther to the side, tilting precariously. My exhausted body trembles as I try desperately to hold on to the spikes before me.

"I can't feel—"

Then my muscles give out.

Winds rush in my ears as I fall off his back and tumble down through the dark night sky.

# BONUS SCENE

Do you want to know what Draven was thinking during that first chapter? Scan the QR code to download the exclusive bonus scene and read the beginning from Draven's perspective.

*Please note*: This bonus scene contains **major spoilers** for the rest of the book, so make sure to only read it after you have finished reading the entire book.

Made in the USA
Monee, IL
07 April 2025

15367928R00239